Ali McNamara lives in Cambridgeshire with her family and her beloved dogs. In her spare time, she likes antique shopping, people watching and daydreaming, usually accompanied by a good cup of coffee!

Ali has the chronic illness M.E./CFS and is a disability and invisible disability advocate.

To find out more about Ali visit her website:
www.alimcnamara.co.uk
Follow her on Instagram: @AliMcNamara
Or like her Facebook page: Ali McNamara

It Always Snows on Mistletoe Square

Ali McNamara

SPHERE

SPHERE

First published in Great Britain in 2023 by Sphere

3 5 7 9 10 8 6 4 2

A CIP catalogue record for this book
is available from the British Library.

ISBN 978-1-4087-2705-8

Typeset in Caslon by M Rules
Printed and bound in Great Britain by
Clays Ltd, Elcograf S.p.A.

Papers used by Sphere are from well-managed forests
and other responsible sources.

MIX
Supporting
responsible forestry
FSC® C104740

Sphere
An imprint of
Little, Brown Book Group
Carmelite House
50 Victoria Embankment
London EC4Y 0DZ

An Hachette UK Company
www.hachette.co.uk

www.littlebrown.co.uk

'A house is made with walls and beams;
a home is built with love and dreams.'
— Ralph Waldo Emerson

Prologue

London

18 December 2023

'Now, let's all give Elle a big round of applause.'

Miss Fitzpatrick encourages her class by beginning the clapping, and a sea of young faces sitting cross-legged on the floor in front of me lift their hands to join in. 'I think you'll agree her talk has been very entertaining indeed.'

It's been an absolute pleasure as always, I think, as I smile back at them all.

My school visits don't always go as swimmingly as this one has today. Sometimes it can take a while to engage the children in my subject, but they usually come around by the end. The majority of today's class of Year Fives, however, were totally enthralled from the start.

'Elle has also kindly agreed to sign some of her books for you,' Miss Fitzpatrick announces. 'If you can all line up in register order beside the Christmas tree, there are enough books for everyone to take one home today.'

Miss Fitzpatrick smiles gratefully at me as the children all clamber to their feet. And I know what she's trying to say. Before I do any of my school visits, I always enquire how many children there might be that won't be able to afford to purchase a book. I then ask my publishers to provide extra copies so every child can take one home. That way I hope no child will feel different or left out. They are all treated the same whatever their background. It's something I feel very strongly about, and I won't agree a visit to a school unless this particular request is met.

Sitting at Miss Fitzpatrick's desk, I happily sign each child's book for them as they queue up. Some of the children are incredibly shy and can't wait to escape from the desk once I've signed their copy. Some ask me funny or insightful questions, like what colour pen I use to write with, what's my favourite word to use, or what snack I like to eat while I'm writing.

'Hello, and what's your name?' I ask a small dark-haired boy currently standing by my side.

'Ben,' he says confidently. 'It's short for Benjamin.'

'Would you like Ben or Benjamin written in your book?' I ask.

'Definitely Ben. Benjamin is far too long. I don't like it.'

'I have a friend called Ben,' I tell him as I write his name and my customary greeting, before signing my name underneath. 'He doesn't like his full name either.'

'Don't blame him,' Ben says, shrugging. 'It's a stupid name. Can I ask you a question?'

'Yes, of course,' I say, closing my book and passing it to him. 'What would you like to know?'

I prepare myself for another question about how I think up my stories, or how long I spend writing each book. But Ben has something different on his mind.

'How do you make it so real?' he asks, his dark brown eyes gazing intently at me.

'Er ... ' I'm slightly thrown by his question. 'I don't know really. I think I'm just good at imagining what it might have been like to live in those particular decades in the past.'

'My mum reads your books too,' Ben continues. 'She says you're really good and despicable.'

Now it's my turn to look questioningly at Ben.

'Do you mean *descriptive*, Ben?' Miss Fitzpatrick asks over my shoulder.

Ben shrugs.

'I think he means descriptive.' She nods. 'I have to agree, Elle, your writing does make it seem like we're actually there with you in the past. The detail is incredible.'

'Thank you,' I tell her, feeling slightly uncomfortable at this praise. 'That means a lot.'

'Can I take my book now?' Ben says impatiently.

'Of course. I hope both you and your mum enjoy it.'

As I sign the last few children's books, the bell sounds for home time.

'Those of you that have your signed books already may go!' Miss Fitzpatrick calls over the hubbub of chairs scraping across the floor. 'Yes, Lucy? What do you mean Dina has your coat? Excuse me a moment,' she says apologetically. 'I'll be right back.'

I look at my pile of books; there's only one left.

'Are you the last?' I say to a bright-eyed little girl gazing inquisitively at me.

She nods and skips towards the table.

'What's your name?' I ask, opening the book and lifting my pen.

'Alvie,' she says cheerily.

'*Alvie*, that's an unusual name,' I say carefully, glancing briefly at her while I write in her book.

'Yes, it is. Do you know what it means?'

'I do.' I look at the little girl and notice for the first time that her eyes are not only bright and inquisitive, but they sparkle like two tiny emeralds.

'It's your anniversary today, isn't it?' the little girl says innocently, but I jump at her question. 'It's five years since you sat on that bench by the Thames.'

'How do you know ...' I begin. But I already know there's no point me asking – there won't be an answer. Not one that makes any sense anyway.

'They just wanted you to know how well you've done,' Alvie says, her green eyes looking keenly into mine. 'Everyone is very proud of you, and what you've done with everything that was left to you.'

I nod slowly. There's so much I want to ask, but I know it will be pointless. Alvie is only ever the messenger.

Alvie glances behind her at Miss Fitzpatrick who is making her way back across the classroom towards us.

'One last thing before I go,' she says quickly. 'It's a bit of a funny one, but I'm to remind you that the star always goes on top of the Christmas tree – not the angel. Does that make any sense to you?'

I smile at her as a warm feeling spreads right through me.

'It does – perfect sense. Tell them not to worry. I will never forget either of them.'

One

18 December 2018

Five Years Earlier ...

What are you doing here, Elle? I ask myself as I gaze out over the River Thames. *It's not like you're actually going to do anything, is it?*

Sitting on one of the wooden benches that line this part of the Embankment, to my right I can see Cleopatra's Needle and the London Eye. Behind me, not too far away, is Covent Garden and Trafalgar Square, and to my left is Waterloo Bridge.

So much history, I think, looking around me. *So many people must have either stood or sat here over the years, the centuries, even, looking out over this river just like I am. Perhaps some of them felt even worse than I do right now.*

I glance back at Waterloo Bridge again. There are so many bridges that span the length of the Thames, but I chose to sit next to this particular one today because I once read something about desperate people jumping off it when they could see no other solution to their problems. I also read about the brave passers-by that would stop and attempt to talk the distressed down when they were about to jump.

Don't be daft, Elle. You're not brave enough to be either of those people – the jumper or the saviour! If you were, you'd not be sitting here now wallowing in the miserable quagmire called your life.

My problems really weren't so bad that I should ever be contemplating jumping from a bridge into the freezing cold Thames. *You've just had a run of bad luck lately, that's all*, I tell myself sternly. *You simply have to find a way out of this deep dark hole you're currently trapped at the bottom of – and fast.*

But right now, there was no one dangling a rope, or a ladder, or anything useful that was going to help me to escape from my deep, dark pit of despair.

'May I sit here?'

I look up to see a smartly dressed city gent gesturing towards my bench with his folded black umbrella. He's wearing an expensive suit that looks like it was probably tailored for him in Savile Row, and, very unusually these days, a black bowler hat, which he lifts politely while he awaits my answer.

'Er ... yes,' I say in surprise, as I'm jolted from my self-imposed misery. 'I don't see why not?'

But, as he smiles and settles himself and his bowler hat on the bench next to me, I can think of several reasons why not.

Firstly, there are a number of unoccupied benches either side of us that he could have chosen to sit on and not disturb me. Secondly, the guy looks like he might be a bit of a weirdo. Along with his three-piece suit and bowler hat, he's carrying a bright red leather briefcase, which he's already making a lot of fuss about opening up so he can retrieve his copy of *The*

Times newspaper, which he then very deliberately folds to a particular page. And the third and main reason – I really just want to be alone right now. But as usual I'm not brave enough to say anything.

'Beautiful view,' the man comments, sadly not lifting his newspaper to read in silence as I hoped he might. 'The Thames never fails to delight.'

'Yes,' I agree quickly, hoping that's the end of any polite chit-chat.

'Are you local to this part of London?' he asks now. 'You don't look like a tourist.'

Internally I sigh. But I can't be rude and tell him to bugger off, can I? Even though I desperately want to.

'Kind of,' I answer as briefly as I can. 'I wasn't born here, but I live here now.'

Not for much longer, unless you sort something out fast.

'Do you work in the city?'

I turn towards the man, hoping he'll get the message from my annoyed expression and terse answer that I'm really in no mood to chat. Perhaps then he'll leave me alone.

'I did. But I've just lost my job and my home, and I'm currently trying to figure out what I'm going to do next. So, if you don't mind, I'd prefer to sit in silence.'

But the man just doesn't take the hint.

'Gosh, how awful for you, to lose both at the same time? That's some bad luck.'

'Add in my fiancé and best friend too and you've got more than a full set,' I add, wishing immediately I hadn't, as I turn to face the river again.

'Your home, job, best friend *and* fiancé? I'm guessing they must all be linked in some way?'

I sigh again, this time out loud. 'Not that it's any of your business, but if I tell you, will you please just go?'

The man folds his newspaper in half and lays it down between us on the bench. 'Of course, if that's what you want?'

'Right, I'll keep this as short as I can. I was recently forced to break up with my fiancé after I discovered he'd been cheating on me with my supposed best friend.'

'It happens,' the man says, nodding sympathetically. 'You've done the right thing.'

I glance at him. I have no idea why I'm telling him all this, but for some reason it feels good to share it with a total stranger. Someone who has no vested interest in either the outcome, or my feelings. The couple of friends I've shared this sorry tale with tried to say all the right things, but, since they were also friends with my ex too, none of what they said or suggested felt very genuine.

'You'd think that, wouldn't you? There's a bit more to it, I'm afraid. The slight twist to my tale is my ex-best friend and my ex-fiancé both happen to be men.'

I wait for his reaction. But it's surprisingly mild. 'Again, that happens too.'

'If only that were where my sorry tale ended,' I continue, surprisingly irritated I've not got what I consider an appropriate reaction from him. 'My ex-best friend was also until very recently my editor and therefore technically my boss on the magazine I wrote for. So now I not only find myself about to become homeless as a result of breaking up with my fiancé, I also find myself jobless too. Apparently, my services are no longer required on the magazine. No guesses needed as to why.'

'Freelance?' the man asks, still calm.

I nod, still a tad irked he hasn't reacted more. 'Sadly, yes.

So even though I was writing for them practically full-time, I have no rights of employment.'

'No wonder you were thinking about jumping. That's a lot of hurt, anger and change to take on in one hit.'

'Yes ...' I say, glancing back at the bridge again. 'It is ... Wait, how did you know I was thinking about jumping? I mean, I wouldn't, obviously, but I can't deny it did cross my mind briefly.'

'I've a few more centuries on this earth than you.'

'Decades, you mean? Not that many, looking at you.'

'You're very kind, but over those many ... years I've witnessed a few jumpers. Very few actually want to end their life, you know? Most can't see any other way out of their problems. What they don't understand, though, is the ripple-like effect their actions have on others – both good and bad. A bit like our friend, the Thames, there.' He nods towards the river. 'It's tidal, so it often has tiny waves on the surface – ripples that start small and then build all along its vast length. The Thames is London's one constant – it's always there winding its way through the capital. Sometimes people notice it, sometimes they don't, but it still remains, ebbing and flowing, just like the city does either side of it. Usually it's calm on the surface, occasionally there might be rough patches, but if you trust in the river and allow it to guide you, you'll never be truly lost.'

I stare at the man. 'That's very profound, you know?'

He shrugs. 'I try. You see those boats out there?' He gestures out to the river again, and my gaze follows the line of his hand out towards several passenger boats and barges on the water. 'They trust the river to guide them safely to their destination every day. If you have the courage to trust and follow your own path, Elle, instead of fighting it, you'll never be truly lost in life.'

I watch the boats for a few seconds while I absorb the man's words.

'Wait, how do you know my . . .' I begin, turning back to the man. But to my astonishment he's vanished. 'Name,' I finish to the empty bench.

I turn and look all around me along the Embankment, but I can't see anyone in either direction who looks anything like my dapperly dressed acquaintance. Only a few tourists taking photos, and a group of boisterous office workers who look like they might have come from their Christmas party.

That's odd, I think, turning back towards the river. *Where did he go?*

While I look out across the Thames and think about what just happened, I watch some of the boats drifting past. Among the motorboats and passenger ferries, an old-fashioned schooner passes, its sails billowing in the chilly December wind.

Painted in old-fashioned script on the side of its hull are the words: *The Spirit of Christmas*.

Christmas. I roll my eyes. Bah humbug, more like! What sort of a Christmas am I going to have this year – lonely, jobless and, most importantly right now, homeless?

I look down at the bench where my eccentric companion had been sitting a few moments ago, and I notice that although he's remembered to take his bowler hat, he's left behind his newspaper.

You might have been wearing fancy clothes and spoken with a fancy accent, but you're a litter bug in disguise! I think, smiling to myself as I lift the newspaper ready to toss it into the nearest bin. But something on the folded page catches my eye. Circled in green ink is a large advert printed in an elaborate font:

WANTED:
Experienced Writer

An experienced and published wordsmith is required to
write the story and history of one house and its family.

Live-in is essential. Accommodation and all
meals will be provided free of charge.

The successful applicant must be available between
1755 and 1984 daily, and essentially
MUST LIKE CHRISTMAS.

Immediate start.

To apply, please visit: 'Christmas House', 5 Mistletoe
Square, Bloomsbury, London WC1 and ask for Estelle.

Closing Date:
18th December.

I read the advert twice through to try to find a catch some-where. But other than the slightly strange sounding hours, which I assume must be a typo, it sounds absolutely perfect – the answer to all my current problems.

Don't get carried away, Elle, I think as I stare at the advert. *It sounds a little bit* too *perfect! Estelle is probably the cover for some freak who collects empty baked-bean tins and used teabags. He likely never leaves the house, and I'll probably find myself running away as quickly as I arrive.*

I toss the newspaper back down onto the bench and gaze at the river again.

And who puts Must like Christmas *in an advert, what's that all about? That's weird in itself. I know I'm pretty unusual in not liking Christmas, and I have my reasons for that. But most people do, don't they? So why would you need to write it?*

Have the courage to trust and follow your own path, Elle . . . The stranger's words still ring annoyingly in my ears while I try and forget all about the curious advert.

My path is leading to a house in Bloomsbury, is it? To a rent-free, live-in writing job in the millionaires' mansions of WC1 . . . ? I roll my eyes. *Yeah right.* Miracles like that never happen. Even if it is nearly Christmas.

Another boat passes under the bridge, then continues on its merry way along the Thames. But this time the words painted on its side make me catch my breath . . .

The Courage of St Nicholas.

Two

St Nicholas – he's the Patron Saint of Christmas, isn't he? I try and remember. Or is it St Nicholas that's supposed to be Santa Claus?

I shake my head.

Whichever it is, what are the chances that that boat should be passing me right at this very moment, especially after what that man just told me and what it says in the newspaper advert?

I think a bit more.

'Come on, Elle,' I say sharply, surprising a couple of pigeons happily pecking away on the remains of a mince pie. 'What does it matter whether it means something or if it's simply a coincidence? If this ad is genuine, this is a job you can do standing on your head, and more importantly, it will be a roof over that same head until you can find something better. Have some courage for once in your life. You can do this!'

Suitably buoyed up I check the date on the newspaper, and I'm pleased to see it's today's issue. *Wait, wasn't that also the closing date for applications?*

I quickly read the advert again and look for a telephone number, but there's only an address.

I pull a compact from my bag and try to look at as much of myself as I can in the tiny mirror. I've looked better. Under my long winter coat I'm wearing a baggy wool jumper and tight black jeans. There are dark circles under my eyes caused by too many sleepless nights, and my face looks pale and drawn from worry. But it will have to do. A bit of make-up will help, and luckily my coat will cover most of my clothes. I don't have time to go home and change into something smarter.

Home. It won't be for much longer.

I simply can't continue living there – even though Owen wants me to. I shake my head. The nerve of him, asking me to stay after what he's done. He even tried to make out in some way it was my fault! I have to get away from this toxic relationship once and for all, and I have to do it now. I just hope the job hasn't been taken already – they must have been advertising it a while if the closing date is today.

While the pigeons keep a beady eye on me, I quickly brush my long dark hair and tie it into a loose ponytail. Then I brush on some mascara and a smudge of lip gloss, adding a little to my cheeks as well to give them some colour. 'Right, I guess you'll do,' I say as I check myself again in the mirror. But as I snap the compact shut, a thought suddenly occurs to me. When did I start disliking the way I looked so much? Not long after I met Owen, I now realise. God, that man has a lot to answer for.

After a few minutes of attempting to hail a taxi, I almost give up. *Maybe it's just not meant to be,* I think, almost allowing myself to slide slowly down the same easy path I've been on for far too long. *No, you're not taking the easy option this time, Elle! Have courage.* I remember the man's words. *You're going to find this Mistletoe Square and you're going to get this job!*

I consider taking the Tube, but decide by the time I've got

down into the station and waited for a train, it will probably be just as fast to walk. Plus, it will save me money. If this job doesn't happen, I don't know how long I might be out of work. I need to save pennies where I can.

I set off towards Bloomsbury. I'm desperate to hurry, but I don't want to arrive at the house all hot and sweaty in my big winter coat and fur-lined boots, so I try and walk at a brisk but steady pace. As I walk along the busy London streets, many of them decorated for the festive season with twinkly lights and the odd Christmas tree, I pass theatres advertising the latest West End shows, brand-name coffee shops offering their latest festive drinks in the obligatory Christmassy cup, and well-known chain stores and independent shops, with their windows full of shiny baubles, colourful lights and the perfect gifts for friends and family.

The traffic, as always, is congested, and I often find myself moving faster on foot than the many red buses, black cabs, delivery vans and motorbikes all queued up at junctions and traffic lights.

Now, where is this square? I look again at my phone and the route Google Maps has plotted for me. I'm not sure I've heard of a *Mistletoe* Square before.

And not for the first time since I left Waterloo Bridge, I begin to doubt the validity of the advert. That guy with the briefcase had been very odd. *Perhaps I should be a little more wary about this …*

My phone rings in my hand, and I'm surprised to see it's Kate, one of my ex-colleagues from the magazine.

'Elle!' Kate says brightly. 'Can't chat long, I'm afraid, have a really tight deadline. But I've just seen an ad in the *Telegraph* and it sounds perfect for you.'

She then reads the exact same advert as the one I've torn from the copy of *The Times* the man had left on the bench.

'What do you think?' she asks eagerly. 'Sounds a bit odd, but it might be something?'

'I'm actually on my way there at this very moment,' I tell her. 'I saw the advert a little while ago.'

'Are you? Wow, amazing! Let me know how you go? And . . . listen, it was bloody awful what happened. Everyone here is still in a state of shock about Liam and Owen.'

'Yes, well . . .'

'About time you saw that ex of yours for what he really is, though. We've all been saying you need to stand up to Owen for ages. You go, girl – that's what I say. Girl power and all that!'

'Thanks.'

'And Liam . . . well I never saw that coming. But he's kept a low profile here since you left, I can tell you. I don't think he dare show his face!'

'I can imagine.'

'Anyway, got to go. Chin up, lovely! Wishing you lots of luck with that job! Speak soon, yah?'

'Yes,' I reply as Kate ends the call.

I think about the office for a moment. I dread to think what all the gossips will be saying right now. My situation will be the most exciting thing to happen there in ages. But for once I decide that I don't care. Let them gossip. I won't be going back there again. However, I'm glad Kate called; she had always been one of my more trusted colleagues and knowing she too saw the advert makes me feel a little happier about its validity.

I'm about to pop my phone back in my bag when notifications for two emails and a text arrive on the screen. They all inform me of exactly the same thing, that the sender has just seen an advert that sounds 'perfect for me'.

'Okay, I get it, I get it!' I call, looking up, and an old lady pulling a tartan shopping trolley gives me a strange look as she passes me on the pavement.

So, which way now? I think, silently this time, as I hurriedly consult my map again.

I follow the route on my phone until I reach the end of the street. As I turn a corner, the road suddenly opens out into the most beautiful Georgian square.

'Wow,' I say, looking around me. 'This is beautiful.'

The square is much like many of the others I've occasionally passed through in this part of London. A small area of grass and trees – like a tiny park – is surrounded by black wrought-iron railings. It's then protected from the outside world even further by terraces of elegant Georgian houses that line its four sides.

These attractive little squares usually come as a welcome respite from the stark, grey, modern buildings that have taken over much of central London, but this one I find myself in now is particularly lovely.

I see where you got your name, I think as I look up at the tall trees dotted through the park, most of them now almost bare for winter. Each one has at least one bunch of mistletoe clinging to its high branches.

Now, which way is number five?

I follow the pavement, and the distinctive Victorian gas lamps, around the edge of the square, trying not to get too distracted by the stylish houses, all with shiny black front doors and pristine cream-coloured steps leading up to them. Some have cheerful window boxes planted with berry-rich winter plants or winter-flowering pansies, and all of them have freshly painted black railings and bright white lattice windows.

'Three … four … ah, number five.'

The brass plaque at the side of the door not only has the number five etched into it in black, but the words *Christmas House* too. I stand a little way back from the house to see if it looks any different from all the others in the square. But there appears to be nothing unusual about this particular house except that it has a bright red door instead of a black one. It's five storeys high – a basement, three floors with tall windows, then what I assume is a little attic room at the top of the house. It has the same black railings as the others, and the same fan-light window over the top of the door. Except in the middle of this particular house's fanlight, etched into the glass in gold, are the words *St Nicholas*.

How interesting can one house's history be? I stare up at the tall building in front of me. Yes, I'm sure it's had many owners over the years, but they can't all have a story to tell, can they? I can't see how there will be enough content for me to write about for any length of time. However, beggars can't be choosers, I remind myself. I need this job, otherwise I'll have no choice but to go back to Owen.

Besides, it might be quite nice to live in a large house in an affluent central London neighbourhood for a while, instead of Owen's poky little flat in North London.

'Right, then,' I say, bracing myself for immediate disappointment when I tap the house's brass door-knocker. 'Let's find out what lies behind this red door.'

I move towards the house and climb the four shallow steps. Then I reach out to grab the knocker, but before I get to it the door suddenly opens and I stumble forwards.

'Oops, sorry!' A well-dressed man with neat chestnut-coloured hair has to put his hands out to stop me from falling into him. 'Didn't see you there.'

'H-hi,' I manage to say as I recover my balance and my composure. 'I-I'm here about the advertisement.'

The man looks blankly back at me.

'Sorry, I don't actually live here,' he says awkwardly. 'I've just been helping them get their tree in. Estelle always insists on a real tree every Christmas apparently, and this year's one is a monster.' He gestures to the window to his right, and I see a lush, green, undecorated Christmas tree filling it. 'I'm just the next-door neighbour.' He gestures to the other side of him. 'That's me on the name plate,' he says proudly, pointing to a brass nameplate on the house next door. 'Ben Harris. I'm a solicitor. My office is next door here at Holly House, and my flat is upstairs. I've just moved in.'

'Oh ... that's nice.' I don't really know what to say. 'I ... I might be moving in here too. I believe there's some sort of job available. I just hope I'm not too late. Do you know if they've had many applicants?'

Ben shrugs. 'Sorry, like I said I just moved in a couple of days ago. All a bit weird actually – the office and house suddenly came up for rent and I just happened to see the advert. They wanted a tenant to move in quickly, so I was able to get it at a great price. Well, a great price for around here.' He grins, and his kind, dark eyes twinkle.

I can't help but smile coyly back at him. Ben is a bit too good-looking, a bit too confident, and, if he can afford to rent in this square, a bit too rich as well. A deadly combination in my experience and one usually to be avoided.

'Angela, is there someone at the door?' a commanding

female voice calls from inside the house. 'That barrister chappie seems to be talking to someone on our steps!'

Ben grins. 'I'm a lawyer, Estelle,' he calls back over his shoulder. 'A solicitor if you prefer, now I'm back in the UK again. Not actually a barrister. And don't worry, I'm just going.'

A cheerful-looking older woman appears behind Ben. She has red curly hair pinned wildly to the top of her head and she's wearing a brightly patterned apron over her blue denim dungarees. She looks a little flustered as she wipes her floury hands on her apron.

'Sorry about that,' she says as Ben moves aside. 'I was in the kitchen. Are you here about the job by any chance?' she asks me hopefully.

'See you around,' Ben says, lifting his hand as he makes his way past me down the steps to the pavement. 'Good luck with the job. Bye, Angela!'

Angela waves hurriedly at him and turns her attention back to me.

'I am here about the job,' I tell her. 'I'm sorry to call unannounced, but there was only an address on the advert. I'm not too late, am I?'

'No, my dear, you'll never be too late,' Angela says, smiling warmly at me. 'Come in. Come in.'

I follow Angela into the hallway of the house.

'Just wait there a moment, and I'll see if Estelle is ready to see you.'

While I wait awkwardly in the hall, I take a look around me. Like the outside of the house, the hallway is decorated completely in keeping with the house's age. Underneath my feet there is a prettily patterned black-and-white tiled floor, the walls are papered in a classic but understated pale floral print, and above me there's a dusty glass chandelier hanging from the high ceiling. On the right of the hall there's a staircase with a mahogany banister leading up to the next floor, and a little further along a few panelled wood doors lead presumably to further rooms. As I look a little more closely, I notice some of the decor is a little tired in places; the painted skirting boards are chipped where they've come into contact with shoes or furniture, and some of the wallpaper is just beginning to peel off the old walls.

'Estelle is ready for you now,' Angela announces, opening the first door on the left of the hall. 'Don't worry,' she says as I walk tentatively past her into what once would have been the drawing room of the house. 'Estelle's bark is far worse than her bite.'

I smile gratefully at Angela, and I notice for the first time that along with her dungarees Angela is also wearing burgundy Doc Marten boots. Hardly the footwear of your average house-keeper – especially one who looks like they could possibly be in their sixties.

An older lady, her white hair pinned elegantly into a chic bun at the back of her head, is sitting in a supportive but comfortable-looking high-backed chair next to a large, ornate white fireplace. The fire is lit and burning cheerfully away in the grate, and on her lap is a hairy little dog, who looks up expectantly at me as I walk into the room.

'Good afternoon,' the lady, who I'm assuming is Estelle, says, looking up too. 'Angela tells me you're here about the position?'

'Yes, that's right,' I say. 'It's a bit short notice, I know, and I'm aware today is the last day to apply, but I saw the advert and I think I'd be perfect for the job.'

Estelle considers me over her gold half-moon spectacles, and I wonder if that last part was a bit too presumptuous. She nods. 'Please, take a seat.'

I take a brief look at my surroundings as I walk towards the chair she's gesturing to. The room is quite an eclectic mix of styles and periods. There is dark, glossy, mahogany furniture – a large dining table and chairs, a tall heavy bookcase and a china cabinet with glass doors, alongside more modern fixtures and fittings – a flat-screen television, a DVD player and a vintage-style, pale blue digital radio. My eye catches on the huge Christmas tree standing undecorated in front of the window. It reaches almost the full height of the high ceiling.

'I always like a real tree at Christmas,' Estelle says, seeing me looking. 'Angela is going to decorate it later for me, aren't you, Angela?'

Angela rolls her eyes. 'I guess I am. That's after I get the pie finished for dinner, and all the hundreds of other things I've still to do today!'

'Perhaps you'd be better served getting on with some of them, then?' Estelle suggests. 'I'll be fine here with our guest.'

Angela gives a dismissive shake of her head as if she's dealt with Estelle's requests many times before.

'Perhaps you could bring us some tea, when you've a moment in your busy schedule?' Estelle asks. 'If it's not too much trouble, of course,' she adds, giving me a knowing look.

I smile, but I feel a tad uncomfortable in the middle of this bickering as I hesitate next to the armchair Estelle suggested I sit in.

'Of course!' Angela says, heading out of the room. 'Just a skivvy, aren't I?' she grumbles as she heads down the hall.

'Don't mind her,' Estelle says, gesturing once more to the

armchair opposite her. 'Her bark is always worse than her bite. Now, please sit down, won't you?'

I smile as I arrange myself in the seat next to the fireplace. What a strange pair these two are.

Estelle adjusts the pale blue cardigan neatly arranged over her narrow shoulders and the little dog sitting in the lap of her green tweed skirt happily wags his tail at me.

'A very good sign,' Estelle says approvingly, stroking the dog. 'Alvie is a very good judge of character. You're all right with dogs, are you?'

'Oh, yes,' I insist. 'Love them.' I smile at Alvie. He gives me such a knowing look from his bright green eyes, that it makes me jump in surprise.

'I'm Estelle, by the way,' Estelle says, clearly not missing any of this, but choosing not to mention it. 'I think you know that already, though, don't you?'

I look away from Alvie – I've known many dogs in my life, but I've never known one look at me quite like that before – to concentrate on Estelle.

'Yes. Yes, I do,' I reply hurriedly. 'It was in the advert.'

'And your name is?' Estelle politely prompts.

'I'm Elle. Elle McKenzie. I'm so very pleased to meet you, Estelle.'

Estelle nods. 'Elle, what a lovely name. What is it short for, my dear?'

'It's just Elle.'

Estelle regards me for a moment over her glasses. 'Now I don't think that's quite true, is it?'

How does she know that?

'Okay, you got me,' I admit quickly. 'It's just I really don't like my full name – that's why I always go by Elle.'

23

'I'm sure it can't be that bad?'

'It is.'

Estelle waits, and I realise this interview is not going to continue if I don't tell her.

'All right, my full name is Noelle.'

'Christmas baby?' Estelle enquires, not seeming to find anything odd in the name I find so embarrassing.

'Yes, my birthday is Christmas Eve.'

'How lovely. In just a few days' time. Do you have any plans?'

'Er, no. I've been a bit . . . busy this year. I haven't really had time to plan anything.'

'I see.' Estelle nods, but is polite enough not to press me further, which I deeply appreciate. 'So perhaps we should talk about the position now?'

'Yes, please,' I reply gratefully.

Alvie jumps down from Estelle's lap and heads over towards the Christmas tree.

'Now, Alvie, be good. Don't you go tinkling up the tree or Angela will be very cross with us.'

'Angela will be very cross about what?' Angela comes back into the room with a silver tray laden with a full china tea service. She puts the tray down on a small wooden table behind Estelle. 'Now you stay away from that tree, Alvie!' she calls. 'I haven't time to be clearing up your doings today!'

Alvie just wags his tail amiably and continues sniffing around the tree.

'How do you like your tea?' Angela asks me.

'A drop of milk, one sugar, please.'

As Estelle begins to tell me about the job, I find my gaze drawn back to Angela. It's fascinating how much effort goes into her tea-making. I'm used to tea made with a few dunks of a bag in a mug. But Angela is very elaborately pouring the tea from a china teapot, through a strainer, before it's allowed anywhere near the fine-bone-china cup and saucer.

'This house,' Estelle continues, 'has been in my family for many generations. But I am the last in a long line of owners. Unhappily, I was not blessed with any children, and I have no other immediate relatives to pass this house on to.'

'I'm sorry to hear that,' I say as I'm offered my cup of tea by Angela. 'Thank you.' She holds out a bowl of sugar cubes and I take one with a tiny pair of silver tongs. 'So how long has this house been in your family, Estelle? It's all right if I call you Estelle?'

'Please do,' Estelle says. 'It's been in my family since it was first built in 1750.'

'Gosh, that long?' I say, genuinely surprised to hear this. 'That's over two hundred and fifty years.'

'Yes, it is a long time for one house to belong to a single family.' Estelle takes her own tea from Angela now. 'Thank you, Angela. Won't you stay and have a cup with us?'

'I will, thank you,' Angela says without a hint of surprise, and immediately I get that their relationship is a little more than simply employer and employee.

'A house this size, anyway,' Estelle continues. 'We're hardly a stately home.'

'I bet you've got many more interesting tales to tell than one of those bigger houses though.'

Estelle smiles. 'I have indeed. And that is why I need your help.'

I like the way she says help, as if it's me doing her a favour, and not the other way round.

Angela has now poured herself a cup of tea. She draws up

a chair and sits down between Estelle and me, facing the fire, and I wonder if she usually sits where I am, companionably chatting with Estelle about their day.

'I want all the stories I know to be written down in one place for posterity,' Estelle explains. 'I have a friend in a publishing house that has promised to publish this book when it's finished. It won't be a bestseller, I know that, but just to know that my family and this house's story won't simply disappear when I go will be more than enough for me.'

Suddenly I feel quite sad that this old lady should have to pay someone – a stranger – to listen to her stories, instead of having children, grandchildren and even great-grandchildren to share them with.

'That's where you come in,' Estelle continues. 'I need someone to sit and listen to all my stories and write them down – in a way that will make them interesting for future generations to read. I don't want my family's history to disappear when I do.'

'I'm sure I could do that,' I reply keenly.

'I know you can,' Estelle says. 'That's why you're here.'

'What Estelle means,' Angela pipes up, 'is that's why we're looking for the perfect person to tell the stories, because they're so important to Estelle.'

'I completely understand,' I say with conviction. 'I assure you I have plenty of writing experience. I got a first at Cambridge in English and History, then after I left university I worked at various publications – mostly local newspapers to begin with, before I took a job at *Pig Breeders Monthly*.' I look at them to see if they've heard of it. But unsurprisingly they both look blank. 'After that I went freelance, and took work wherever I could get it, mainly on London-based newspapers like the *Evening*

Standard and the *Metro*, and most recently I've been writing full time for *Your Home and History* magazine.'

'That sounds more like it,' Estelle says approvingly. 'My doctor always had a copy of that in his waiting room whenever I visited, and he was a most discerning man. You have some experience in the history of houses then?'

'A little, yes.' I say, choosing not to mention that much of what I covered on the magazine was home makeovers with a period twist. 'I can already tell this house will have the most amazing history, though. It's totally understandable that you'd want to record it for the future.'

Estelle nods approvingly. 'Would you be able to start immediately?' she asks. 'Am I right in thinking you have no ties keeping you elsewhere?'

I'm surprised by Estelle's assumption. 'Er, yes, you are right. No ties.'

'Good. Good.' Estelle nods. 'Quite unusual for someone of your age though? I'm guessing you must be what, thirty-four?'

'Wow, yes, spot on again, I am. I'm as free as a bird, I can assure you.'

'And you would be happy to live in?'

'Of course.' I look around. 'You really have a beautiful home. I'd have my own room, would I?'

'You'd have the run of the whole first floor if you want it. I can't get up the stairs any more, so we've converted the room adjacent to this one into my bedroom. Angela is on the top floor and she's quite happy there – aren't you, Angela?'

'Yep, like all the poor housemaids before me, I live in the attic accommodation,' Angela grumbles.

'Oh, don't listen to her. She loves it up there really.'

'It does have some pretty special views,' Angela agrees begrudgingly.

'What's on the second floor?' I ask.

'Nothing really – just my old junk and knick-knacks,' Estelle says quickly. 'Books, fancy china dinner services we no longer have the use for, that kind of thing.'

I nod.

'My days of entertaining have long since passed,' Estelle says sadly. 'It will be good to have a new face in the house. You're welcome to bring any friends round, or gentleman callers?' she ventures. 'I may be old, but I'm not a prude.'

I smile. 'That won't be necessary. I'm sworn off men right now, and friends for that matter,' I add, thinking of both Owen and my now ex-bestie and ex-boss, Liam.

Estelle and Angela exchange an uneasy look, and I wonder why.

'So there's just one more thing I have to ask,' Estelle says, her bright green eyes looking intently at me. 'It's actually one of the most important questions I have for you.'

'Sure, go ahead.' This interview has been so different from any other I've ever attended, Estelle could be about to ask me anything.

'Do you like Christmas, Elle?'

For a moment there's silence in the room as I confirm with my brain that is what Estelle has actually just asked.

'Er . . . yes, I guess so.' I lie for the first time since I arrived.

Estelle stares at me with even more focus. 'You guess so?'

'I mean, who doesn't?' I try. 'Everyone likes Christmas, right?'

Estelle looks across at Angela.

Angela simply shrugs.

'I mean,' I say, suddenly seeing this opportunity slipping

away from me if I don't do something fast. 'Look at your beautiful tree there – it's the spirit of Christmas, isn't it.'

'Indeed it is.' Estelle looks at the tree with pride. 'It's my favourite time of the year when the tree is finally all decorated and lit up. It brings back so many memories for me seeing it glowing with so much happiness and joy.'

'And that is why I promised to do it later for you, didn't I?' Angela raises her eyebrows at Estelle. 'But it's such a big tree,' she says turning to me. 'Takes me bloomin' ages to decorate it every year.'

'I could help you if you like?' I offer, hoping this act of kindness might seal the deal for me. 'If I get the job, of course.' I look back at Estelle hopefully.

This may be the craziest job I've ever applied for, but strangely, I find myself wanting it more than any other job I've ever gone for. There's something about the square, and this house, and the people who live in it, that I really like, and I want to spend more time getting to know them.

'I don't think we need to discuss it any further,' Estelle says abruptly, and I think I've pushed it too far. 'If agreeable to you, you can start tomorrow, and your first task, Elle, if you're still willing, is to help us to decorate our Christmas tree.'

Three

19 December 2018

After Owen leaves for work, I emerge from his spare room and begin to pack up my belongings from the flat I called home for the last two years. The flat was Owen's before I moved in, so most of the furnishings belong to him. It's quite sad when I realise how little I'd put my stamp on the place in the time I lived here. But that was a bit like our relationship. It revolved for the majority of time around him and his life. *How had I ever let myself get into that situation?*

If it wasn't for Estelle, I'd now be homeless, jobless, with no one to turn to. Nearly everything in my life, including my friends, were Owen's first. So now we aren't a couple any more, I realise just what an unhealthy and unbalanced relationship it was.

As I post the key back through the letterbox, I make a pact with myself never to get into this sort of mess again. From now on I will look after me, and not worry about anyone else, not until I get back on my feet again.

Even though I leave the flat with minimal possessions, this time I have no choice but to take a taxi to Mistletoe Square – there are just too many bags and suitcases to even consider attempting the Tube. But now I know I am going to be earning some money again, I don't feel quite so worried about the expense. Last night, after I agreed to take the job, Estelle and I ran through a few of the finer details, such as my fee. It's not the highest paid job I've ever done, but since I'm getting free meals and board thrown in, I'm more than happy with the terms she offered.

My taxi driver, wearing a festive Santa hat, looks decidedly un-jolly when he pulls up next to all my luggage on the pavement. But he soon cheers up at the end of my journey, when we unload all my luggage and I give him a good tip and wish him a Merry Christmas as he pulls away from the square.

With Angela's help, I haul all my cases and bags up the steps outside the house and then up a further flight of stairs inside, to my promised lodgings on the first floor.

'This do for you?' Angela asks as we move the last of my things into one of the rooms.

'It's wonderful,' I gush, still hardly believing I've fallen on this sort of luck.

I've been given two rooms on the first floor – a bedroom containing some enormous, heavy pieces of antique furniture, including a large double bed, chest of drawers, wardrobe and dressing table, and a pretty sitting room, with a fireplace, chintz sofa and, by the window looking out over the square, an ornate oak writing desk. Just along the landing there is a small bathroom for me to use – again with period fittings.

'Glad you like it. The bathroom is all yours. I have my own

rooms upstairs and Estelle keeps herself on the ground floor now she struggles to climb the stairs.'

'Have you worked here long?' I ask, keen to know a little more about the people I'm going to be living with. Today, Angela is wearing an outfit that evokes the 1950s. Her auburn hair is tied into a high ponytail with a white ribbon, and on her bottom half she's wearing a full skirt with a red-and-white poodle pattern, matched with a red polo-neck sweater. On top of this she wears another bright kitchen apron.

'Long enough,' Angela says briefly. 'Me and Estelle go way back.'

'Really?'

'I'm sure we'll tell you all about it sometime. Now, I'll leave you to get settled in. Lunch will be at one o'clock sharp. It's homemade chicken soup and freshly baked bread – is that all right with you?' She looks me up and down thoughtfully. 'You're not one of those vegan types, are you?'

'No, I eat most things.'

'Good,' Angela says approvingly. 'That'll make my life a lot easier. I mean, if you had been I'd have coped, of course. I can cook most things, and quite well if I do say so myself.'

'I'm sure you can.' I smile at her. 'But I'm easy when it comes to food.'

'Lovely.' Angela nods. 'See you in a bit then.' She then hurries back down the stairs to the kitchen, leaving me to unpack.

Unpacking is the last thing I feel like doing after moving all my stuff, so instead I take a seat at the desk and gaze out of the window, ruminating on how my life has changed so suddenly.

How can it be only yesterday that I was sitting on the banks of the Thames at my wits' end, and today I've got rooms in a Georgian townhouse in Bloomsbury? My mind wanders back to the man who sat down next to me on the bench. 'You said to follow a new path,' I murmur as I watch the comings and goings on the square below me. 'And so far I'm liking this one very much indeed.'

As I speak, I see a familiar figure crossing the road outside the house. It's Ben, our next-door neighbour. He's wearing a long dark wool coat over his suit today, with the collar turned up as he hurries to get out of the cold. He glances up and sees me watching him, and he pauses for moment to smile.

'Hi,' he mouths silently up at me.

'Hello,' I whisper back, waving my hand.

He briefly lifts his own hand in reply, before disappearing out of view as he heads up the steps to his front door.

My heart is beating far too quickly for my liking at the end of this brief exchange.

Oh, no, you don't! I tell myself sternly. 'You've just escaped one disastrous relationship. You are not heading straight into another. You are taking a long-extended break from men – even if they are as handsome as your new neighbour!'

To take my mind off Ben, I do a little necessary unpacking, and just before one o'clock I head downstairs. I'm about to go into the sitting room when I hear Estelle and Angela talking to each other. Not wanting to interrupt, I pause outside the door.

'Already?' I hear Angela saying. 'Are you sure? She's just arrived. Isn't it a bit too soon?'

'No, we've got a lot to get through,' Estelle replies firmly. 'We need to start as soon as possible.'

I assume they are discussing Estelle telling me her stories of the house and her family. It feels rude to disturb them, so I decide to take a quick look around my new home.

I walk a little further down the hall, pausing to glance at

a painting and some photographs hanging on the wall. The painting, which looks quite old, is of a kind-looking man, wearing a long black jacket with an embroidered waistcoat and britches that end just under his knee. He is standing next to a seated, pretty, pale woman wearing a long cream embroidered dress, with a big skirt and long puffy sleeves. The plaque underneath reads: *Joseph and Celeste Christmas 1750*. I wonder if the house is named after them? I think as I gaze at the portrait for a few moments.

Next to them hangs a sepia photograph of a Victorian couple posed in a similar way to the painting, the man again has a kind face even though he's not smiling – as was the way back then – and the woman has a European look about her. Then next to that some black-and-white photos. A man in uniform that looks like it's from the First World War. An elegant but fragile-looking woman wearing a pretty dress, that looks like it might have been taken in the late twenties or early thirties, and a few colour photos that look like they could be from the sixties and seventies judging by the clothing the young people grouped in them are wearing, including one of a young man in graduation robes.

After I've looked with interest at all the photos, I continue on past the closed door that Estelle had said was her bedroom, past the downstairs bathroom and towards the kitchen, which I can just see at the end of the hall through a door that's been left ajar.

I pause in the doorway. It looks pretty spacious for a kitchen. The spotlessly clean floor is tiled in a black-and-white check. Traditional stripped-oak cupboards line two of the tall, white-washed walls. Against the third wall, a large Aga-style stove stands, with a pot of soup bubbling away on it, and against the fourth, a tall, modern fridge-freezer stands, looking a little out of place among all its vintage neighbours. Cooking utensils rest in striped ceramic pots along the countertops, next to sharp knives in large wooden blocks. Above them, copper pans and black cooking pots hang on hooks. On a scrubbed wooden table in the centre of the room sit several thick slices of bread on a wooden chopping board, and soup bowls waiting to be taken through to the sitting room on a tray. Angela is clearly ready to serve our lunch.

It's not hard to imagine, as I stand in the doorway, the kitchen as it once might have been when the house was first built. I'm sure a house this size would have had several servants scurrying about in this area preparing meals for the family of the time.

'Can I help you?' I hear Angela say sharply, making me jump.

'I . . . I was just having a look round.' I turn and I'm surprised to find Angela looking quite cross behind me. 'Sorry. I haven't touched anything.'

'Oh, I'm not cross at you,' Angela says to my relief. 'I was just having words with Estelle. She has a way of winding me up with even the simplest of requests.'

'Yes, I heard you . . . chatting,' I say tactfully. 'I didn't want to interrupt.'

Angela looks surprised, then immediately suspicious. 'What did you hear?'

'Nothing really, honest. Just you both discussing when Estelle was going to start telling me her stories.'

Angela considers this. 'Of course. That was it.'

'Should I go in there now?' I ask, wondering why she's reacting oddly. 'The sitting room?'

'Yes, I think you should. I'm about to serve the lunch.'

35

'Would you like a hand?'

Angela looks surprised, then pleased. 'That's very kind of you, lovely,' she says. 'But I'll be just fine. You go on and find Estelle – she's waiting for you.'

As I head back down the hall, I can't help wondering why Angela had seemed so on edge. I hesitate at the sitting room door for a moment, wondering whether I should knock. 'Do come in, Elle,' I hear Estelle call. 'You don't need to stand on ceremony here.'

'Hi.' I open the door, suddenly feeling a little awkward as I enter the room. 'Angela said lunch was almost ready, and I should come through.'

I'm pleased to see the dining table at the back of the room has been laid for three. It's difficult trying to work out just what Estelle and Angela's relationship is – sometimes it seems like employer and employee, but more often it seems like old friends and I much prefer the second pairing.

'Angela will be joining us for lunch,' Estelle says from her chair by the fireplace, seeing me glance at the table. 'I hope that's all right?'

'Of course, it is. You two are obviously old friends?' I move towards the chair I sat in yesterday, and Estelle nods for me to sit down.

'We've known each other for a long time,' is her considered reply as she strokes Alvie, who is sitting on her lap. 'She helps me out now I can't do as much for myself any more.' Estelle lowers her voice. 'Just between the two of us, I'd be lost without her. But don't tell her I said that, will you?' She winks.

'Too right you'd be lost without me.' Angela enters the room with a large tray full of our lunch. 'Indispensable, that's what I am.' She places the tray on the table and unloads a soup tureen and the slices of buttered bread on a plate. 'Why don't you go and sit down at the table, Elle?' Angela suggests while she helps Estelle from her chair.

'Where would you like me to sit?' I ask, positive they will already have their usual seats.

'On the left there.' Estelle points with her stick towards a chair.

I take my seat, while Angela guides Estelle to the table. Then Angela ladles the soup into our bowls and we all help ourselves to bread.

'So I thought we might start talking about the history of the house later,' Estelle says when we've all tucked into a delicious chicken soup, and some of the nicest homemade bread I've ever tasted. 'After we've decorated the tree, of course.'

'Sure,' I agree, taking a drink from my glass of water. Even the water tastes amazing here, and I make a note to ask Angela what brand it is. It's definitely not London tap water, of that I'm certain. 'I'm keen to get going with the project.'

'Good, good,' Estelle says. 'After lunch perhaps you can bring in the boxes of decorations, Angela?'

Angela nods. 'Of course. I might complain about it, but it's always a good day when we decorate our tree for Christmas.'

I notice she says *our* tree.

'Yes, it's always the start of something good,' Estelle agrees. 'And this time more than ever it's important we get it right.'

Angela nods, and I'm left, as seems to be becoming the norm, slightly bewildered as to what exactly they are discussing.

After lunch I insist on helping Angela clear the table and fill the dishwasher. I am surprised to find, along with a washing machine and tumble dryer, a modern dishwasher in a sort of utility room off the kitchen. I'm sure this room would have originally been called a scullery, I think, calling upon my limited knowledge of period houses gained on the magazine. But now with its very modern equipment, a utility is the best name for it.

When I return to the sitting room Angela has got a wooden box of Christmas decorations down from the attic, and she and Estelle are sitting at the table already carefully unwrapping some very old and very delicate-looking tree decorations, while Alvie is curled up in his basket at the side of the fire.

'They look beautiful.' I walk over to them. 'Are they all antique?'

'Most of them, yes,' Estelle says. 'Each one represents a person or a time in this house's history. They've been passed down through the generations with each new owner adding to the collection.'

'Gosh!' I look at what they've already unwrapped. 'That's really lovely. How far do they go back?'

'Some to Victorian times when the first Christmas tree would have been brought into the house,' Estelle explains. 'Did you know, before that, trees were never usually a part of Christmas in England? Families decorated their homes, but mainly with greenery and berries brought in from outside.'

'Wasn't it Queen Victoria who started the tradition for trees here?' I add, keen to share what knowledge I have.

'Close. Her husband Albert brought the first one into Buckingham Palace, and it began there. Victoria and Albert also began the tradition for sending Christmas cards.'

'Some of these decorations could be over one hundred and fifty years old, then?' I say, quite amazed by this fact. The decorations are really intricate, beautiful and extremely delicate-looking.

'Which is why I'm not quite as keen as Estelle is on decorating the tree,' Angela says wryly. 'I'm always worried about dropping one of the decorations and it smashing.'

'You've never dropped one before,' Estelle says.

'I daren't!' Angela grimaces. 'I'd never hear the end of it!'

'While we unpack the rest of the decorations, why don't you start hanging them on the tree, Elle?' Estelle suggests. 'You're a little taller than Angela, you won't need the stepladder as soon.'

I look over at the tree and see a small wooden stepladder has been placed at the bottom of it.

'And that's another thing,' Angela grumbles. 'I'll break my neck on that thing one day. Why we have to have such a big tree, I don't know.'

Estelle sighs like she's heard this complaint a few too many times before. 'It's tradition,' she explains patiently, I feel as much for my benefit as Angela's. 'There's always been a real Christmas tree at Five Mistletoe Square, and I'm not going to be the one to break that tradition.'

Over the next hour, Angela and I, under Estelle's watchful gaze and many directions, carefully decorate the tree. I am a bit wary of the ancient-looking lights we twist first from the top to the bottom of the tree. But Estelle assures me they are perfectly safe, and they use them every year along with everything else in the box.

We then move on to all the decorations that are unwrapped one-by-one from the wooden box. Among the many ornaments we hang are china cherubs, a baby in a manger, a snowflake, and the three wise men, or in this case they look more like three kings.

As I tried to hide from Estelle, decorating a tree has never been high on a list of things I enjoy, along with most things to do with the festive season. My parents never made much of a fuss at Christmas, so I never really experienced as a child the simple joy of decorating the family Christmas tree. But this time is different. As we gradually adorn the full green branches with the trinkets and memories of past festive seasons, the smell of the pine needles and the ever-growing look of delight on Estelle's face makes it so much more enjoyable than the few times I tried to join in with similar activities before.

While we take a short break so Estelle can visit the bathroom, Angela and I stand back to admire our work.

'Only the angel and the star to go,' Angela says, hurrying back over to the table to pick up a cheerful-looking angel with pale pink wings, a white dress and a gold halo over the top of her head. Angela glances quickly at an ornate gold star edged with sparkling crystals, but leaves it on the table.

'Can you reach?' I ask her as she climbs up the wooden ladder.

'Just about.' Angela wobbles a little as she attempts to stretch up to the top of the tree.

'Shall I do it?' I offer. Angela looks precariously balanced on top of the ladder with the angel at the very end of her fingertips. 'I'm a bit taller; it might help.'

'I think you might have to.' Angela says, sighing with frustration as she climbs back down the steps of the ladder. 'But be quick,' she says, looking towards the door to see if Estelle is on her way back yet.

I wonder why she's so concerned, but as I take the angel from her and climb the ladder, I find out why.

'Angela!' Estelle bellows, as she pauses with her walking stick in the doorway. 'You know the rule. The star always goes at the top of the tree. Not the angel.'

I pause awkwardly at the top of the ladder, not knowing what to do.

'Never the angel, is it?' Angela grumbles as she begrudgingly collects the star from the table and heads back over to me. 'Always the bloody star that shines the brightest in your eyes. Here you go,' she says, exchanging the angel for the star. 'Best do what she says.'

While Estelle shuffles across the floor back over to her chair, I place the star on the top of the tree, my arms just long enough to reach. Then Angela passes me the angel, and I hang it as close to the top of the tree as I can.

'There now,' Estelle says, looking proudly up at the tree from her chair. 'We're nearly ready – only the lights to go. Would you like to do the honours this year, Elle?'

'Me?' I ask in surprise as I climb down from the ladder. 'Wouldn't you like to do it, Estelle? It's your tree.'

'This year the tree belongs to all of us,' Estelle says, smiling. 'Unfortunately I can't get down there to switch the lights on.' She gestures with her stick to the switch at the bottom of the wall where the set of lights are plugged in. 'And Angela is too busy sulking.'

'I'm not sulking,' Angela says petulantly. 'I just don't know why the angel can't be on top sometimes, that's all. You do it, Elle. I'm not bothered.'

'As I said – *sulking.*' Estelle tuts, shaking her head. 'Please, Elle, you do it. It's just about dark enough now for them to show up.'

I glance out of the window and sure enough it's just starting to get dark outside. The gas lamps I noticed yesterday around the outside of the square are now lit, making it look quite festive and cheerful in its own right.

'Okay then,' I say, heading over to the plug. I kneel down next to the switch. 'Are you ready?' I look up at Estelle and Angela.

They both nod.

'Right then. Three. Two. One!' I announce, pulling the old black switch down. But the pretty show of lights I expected to see doesn't appear.

'Wait, I'll try again,' I say, lifting the switch up and down a couple of times.

'No,' I hear Estelle call, as I jiggle the switch. 'Don't do that, Elle!'

But instead of my eyes being dazzled by colourful Christmas tree lights, I see a bright white light dart from the plug, at the same time as I feel a sharp pain shoot up my arm and through my body. The force of it strong enough to propel me away from the switch, a little way across the floor.

The last thing I see before everything goes black is Estelle and Angela's stunned-looking faces. *Which is odd*, I think, as I pass out into oblivion, *because it's very clear to me just who has had the biggest shock here.*

Four

I open my eyes and see Angela's concerned face looking down into mine.

'She's alive!' she cries jubilantly as Alvie licks my cheek.

'Of course she's alive.' I hear Estelle's down-to-earth tone behind her. 'She's had a shock from the lights, that's all. The plug must need rewiring.'

'What happened?' I ask, sitting up, feeling a bit woozy. 'That must have been some electric shock to throw me across the floor.'

'That's the trouble with these old buildings,' Estelle says, lifting Alvie onto her lap while Angela helps me up and into the chair by the fireplace. 'The current does have a tendency to surge occasionally.'

'It does if you won't pay an electrician to come and fix it properly,' Angela grumbles.

'Electricians cost money,' Estelle says while Angela pours me a glass of water. 'The last one said the whole house needed rewiring, and in the short time I have here I'm not paying for that. Now, are you all right, Elle?' she asks, looking at me with concern. 'Any damage done?'

'I don't think so,' I reply, moving my head and arms around. 'I feel much the same as usual.'

Estelle and Angela glance briefly at each other.

'Good. Good,' Estelle says. 'We'll leave the lights for now. Maybe that nice barrister chap from next door will come in and take a look at them for us if we ask him nicely?'

Angela sighs. 'Ben is a solicitor, not a barrister. And he's definitely not an electrician.'

'They probably charge similar amounts if the last electrician we had here is anything to go by.'

The large brass knocker rattles on the front door.

'I'll go, shall I?' Angela says when Estelle and I don't move.

'That is part of your duties,' Estelle reminds her.

'Duties . . .' Angela mutters, heading towards the door. 'I'm sure this wasn't what I agreed to . . .'

Estelle rolls her eyes at me and quietly shakes her head.

'Hello there! Come in! Come in!' we hear Angela say with an unusually enthusiastic tone. 'Yes, they're just through here.' She reappears at the sitting-room door. 'It's Ben . . . I mean Mr Harris from next door,' she announces.

'Ben is just fine,' Ben says amiably, walking into the room. 'I hope I'm not intruding, but I was just on my way out when I couldn't help but notice what looked like a rather large electrical spark shoot across your room. It lit up your whole front window. Is everything all right?'

He glances at me and half smiles.

'How kind of you to call and check on us,' Estelle says, her green eyes looking even brighter as she speaks to Ben. 'I'm pleased to say we're all absolutely fine. Elle here was just finishing off our tree. As you can see, we've got it decorated now.' She gestures to the Christmas tree.

'Wow, that looks great,' Ben says approvingly. 'I did wonder when I was lifting it in yesterday why you were getting such a big tree, but now it's all decorated I can see why – it's quite the statement with all your vintage decorations. So, just your lights now, is it?'

Estelle nods. 'That is the problem, I'm afraid. Our lights seem to have malfunctioned. That was the spark you witnessed. It caught poor Elle here quite unawares.'

'Crikey, are you all right?' Ben looks quite concerned. 'That looked like a nasty electric shock.'

'I'm fine – really,' I tell him. 'It was the shock more than anything – I mean, obviously it was a shock ... oh, you know what I mean.' My cheeks flush.

'Yes.' Ben smiles properly at me this time, and to my annoyance my stomach does a little somersault of pleasure while he holds my gaze. 'I know exactly what you mean. Shall I take a look? I'm not much of a sparky, but my dad was, and I learnt a little from him.'

'That would be most kind of you,' Estelle says, her sharp eyes clearly noticing the plug socket isn't the only thing in the room where there's a spark.

Ben heads over to the plug socket.

'Do you possibly have an electric screwdriver and some rubber gloves?' he asks Angela. 'Just in case it's still live.'

'I think so,' Angela says. 'The electric one has a clear handle, yes?'

'That's exactly right,' Ben says. 'Clear handle, small head.'

Angela hurries off to the kitchen. She quickly returns with a screwdriver and a pair of yellow washing-up gloves, which Ben pulls tightly over his hands.

'Now then,' he says, gently removing the plug. 'Let's have a look.'

Ben carefully unscrews the plug, and then the socket, and examines them.

'I can't see anything wrong with either of them. Perhaps I should try the plug in the socket again.'

I'm about to ask him if that's a good idea after what happened to me, but before I can say anything I hear Estelle and Angela's words of encouragement.

'Right then,' Ben says, pulling off the gloves and putting the plug in the socket once more. 'Here we go. Three, two, one!' He flicks the switch, and I see the same thing happen to him that happened to me just now – a bright light that fills the whole room, followed by a body shooting a little way across the polished wooden floor.

'Whoa,' Ben says, blinking a little and sitting up as I rush to his side. 'I think you might need to get that socket looked at. But it seems my efforts haven't been in vain – look.'

I follow his gaze and realise that unlike when I tried to switch the socket on, this time the lights have actually lit up. The tree, which had looked pretty good before, now looks amazing. Tiny, coloured lights illuminate all the ornaments we'd hung so carefully, so they shine and sparkle like precious gems.

'Merry Christmas!' Ben sings, looking up at Estelle and Angela gazing at the tree. 'May the season of goodwill bring you everything you both desire.' He glances at me sitting next to him on the floor. 'It seems the festive season has started with a bang for both of us, Elle.'

'It certainly has,' I agree.

'Now Christmas can really begin,' Estelle announces from her chair. 'And I've a feeling this year is going to be a magical one for us all.'

After dinner – which Estelle tried to persuade Ben to stay

for, but he politely declined, explaining he already had other plans – I settle down in the sitting room for the first of what Estelle is insisting we call 'Christmas Story Time'.

I baulk a bit at the name, but this is what I'm being paid for, so if Estelle wants to call it that, then who am I to argue?

The fire is burning brightly in the hearth, making the room feel warm and cosy. Surprisingly, the tree lights have remained on, making the atmosphere in the room feel very festive, and Alvie, curled up on top of his red tartan blanket in his basket by the fire, only adds to the scene, making it look very much like a charming vintage Christmas card.

Also surprising is the fact I'm feeling no after effects of my earlier electric shock. Before Ben had left we'd had a brief word with each other about our shared experience. But as neither of us felt any worse for wear, we decided to let it go as just 'one of those things'.

So, as we settle down to hear the first of Estelle's stories, all is well in Five Mistletoe Square.

'What's that?' Estelle asks as I put my smartphone down on the table to record our conversation.

'It's my phone – I'm going to use it as a Dictaphone to record what you tell me. It will make it easier for me to type up my notes later.'

'What's wrong with paper and a nice fountain pen?'

I smile. 'Nothing, I just find this is a lot easier.'

'Hmm …' Estelle looks suspiciously at the phone. 'I've never trusted those things. They have a tendency to malfunction in my experience.'

'I'm sure it will be fine,' I assure her. 'Now, let me worry about how I'm going to record your stories, and you worry about recalling them for me.'

Until now, everything that went on in the house felt like it was very much at Estelle's behest. Now we are finally about to begin my part in this agreement, I suddenly feel a little more in control.

One of the reasons I wanted to become a journalist was because I liked hearing people's stories. Not necessarily exciting or adventurous stories, but just everyday tales that meant something to the person telling them.

I get the feeling from what Estelle has said so far that the stories she's about to tell me mean a lot to her, and I'm determined to record them as best I can.

Angela returns to the sitting room with a pot of tea for us all, which she insists on pouring into more china teacups – this time with a suitably festive holly and ivy pattern on them – before finally she settles down in a chair next to Estelle and me by the fire so we can begin.

'Right, where shall we start?' I ask, setting the voice recorder on my phone running. I lift my tea and take a sip.

'I always find it's best to start at the beginning,' Estelle says. 'Now, if you'll make sure the first decoration is in exactly the right place, please, Angela.'

Angela goes over to the tree and lifts a bauble shaped like a newborn baby in a pale blue crib. She moves it across to the side of the tree.

'Now, we wait,' Estelle says, lifting her tea from the little table next to her chair, and I wonder what we're waiting for.

Estelle glances at the clock on the mantelpiece while she sips her tea, and as she does I notice the moon through the window outside. Slowly it begins to peek out from behind the bank of cloud it's been caught behind. At exactly the same time as the clock strikes eight, the moon shines through the window, its luminescent glow landing directly on the baby in the crib.

'Now we are ready,' Estelle announces. 'For our first story I'd like to take you all the way back to the London of Georgian times.' She puts her tea back down on the table and happily settles into recalling the first of her stories, but as she does something odd begins to happen. 'I'm not sure if you're aware, Elle,' she says as the furniture in the room suddenly begins to fade away. 'But this house, along with all the other houses on Mistletoe Square, was built in 1750 by a renowned architect of the time called Joseph Christmas. He designed buildings all over London, but Mistletoe Square was his pride and joy.'

I glance across at Angela to see if Estelle's words are having the same effect on her and she's seeing what I am. But Angela just appears to be listening calmly alongside me. She doesn't seem to notice that as Estelle speaks the room is changing all around us.

'Joseph,' Estelle continues, while the dining table begins to slide through some newly formed double doors into the room that was Estelle's bedroom, but now is transforming into a formal dining room, 'not only put his time and energy into this square, but his heart too. He built Number Five to live in with his wife, Celeste, and their only child, Nora.'

The chairs that were around the disappearing table slide seamlessly into a new position with their backs firmly against the walls, their upholstery changing from a light chintz pattern to a heavy velvet, and they now rest in between a couple of small card tables.

'Joseph was not only a successful man in his own right,' Estelle says calmly, seemingly unaware of the changes taking place in her own house, 'he was a philanthropist too. He supported many good causes and charities of the time.' Much of Estelle's furniture has now faded away, only a few pieces made from dark mahogany remain. In its place, different pieces of furniture, again much of it crafted from shiny, dark wood, fill the room – it's very clearly antique in style, but somehow it manages to look brand new.

'But, sadly, Joseph passed away suddenly in 1753, and, in 1754, Celeste remarried, to a man who was not as kind-hearted as Joseph. We join their story on Christmas Eve 1755 ...'

The room becomes colder, even though a fire still burns merrily away in the hearth. The Christmas tree that Angela and I spent so long decorating earlier has now vanished, and in its place, fresh winter greenery mixed with the sharp spikes and red berries of holly is positioned on top of a large sideboard and an expensive-looking chest of drawers. More greenery is also hung over the frames of oil paintings and watercolours, which hang from a new picture rail running the length of the dark red walls.

I shiver and blink a few times, then I rub my eyes, but nothing changes.

Except everything has. Everything is different.

'Watch,' I hear Estelle say next to me as I open my mouth to question what I'm seeing. 'This is where our story begins ...'

Five

24 December 1755

A Child is Born ...

'Ooh, it's criminal,' a stout, red-faced woman says, bustling into the room. She's followed by a slim young girl. Both of them wear long dark dresses, white aprons and white mob caps. 'That poor girl up there in all that pain, and for what? I'll tell you for what?' the older woman continues when the younger one doesn't speak. 'For them to give the child away as soon as it arrives in this world.' She looks up and crosses herself. 'Heaven help us.'

The younger woman simply nods in agreement.

'Now, Beth, you make sure that fire is well stoked,' the older woman instructs. 'You know the master likes a roaring fire to sit beside after dinner.'

The young woman comes over to where we're sitting, walks directly between us and begins tending to the fire.

Estelle and Angela don't even flinch. They simply watch her.

Okay, this is just getting really weird now.

I'm about to try and find out what on earth is going on when another woman comes into the room. This one is wearing much smarter clothes than the other two – a long dress again, but in a much more expensive-looking fabric – a blue-and-green striped silk. It has a long full skirt, fitted bodice and three-quarter length sleeves. Her hair is pinned up artistically on her head in a style reminiscent of a very ornate sixties beehive. I recognise her immediately from the painting in the hall.

'This is Celeste,' Estelle says, as though there is nothing unusual in any of this.

'Are you finished in here, Edith?' Celeste asks.

'Not quite, m'lady.' Edith, the older maid, bobs a little curtsey. 'We're just getting the fire ready for the master – we knows how he likes to add the yule log himself.'

'Thank you.' Celeste sighs wearily. 'Do forgive me, it has been a trying day for all of us.' She goes over to the window and gazes out into the square. 'It's starting to snow. Usually that would bring me so much joy. Especially at this time of year.'

'Yes, m'lady,' Edith agrees quietly. 'Are you done yet, Beth?' She looks impatiently over at the young girl.

'Almost,' Beth mumbles.

Edith stands awkwardly, her hands clasped in front of her as she waits for Beth to finish the fire.

'Edith, I want to thank you for your help with Nora earlier,' Celeste says, turning back from the window.

Edith nods. 'Least I could do when the young mistress was in so much pain and there wasn't a midwife or a doctor nowhere to be seen.' Edith immediately looks like she wishes she could take back the last part of her statement. 'I . . . I mean, I knows you had your reasons m'lady. Banning mistletoe at Christmas is one thing, but medics too?'

'You know why Jasper disapproves of mistletoe in the house at this time of year,' Celeste says, avoiding the question.

'It reminds him of the old master, God rest his soul.' Edith closes her eyes for a moment and crosses herself. 'Because he built Mistletoe Square. Yes, I knows that. But having a doctor in the house wasn't going to do that, and with such a difficult birth too . . . ' Edith looks a little accusingly at her mistress.

'Nora did very well in the circumstances. I am so proud of her.' Celeste's voice breaks slightly and she hurriedly looks out of the window again.

'What time are they coming?' Edith asks. 'To take the baby?'

Celeste's head whips round. 'You know about that?'

'We all knows, m'lady.' Edith dares to sound a little reproachful now.

Celeste glances over at Beth, but although she must be listening to this conversation, she silently continues tending to the fire. 'I suppose you all think we are doing a terrible thing?' Celeste asks.

'It's not any of our business what to think, m'lady,' Edith says, clearly wanting to say more, but this time managing to hold back her words.

Celeste sighs. 'Speak your mind, Edith. I will not hold what you say against you. I promise. We have known each other a long time now, have we not?'

Fire complete, Beth stands up, straightens her apron and comes and stands by Edith's side.

'We certainly have,' Edith agrees. 'Way back before you and the master, I mean the old master, moved into this house.' She pauses, then she nods quickly, as if she's allowing herself to speak her mind. 'It's just … it's Christmas tomorrow, m'lady. You can't allow the young mistress to give her baby up at Christmas. It's just not right.'

'Does it make a difference?' Celeste asks, a look of despair on her pale face. 'It is going to happen whatever. So why not at Christmastime?'

'The old master wouldn't have let it happen,' Edith mumbles. 'Whatever the time of year.'

Celeste stares hard at Edith, a mix of sorrow and grief on her face now. 'You are absolutely right, Edith, he would not. But things are different now; Joseph is no longer with us. Jasper is master of this house now, and we must abide by what he wants.'

'But Nora is your daughter, m'lady,' Edith says desperately, 'and that little one up there is your grandchild. You can't just let the master get rid of him.'

'Get rid of who?' Another much louder and more powerful voice joins the women now, as a tall, disagreeable-looking man with black hair enters the parlour. He's wearing breeches, a long tail coat with a matching waistcoat and black knee-high boots. 'What are we discussing, Celeste?'

The two maids immediately bow their heads.

'Nothing for you to concern yourself with, husband. We were just discussing a small rat problem that Edith and Beth have brought to my attention. Thank you, Edith. That will be all for now.' She nods hurriedly at Edith.

'Yes, m'lady,' Edith says, bobbing a curtsey before grabbing Beth and making for the door. I watch them leave, quite forgetting how strange this all is, but so entranced already by this story my only thought is, what happens next?

'Quick, stand up!' I hear Angela say, and I turn to see Estelle nimbly leap up from her chair.

'What? Why?'

'Just do it,' Angela instructs.

I stand up and quickly follow them over to where they're now standing on the other side of the room, right where the dining table had been until a few moments ago.

'Jasper is heading towards the chairs and you don't want them sitting on you,' Angela whispers, as we watch the man walk across to the fireplace. 'It's really not pleasant at all.'

I'm about to ask her what she means, when Jasper speaks.

'Why are you frequenting that window, Celeste?' He sits down in the chair Estelle always favours. Except, I notice now, the chairs have also changed, and are nothing like the floral fabric ones we were sitting in before. They are now much more upright wingback armchairs in a dark green leather. 'You will catch your death of cold standing there, especially now it's snowing outside. Come, sit by the fire with your husband.'

Celeste looks over at him, clearly wanting to be anywhere else than by his side right now. But she does as she's told and sits down in the chair opposite.

'Now, what is making my wife look quite so sad on this eve of Christmas?' Jasper asks, warming his hands in front of the fire. 'This is the season of joy, my dear, not of melancholy.'

'It is nothing, husband.' Celeste sits with perfect posture in the chair, her hands clasped neatly in her lap.

'It must be something, dear wife. Pray tell me?'

Celeste swallows hard, then bravely she takes a deep breath.

'My child is upstairs having given birth to my first grand-child today,' she says quietly, looking down into her lap. 'I wish to know my grandson. I do not want him to go to strangers.'

Jasper doesn't say anything as he continues to warm his hands. But his silence makes the room feel even chillier.

'The child upstairs may well be your grandson, but he is also a bastard,' Jasper says in a quiet but steady voice, still looking into the flames. 'Your daughter is not married, and is unlikely to become so now she has lost her virtue. When you told me she was with child, I was more than generous in letting her stay under my roof, was I not?'

Annoyingly, Celeste nods. 'You were, husband.'

'And did we not agree that, on the birth of the child, it would be removed from this house immediately?'

'We did, but—'

'But nothing!' Jasper bellows. 'I have a reputation to uphold, Celeste,' he continues in a lower, but no less menacing voice. 'I cannot and will not allow that bastard to remain in my house.' He pulls a pocket watch from his waistcoat. 'They will be here at a quarter past the hour, and we will never talk of this again. Do you hear?'

Celeste nods hurriedly, then she stands up.

'Where do you go now?' Jasper asks.

'I have things to attend to,' Celeste says, clearly trying to hold back her tears.

'What things?'

'For the handover.'

Jasper nods. 'Very well.'

Celeste leaves the room.

Forgetting for a moment just how strange the situation I currently find myself in is, I turn quickly towards Estelle and Angela. 'What happens next?' I demand.

'We simply watch the story unfold.' Estelle says calmly. 'All will be explained. Come, we move forward a few minutes.'

Walking with incredible ease, Estelle leads us out of the sitting room and into the hallway.

'The tiles are still the same!' I say, looking down at the black-and-white patterned floor tiles that are in Estelle's house. 'Yours must be the originals.'

But Angela and Estelle are looking at the front door.

Seconds later someone rattles on it.

Edith hurries past us to open it. 'You must be from the hospital,' she mutters, clearly trying to hide her anger. 'I suppose you'd best come in.'

A gentleman wearing a long, grey woollen coat, gloves and a top hat steps into the hallway. He brushes the snow from his coat and his hat before he enters.

'Wait here,' Edith says, heading for the stairs. 'I'll let the mistress know you have arrived.'

'No need, Edith.' Celeste is already walking slowly down the stairs carrying a tightly wrapped bundle, which she presses tightly to her body.

'You must be Mr Jenkins,' she says as she reaches the bottom of the stairs.

The man gives a small bow. 'I am indeed, madam.'

'I understand my husband has made all the necessary arrangements,' Celeste continues in a formal voice.

'He has.' The gentleman nods. 'We are most grateful to him. Your husband was very generous in his donation.'

'I'm sure. You'll take care of him, won't you?' Celeste asks, clearly prolonging the awful moment a little longer.

'Madam, I can assure you we take care of all our children extremely well.'

Celeste nods, but as she gazes down at the baby in her arms she looks heartbroken.

The gentleman holds out his arms. But Celeste isn't ready to let go.

'I understand this is difficult,' the man says gently. 'But it is for the best.'

'Is it?' Celeste asks, her pale cheeks flushing. 'For who? Not for myself or my daughter upstairs sobbing her heart out. Not for this little one, so new to the world, so innocent, so very, very loved.'

Celeste begins to shake, and inside the bundle of blankets the baby wakes, and a tiny hand emerges.

'Madam, please.' The man holds his arms out again.

'The token, m'lady?' Edith suggests, buying Celeste a few more precious moments with her grandson. 'Why don't you give him the token?'

'Yes, the token,' Celeste says gratefully. With one hand she reaches into a small pocket at the front of her dress. 'Please take this as a token of our love for the boy.' She gazes down at a tiny piece of red velvet in her hand. 'Just in case one day . . .' But it's suddenly all too much for her. As the tears begin to roll down her cheeks she buries her face in the baby's blankets.

Edith quickly takes the token from her. 'The young mistress upstairs embroidered it herself,' she says to the man, holding out a tiny red velvet heart, no bigger than the silver locket Celeste wears around her neck. 'So we stitched it into this token to carry with him.'

The man takes the heart from Edith. He pulls out an eye-glass from his waistcoat pocket so he can examine it more closely. 'It is indeed a work of art. Mistletoe, holly and ivy, and is that the words *St Nicholas* stitched in gold?' he asks, squinting so he can pick out the tiny details.

'It is,' Celeste says, recovering a little. She still holds the baby so close to her, I can't imagine she will ever be able to let him go. 'The winter greenery is to remind him when he was born,' she continues, her voice beginning to crack again. 'And St Nicholas, because he's the patron saint of children. Which is why my first husband had it painted over our door.' She points up to the fanlight, and I can just make out the words etched in gold over the glass. 'When he was alive he felt very passionately that children must be protected and looked after. So we have included it on the token in the hope this little one will be protected too, and if such a time ever came, and he was able to return to us . . . ' Her voice falters again.

'Please do not fret, madam,' the man assures her. 'It will be kept safe. As all our children's tokens are.' He tucks the token away safely inside his jacket with his eyeglass, then he holds out his arms again. 'Please?'

This time Celeste nods. She gently kisses the baby, and allows the man to take him. As the baby is removed from her arms, we see her visibly wilt as her legs buckle underneath her, and Edith immediately rushes over to support her.

'I will keep him safe, I promise you,' the man says, looking quite moved. The baby now safely in his arms, he moves towards the door. 'And I will make sure the heart stays with him always.'

Celeste has now collapsed on the stairs sobbing, while Edith crouches next to her, trying to provide some comfort.

The man opens the door ready to let himself out; some flakes of snow blow in through the open door as he does. He turns back to the women, bows quickly, then puts his top hat back on before beginning to back slowly outside.

'Good evening to you both.' He pauses on the steps and I feel a chill wind whistle through the entrance to the house. 'I wish you a merry . . . my apologies . . . a *peaceful* Christmas may be more appropriate in the circumstances.'

'Let us return,' Estelle says, her head bowed as she turns towards the sitting room.

Six

19 December 2018

I follow the other two back into the sitting room and I'm amazed to find that the room has transformed back to its original decor.

'How is this even possible?' I ask, looking around me. 'It can't go from one thing to another and back again so fast?'

'Why don't you sit down?' Estelle gestures to the armchair opposite her as she eases herself into her own chair.

Reluctantly I do as she says, but I still have so many questions.

'How did all that just happen?' I demand, still looking around me. The Christmas tree is back in front of the window again – decorated with all the decorations that Angela and I originally hung on it. 'One minute you're telling me a story about your ancestors and the next . . . well, it was like we were there with them. Except how could we have been – that was over two hundred and fifty years ago!'

61

'Estelle *is* a very good storyteller,' Angela says calmly, picking up her cup of tea again. 'I'm always amazed at her level of detail.'

'That wasn't just good storytelling.' I look suspiciously at them both. 'That was like some magic trick, at the very least a trick of the mind.' I see my own cup of tea has miraculously appeared next to me again and I frown. 'What's in this?' I pick up the cup, which is still warm. 'Some sort of hallucinogenic drug – is that it? Did you drug me?' I lift the cup to my nose, but nothing unusual wafts up my nostrils, just the usual aroma of tea.

Estelle looks at Angela and smiles.

'This isn't funny!' I cry, my china cup clanking back down on its saucer as I leap up. 'One minute we're here by the fire and you're telling me a simple story, and the next ... it's like we're in a Jane Austen novel. Now you tell me exactly what went on just now, or ... or I walk!' I point towards the front door. 'I walk out of this house right now, away from this hocus-pocus, and away from writing your family history, Estelle!'

I stare challengingly at them both.

As they both look back at me, Angela has the good grace to look worried, possibly even a little ashamed. But Estelle just seems cool and collected as always.

'Where would you go?' she asks calmly, to my surprise.

'What do you mean?'

'I mean where would you go? It's the nineteenth of December. I doubt you'd get lodgings now right before Christmas, and we both know you can't afford a hotel – especially not during the festive season.'

'You don't know anything about me,' I say, quite unnerved by both Estelle's cool questioning and also her accuracy. She's spot on, of course. But how? 'You don't know what I can or can't afford. Or how many people I could go and stay with.'

'Well, it won't be your family, will it?' Estelle says, lifting her own tea and taking a sip. 'You've fallen out with them.'

'H-how could you possibly know that?' I ask, still aghast at her knowledge of my life.

Estelle shrugs. 'I know many things.'

'But you can't possibly . . . Who have you been talking to?'

'Maybe you could go and stay with one of your many friends,' she continues. 'I'm sure they'd be overjoyed to have you. Or would they be quite so keen when they're mostly your ex's friends?'

I stare at Estelle. This was just plain weird now. How could she possibly know any of this?

'I don't think you have an awful lot of choice, do you, Elle? It looks to me like Christmas House is your best bet right now.'

I feel my legs buckle underneath me, like I'd seen Celeste's do just now. But unlike Celeste, I don't have an Edith to fall back on, so instead I fall back into the chair.

'I think that's enough now,' Angela says, raising her eyebrows at Estelle. 'Are you all right, Elle?' she asks gently. 'The last few minutes must have been quite a shock.'

I'm not sure if she's talking about our trip into the past or Estelle's all too accurate summing up of my life.

'I think it might be time to break out the whisky,' Estelle announces. 'Elle looks like she needs a pick-me-up. She's gone quite pale.'

'Oh no,' I say, waving my finger at them. 'I'm not taking anything else from you two until you tell me exactly what's going on.'

Estelle glances at Angela.

'Ah-ah, don't look at me.' Angela shakes her head. 'I said to take it slowly. You were the one who said she'd be all right with it.'

'All right with what?' I demand. 'Will you please tell me what's going on here – the truth this time.'

'It's really nothing to be concerned about,' Estelle says kindly, after she's cast an irritated look in Angela's direction. 'Everything I've told you so far is absolutely true. I do want you to write the history of this house and my family, and I do want you to stay here with us while you do.' Estelle glances at Angela again, and Angela nods her encouragement. 'I'm sorry if I was a little harsh with you just now, Elle. I didn't mean to be rude, even if I came over that way. Perhaps my methods might be ... how can I put this ... a little *different* than you're used to. But please trust me when I say that everything we do is for your benefit, Elle. We will never put you at any risk, or let you come to any harm.'

What a strange thing to say – 'it's for my benefit'. Why is any of this for my benefit? Unless Estelle means so I can understand her stories better? But that still doesn't explain how what happened just happened!

But Estelle seems so genuine as she speaks, it's hard for me to disbelieve anything she's saying. I've met and interviewed enough people in my time to know when someone is lying, and I really don't think Estelle is.

'That's good to know ... I guess,' I reply tentatively. 'But that still doesn't explain how you know so much about me. I haven't told you any of that about my friends, or my family.'

'No, *you* didn't ...' Estelle looks to Angela for assistance.

'People talk,' Angela says quickly. 'We couldn't just let you come and live here without checking on you first, could we?

64

We didn't ask for references, so I spoke to a couple of people at the magazine you worked for and they probably told me more than they should have when I pushed them a little. I'm sorry.'

I think about this. If Angela had spoken to Michelle in Accounts, or Gemma in Advertising, then they would have told her everything – they're such gossips. But that still doesn't explain how Estelle knows about my family. I never talk to anyone about that. Or why I don't want to spend Christmas with my parents any more.

'I guessed about your family,' Estelle says, reading my mind. 'It doesn't take a genius to work out if you would rather spend Christmas here with two strangers rather than your family, it means you've likely fallen out with them.'

I suppose that makes sense.

'I'm very sorry if I touched a raw nerve, Elle.' Estelle looks genuinely sorry. 'I may seem a little brusque at times, but it's just my way. My heart is in the right place, though, isn't it, Angela?'

Angela nods. 'You'll get used to Estelle. Her bark is *always* worse than her bite.'

Alvie, on cue, gives a little yap from his basket.

'You're absolutely right. I don't see much of my parents these days,' I say, watching Alvie settle down in his basket again. 'It's been a gradual thing over time though, so I'd really rather not talk about it if you don't mind?'

Estelle and Angela both nod.

'But that still doesn't explain how you made your first story seem so real tonight. What's the trick?'

'There is no trick,' Estelle says. 'Is there, Angela?'

Angela, a little reluctantly, shakes her head.

'I just feel it's important to make history seem as real as

possible. Did it seem real?' Estelle cleverly turns the questioning back to me.

'A bit too real,' I reply, still not happy with this explanation, but I'm quickly realising Estelle isn't easily going to reveal the secret of how she's doing this. So I decide to bide my time for now and change my line of questioning. 'So, what happened to the baby in the end? Did they get it back? Please tell me that awful Jasper met a grisly end and they were able to rescue the baby from the children's home or wherever it went to?'

'Elle, this isn't a fairy story I'm telling you,' Estelle says solemnly. 'This is real life, and real life doesn't always have a happy ending. The baby didn't go to a children's home, it went to a foundling hospital. Back then there was one not too far away from here. Foundlings were usually children rescued from poverty, or babies that were thought would die if left with their mother. The majority of the children that were cared for by the hospital that Celeste's grandson went to were given up by their mother voluntarily, when circumstances meant they were unable to care for them. Foundlings that young were usually sent to a wet nurse in the country, returning at around five years old to be schooled if they were lucky.'

'But the baby we saw had a wealthy family – he wasn't poor or at risk?'

'No, but pregnancy out of wedlock back then wasn't just frowned upon, it was positively despised. There was no way Jasper could have let that baby stay, and uphold his position in society. If the secret had got out, his reputation would have been ruined. It was quite common back then for babies born in these circumstances to be quietly taken away, in exchange for a large donation to a charity such as the foundling hospital.'

'But he was wanted by his mother, and by Celeste,' I say,

angry that Jasper had got his own way, without the women having any say in what happened. 'Was Edith right, would Celeste's first husband have let him stay?'

'Possibly. He was a much kinder man than Jasper and less bothered by what society thought. But once Celeste remarried after Joseph's death, Jasper became the head of the family; he was in charge and made all the decisions. Back then Celeste had no choice but to abide by his wishes or she would have found herself and Nora destitute, and without a home.'

'Bloody men,' I say, thinking of Owen. 'They think they can get away with everything, and we'll just forgive them and carry on as normal.' I stare at the baby in the crib hanging innocently from the Christmas tree. 'Not this time!' I bang my balled fist on the top of my thigh. 'Not this time,' I murmur again, frustrated not only for Celeste but for myself too. Suddenly I remember where I am. I glance hurriedly at Estelle and Angela, wondering what they must be thinking. But they both just look at me with sympathy. 'It was so much worse back then, wasn't it?' I add, hoping they'll quickly forget my outburst. 'For women, I mean.'

'Indeed it was,' Estelle says, continuing on as if nothing unusual has happened. 'Luckily things have changed somewhat since then. Thanks to the effort of our forebears, we're seen a little more equally now. Even if things still go a little wrong for us at times.' She gives me another sympathetic look.

'So what became of the baby?' I ask quickly, keen to keep the focus on the house and Estelle's family, and not me. 'Did they ever get him back? And his little heart token – what was that about?'

'Babies given up back then were usually given a token of some sort,' Estelle explains. 'This enabled them to be easily identified if the parent should want to come back and claim them again in the future. Because their names were changed immediately on entering the hospital, it was the only way to differentiate one child from another as they grew. But as you can imagine, the tokens, which were anything from an engraved coin to a ticket stub, or even jewellery in some cases, often went missing – so it wasn't a great system, but back then the only one they had.'

'Poor Celeste,' I say, thinking of her sobbing in Edith's arms. 'And poor Nora. What became of them?'

'Jasper died some years later, not from a grisly death as you suggested, Elle,' says Estelle, looking reprovingly over her glasses at me, 'but simply from heart failure. Celeste, probably sensibly, never married again, but continued to live in this house. Nora went on to have a family of her own with a very kind man who was quite high up in the world of banking. When Celeste died, and Nora inherited the house, she moved back in with her husband and family, and it's been passed down through our family ever since.'

'I'm so pleased both Celeste and Nora had a happy life in the end.'

'They did. Nora's husband was a good man, like her father was. But I don't think Nora ever truly got over having her first child taken away – even though she was very young when it happened. So she persuaded her husband, who was very wealthy, to become a patron of a children's hospital, and they helped to raise significant and much-needed funds over the coming years for charity. So some good did come of Jasper's decision eventually.'

'Hmm, but at what cost?' I say, thinking of Nora. 'I wonder what became of the baby if they never managed to trace him?'

'I guess we'll never know,' Estelle says quickly. 'Now, I'm feeling a little tired after our story tonight. I think I might have an early night if that's all right with the two of you?'

'Of course.'

'I'll help you to your room.' Angela hurries over to help Estelle up.

'Goodnight, Elle,' Estelle says, as she shuffles towards the door using her stick, followed by Alvie. 'Have a good evening. I will see you tomorrow, and my apologies again if anything tonight shocked you too much.'

'Goodnight, Estelle. Sleep well.'

'And you, my dear, and you.'

I watch Estelle, Angela and Alvie leave. Then, not really knowing what to do next, I glance around the room, and my gaze falls once more upon the beautifully lit Christmas tree.

I stand up and go over to examine in more detail the decoration the moonlight had fallen on earlier tonight. 'If all that can come from one baby in a cradle, I wonder what all you others have in store for me?' I whisper, looking at the other vintage decorations with interest.

Then I head back over to the chairs by the fire, and tidy up the tea things, loading them onto the tray. 'My phone!' I exclaim as I see it still sitting on the little table. 'And it's still recording, too. I'll have some very interesting stuff to write about when I listen back to it later.' I pop my phone into my pocket, then I lift the tray and head through the hall down to the kitchen. I decide the china tea set is a little delicate for a dishwasher, so I run a bowl of soapy water and wash the cups and saucers by hand. I'm about to head up to my room when Angela appears in the kitchen.

'You needn't have done that,' she says, seeing the cups and saucers on the draining board. 'But thank you.'

'It's fine, I don't mind helping out. If it's all right I'm going to go up to my room now,' I say, wondering what Angela does of an evening when Estelle goes to bed. 'I'm going to start writing up this first story immediately. Is that okay?'

'Of course it is. What you do with your free time is no business of mine. I won't be late to bed either once I've let Alvie outside to do his business. Estelle is always an early riser.' Angela pauses. 'I'm sorry if tonight was a bit of a shock for you, Elle. It can take a while to get used to Estelle's storytelling methods. They may seem strange at first, but once you stop trying to make sense of it, and you simply let it happen, it's much easier to come to terms with, believe me.'

'Right . . . ' I say, not knowing quite how to respond to this. 'I'll try. I guess I'll say goodnight then?'

'You're welcome to use the sitting room to write in, if you'd rather?' Angela suggests. 'I always enjoy sitting by the fire in the evenings, especially now the Christmas tree is up. But I won't be tonight. I'm quite tired, so it's all yours.'

'I might do that. Thank you.' I leave Angela in the kitchen and I head up to my room, deciding when I get there that an evening by the fire writing up this first story might be preferable to sitting up here in my room alone. Which, although perfectly warm and comfortable, isn't anywhere near as cosy as the sitting room with a roaring fire for company.

So I take my laptop, a notebook and my phone downstairs and get settled in a chair by the fire. I open my notebook ready to jot down a few things before I type up the story and then I press play on the voice memo.

I listen to Estelle tell the background of the story about Joseph and Celeste, and Joseph building the house. 'We join their story on Christmas Eve 1755 . . . ' she says. But then the voice memo goes silent.

'What? You're kidding me!' I lift the phone up and adjust the volume, but there's nothing. I push the memo on a bit to see if it's picked anything up a bit further along, but still nothing. It seems no amount of fiddling with the memo will produce any sound in the middle of the recording until I hear my own voice say: 'How is this even possible? It can't go from one thing to another and back again so fast?' Then the conversation between myself, Estelle and Angela is recorded until Estelle goes to bed and I go over to look at the Christmas tree.

Hmm ... something very odd is going on here, I think as I desperately begin to scribble down everything I can remember about Estelle's first story in my notebook. *And I'm going to find out exactly what that is.*

Seven

20 December 2018

The next morning, I breakfast alone.

Angela tells me Estelle isn't feeling too well, so she's going to stay in bed for a few hours and rest in the hope she will be up to telling me another story later.

My hope that Angela will join me for breakfast, so I can ask her more about last night without her fearing what Estelle might say, is also quashed when she says she's already eaten earlier this morning. 'Always up with the lark, me,' she says proudly as she brings me my breakfast at the table. Today Angela is wearing an outfit that could have stepped right out of the 1960s. She's wearing her hair up again, but instead of the ponytail of yesterday, today it's piled up into a semi beehive reminding me of Celeste's hairstyle from last night. Under her apron she wears a black-and-white mini dress with thick black tights and long black boots, and I marvel at how someone of Angela's age can carry all this off, and still look fabulous.

'Early to bed and early to rise makes me healthy, wealthy and wise! Two out of three isn't bad, I suppose!' she adds with a grimace. 'Estelle prefers to tell her stories at night, so you're not missing out on anything. You have the day to yourself.'

After I've had breakfast, I decide to take a walk to explore the local area. Even though I've lived in London for nearly ten years, the affluent and often bohemian area of Bloomsbury is not somewhere I've ever had the occasion to frequent that often.

It's a beautiful, crisp, cold December day as I wrap my scarf around my neck and head down the steps into Mistletoe Square, wearing my long red winter coat and a pair of long black boots over my jeans.

I take a trip around the square first, admiring the neat, precise Georgian architecture and the tall, elegant houses that surround the little fenced garden in the middle. After last night, I now have a new understanding of what the people who first lived on this square might have been like. Many of the buildings now contain businesses and companies rather than families, and I find myself wondering who else might have lived here when Celeste, Edith and Nora did.

Eventually, I leave the square and head out into the surrounding streets, hoping that a long walk on a cold winter's morning will clear my head a little and allow me to think with more clarity about Christmas House and the people who live there.

Sadly for me, Estelle was spot on last night. If I did leave Mistletoe Square, where else was I going to go right now? With Christmas fast approaching it wasn't going to be easy to find somewhere else to live, or someone to stay with. Not somewhere I wanted to be, anyway. Part of me thinks I should get out of there as fast as possible. It's clear something strange is going on. But part of me – my journalist's nose, as I like to call it – smells a story, and not simply one of Estelle's strange tales. I find myself intrigued by Estelle and Angela and their large Georgian house. How can they afford to live there, when all the other houses in the square have been sold off or rented out to businesses wanting a fancy Bloomsbury address? Why do they live there together, and what exactly is their relationship – friends, colleagues, employer and employee? I desperately want to know more about them.

But it's not just that, I realise, as I walk past the British Museum with its majestic frontage of Greek-style temple columns, the renowned Great Ormond Street children's hospital, and a number of other Georgian squares, similar to, but not quite as pretty as, my new home. I've grown quite fond of Estelle and Angela in the short time I've known them. There's something I really like about the two of them and their quirky relationship. They both made me feel so welcome in their home, and it's been a long time since I felt so comfortable or so wanted.

A warm feeling spreads through me, even though the temperature out here can't be more than three or four degrees. For some reason the thought of spending this Christmas with Estelle and Angela makes me happy. They clearly adore this time of year; perhaps some of their festive cheer will rub off on me if I allow it to?

I smile to myself as I walk. There are a lot of strange things going on in Mistletoe Square, but nothing would be stranger than if I suddenly started liking Christmas.

I glance at the Christmas decorations I pass in office and shop windows, and the flats above them. Everywhere is decorated or lit up in some way with tiny twinkling lights in the shape of stars and angels. Reindeers whose noses glow red, and Santas who wave at me as I pass. Christmas is everywhere right now and there is no getting away from it. But then most people don't want to get away from it, do they? Most people love it. They've probably loved it from when they were small children.

But I'm not most people, and I really can't remember a time when I did like Christmas. Perhaps when I was very young I had, or perhaps I never liked it at all.

But then why would I? When your parents don't have time to celebrate Christmas with you, what reason would you have to enjoy it if you've never made any happy memories at this time of year?

I walk around Brunswick Square with the usual small garden in the middle and black wrought-iron railings around the outside, quickly forgetting all about my negative Christmas thoughts as I pause outside a large building. But this time it's not the architecture that makes me stop walking, it's the yellow sign outside. *The Foundling Museum*, it says in bold black font.

Foundling – that's what Estelle called the little boy that Celeste and Nora were forced to give up.

'You should go in,' a man walking a dog says as he passes by on the pavement behind me. 'It's very good. Much better than some museums I've been to. This one has some meaning, some heart, you know?'

'Thanks,' I tell him, looking up at the building again. 'I might just do that.'

The man carries on his way with his dog, and I head up the steps.

Inside the building, which I quickly discover once originally housed a children's home, is a museum dedicated to telling the story of the foundling hospital, and the children who once lived here. After I pay my entrance fee, I walk through wood-panelled galleries, admiring the many works of art that have been donated to the hospital over the years. I'm intrigued to find that famous and not so famous artists of their time have donated art in support of the hospital. There are works by William Hogarth and Thomas Gainsborough; even Handel's last will and testament is on show. I'm also surprised to discover as I wander that the charity is still in existence today, but it now runs as a successful adoption charity, placing children with a family who will love and care for them as they grow. A fate most of the children who lived here in the early years of the hospital's existence sadly didn't ever get to experience.

But by far the most moving part of my visit is when I come to the galleries telling the stories of the foundling children who lived in the hospital. There are accounts written in their own voices of their daily lives, photographs of the stark dormitories they once shared, and the tiny austere wrought-iron beds they would have slept in. There are stories of what happened to some of them if they were able to be traced, and, perhaps the most moving of all, some of the actual tokens that were left with the children, usually by their mothers, in the desperate hope that one day they would be reunited again.

As I gaze at the many tokens pinned up in a large display cabinet, I'm touched by the vast diversity of things that were used as a possible way of identifying one child from another. There are tiny pieces of fabric and coins, thimbles and playing cards, jewellery and medals. A small walnut has been engraved by one mother with a message to her child. It's clear that very few of the children who ended up here were unwanted by their parents – they were simply incredibly unlucky to be born into difficult circumstances that led to them being orphaned in this way.

I think about what I saw last night, the desperation and grief etched in not only Celeste's face as her grandchild had been taken from her, but in Edith's too.

Children should be with people who love them, I think, as I wander further through the museum. *Whether that be their actual family, or someone who is willing to give them the love they deserve. They should never be somewhere like this.* And for the first time in ages, I think with fondness about my own parents. Did I experience the best upbringing? Perhaps not. But at least I was loved and cared for, even if it was in a slightly unusual way.

After I've spent a couple of hours wandering around the museum, I decide to make my way back towards the house. I still have many things I want to write about from last night, and after my visit to the hospital there's now so much more detail I can add.

I buy a takeaway coffee from a stall just outside Mistletoe Square, with the intention of drinking it on one of the benches inside the gardens before I go back inside.

'You want marshmallows on that?' the vendor asks me. 'Christmas special?'

'No, thank you.'

'Cream?' He holds up a can ready to squirt on my coffee.

'No, just as it is thanks.'

'Sure.' The vendor shrugs at me. 'Nothing wrong with a simple coffee. Especially when it's as good as mine!'

I take my coffee and walk along the path that cuts diagonally through the centre of the garden. I gaze up at the bunches of mistletoe that so many of the bare trees have at their tips. My mind is still partly on what I saw and read about in the museum as I walk, so I'm not really concentrating enough on what's around me.

'Careful!' I hear, right before I collide with a man out jogging. I feel our shoulders catch each other, and I have to steady myself to avoid spilling my coffee.

'I'm so sorry!' I say automatically, as I turn round. 'I didn't see ... Oh, it's you. Gosh, are you all right?'

Ben looks very different today to when we first met. Whereas before he was wearing smart office clothes, today he's wearing running shoes, a sweatshirt and jogging bottoms as he picks himself up off the path.

'Yeah, no harm done,' he says, brushing some leaves off his trousers. 'You caught me off guard or I wouldn't have gone down. Perils of wearing these things,' he says, removing a pair of white Apple AirPods from his ears. 'I should count myself lucky you didn't spill your coffee down me, I suppose.'

'I'd never spill my coffee,' I say with a straight face. 'I'm a bit of a caffeine addict.' I lift my coffee cup and take a sip.

Ben stares at me for a moment, clearly trying to figure me out. Then he grins. 'Nice one,' he says, nodding. 'Me too, actually – you can never have too many cups of coffee. So what were you looking at just now?' he asks. 'You looked totally absorbed in whatever was in those trees.'

'Mistletoe.' I look up again. 'That's what all those balls are high up there in the branches.'

'So they are; I hadn't really noticed before. I guess the square must have been named after something similar – possibly when these trees were first planted?'

'Yes,' I say, thinking of Celeste again as I look up at the branches above us. 'You might be right.'

'Did you know mistletoe is a parasite?' Ben asks

78

matter-of-factly, breaking me from my thoughts. 'It attaches itself to trees and lives off them even though it doesn't belong there. Sometimes it can actually kill the tree as a result.'

'That's not a very romantic view.' My gaze turns back to Ben. 'We all need support sometimes to thrive – even mistletoe.'

'I can tell you're a writer,' Ben says, grinning.

'What's that supposed to mean?' I ask, not mirroring his amused expression.

'It means you have a writer's romantic view of the world – you see things through rose-tinted spectacles. Whereas I'm more practical.'

'Practical ...' I repeat slowly, eyeing him. 'Is that right? Many might use the word "dull" or "boring", even, when describing a solicitor ...'

'Nice one!' Ben replies, not looking in the least bit annoyed. 'I prefer the term lawyer, when I can get away with it. As you rightly pointed out, when you tell people you're a solicitor it can sound a little dull. At least you didn't say "barrister" like Estelle insists on. My colleagues at the bar would be very irritated if they heard me referred to as that. However, you counter very well m'lady, touché!' He suddenly takes up a dramatic pose and pretends to stab at me with an imaginary sword.

I jump at his use of the word 'm'lady', as yet again I'm transported back to last night.

'What's wrong?' Ben asks, looking a little affronted that I don't appear to find this as amusing as he does. 'I haven't actually stabbed you with my imaginary fencing foil, you know?'

'I know. It's nothing, really.'

Ben still looks confused.

'I just don't appreciate your choice of words to describe me,' I say hurriedly. 'I'm a journalist, not a romance writer.'

'Golly,' Ben says, still clearly joking around. 'I didn't realise a journalist's worst enemy is Barbara Cartland.'

'That's not what I mean, and you know it. Anyone who writes at all successfully in their chosen field is equally talented. It's a tough world to break into, whatever you choose to do with your words.'

Ben nods solemnly. 'And currently, you are using your words to tell the story of Estelle's family?'

'That's right.'

'How's that going?'

'It's ... interesting,' I reply diplomatically.

'That good, eh?' Ben grins. 'Perhaps you would rather use the words "dull" or "boring" to describe it?'

'Funny. Actually, no, I wouldn't. I'm enjoying living with both Estelle and Angela; they're teaching me a lot.'

'Really?' Ben grins. 'Oh ... *really*. You mean it?' he asks when my face suggests otherwise. 'Sorry, I thought you were joking.'

There's a slightly awkward pause, but luckily a lady walking a Pekingese dog needs to pass us on the path, so we move aside to let her past.

'Thank you,' she says, smiling. 'Merry Christmas.'

'Merry Christmas,' Ben calls as she walks on with her dog. 'And a Happy New Year! Talking of which,' he says, turning back to me, 'are you staying here on the square for the festive season, or are you going to family ... or friends, perhaps?'

'I'm staying here,' I say, without adding any further detail.

'Right ... ' Ben says, clearly considering something.

'Is there a problem in that?'

'No, not at all. Funnily enough, I'm doing the exact same thing.'

'Are you?' I ask, surprised to hear this. 'Do you have people coming to you?'

Ben shakes his head. 'Nope, it's just me this year.'

'I'm sorry,' I say automatically, a tinge of sadness to my voice. 'Apologies,' I hurriedly add when I realise what I've done. 'I didn't mean to sound like it was a bad thing. If you want to spend Christmas on your own, that's your choice of course.'

'It's fine.' Ben shrugs. 'No apology necessary. I've just had a fairly major relationship break-up. That was partly why I moved here to the square. I suddenly found myself needing a place to work and live, and this was perfect. Came at just at the right time.'

Interesting. Like it did for me . . .

'I'm sorry to hear that,' I say, meaning it. 'Break-ups can be tough. Really tough.'

'You sound like you know what I'm talking about?'

'Yeah . . . a similar thing happened to me recently. I was very nearly spending Christmas on my own too, until I came here.'

Ben and I gaze silently at each other for a moment, and I wonder if he's thinking the same thing as me. There are a lot of similarities in our situations. We might have more in common than I first thought.

'Where did you get your coffee?' Ben asks suddenly. 'I quite fancy one myself. Maybe we could drink it together on that bench over there and compare tales of heartbreak?'

'Er . . .' This is the last thing I feel like doing right now. I've been trying very hard to keep my personal problems under wraps since I came to Mistletoe Square. I like to think I've locked the whole sorry tale somewhere in the depths of Estelle's basement so I don't have to think about it any more, let alone discuss it with a stranger, even if he is my new neighbour.

But Ben's face suggests he really needs someone to talk to right now. 'Sure,' I reply as brightly as I can. 'The coffee place is just over there.' I point to the corner of the square where my vendor was.

'Is it good?' Ben asks. 'I'm quite particular about my coffee.'

'Yes, it is actually. They do marshmallows and cream and stuff if you like that sort of thing?'

'Nah, I like it just as it comes. None of this festive nonsense on top.'

I smile and hold up my cup. 'Me too.'

'Would you like another?'

'I'm good, thanks. Still got most of this one.'

'Of course, you didn't spill any when you carelessly knocked me over, did you?' He winks. 'I'll go and grab a cup and I'll be right back.'

While Ben jogs off, I sit down on one of the benches that are dotted about the garden and sip my coffee, waiting for him to return.

Mistletoe Square really is timeless. If it wasn't for the constant hum of central London on the other side of the buildings, and the occasional vehicle driving around the square, or aeroplane flying overhead, the houses, railings and ornate black gas lamps could easily be dropped into any era and you wouldn't immediately be able to identify what year you were in.

Nothing about this square has probably changed all that much since Celeste, Edith, Beth and Nora lived here. I wonder what they'd make of it now if they could see it as I do. Just as I saw a tiny part of their life last night.

'You looked completely lost in your thoughts just now,' Ben says, as, coffee in hand, he sits next to me on the bench.

'I was just thinking that this square probably hasn't changed all that much since it was built in the eighteenth century.'

Ben looks around. 'Yes, I think most of these features are probably original. Did you know a man from the gas board comes around to light these street lamps every night? Just like in the old days.'

'Gosh, really? No, I didn't know that.'

'No, I'm kidding, they don't do that any more. But someone comes every fortnight to maintain them – they have to be cleaned and their mechanisms have to be wound manually to allow their timer to work. There was someone doing it the day I moved in. That's the only reason I know so much about it – he was very keen to share.'

I look up at the lamps. 'I can imagine someone arriving to light them, though, can't you? With a long pole or something similar. Perhaps they climbed up the posts to get to the light?'

'Is this your romantic side coming out again?' Ben asks, smiling at me.

'Possibly. I've always been interested in history, though – modern history – I like stories of how people used to live. Their daily lives, not battles and wars and stuff. However important they were. It's real people's stories I'm interested in, not who led their troops to victory.'

Ben watches me for a few seconds.

'What?' I ask, feeling a little uncomfortable under his gaze.

'You're really quite interesting, aren't you?'

'Am I?' I ask, not really knowing how to respond.

'Yes. You are.'

'So why are you spending Christmas alone?' I ask suddenly, keen to steer this conversation away from me. 'I mean, I know why, you said. But don't you have family or friends you could go to?'

'I see what you did there.' Ben grins. 'I asked you the same thing earlier, and you managed to neatly sidestep my question.' He raises his eyebrows. 'I however will not do the same to you. Like I said before, I've just got out of a long and difficult relationship, and many of my friends were my ex's friends too, so it makes things a little *complicated*.'

'I see.' *More similarities ...*

'I've had a couple of invitations from colleagues asking me to spend Christmas with them. But who really wants a stranger turning up on their doorstep on Christmas Day? It's a time for families. I'd feel like a spare wheel, and I'd much rather ride a unicycle than be an extra on someone else's car. Does that make sense? I literally made it up just now after I said spare wheel!'

'It makes perfect sense. I know just what you mean; it's only because I've come here to live with Estelle and Angela that I'll be spending Christmas with anyone this year.' I hesitate. Am I ready to discuss this? 'I half-mentioned it before,' I continue before I change my mind. 'But I've recently come from a very similar situation myself. Mine was a nasty break-up too.'

'You have my utmost sympathy – miserable, isn't it?'

I nod.

'So, no family to go to then?' he asks. 'For the festive season I mean. Not permanently.'

'Er ... not really. You?'

Ben shrugs. 'Yes, but I really don't feel like going this year.'

'I totally understand,' I reply with feeling.

'The thing is I'm not really that big on Christmas.' He holds his hands up as if to protect himself.

I stare at him. How do we have so many things in common? It's quite incredible.

'I know. I know. Don't hate me!' Ben says, wincing.

'No, it's not that.' I smile at him. 'I'm completely in the same camp as you. Never been a big fan of Christmas either.'

Ben lowers his hands and looks at me in genuine surprise. 'Wow. It seems like we might have more in common than simply being neighbours?'

'Yes. It's certainly beginning to look that way.' Again, Ben and I gaze silently at each other for a few seconds. 'There's one thing we do differ on, though,' I say, hurriedly breaking the moment. This is happening way too fast for my liking.

'What's that?'

'I'd never let a cup of perfectly good coffee to go waste, like you have.'

Ben looks down into his paper cup. 'And neither would I.'

He swills the coffee around in the cup a couple of times and then downs, what by now on this chilly day must be a luke-warm coffee, in a few big gulps. He gasps. 'There. That hurdle is removed. I will not have coffee be the thing to come between us. So now, Elle, in the absence of other loved ones. What do you say to us being each other's friend this Christmastime?'

Eight

We don't spend too much longer sitting outside on the bench because Ben has a couple of meetings he has to get back for, and he needs to get showered and changed first.

As we walk towards our respective houses, we see Angela hurrying along the pavement towards Christmas House. She's carrying several shopping bags and Ben immediately rushes over to help her with them.

'What a kind young man you are,' she says, blushing a little, as Ben takes the heavy bags. 'Your mother must have brought you up very well indeed.'

Ben doesn't respond to this. He simply carries the bags with ease up the steps to the house. 'Do you want them in the kitchen, Angela?'

'Yes, please. Now where's my key?' As Angela climbs the steps she begins to rummage in her big patchwork handbag.

'It's all right, I have mine!' I squeeze past the other two on the steps. As I'm about to put my key in the lock, the door swings open and Estelle stands in the doorway with her cane, Alvie at her side as always.

'Goodness, quite the party we have here on my steps,' she

says, eyeing us all over the top of her glasses. 'And I see you have my shopping, Mr Harris?'

'I do indeed!'

'Ben kindly helped me carry it up the steps,' Angela says, walking past Estelle into the house. 'The kitchen is this way, Ben.'

Ben smiles at Estelle and obediently follows Angela along the hall towards the kitchen.

'How are you feeling now?' I ask Estelle as I enter the house. 'Angela said you were a little tired this morning?'

Estelle shakes her head. 'Angela fusses far too much. I'm fit as a fiddle.'

'Good. Good. I'm looking forward to hearing more of your stories tonight.'

'I am very pleased to hear that,' Estelle says approvingly. 'I wondered after last night if I might have scared you off. I know my storytelling style can be a little off-putting.'

'Nope, I'm raring to go,' I tell her. 'Can't wait for the next instalment!'

Estelle nods.

'Right, ladies, I must be off,' I hear Ben say as he comes back down the hall empty-handed. 'See you all soon. I hope?' he asks, raising his eyebrows at me.

'Would you like to join us for dinner tonight, Mr Harris?' Estelle asks suddenly. 'I have not thanked you properly for helping us with the tree. Without you, I fear it might still be stuck at the bottom of our steps.'

'I wouldn't want to impose,' Ben says, glancing at me.

'Nonsense, you will be our special guest for the evening. I like to find out about my neighbours, and it seems we have yet to be properly introduced.'

'Then it would be my absolute pleasure,' Ben says. 'But I do have one condition.'

Estelle nods. 'Yes?'

'You must call me Ben – all my friends do.'

Estelle smiles. 'Of course. It shall be so. I look forward to finding out much more about you this evening, Mr ... *Ben*.'

'And I you, Estelle,' Ben says with a tiny bow of his head, which Estelle clearly enjoys. 'I will look forward to it all afternoon.'

The dinner goes swimmingly. Ben is the perfect guest and arrives on time carrying a bottle of wine and a bouquet of flowers for his hosts. We enjoy lots of cheerful and interesting conversation over the most delicious dinner of homemade chicken-and-mushroom pie with potatoes and vegetables, and we learn a little more about Ben and how he came to be in Mistletoe Square.

'It was very strange,' he tells us. 'The advert for the property appeared at just the right time. I don't even buy that newspaper – I found it lying open on the seat next to me when I was on the Tube. The ad was circled in bright green pen or I might not have noticed it. I assumed I'd either be too late to apply, or they'd have had lots of applications – I mean this is Bloomsbury after all. But the estate agent who showed me Holly House next door said they'd had hardly anyone – so I snapped it up. The rent is very reasonable.'

Immediately, I want to ask him more – my advert was circled in green pen too. Did Ben also bump into the strange man with the briefcase? But Estelle begins talking about a good friend of hers who was a solicitor, and the conversation quickly moves on.

'Angela,' Ben says, after we finish our dessert of apple crumble and cream. 'If I didn't know Estelle relied on you so heavily, I would try and poach you to come and work for me. That dinner was amazing.'

Angela looks as pleased as punch at Ben's praise. Her cheeks flush and she looks adoringly at him.

Ben certainly has a way with the ladies, I think to myself as I take another sip from my wine glass. *The older ladies, anyway . . .*

'So how long have you two known each other?' Ben asks Estelle and Angela. 'I would guess quite some time?'

'We've known each other a long, long time, haven't we, Angela?' Estelle says, slowly nodding as if she's been asked this question many times before.

'We surely have. I was just a young girl when we first met, wasn't I, Estelle? And a bit of a tearaway back then too.'

Estelle casts a warning glance in Angela's direction. 'Yes, indeed you were. Now, Ben, would you care to stay for a night cap?' she asks, abruptly ending the previous line of conversation.

What is it with these two? Why can't they talk about how long they've known each other, or when they first met?

'We will be retiring to the comfortable chairs by the fire after dinner,' Estelle continues. 'I remember a time when it would have been a different room we would adjourn to, rather than the same one we've just eaten in.' She looks wistfully over at the chairs for a moment as she remembers. 'But needs must, and the comfortable chairs it is. I have more tales of this house and my family to share with Elle tonight, and you'd be more than welcome to join us, Ben?'

Earlier, Ben expressed an interest – I thought perhaps only a polite one – in Estelle's stories, and how we were working together on the book.

'If you don't want to, I'm sure we won't be offended,' I say hurriedly, in case Estelle has put him on the spot. 'You probably have better things to do than listen to us wittering on.'

'I can assure you I don't witter on,' Estelle says reprovingly. 'Angela perhaps ... '

'Hey!' Angela pipes up, putting her glass down, which unlike ours has contained water all night. 'You aren't the only one who can tell a story, Estelle. You seem to forget that I know all your stories almost as well as you do.'

'Some of them, perhaps,' Estelle concedes. 'But not all. Perhaps you would like to tell tonight's tale, Angela? Since you know them so well.'

I expect Angela to decline, but instead she accepts the challenge. 'I might just do that!' she says defiantly as she turns to us. 'When you've heard Estelle's stories as many times as I have,' she whispers, 'they become second nature.'

'Then we will make ourselves comfortable by the fire,' Estelle announces, unperturbed. 'And await your storytelling prowess.'

'I'll help you clear up first,' I say, keen that Angela doesn't resort to maid mode again.

'Me too.' Ben stands up.

'Ben, you are a guest,' Estelle says disapprovingly. 'It is most kind of you to offer, but I simply can't allow it.'

'Whereas I'm now part of the staff,' I say, winking at Angela.

'Correction, Elle, you are now part of the *family*.' Estelle gives me a stern look that is in contrast to her kind words. 'Isn't that right, Angela?'

'Indeed you are,' Angela says warmly. 'And family is allowed to help.' She winks back at me.

Ben accompanies Estelle to the chairs by the fire. He

gallantly offers his arm for her to hold as they walk, which Estelle graciously accepts.

After Angela and I have cleared the dinner things, Ben helps Angela pull up a fourth comfortable chair to the fireplace, so there are now two chairs on either side of the fire.

Then Angela pours three large measures of whisky from an Art Deco drinks trolley into some crystal tumblers and carries them over to us on a silver tray. I hesitate when she offers me one but it's obvious that Estelle is very much enjoying playing the hostess this evening and I don't want to spoil her night, so I take a glass, intending to sip at it incredibly slowly, and only if I have to. The one glass of wine I drank with dinner is already plenty of alcohol for me, and I know adding spirits to the mix will only end in trouble.

'Are you not having one yourself?' I ask, as Angela passes her tray to Ben and Estelle.

'No, I'm not a drinker, me,' Angela says. 'I've got a nice glass of orange juice instead.' She fetches her own glass from the cocktail cabinet.

'Here's to good neighbours!' Ben lifts his glass as we all settle down next to the fire.

'Good neighbours!' everyone replies, lifting their glass and taking a gulp of whisky.

I take the tiniest of sips. I know what Estelle's stories are like, and, if tonight's tale is anything like last night's, I need to keep my wits about me. I wonder what Ben will make of it all? Perhaps I should have warned him. But how silly would I have sounded trying to explain what happened last night, when I don't really understand it myself yet.

'No telephone tonight, Elle?' Estelle asks, looking around. 'Elle had a gadget to record me last night,' she explains to Ben.

'No, I'm going old school.' I hold up my notepad and pen. 'The voice recorder didn't work very well last night for some reason.'

'What a shame,' Estelle says, glancing at Angela. 'Angela, do you still want to tell the story tonight?'

'Nah, moment's gone now.' Angela shrugs. 'You do it, Estelle. I'm happy just to sit here and listen.'

'Right then. Now we just need to wait a few moments ...' She looks towards the window as she calmly strokes Alvie who's sitting on her lap as usual, and I know she's waiting for the moon again. Ben, sitting to my right, looks at me with a mystified expression.

'You'll see in a minute,' I whisper.

As the clock strikes eight again, the moon, just like last night, comes out from behind the clouds and shines down through the window. Tonight, it casts its glow over the decoration hanging on the Christmas tree of two entwined theatre masks.

'Comedy and tragedy,' Estelle says, watching the illuminated masks glisten in the moonlight. 'For tonight's story we will be visiting Victorian London. Christmas House is now owned by one Robin Snow, the great-grandson of Joseph and Celeste, whom we met in the first story, if you remember?'

How could I forget?

'Joseph Christmas built both this house and the whole of Mistletoe Square in 1750,' Estelle explains for Ben's benefit. 'Robin lives here with his young wife, Carola, and his two children, Timothy and Belle. We join the story in December 1842.'

Just like yesterday, as Estelle begins to talk, the room begins to change around us.

Some of Estelle's lighter, more modern furniture disappears, and is replaced by darker, much larger pieces of furniture that match with a few of her other items. The wallpaper becomes a deep shade of green with bold gold leaves, and the mantelpiece in front of us fills with many ornaments and tiny knick-knacks. In fact, the whole room is now packed with what looks like junk to me – but I know is the height of Victorian style. The end result makes the room feel very oppressive, dark and heavy.

I glance at Ben. He looks just as shocked and surprised as I was last night.

I watch as our Christmas tree disappears with the rest of the furniture, but this time it is replaced by a tree decorated in colourful paper decorations and unlit candles.

'What the hell is going on here?' I hear Ben mutter. But as I turn to look at him the door to the sitting room swings open.

Nine

20 December 1842

God Bless Us Every One

In the hall stands a woman buttoning a small boy into his coat.

'Yes, you must wear your coat, Master Timothy,' the woman says. 'It's very cold outside today. I think it might snow.'

'Ooh, I hope it does, Nanny Avery,' Timothy says, his dark eyes shining. 'I love to play in the snow.'

'Well, I don't know about that – you might catch cold.'

'Please, Nanny Avery!' A younger girl jumps up and down. She has on a long navy cape over her full dress and laced brown boots. She wears a navy bonnet on her head, and her hands are inside a matching muff edged in white fur. 'I love the snow.'

'Let's see if it actually does snow first, shall we, Miss Belle?' Nanny Avery says firmly, as she finishes wrapping Timothy up with a red scarf and a tweed cap. Finally, she checks her own reflection in the hall mirror – in exactly the same place as

Estelle has a mirror hanging today. Nanny Avery neatens the bow holding a thick grey cape over her long dress. She then pulls a matching grey bonnet over her neatly pinned-up hair, and ties the ribbon tightly under her chin. As she takes one last look at her appearance in the mirror, she jumps.

'Goodness!' she says, immediately turning and peering behind her into the sitting room where we all still sit. She shakes her head and looks suspiciously into the mirror again. 'Trick of the mind,' she says sharply to her reflection. 'That is all.' She shakes her head. 'Goodness if we don't already have enough nonsense in this house to contend with.'

'What are you talking about, Nanny Avery?' Timothy asks. 'What nonsense?'

'Nothing for you to worry about, Master Timothy.' She glances in the mirror one last time, but this time seems happier with what she sees reflected back at her.

'Is it the Christmas tree?' Belle asks. 'It does seem quite odd to have a real tree in our parlour. But it's pretty. I like it.'

'So do I,' Timothy agrees. 'At night it looks magical when all the candles are alight.'

Nanny Avery nods. 'Yes, it is very pretty. It is a little odd too. But your mother likes it, and therefore so must we.'

'Mother says it's traditional in Germany,' Belle says, peering back around the door to look at the Christmas tree. 'And our royal family will have one every year at Windsor Castle now that the Queen has married Prince Albert.' She also looks across at us a little suspiciously, like Nanny Avery did, but says nothing and returns back to the hall.

'I'm not sure about that,' Nanny Avery says with a small purse of her lips. 'It is not for us to suppose what our queen does or does not do. I am sure the German people will have many

Christmas traditions that we know not of here in England. Now we really must leave or we will miss the pantomime.'

Timothy claps his hands in excitement. 'Ooh no, we mustn't do that. Come on, Belle. Let's go! You're going to love this.'

'Shush,' Nanny Avery says, holding her finger to her lips. 'Your mother is resting before her dinner party tonight. We mustn't wake her.'

Timothy silently puts his gloved finger to his own lips. 'Let's tip-toe,' he whispers as the two children and their nanny creep out of the house together.

I turn back towards the others.

Estelle looks calm and composed as always in her chair, which has now changed into a high-backed carved walnut chair with green silk upholstery. Angela is examining the Victorian Christmas tree decorations, and Ben is sitting in his chair next to me looking shell-shocked.

'Are you all right?' I ask him gently.

He turns slowly towards my voice. 'What … is … going … on?' he asks, staring at me with wide eyes. 'Where are we?'

'We are still in Christmas House,' Estelle explains. 'We are just seeing it as it was in the past, that is all.'

'How … ' Ben begins, but he is interrupted by Estelle.

'No time for questions! Do you want to see what's going on in the rest of the house right now?'

'Ooh, yes!' Angela says. 'Kitchen?'

'You read my mind,' Estelle replies, climbing with ease once more from her chair. 'This way.'

We all follow Estelle out into the hall where just a few moments ago the two children and their nanny stood.

'Did she see us?' I hear Angela quietly ask Estelle as we head along the hall. 'Through the mirror, I mean?'

96

'She may have done briefly.'

'But I thought it was just children and animals.'

'Not now, Angela,' Estelle whispers, glancing back at us. But Ben is still in a daze, and I pretend to be busy looking at the decor in the hall, which is almost as busy as the newly transformed parlour. The floor tiles are still the same pattern, but the walls are dark like the parlour, half wallpaper and half thick green tiles. The top half of the walls are decorated with watercolour paintings, complicated embroideries and a few framed black-and-white portraits of the family's faces in silhouette.

Estelle leads us down a set of stairs that usually would lead to her basement, but instead we find ourselves in a large Victorian kitchen.

'The kitchen is down here now,' I whisper, looking around me. For some reason I assumed the kitchen would have always been at the end of the hall like it is now, but of course it would have been downstairs in Victorian times. This Victorian kitchen consists of a huge black range cooker, a basic square sink with a hand pump over it to provide water, a set of brass servants' bells on the wall, with plaques underneath them that correspond to various rooms in the house, and in the middle of the room a wooden table where two women – who remind me a lot of Edith and Beth – stand wearing plain grey dresses, white aprons and white mop caps. They are busily chopping and mixing, while pots boil and bubble on the stove. There's an unpleasant smell in the kitchen and it's also roasting hot.

'Now, Iris,' the older woman instructs. 'You chop up that ox tongue really well now, won't you, while I prepare the fruit and spices.'

'Yes, Mrs Bow,' Iris says, using a fork to prong some grey-looking meat and wielding a sharp knife to slice it with.

'Is that really a cow's tongue?' I ask, wrinkling up my nose as we watch Iris cut into the meat. 'It stinks.'

'They're making mince pies,' Angela says, going over to the table to peer over Mrs Bow's shoulder. 'The traditional way too.'

'With meat?' I pull even more of a disgusted face.

Angela grins. 'Yep, they made them with fruit and spices – just like we have them today, but with the addition of meat, usually ox's tongue.'

I hear Ben make a retching sound next to me.

'Are you all right?' I ask.

'Are you?' Ben holds a white handkerchief over his nose and mouth. 'This was crazy enough before we came down here, but that smell is enough to finish me off.'

'We won't be here long,' Estelle says. 'I just wanted you to see some of the preparations for tonight's dinner party.'

Mrs Bow finishes mixing the fruit and spices, and begins rolling out some pastry while instructing Iris. 'That's it – now mix the meat into the bowl with the other ingredients.' Iris does as she's told and then Mrs Bow takes a spoon and scoops up some of the mixture. 'Now for a little taste,' she says, popping the spoon in her mouth. 'Mmm, now that is good.'

'Can I try some, Mrs Bow?' Iris asks.

'No, you certainly cannot. Tasting is the cook's prerogative. We can't be wasting it – the master has some important guests coming for dinner tonight.'

'Do you know who?' Iris asks, agog.

'I do.' Mrs Bow looks smug. 'But I can't tell.'

'Please do,' Iris says. 'I like a bit of excitement. Is it a star of the music hall?'

'It most certainly is not,' Mrs Bow says with disapproval. 'We don't want none of them sort in this house.'

98

'Then who?'

Mrs Bow looks behind her in case someone might be listening.

'He writes books.'

Iris looks disappointed. 'I don't read books.'

'Do you read anything?' Mrs Bow asks.

Iris shrugs.

'Can you read?' she asks, this time a little more gently.

Iris shakes her head.

'Would you like to be able to?'

'Oh, yes, very much I would.'

'Then I shall teach you.'

'Really?' Iris asks, her eyes wide. 'You'd do that, for me?'

'Everyone should have the best chances in life,' Mrs Bow says stoutly, but I can tell she's moved by Iris's reaction. 'I wasn't at school for long when I was a gal. But long enough to learn the basics. Everything else I've taught myself. The master upstairs, he's a good, kind man. He lets me borrow books from his library, so I can keep improving my reading.'

Iris stares at Mrs Bow. 'Really?'

'Yes,' Mrs Bow says proudly. 'But don't you be getting any ideas though. I've known the master since he was a young boy. My mother was the cook here before me, just like her mother was before her, so the master and I grew up together in this house. I like to think he trusts me. So now I'd like to help you, like he helps me.'

'Gosh. Thank you, Mrs Bow.' Iris smiles. 'It's ever so kind of you.'

Mrs Bow looks pleased. 'Not at all. We'll have you reading in no time, young Iris.'

'When can we start?' Iris asks eagerly.

'Not today, girl, that's for sure!' Mrs Bow replies, returning to her sharper tones. 'We have far too much to prepare for this dinner party, and we haven't even started peeling the potatoes yet. We'll start as soon as we can, though,' she adds softly. 'Don't you fret.'

'Let's leave them now to their preparations,' Estelle says as she moves towards the kitchen door.

'Thank goodness.' Ben's voice is muffled by his handkerchief. He allows Estelle to pass, then quickly follows behind. 'I have no idea what's going on right now, but the sooner we leave that God-awful smell behind the better!'

'Now,' Estelle says as she climbs the stairs with ease. 'We're moving on a little timewise. When we arrive upstairs again it's a few hours later the same day.'

We all follow Estelle to the top of the stairs.

'Are we feeling brave enough to step outside for a little while?' Estelle asks as she heads towards the door.

'Ooh, yes!' Angela cries eagerly. 'I love it when we go outside.'

I glance at Ben. He has popped his handkerchief back in his pocket now and is peering at the pictures and embroideries on the walls. He puts his hand out to touch them.

'No!' Estelle calls sharply. 'You can't touch anything!'

But Ben's fingers are already heading towards the frame. Instead of stopping when they reach something solid, they continue through the painting into the wall.

'Whoah!' Ben pulls his hand back. 'That was weird.'

'We're not really here,' Estelle tells him. 'This is simply a trick of the mind.'

'It's like we're in some really strange, but really lifelike virtual reality game,' I say, suddenly getting it. 'Everything seems real around us. But it's not actually here at all.'

Estelle looks puzzled and looks to Angela for an explanation.

'Don't worry, Estelle,' Angela says. 'It's something the young people use today. That's exactly what it's like, Elle,' she says, turning to me. 'Only without the goggles.'

Ben reaches out towards the wooden bannisters, but, again, when he touches the shiny mahogany, his hand doesn't stop and simply goes straight through it.

'Please stop that, Mr Harris,' Estelle says crossly. 'Otherwise I will not be able to continue with my story.'

'Sorry, Estelle. And it's Ben, remember?'

'I only address my friends by their Christian names.' Estelle eyes him sternly over her glasses. 'Of which you will soon not be one if you keep fiddling with things that do not concern you.'

Ben nods. 'Sure, I get it. I'll be good from now on.'

'I do hope so. This is Elle's second story and she is not messing about with the past.'

'To be fair, I didn't know we could touch things. This story feels even more real than the first one. We didn't even leave the sitting room for that.'

'You can't actually touch anything,' Ben says. 'I've tried, remember?'

'I am easing you both in gently,' Estelle says in the tone of a teacher to a couple of naughty pupils. 'Story by story. But if you do not abide by the rules, then I'm afraid there will be no further tales of this house.'

'Sorry, Estelle. We really want to know more, don't we, Ben?'

Ben nods. 'Of course we do. Crazy as this is, I'm fascinated. I'll behave, I promise.'

'Right then.' Estelle seems satisfied by our suitably repentant responses. She reaches for the handle on the door. 'Outside we go.'

101

'Wait!' Ben says as Estelle turns the handle and the door swings open. 'How come she can do that and we can't?'

'Practice,' Estelle says. 'And it's too early to ask you both to walk through a door just yet. That will come later with experience. Now, please, some hush. This next part is very important.'

We follow Estelle out onto the steps, and I can't help but let out a little gasp by the scene that greets us.

Snow has been falling heavily from the now darkened sky. Huge white flakes are still occasionally floating down, lit by the glow of the gas lamps around the square as they fall. The rest of Mistletoe Square, aside from the blanket of snow, looks exactly the same, though – four rows of houses with a grassed area in the middle surrounded by black railings. In the centre of the little park the bare branches of the trees are covered in snow, along with copious bunches of mistletoe just like they are today. The only differences from the modern-day square and this one, is instead of electric lights shining out of the many Georgian windows, the flicker of candles or small gas lamps light up the panes of glass. And where we'd usually see cars and vans driving around the square looking for somewhere to park, there are horse-drawn carriages instead. They pull up at houses and women in bonnets and long dresses alight, alongside men in top hats and long tail coats.

It's like we've stepped right onto the front of a Victorian-themed Christmas Card.

A man carrying a ladder passes by.

'You all done, Wilf?' he calls to his mate down the road.

'No! Some fella's nicked me ladder,' Wilf calls back angrily. 'I only stopped for a smoke, turned me back for a minute and it was gone.' He marches purposefully towards the first man. 'That's me livelihood, that is.'

The first man looks around and points towards one of the trees in the park. 'What's that over there up against that tree?'

'It's me ladder!' Wilf says, immediately heading over towards it. 'How'd it get there?'

He retrieves his ladder, then they finish lighting the rest of the street lamps before leaving the square

'Watch.' Estelle points and we see Nanny Avery with Timothy and Belle returning from the pantomime. When they get near to the house, a young, incredibly pale and thin boy pops up from behind the park railings.

'Buy some mistletoe, miss?' he asks, thrusting a bunch of mistletoe at Nanny Avery.

'Certainly not,' Nanny Avery says, pulling the children behind her. 'Be away with you now!' She wafts her hand at him like she's swatting away an annoying fly. 'And where did you get that mistletoe?'

'Did he steal the lamp-lighter's ladder to get the mistletoe down off the tree?' Ben asks, watching the boy.

'Hush,' Estelle says. 'Listen.'

Belle hides behind Nanny Avery's skirt, but Timothy walks boldly back out in front of her. He takes a few steps towards the boy, watching him carefully.

'Want some mistletoe?' the boy asks brazenly, holding the bunch up again. His dark eyes are sunken and he's so thin he looks like the slightest breath of wind might blow him over.

Timothy shakes his head. 'Aren't you cold?' he asks, staring at the boy's torn and ragged clothes.

'Timothy!' Nanny Avery admonishes him. 'Come here at once.'

The boy shrugs. 'Used to it, ain't I?'

'Are you hungry?' Timothy asks.

The boy nods.

Timothy reaches into his pocket and pulls out a half-eaten bar of chocolate. He hands it to the boy, who stares at it for a moment, then grabs it and begins devouring it hungrily.

'Timothy, what are you doing?' Nanny Avery positions Belle on the steps in front of us, then heads over to rescue Timothy.

'He's hungry, Nanny,' Timothy says, still looking at the boy, 'And cold. And he has no shoes.'

Nanny Avery looks down at the boy's bare feet.

'Goodness,' she says, looking shocked. 'You truly are a poor waif.'

'Have my boots.' Timothy begins to untie his leather boots.

'No, Timothy. How will I explain to your mother where your shoes are?' She looks around her to see if anyone is watching. 'Come around to the back of the house in a few minutes,' she says quietly to the boy. 'It's Number Five. I'll see if Cook can provide you with some scraps to eat and a warm in front of the fire while you eat them.'

The boy, whose face is covered in so many dark smudges it's difficult to see where the chocolate ends and the dirty marks begin, looks suspiciously up at her.

'It's not a trick,' she says kindly. 'Mrs Bow will look after you.'

'Yes, she will,' Timothy says eagerly. 'Mrs Bow is very kind to me, I'm sure she'll be kind to you too.'

The boy nods.

'Come now, Timothy,' Nanny Avery says. 'We need to get you bathed and fed early tonight if you're to see your parents before their dinner party begins.'

Reluctantly, Timothy leaves the boy and returns to the house.

We stand back to let them pass us on the steps, while the

boy still carrying his mistletoe makes his way to the back of the house.

'Now,' Estelle says, taking charge as usual. 'We will skip on a little to the evening's events.'

As we head back through the open door again, the house that was pretty dark before due to its decor, is now even darker. The hall is dimly lit by a glass oil lamp, and there's a warm glow coming from the sitting room – now the parlour. As we enter and the clock on the mantelpiece strikes a quarter to seven, I realise the glow isn't only coming from the fire, but the Christmas tree too, which is now lit with real candles. Their holders are clipped to the end of the branches, while their flames flicker dangerously close to the other decorations.

'Ooh,' Angela coos, immediately going over to the tree. 'Now that is brave.'

'Dangerous, more like,' Ben says, following her. 'It'll go up in flames if one of them catches.'

'That is what they did in Victorian times,' Estelle says calmly. 'All will be fine I'm sure on this occasion.'

'On this occasion?' I ask, picking up on her choice of words. 'There were fires then?'

'Sadly, yes – too many, until the invention of electricity. Angela, come away from the mantelpiece now – our hostess is here.'

I follow Estelle's gaze and see a small, pretty, fair-haired woman enter the room. She's wearing a long, tiered, forest-green gown edged with white lace that shows off her slim shoulders, and her hair is braided into two complex, but artistic displays either side of her head.

'It's the woman from the Victorian photo in your hall,' I whisper to Estelle.

Estelle just nods.

The woman looks around the room giving it the once over, then she runs her finger over one of the sideboards to check for dust. Satisfied it's clean, she goes over to the window and peeks out through the branches of the Christmas tree.

'Do not worry, my dear,' a commanding male voice says, as a middle-aged, dark-haired man with a moustache appears in the doorway of the room. He's wearing full evening dress – a dark suit, high-collared white shirt, a waistcoat and a flouncy bow tie. Again, it's the same man from the sepia photo in Estelle's hall. 'Our guests will be here shortly. Now, where are my children before they arrive? Nanny Avery!' he calls up the stairs. 'Will you bring the children down, please.'

'They can't be here long, Robin,' the woman says with a strong German accent. 'The guests must not see them.'

'Is it not the want of every father to spend a little time with his children?' Robin says. 'Even you, Carola, must wish to see them sometimes?'

'Of course. But what is it you English say, though? Children should be seen and not heard? Surely it is not right having the children here when our guests arrive?

Robin smiles. 'That silly phrase means that children should not be noisy in polite company. It doesn't mean they shouldn't be here at all. Anyway, I love to hear our children happy and enjoying themselves. Don't you, my dear?'

'Robin, I am simply trying to fit in with your English society. You have so many rules and traditions I do not yet understand. I do not want to be seen to be doing the wrong thing.'

'And yet you insist on a lit tree in our parlour, my dear.' Robin smiles, looking over at the tree.

'And this is the German way,' Carola says proudly, admiring the tree. 'I am sure it will soon be the way of the English now that Prince Albert is in the royal court. You will see.'

Robin walks over towards Carola and takes hold of her hand, kissing the back of it. 'It looks beautiful, my dear, as do you this evening. Tonight, our dinner guests we will be incredibly happy and most contented with everything we provide for them, I am sure of it.'

'I do hope so,' Carola says, glancing at the clock. 'We have more time than I thought. Perhaps enough time to see the children after all.'

A knock at the sitting-room door announces the arrival of Nanny Avery and the two children.

'Come, come!' Robin sits down in a chair by the fire and pats his legs.

The children run immediately to their father. 'Now,' he says, lifting one then the other onto his lap. 'Tell me all about your day?'

'We went to the pantomime!' Belle says excitedly, while Nanny Avery silently enters the room and stands by the door with her hands folded neatly in front of her.

'Did you now? And what did you see?'

'Spinderelda,' Belle says, looking up adoringly at her father. Robin looks questioningly at Nanny Avery.

'She means Cinderella, sir.'

'Cinderella! A classic, and it sounds like you enjoyed it?'

Belle excitedly recounts her afternoon at the theatre.

'And did you not enjoy the pantomime?' Robin asks Timothy, who has sat silently on his lap while Belle does all the talking.

'Yes, it was very good,' Timothy replies quietly.

Robin looks questioningly over at Carola.

'Are you feeling quite well, Timothy?' Carola comes over to him and touches his forehead. 'He's not running a fever, is he, Nanny?'

'I'm sure he's not,' Nanny Avery says, looking concerned.

'I'm fine.' Timothy pushes his mother's hand away.

'Perhaps he's a little overtired from his outing,' Nanny Avery says. 'Shall I take them both back to the nursery now?'

'No! Not yet,' Belle whines, gripping on to her father's arm. 'We've only just got here.'

'But your parents' guests will soon be arriving,' Nanny Avery says kindly.

'Nonsense, we still have plenty of time,' Robin says, glancing at the mantelpiece clock. 'It's only a quarter to the hour. Our guests are not due until seven.'

How is it only a quarter to seven? I wonder. Hadn't the clock struck that when we entered the room?

'Now, Timothy, what is troubling you, child?' Robin asks gently. 'Please, tell your father.'

Timothy glances at Nanny Avery. She gives the tiniest shake of her head.

'We saw a boy earlier,' Timothy tells his father, ignoring his nanny. 'Outside the house. He was selling mistletoe.'

'We already have plenty of mistletoe,' Carola says hurriedly, her eye on the clock again. 'Look, our kissing ball is full of it.' She holds her hand up to a ball of greenery hanging near the doorway covered in holly, ivy, herbs and mistletoe. 'We do not require any more.'

'Go on, Timothy,' Robin encourages, realising his son is not finished.

It's clear to me from watching Robin and Carola with their

children that their father is clearly their favourite. Carola seems more concerned about her guests' impending arrival than the troubles of her own flesh and blood.

'The boy was very thin, Father,' Timothy continues, 'and he was very hungry. I gave him the rest of my bar of chocolate that Nanny bought for me at the theatre, but he was still hungry when he'd eaten it.'

Robin glances at Nanny Avery, whose usually pale cheeks have pinked a little. 'It was a waif,' she explains hurriedly. 'He accosted us outside the house and tried to sell us mistletoe from our own gardens across the street.'

'Mrs Bow gave him some food from the kitchen,' Timothy tells his father.

'Scraps that were to be thrown away,' Nanny Avery explains, clearly worried by this tale her charge is telling her employers. 'Nothing else.'

'But he still looked so tired, so ill and so sad, Father,' Timothy says, looking quite weary himself. His meeting with the boy outside has obviously affected him deeply. 'He had no shoes. His feet were bare – and in the snow too.'

'Timothy gave him his boots!' Belle pipes up.

'You did what?' Carola cries, looking shocked. 'You gave your good boots to a street urchin?'

'I am very sorry.' Nanny Avery looks equally as shocked. 'I had no idea that particular incident had taken place.'

'He did it when you were bathing me,' Belle says. 'He went down to the kitchen and gave them to the boy before he left the house.'

'I am sorry if I did the wrong thing, Father.' Tears form in Timothy's eyes and slowly roll down his cheeks. 'But I thought he needed them more than me.'

Robin, looking quite emotional himself, puts his arms around both his children and pulls them close.

'We are very lucky,' he tells them, his head level with theirs. 'We live a privileged life, where we do not want for food or shelter or warmth. Some of our fellow Londoners are not so lucky as us. Let me tell you, Timothy, you did exactly what I would have done in the same circumstances. Caring for others when they are in need is never the wrong thing to do, and I am proud of what you did today for that boy. Never feel guilty for helping those less fortunate than yourself. It is to be applauded, not apologised for.'

There's the sound of hands clapping together in the hall, and a handsome young man with wavy dark hair enters the room, still applauding.

'Bravo! Bravo!' he calls.

'Mr Dickens!' Carola cries, looking horrified. 'How ... how did you get in?'

'Your charming housekeeper let me in – although she said she was the cook,' he says, winking at Carola. 'Do not admonish her. I insisted we come through when she asked us to wait.'

'He did.' A small young woman with loose blonde tendrils framing her face enters the room behind him. 'And as you know Charles can be very persuasive.'

'I like to call it charming, my dear Catherine,' the man says, smiling at her. 'Now, dear Mrs Snow, how are you keeping?' He goes over and kisses Carola's hand. 'I do hope we've not arrived early? But we did wait until we heard the church clock strike seven outside.'

'No way ... ' I hear Ben gasp as all this is going on. Ben, myself, and the two children all stare at this energetic, cheerful-looking man, who has completely taken over the room with his enigmatic presence. 'That can't be *the* Charles Dickens, can it?'

'Charles, Catherine,' Robin says, popping Timothy and Belle down on his chair while he stands up to greet his guests. 'How good you could both come.' Robin pulls his pocket watch from his waistcoat. 'It seems our mantel clock has not been wound properly. It is running late by a quarter of the hour.'

Carola looks with annoyance at the clock. 'Nanny, would you take the children back up to the nursery now our guests are here.'

'Certainly not!' Charles says with a flourish of his hand. 'I will not be the cause of the young man going to bed upset. I heard what your father said to you, and he is quite right. We who are in a privileged position such as this must help those that are less fortunate than ourselves. But what I did not hear, and I would very much like to if your parents agree, is what you did to deserve such praise?'

Robin helps Timothy to his feet, and Timothy recounts somewhat shyly what had happened with the boy. The ladies, with Carola looking quite horrified that this is taking place, and Catherine looking quite enchanted by Timothy, sit on an elegant, gold silk double-ended chaise lounge while the men both stand.

'I will say it again,' Charles says when Timothy has finished his tale. 'Bravo, young sir. If only everyone cared as much for our poor and needy, this country would be a better place. I wish I could do something for you in return for your kindness.'

'Can you tell us a bedtime story?' Belle pipes up. 'Nanny Avery says you write really good storybooks.'

Nanny Avery, who has been standing quietly in the corner

of the room while all this takes place, flushes a shade of red to match the decorations on the Christmas tree.

'Belle!' Carola snaps. 'Don't be rude. Mr Dickens is our dinner guest. He is not here to tell you bedtime stories.'

'Please.' Charles holds up his hand. 'It would be my pleasure. Children are our future; they need to ask many, many questions, so they can grow into the good, brave citizens of the future. I wish I was clever enough that I could make stories up on the spot,' he says, kneeling down next to Belle. 'But I'm not quite that good, as your father will tell you. Otherwise my publishers might pay me a little more.'

He raises his eyebrows at Robin, who simply smiles back. 'Write another bestseller, and maybe we might.'

'What do you think I should write about next?' Charles asks Belle.

'Ooh ... ' Belle says, thinking hard. Her gaze falls on the Christmas tree. 'Christmas!' she shouts excitedly. 'Write a story about Christmas, Mr Dickens.'

'Christmas ... ' Charles says, pondering this. 'That would certainly be different. What else should I put in this story? What do you think, young Master Timothy?'

Timothy thinks carefully. 'Something that helps the poor people,' he says quietly. 'There are too many mean rich people out there. Why can't we share all our money so no one has to be cold or hungry, especially at Christmas.'

Charles nods. 'I will do my very best, young sir, and I shall call one of the characters after you, Master Timothy, and also you, Miss Belle. Would you like that?'

Belle claps her hands with glee, and Timothy nods solemnly. 'You promise?'

'I promise,' Charles says formally shaking Timothy's hand.

'Why don't you call one of them Ebenezer too?' Ben jokes.

'Ebenezer,' Belle repeats as though she heard him. 'That is a funny name.'

While Ben stares at Belle in astonishment, Charles Dickens looks up into the air. 'Ebenezer ...' he says, considering this. 'Yes ... yes, I like it. Ebenezer, it shall be.'

'And on that note, I think it's time for us to leave,' Estelle announces.

Ten

20 December 2018

Estelle once more takes her seat by the fire in the more familiar surroundings of her 2018 sitting room. She pats her lap and
Alvie jumps up on to it. But while Angela and I join her by the
fire, Ben still paces agitatedly around the room.

'Will someone please explain to me exactly what just happened here?' he asks with a bewildered expression. He stares at
the Christmas tree, where just moments ago there were candles
illuminating the branches, but now there are small electric
lights again twinkling in the light from the fire.

'I simply told you the story of the inhabitants of this house
in 1842,' Estelle says calmly, lifting her glass and finishing off
her whisky.

'Yes, but that wasn't just storytelling.' Ben's voice sounds
part disbelieving, part accusatory. 'It was like we travelled in
time back to Victorian London.'

'I can assure you we are not time-travellers,' Estelle says, smiling. 'Simply storytellers.'

'But it was so real.' Ben starts pacing around the room again. 'The candles on the tree for instance,' he says, pausing by the Christmas tree once more. 'You could feel the warmth of the flames when you stood next to them. And what about when we went down to the kitchen. You can't conjure up a smell as awful as that in a story. It's just not possible. It's ... magic ... no, it's not, it's witchcraft! Yes, that's a much better name for it.'

'I can assure you, neither Angela nor I are witches, Ben.'

'Don't look at me.' I shrug when Ben turns towards me. 'I'm not a witch, either. The only reason I seem calm is because I went through all this last night with Estelle's first story. I can assure you I'm just as amazed and mystified by this as you are.'

Ben nods. 'Sorry. I forgot that, and it was just like this last night?'

'Pretty much, except we went back even earlier, to 1755.'

'Blimey.'

Oddly, it was strangely reassuring to see Ben's reaction to the story, because it completely mirrored my own reaction from yesterday.

'Angela?' I ask while Ben is still thinking. 'Can I ask if it was you who put the clock on the mantelpiece back a few minutes? So the children were still in the parlour when Charles Dickens arrived?'

Angela smiles secretively. 'Perhaps.'

'So you can touch things too, like Estelle can?' But my question goes unanswered as Ben stirs from his silent contemplation.

'I knew there was something else,' he says, turning to

Estelle again. 'Am I supposed to believe that was the real Charles Dickens we saw just now?'

'What you choose to believe is up to you, Ben,' Estelle replies calmly. 'I can assure you, though, that Charles Dickens did visit this house a number of times. Robin worked for the company that published Mr Dickens's books.'

'Was that really how he got the idea for *A Christmas Carol*?' I ask, 'Or is that just a bit of embellishment on your part?'

'What do you think?' Estelle smiles serenely.

'Well, I certainly didn't give him the idea for the name Ebenezer,' Ben says. 'No way would I do that.'

'How can you be so sure?' Estelle asks innocently.

'I just wouldn't, that's all,' Ben says, folding his arms. 'Not in a million years.'

We all look questioningly at him.

'And why is that, Ben?' Estelle continues to probe. 'Do tell us.'

Ben stares hard at her, then, like we all do, quickly folds under Estelle's watchful gaze. She certainly has a way of getting secrets from people. 'Because it's my name, isn't it?' he mumbles uncomfortably.

'Sorry, Ben.' Estelle cups her ear. 'I'm a little hard of hearing. What did you say?'

'I said, it's *my* name,' Ben repeats in a much louder voice. 'Ebenezer Frederick Harris. I can only assume my parents thought it a tremendous lark calling their son that.'

'Were you born near Christmas?' I ask. Was this another thing we were going to have in common? Surely not?

Ben nods. 'Yup. Christmas Eve, unfortunately.'

'Gosh, same here,' I reply, pointing at myself.

'Really?' Ben says. 'That's pretty amazing – another thing

116

we both share. At least you didn't get called after a miser in a Christmas book, though.'

'No, but my name is still bad enough.'

Ben looks puzzled for a moment. 'Don't tell me … don't tell me … Got it! Noelle, right? But you call yourself Elle because it's more normal and less … '

'*Christmassy!*' we both say at the same time, and we smile.

'Noelle is not quite as bad as Ebenezer, though, is it?' Ben says, grimacing.

I grin. 'No, you definitely win that one.'

'I think I might retire,' Estelle announces while Ben and I are still smiling at each other. 'I'm feeling quite worn out after tonight's storytelling. Angela?'

Angela jumps from where she's been gazing with a dopey expression at Ben and me, and rushes over to help Estelle up.

'I hope you both enjoyed this evening's tale?' Estelle asks us, as Alvie hops off her lap, and she rises to her feet with Angela's help. 'And it has given you much to write about, Elle?'

'It has indeed,' I tell her. 'Yet again.'

'I'm sure you still have many questions, Ben,' she says as she takes hold of her cane. 'I appreciate my storytelling techniques are quite … full on.'

Ben nods. 'You can say that again.'

'But perhaps you'd like to join us again tomorrow, if you're free? When I will be telling Elle the third of my stories.'

'I would love to,' Ben says, smiling graciously. 'I don't know how you did what you did tonight, Estelle. But if it's going to happen again, I definitely want to be a part of it.'

'Then it shall be so. Elle,' Estelle says, turning to me. 'You are very quiet. Is everything all right?'

'I was just wondering about Timothy,' I say hastily, though

in truth I was thinking about Ben and the way he just smiled at me. 'Did his experiences that day change him in any way? In the first story you said that Nora and her husband went on to donate a lot of money to children's charities. So I wondered if something similar happened to Timothy and his family?'

Estelle smiles. 'Yes, you are correct. Timothy went on to support many of the charities that Charles Dickens was involved in. Eventually he became a member of parliament and campaigned tirelessly for help and assistance for under-privileged children. Many important social reform bills were passed as a result of his efforts.'

'And Belle – what happened to her?'

'Belle went on to marry a doctor, and they were both involved in raising the funds to open Great Ormond Street Hospital for sick children. Their son, Charles, went into publishing like his grandfather, and was eventually involved in publishing the original *Peter Pan* novel, which, as you might know, now helps support the hospital with royalties from the book and the subsequent play.'

'Gosh, so they were both involved in helping needy children in the future – that's great.' I smile. 'It's really cool to see how one little moment can change a person's life. I'm pleased there was a reason for that story.'

'There is a reason for all my stories,' Estelle says with mean-ing. 'It might not be immediately obvious every time. But believe me, all this,' she waves her hand around the room, 'is for a reason. Now, I must bid you both goodnight.'

We both say goodnight to Estelle.

'I'm going upstairs soon as well,' Angela says as she helps Estelle through the door. 'So you've got the place to your-selves.' She winks at us. 'Don't do anything I wouldn't do ...'

I shake my head as they both head along the hall with Alvie trotting after them.

'Sorry about that,' I say as Ben sits down opposite me in Estelle's vacated chair.

'Which particular thing are you referring to?' Ben asks. 'So much has happened here tonight, I'm not sure what's real and what's not any more.'

'I felt exactly the same after Estelle's first story.'

'How is she doing it? Have you any theories? Was it the whisky?' He picks up one of the glasses on the table next to him and sniffs it. 'Did we take hallucinogenic drugs without knowing?'

'I wondered something similar last night. Except last night we were all drinking tea just before Estelle's story, not whisky. They both swear blind it wasn't drugged, though, and I believe them.'

'Yeah, I guess that's a little extreme. But ...' Ben looks around the room again. 'How did what just happened ... happen? It's impossible, isn't it? You were there – it was so real.'

'I know. In a way, tonight's story was even more real than last night's.'

'How so?'

'It was longer, for one thing. Yesterday we really just stayed in this room and the hall. Tonight we went much further around the house – even outside, for goodness' sake.'

'Yeah, that was really odd, wasn't it? Seeing Victorian London like that.'

'It felt like we were in a Christmas card.'

'The square was really pretty with all the snow. But is that how it would have looked back then, or how Estelle wants us to see it?'

'How do you mean?'

'If we don't know how she's doing this, are we seeing history as it actually would have been, or a version of history that Estelle wants us to see?'

I think about this. 'I used to write about period interiors for a magazine, so as far as that side of things goes, it's pretty accurate. But as for the stories and the people, who knows?'

Ben stands up again and walks around the room, feeling the furniture and tapping lightly on the walls. 'There doesn't seem to be anything dodgy going on,' he says, turning back towards me. 'No false walls, et cetera.'

'Estelle's not a master magician, then,' I say, smiling at him. 'With Angela as her glamorous assistant.'

'Sadly it appears not. At least that would explain it.' Ben shakes his head. 'How are they doing this then, if it's not some clever trickery?'

'I really don't know.'

'Doesn't it bother you, not knowing?'

I consider this for a moment. 'It did at first,' I tell him honestly. 'Yesterday I really freaked out after Estelle's first tale. Going back to the eighteenth century was incredibly odd. They didn't even have a Christmas tree that time – it simply disappeared. Totally correct, of course. Christmas trees didn't become popular among the masses until the mid-Victorian times.'

'But you didn't freak out tonight?'

'I thought about it a lot today when I was out walking, and I realised whatever is going on here – and clearly there is something very strange or extremely clever happening in this house – going back in time to really see how people lived, dressed and spoke, even, is an incredible opportunity – however it's being achieved.'

'I guess so . . . ' Ben considers this. 'But why?'

'Why what?'

'Why us?' Ben comes and sits down in the chair again. 'More particularly, since you've been involved from the beginning it seems, why you?'

I shrug. 'Dunno. Right place at the right time? Could have been anyone that answered that advert for a writer.'

'Hmm . . . ' Ben gazes into the fire. 'Make that adverts. Remember how I came to be here too? It can't just be a coincidence that we both answered adverts that no one else replied to, can it?'

'What other explanation is there?'

'I don't know,' Ben says, leaning forward in his chair so I can see the flames from the fire reflected in his dark eyes. 'But I *really* want to find out – don't you?'

Eleven

21 December 2018

The next day is a quiet one.

Last night, Ben and I sat chatting for a further hour or so about what we saw when Estelle took us back to Victorian times in her latest story, and once again we tried to fathom out just how this was being achieved – but we simply kept going round in circles, getting absolutely nowhere with our ideas and theories.

We'd even spent time discussing if our electric shocks from a couple of days ago, might have something to do with our apparent new abilities to travel back in time. But we'd finally come to the conclusion they were simply the result of the house's old, and likely faulty, wiring, and not some new-found superpower.

Eventually Ben reluctantly decided he must leave as he had a couple of early meetings the next morning.

I saw him to the door, and he told me he was really looking forward to joining me again for the next instalment in Estelle's lengthy volume of stories.

As I closed the door behind him and headed back into the sitting room to tidy away the now empty glasses, I couldn't decide whether he meant he was looking forward to seeing me or hearing the story. In the end I decided that hopefully he meant both.

It rains for most of the day, so I spend my time in my room typing up what I know so far about Estelle's family.

I have lunch on my own, because Estelle and Angela have gone out to take Estelle to an appointment. They don't say what sort of appointment, so I don't ask. But they take Alvie with them, so for the first time I really do have the house to myself.

After lunch it's still raining, so I decide to have a bit of a nose around the house. I've already taken a good look at most things in the hall and the sitting room, as other than my own room those were the two rooms I spent the most time in. Angela never seemed that comfortable when I went along to the kitchen, so I tended to keep away from there.

Estelle has a classic, but eclectic mix of decor and objects that seem to date from as many decades as the house has stood in Mistletoe Square. From the periods in the house's history I've already visited with her, I recognise a few things – a couple of ornaments from the Georgian story that stood on the mantelpiece, and one of the tapestries from the hall in the Victorian tale. On a large bookshelf at the back of the sitting room I find a very old and worn hardback copy of *A Christmas Carol*, along with a few other Charles Dickens novels. These can't be first editions, can they? I wonder. They do look incredibly old.

I carefully open the copy of *A Christmas Carol*; at the front on the title page there's a dedication and a signature written in black ink:

To Timothy, Belle and the Snow Family.
Thank you for the inspiration.
Your friend,
Charles Dickens

'Wow,' I say out loud. 'Double wow. That's incredible if it's real?'

But it certainly looks genuine. What possible reason would Estelle have for faking it? Carefully, I put the book back on the shelves.

After I've had another good look around the ground floor, avoiding Estelle's bedroom to which the door is always closed, I head back up the stairs to the floor where my own rooms are. Then, for the first time, I continue up the next flight of stairs to the floor above, to the area of the house that is in between mine and Angela's right at the top.

The landing on this floor looks much like mine does, with the same carpet and wallpaper. But unlike my floor, where the doors are usually ajar where I come and go in between rooms, here the doors are all tightly shut.

I pause outside one of them. *I probably shouldn't . . .* I think, my hand hovering close to the doorknob. It's likely to be locked anyway.

Before I can talk myself out of it, my hand grabs the brass doorknob and I turn the handle.

To my surprise the door swings open with no resistance at all. Inside the dark room the blind is turned and the curtains are pulled, but I can just make out a small tower of packing cases stacked up in one corner, alongside several pieces of furniture with dust sheets thrown over them.

I reach for the light switch and flick it on.

'Oh,' I say, not sure why I'm disappointed. 'Looks like stuff they don't use any more.'

I walk further into the room and lift a couple of the dust covers. Underneath there's more antique and vintage furniture – a couple of side tables, a set of bookshelves, a china cabinet and some chairs. Some of it looks really old, some more retro, like it's come from the 1960s and 1970s.

I carefully place the covers back over the furniture, thinking how sad it is that Estelle doesn't have a use for any of this now. And yet she still holds on to it, as many older people do. Memories of past times, happy times, that have now long gone.

The boxes contain similar – a mix of china ornaments, silverware and paintings from various eras that once would have graced the parlour, sitting room, hall or even dining room of this house when Estelle's family and ancestors lived here.

When Estelle spoke to Ben last night about how she would have adjourned from the dining room into another room many years ago, she looked quite forlorn. So seeing Estelle's past all covered up like this, unused and gathering dust, makes me sad for her.

Even though we are still quite a few decades away in Estelle's stories from when she began living in this house, I'm pretty sure she must have been used to a lifestyle similar to those family members we've already met. So the quiet life she now lives with Angela, although happy, must seem a long way from her opulent past, and it makes me even more determined to do justice to her stories with my own words.

Quietly, I back out of the room, and pull the door shut behind me.

I don't attempt to open any further doors. These rooms might only contain some old furniture and a few ornaments wrapped in newspaper, but, to Estelle, these rooms contain her memories, and I wouldn't want to disturb or intrude on those for anything.

After Estelle and Angela have returned from their outing, Estelle takes a rest in her room while Angela prepares dinner for us all. She shuns my offers of help, but allows me to set the table with the silver cutlery and white bone-china plates we always use for meals.

'You all right, Alvie?' I ask as the little dog watches me from the chair. 'Did you enjoy your excursion today?'

Alvie is usually at Estelle's heels twenty-four seven, so it's strange to find him in the sitting room without her.

He looks up at me with a pair of wise eyes that I feel have seen more than people probably give him credit for. I go over and kneel down next to his chair so I can fuss him. He gives me a welcoming lick on my hand.

'This is a funny situation we find ourselves in here, don't you think?' I ask him as I rub his head. From my limited knowledge of dogs, Alvie doesn't actually seem that old, and I wonder how long Estelle has had him. Other than for company, why would someone of her age take on a young dog in what she must know are her twilight years? Estelle is incapable of walking very far, even with her cane. Angela seems to take Alvie for most of his walks as far as I know. 'You seem to be all right with Estelle's strange stories, though, don't you?' The little dog rolls over on his back so I can tickle his tummy. 'I guess I'm going to have to get used to them too, if I want to make a success of this job.'

After dinner, I insist on helping Angela clear away and then we settle down to wait for Ben to arrive, and for Estelle's next story. The chairs have been left, I notice, in the same position as last night – two either side of the fire.

I look at the tree and wonder which of the many decorations would be next on our journey through this house's history.

'There's more cloud out there tonight,' I say, glancing out of the window as we wait for Ben. 'Are you sure the moon will be able to shine through the window onto the tree?'

'It will find a way,' Estelle says with confidence. 'It always does.'

There's a knock at the door, which Angela answers, and then she and Ben come through into the sitting room.

'Hey,' he says, smiling at us. 'I hope I'm not late, am I? My apologies if I am, but I've had a heck of a day.'

'Not at all.' Estelle pats the seat next to her. 'Right on time as always.'

'We're just about to have some after-dinner coffee,' Angela says. 'Would you like a cup, Ben?'

Ben glances warily at me. 'Er, okay, yes. Thank you.'

Angela, wearing a long kaftan-style dress tonight straight from the 1970s, fetches the coffee while Ben tells us about his day.

'Bit dull really,' he says, warming his hands in front of the fire. 'A few meetings and lots of paperwork. But it was the three hours I spent trying to get my heating fixed that was the killer. This fire tonight is very welcome, I can tell you.'

'What's the problem?' I ask. 'Have you got it fixed now?'

'Nope, it seems my very old boiler has finally decided to retire. It had to wait until I moved in, didn't it?'

'You're without heat in December?' Estelle asks. She glances at Angela as she comes through the door carrying a tray filled with cups of coffee. 'We can't have that, can we, Angela?'

'Definitely not. Ben, you can't be without heat and hot water at this time of the year. The winters aren't as cold as some I can remember.' Again, Estelle and Angela exchange a knowing glance. 'But it's cold enough.'

'Why don't you come and stay with us until you get it fixed?' Estelle offers. 'We have plenty of room here as you can see.'

'Gosh,' Ben says, looking surprised. 'That's very kind, but I couldn't intrude on you like that. I'll be fine. I'll just need to wrap up a little warmer, that's all. I can meet any clients in a coffee shop for the time being. The plumber said it wouldn't take long for him to source a new boiler. They say cold showers are good for you, don't they?'

'Nonsense, it would be our pleasure,' Estelle insists. 'We haven't had guests here for . . . well, for a very long time.'

I clear my throat.

'Except for you of course, dear Elle. But like I said yesterday, I consider you family now. Ben, it would be our absolute pleasure to have you here with us. Wouldn't it, Angela?'

'Absolutely.' Angela nods.

'Well, if you really don't mind . . . ' Ben still looks unsure. 'I'm sure it would only be for the odd night.'

'I'll go and make a bed up for you right after Estelle's story,' Angela says, looking pleased. She glances at the clock on the mantelpiece. 'We need to get ready – it's almost time.'

Angela sits down in the chair next to me, and we wait for the clock to strike eight. Right on cue, as I hear the chimes, the moon appears from behind the thick bank of cloud it's been stuck behind all night. Immediately, it shines down through the glass, and tonight its rays land on a tree decoration that hangs from the branches by a purple-white-and-green-striped ribbon. The beam illuminates the matching coloured jewels that hang from the ribbon, so they sparkle and glisten like fine gems.

'Tonight,' Estelle says, looking proudly at the decoration. 'I would like to share with you a story from December 1918 that involves the brooch you see hanging before you, which belonged, I'm extremely proud to say, to my mother.'

Twelve

14 December 1918

Peace on Earth, Good will to all (Wo)Men

As has happened for the past two nights, the furniture begins to move as the decor in the sitting room changes. Even though I'm prepared for it tonight, it's still amazing to witness the room morph before our eyes.

Estelle's eclectic mix of styles all simultaneously change into one I easily recognise from my time on the magazine – Art Nouveau.

The fireplace surround changes to a pale cream, with ornate leafy scrolls carved either side of the fire. The wallpaper is now pale blue, with a yellow-and-pink floral pattern interspersed with birds and insects. In fact, everything in the room is based around nature and plants, with long leafy vines carved into the chairs, picture frames and a newly placed sideboard.

'I love Art Nouveau,' I whisper as I watch everything

change. 'It's so elegant and beautiful. Gosh, is that original William Morris wallpaper?'

The pale, light, inviting Art Nouveau room is so very different to the heavy dark interiors of the Victorian age we witnessed last night. There's much less clutter everywhere, and the room feels much less oppressive, even though a huge Christmas tree still fills the window. It's decorated with brightly coloured glass baubles, beads and ornaments, and is now beginning to resemble the Christmas trees we have today. There are no naked candles this time, but some wicks covered by glass bulbs wait ready to be lit when the evening comes.

'Here he comes,' Angela says, as though she's seen this story before. 'Mind yourselves.'

We all stand up and vacate our chairs as a man enters the room. He's wearing a brown suit made from a tweed fabric, along with a waistcoat, shirt and tie. He has a dark moustache, but no beard, and he's smoking a pipe.

'Nasty, smelly thing,' Estelle says, turning up her nose. 'He always had it on the go.'

The man sits in one of the chairs by the fire and opens up a newspaper.

The front page reads something about a general election, and there is a black-and-white photo of a man with white hair and a bushy moustache, who the paper tells us is David Lloyd George, the current prime minister.

'The man sitting by the fire is my father,' Estelle says without any feeling in her voice. 'Currently, he works for the same publishing house that my great-great-grandfather Robin worked for in our Victorian story. I'm not sure why – he never cared about books, let alone read any. My lovely mother, who you will meet in a moment, is the granddaughter of Timothy, the young boy in our last story.'

A heavily pregnant woman comes into the – what should we call it now? A parlour, a sitting room, a front room? I rack my brains trying to remember what it would have been called in 1918. A drawing room, perhaps? I turn my attention back to the pretty woman who's wearing a calf-length, olive-green pinafore dress and underneath it a white long-sleeved blouse with a large square collar. I've seen her somewhere before, but looking a little older ...

The man looks up from his newspaper. 'Clara, I thought you were resting?'

'I was,' Clara replies. 'But I'm up now, Stephen. I have errands to run.'

'Let Ivy run the errands,' Stephen says. 'It's snowing outside and you're in no state to be running anywhere. You should be in your confinement.'

'Nonsense.' Clara puts her hand on her tummy. 'That's such an outdated practice. Have you learnt nothing from the Great War, Stephen? Women can do so much more than you men ever gave us credit for. We kept this country running while the men were away fighting. Ah, Ivy,' she says as another woman enters the room. Ivy is wearing a similar-length dress as Clara, but it's plainer, and made from a much cheaper navy fabric. Over it she wears a white apron, and on her feet sensible lace-up shoes. 'Thank you, Ivy,' Clara says as Ivy holds out Clara's thick coat for her to put on, which is in the same shade of dark green as her dress.

'And you have been rewarded for it with the right to vote.' Stephen flicks his paper. 'The newspapers are full of the Representation of the People Act and how it will affect the voting today.'

'Thank you,' Clara says again, taking a large, floppy, burgundy velvet hat from Ivy. She goes over to a gilt mirror on the wall and arranges it on her head. 'Representation of the People,' she repeats with a hint of contempt. 'It should be *all* of the people, not *some* of the people – there shouldn't be rules to democracy.'

'At least you have the vote now.' Stephen returns his gaze to his newspaper. 'That's what you and your cronies have been campaigning for all these years, isn't it?'

'They are not my cronies, they are my fellow suffragettes,' Clara corrects him. 'And I only have the vote today because I'm over thirty, and we are fortunate to have some wealth.' She spins around from the mirror to look at Stephen. 'But what about all those under that age who have been fighting with us, or those less fortunate who do not have property worth five pounds or more? They have gained nothing. We will continue the fight until all women have rights equal to those of men.'

Stephen smiles. 'I fear that will be a very long time in the future, my dear. Long after our time, if it ever happens at all.'

'It will happen,' Clara says, a determined look in her eye. 'And we won't stop fighting until it does. Will we, Ivy?'

Ivy, who has been standing quietly by the door while Clara arranges her hat, jumps.

'Er ... yes, madam. If you say so.'

'I do. Do you have my – oh, you do,' she says gratefully as Ivy passes her a pair of burgundy leather gloves.

'What about you, Ivy?' Stephen asks, dipping his newspaper to speak to her. 'Will you be voting today?'

'I don't know about that, sir,' Ivy says. 'I'm not sure it's for the likes of me to choose government.'

'Of course it is, Ivy,' Clara says. 'It's for people like all of us.

But sadly, as I've just pointed out to my husband, you will not be eligible as you do not have property.'

'No, madam.'

'We will get there, though, don't you worry.' Clara pulls on her gloves.

'Where are you going?' Stephen asks again. 'I know there's no point in asking you to go and rest, but at least tell me which of your friends you are going to visit.'

Clara checks her final appearance in the mirror. 'I'm not visiting friends,' she says proudly, and she turns to face her husband again. 'I'm going to vote.'

Stephen looks shocked. 'You're what?'

'I just said, didn't I? I'm going to do what I've been campaigning for all this time. I'm going to place my first vote in a general election.'

'And who may I ask will you be voting for?' Stephen stands up, his hands on his hips, so his newspaper drops to the floor. Ivy scurries over to pick it up for him.

'I do not have to disclose that to you,' Clara says, her chin firmly jutting out.

'As your husband I demand to know. Otherwise you shall not go. I will stand in your way and prevent you from leaving.' He goes over to the door and stands in front of the opening.

Ivy, looking quite anxious, hurriedly tends to the fire, keeping herself well out of the tensions between her employers.

I can see Clara weighing up her options in her head before she answers. 'If you must know,' she says clearly, 'I will be voting for the Liberal candidate. There, does that make you happy?'

Stephen nods. 'As it should be.'

'Now, will you let me pass?' Clara asks.

But Stephen doesn't move.

'I still do not think you should be going out in your condition. Apart from the fact you are due to give birth to our child very soon, and it's freezing cold outside, what about the threat of influenza spreading across the country?'

'I will be fine,' Clara insists. 'It's just the sniffles.'

'That's not what it said in yesterday's newspaper. They are talking about a pandemic.'

'Nonsense. Just journalists making trouble for trouble's sake.'

'Clara, I am very aware I married a strong woman – you made that quite clear from the start of our courtship. But as your husband I am asking you to be careful for your own sake and for the sake of your unborn child.'

'I will be careful, Stephen. Please stop worrying about me.' Clara makes a move towards the door but Stephen still doesn't move aside.

'But I do worry,' he says. 'I worry very much. I don't want you to lose this one, Clara.' He moves away from the door and places his hand on her bump. 'We have had far too much heartache in this house over the last few years, I do not wish either of us to suffer any more.'

Clara's face softens and her expression changes from defiance to sorrow.

'You are right, my husband. We have both lost much as a result of this ghastly war – first my dear brother in the Somme.' She looks across at a photo of a soldier in uniform on the sideboard, which I immediately recognise as the same photo as the one hanging in Estelle's hallway. 'And then, as a result, our first child too.' She puts her hand over his on her protruding tummy. 'This baby means everything to me, as I know it does you. But you must understand why I need to go and do my duty today.'

135

Stephen nods. 'As you wish. May I request that Ivy accompanies you, though? She will make sure no harm comes to you. Ivy? Will you please go with Clara this afternoon?'

'Yes, sir, of course I will.' Ivy glances at Clara. 'If that's all right with you, madam? It may mean dinner is a little later than usual tonight, though.'

Clara hesitates, then realises this is the only way Stephen is going to allow her to leave the house. 'So be it,' she says, sighing as she sits down on one of the wooden chairs by the door. Which I recognise as the same ones I uncovered upstairs earlier today.

Clara pulls off her gloves again and puts her hands neatly in her lap. 'I will wait here while you get your coat and hat, Ivy. Do wrap up warmly. My husband tells me it's now snowing outside.'

'Yes, madam. I'll be as quick as I can.'

'Poor Ivy,' Clara says as Ivy disappears down the hallway. 'She is so put upon now we have lost all our other staff.'

'This is what you get from giving women more opportunities.' Stephen heads back over to the fireplace. 'They demand more in return. Suddenly working in service isn't good enough – they want to work in factories and shops instead of in perfectly good homes.'

'It's not that they don't want to work in homes,' Clara says. 'It's that they get better pay and conditions elsewhere since the Shops Act. If it wasn't for the fact that Ivy has been with us since I was small, I'm sure she would go too. She does so well considering she also has two children to bring up alone since she lost her husband. We are lucky her sister helps to take care of them so she is still able to work here. Ah, here she is now.'

Ivy returns wearing a long navy coat, a hand-knitted scarf and gloves, and a straw hat pinned on top of her hair.

'I shall expect you both back here within the hour,' Stephen says, looking at his pocket watch. 'The polling station isn't far. I was there myself this morning. If I would have known you wished to go, Clara, you could have accompanied me.'

'Perhaps this is something I wish to do alone,' Clara says bravely as she stands up again. 'Women can cope quite adequately, you know, without men.'

Stephen looks like he doubts this very much, but he puts his pocket watch back in his waistcoat. 'I shall expect you back here by twelve at the latest.'

'I do have a few other errands to run as well,' Clara says, pulling her gloves back on. 'So we may be a little later than that.'

'What errands?' Stephen demands. 'I thought we had just discussed this.'

'I need to go to the hospital and drop some things in. They are running a fundraiser this week for the children and I'm taking them some of our old clothes to sell.'

Stephen looks suspiciously at Clara. 'What sort of a fundraiser? It is the first I've heard of it.'

'Just because you're a name on the board at Great Ormond Street, that doesn't make you privy to everything that goes on at the hospital. They're also putting a play on for the children next week too. Mr Barrie has kindly offered yet again to allow his work to be performed.'

'That *Peter Pan* nonsense,' Stephen says, turning his nose up. 'How that man has made so much money from a story about a fairy, I'll never know.'

'Are you sure you're not a little jealous because you didn't buy the rights to his novel when they were offered to you?'

137

Stephen smiles scornfully. 'I hardly think so.'

'Such a shame you turned it down. It's just as well Charles, Great Aunt Belle's son, bought it for the company he worked for,' Clara continues bravely, and I find myself rooting for her as she dares to challenge her husband, albeit very politely. 'I hear the book has been very successful. Ivy took her son and daughter to see the play last week at the theatre, didn't you, Ivy?'

'After you kindly paid for us, madam,' Ivy says, looking down at the ground as if she'd rather be anywhere than involved in this conversation between her employers.

'And you thought it rather good, didn't you? You said as much to me.'

'Yes, me and the children fair enjoyed it, so we did.' Ivy glances nervously at Stephen. 'Holly and Rudy laughed so much, especially when Nanna the dog came on.'

'Hmm,' Stephen says, regarding Ivy with a steely look. 'Since when are we paying for staff to go to the theatre, Clara?' He turns his glare back on Clara.

'Since they deserved it,' Clara says resolutely. 'We've all been through a terrible time in the last few years, and everyone deserves some happiness again. Including the staff and children at the hospital. You know Belle and her husband were great supporters of Great Ormond Street when it first opened, and this family shall continue to support their endeavours while they are in need of our help.'

'It's a shame your grandfather didn't feel the same way about his father's publishing house and follow in his footsteps. The company might be a little stronger now if he had.'

'Grandpapa Timothy had his own reasons for becoming a politician instead of going into publishing like his father,' Clara says. 'He wanted to give help to those that needed it the most.'

'Hmm,' Stephen says again. 'Even if it was for the wrong party.'

I see annoyance flicker across Clara's face, but she chooses not to show it. Instead she simply says, 'Ivy and I will be visiting the hospital first and then the polling station. We will return as soon as possible. Come, Ivy.'

'Please be careful, Clara,' Stephen says, his voice softening, as Clara turns her back and heads through the door to the hall. 'Remember, you are due in a few weeks.'

'I am not due until January, Stephen.' Clara turns round, her voice also softening as she tries to reassure her husband. 'Please do not fret. I will be perfectly fine, and Ivy will watch over me as you have requested. Now, Ivy are we ready?'

'I think so, madam.' Ivy nods. 'Sir,' she says, bobbing her head towards Stephen. 'We will be careful. I promise.'

We watch as they leave the house together.

Stephen settles down again with his newspaper by the fire and the house is silent, save for the ticking of the clock on the mantelpiece.

'As I mentioned at the start,' Estelle says, walking over to the Christmas tree and delicately cradling the suffragette badge in her hand. 'That brave woman was my mother, and that . . . man,' she struggles to say the word, 'sitting there, is my father.'

'Your mother was a suffragette – how fabulous,' I say. 'We have so much to thank her for.'

'Yes, indeed we do.'

'And your father seems like a good man at heart,' I tell Estelle. 'He's strict, but I expect that's the result of a Victorian upbringing when things were different between men and women.'

'Yes, I think they were very much in love back then.' Estelle sighs. 'It's a shame things had to change . . . ' She glances over at Angela, who gives her a sympathetic look. 'I'm not sure when he began to morph into the monster he eventually became. Maybe it began after I was born – I'm the unborn baby, if you hadn't worked that out.'

I nod, but Ben looks puzzled.

'Estelle, if you're that baby, and this is 1918,' he says slowly, 'then that would make you almost a hundred years old now, wouldn't it, if you were born in January?'

Estelle simply nods.

'My goodness, Estelle, I had no idea,' I say, astonished. 'You look amazing.'

'You are very kind.' Estelle smiles at me. 'Now, we must get back to the story. Where were we? Ah, yes, we need to skip forward a few days . . . so let us go into the hall to do so.'

We all follow Estelle into the hall and immediately hear a baby crying.

'Is that you?' I whisper, wondering how this must feel hearing yourself as a baby and seeing your parents as they once were.

Estelle nods. 'I was born early. This is now the eighteenth of December 1918.'

A woman wearing a large white apron, a pale blue dress and a tall, white nurse's cap comes down the stairs looking worried. She knocks on the drawing-room door.

'Come!' Stephen calls impatiently. 'Well?' he snaps before the nurse has a chance to speak.

'Your child has been born, sir, and I'm pleased to tell you, you have a healthy baby girl.'

'A daughter . . . ' Stephen says quietly. 'I have a daughter?'

The nurse nods. 'The doctor is examining her now.'

'Good. Good,' Stephen says, still looking dazed. 'And my wife?'

'Your wife is fine, but she is running a slight fever.'

'A fever? Why?'

'I think it's best to let the doctor decide that, sir.'

Stephen looks puzzled. 'But you are our midwife. I know my wife trusts both you and your opinion, Tabitha. What do you think?'

Tabitha looks down at her sensible lace-up shoes. 'I can't be sure,' she says, looking up again with a worried expression. 'But I think your wife may have contracted the influenza. As I'm sure you know there's an awful lot of it about right now.'

'Influenza ...' Stephen repeats. 'No, she can't have. She has hardly been out anywhere recently. She's been so careful.'

'Hardly?' Tabitha enquires.

'I mean she went to the hospital the other day to drop off some things, and then on to vote. Did she catch cold? It was snowing when she left.'

'You can't catch influenza from being too cold, sir. Both hospitals and polling stations can be busy places. I suspect she caught it there.'

'I voted in the morning and I'm absolutely fine,' Stephen says robustly.

'I don't think it was the actual voting that may have caused her to become infected. More likely someone standing near her at the polling station.'

Stephen nods. 'Yes, of course. So what happens next?'

'We wait. The baby seems to be fine, though, which is good.'

'Thank you,' Stephen says, 'I'm sorry if I was curt with you before, Tabitha, but it's been a worrying time for us. Clara lost our first baby, you see.'

'Yes, I am aware of that. She told me.'

Stephen nods. 'I ... I would offer you some tea and refreshments,' he says, looking towards the kitchen. 'But our maid was taken ill yesterday.'

'Not a problem. I can make some tea for us all if you wish?'

'Oh could you?' Stephen says smiling gratefully at her. 'I'm pretty useless when it comes to the kitchen.'

'Of course. You say your maid is ill?' Tabitha asks, pausing in the doorway. 'What is the trouble?'

'I'm not too sure to be honest,' Stephen says. 'It's very unlike Ivy to suffer illness of any sort – let alone take to her bed.'

'Is she up on the top floor?' Tabitha asks.

Stephen nods.

'Then I will check on her when I have made the tea. You should be able to see your daughter soon. The doctor won't be long.'

Stephen nods. 'Thank you so much, Tabitha, we are all very grateful to you.'

We watch the midwife exit the room and disappear along the hall towards the kitchen.

'Come,' Estelle says leading us back into the drawing room.

Stephen is now standing at the side of the Christmas tree by the window. 'Thank you,' he says looking upwards through the window at the night sky. 'Thank you for blessing me with a healthy baby daughter ... Goodness!' he exclaims. '... a shooting star, that must be a good sign. I should make a wish.' He thinks for a moment. 'Please let Clara be all right. If she has caught this dreaded influenza, then please let her survive. Our daughter needs her. I need her.'

Someone at the door clears their throat.

Stephen spins around as we all turn and see a kind-looking

man, wearing a smart suit, with a white shirt and tie. In his hand he's carrying a brown leather Gladstone bag.

'Sorry to interrupt,' he says apologetically. 'I am finished upstairs now.'

'No, not at all, doctor,' Stephen says. 'Please come in and take a seat. Tabitha is just making us some tea, I believe. I hope you'll stay for a cup.'

'Please, call me Fraser, and that would be very welcome, thank you.'

'How is she?' Stephen asks with a worried expression.

'Are you enquiring after your wife or your new daughter?'

'Both.'

'Your daughter is doing very well, I'm pleased to say. She's a good weight and she seems very healthy indeed.'

'Good. Good. And my wife?'

'Delivery-wise, she did very well. But I'm afraid that she does have signs that suggest a possible influenza infection.'

'She will be all right, though?' Stephen insists. 'Won't she?'

The doctor looks over towards the window. 'A shooting star is always a good sign,' he says quietly. 'I'm glad you made that wish ... '

Thirteen

Bloomsbury, London

21 December 2018

The room begins to get fuzzy around the edges. Stephen and the doctor begin to blur then fade away as the room changes back to its modern-day self again.

'You can't end it there!' I cry out as Estelle begins to hobble over to her chair, as always never as sprightly as she appears during one of her stories. 'I want to know what happened.'

Estelle lowers herself down into her chair.

'Was your mother all right?' Ben asks gently. 'She fell foul of the Spanish flu pandemic, didn't she?'

Estelle nods. 'Yes, like millions of others she caught influenza that year and she was quite ill with it, I'm told. But mercifully she survived, unlike Ivy, who as you've probably guessed also had it, but sadly passed away.'

'Oh no.' I'm genuinely sorry to hear this. 'Poor Ivy. She said she had children too. What happened to them?'

'They went to Ivy's sister, Mary. She also worked here for a while. You'll hear more about them in a future story.'

'Tabitha was very good, though, wasn't she?' Angela prompts, slightly changing the subject. 'Didn't she stay and nurse them all and look after you too?'

'Yes.' Estelle nods. 'Thank you for reminding me, Angela. Tabitha, Mother's midwife, had already had influenza that year. So she stayed with us and helped take care of everyone until my mother was well enough to look after me again. I say well enough – my mother never fully recovered. She developed a condition we would know today as post-viral fatigue, but back then they did not know of this type of illness, and could not diagnose anything wrong with her. My early memories are always of her sitting up in bed in a nightgown. She was always pale and tired, but she always tried to be a good mother to me as best she could.'

'I've read about Spanish flu,' I say. 'It was awful and it killed so many people. Thank goodness medicine is so advanced now, and we know so much about how contagious disease spreads. Hopefully another worldwide pandemic will never happen again on such a scale.'

Estelle and Angela exchange an uneasy look, and I wonder why.

'You didn't catch it though, Estelle?' Ben asks.

'No, I think they removed me pretty quickly from my mother just in case, and my father didn't catch it either – more's the pity.'

'Estelle,' Angela chastises her. 'You don't mean that.'

'I know what I mean.' Estelle folds her hands in her lap purposefully. 'My poor mother suffered terribly, and he didn't lift a finger to help her. However, that story is for another time.

145

I think it's time for me to rest now. Seeing all that again has quite exhausted me. Angela?'

Angela comes over and helps her to her feet.

'I shall see you both tomorrow morning – yes? Ben, please feel free to move your things in tonight. Angela will make a bed up for you.'

'If you're sure that's okay?' Ben says. 'I'm very grateful. These old houses can be very cold with no central heating. I don't know how they managed years ago with just a fire for warmth.'

'It will be our pleasure,' Estelle says. 'Besides, it will be nice for Elle to have someone her own age to chat to.'

I smile at Ben and he grins back.

'Well, no time like the present,' he says, standing up. 'I'll pop back and get a few bits now if that's all right?'

'See you in a while,' I say as Angela and Estelle leave the room with Ben, and I begin scribbling yet more notes in my book about our latest trip with Estelle into the house's past.

'Estelle made us sound like two teenagers earlier,' I say to Ben when he's returned from next door, after packing a bag and leaving it on one of the beds upstairs. Angela has also taken her leave for the night, so now it's just me and Ben again in the chairs next to the fire.

'You mean when she said you'd have someone to chat to your own age?' Ben grins as he sips on one of the mugs of cocoa Angela insisted on making for us before she went up to her bedroom. 'Yes, I thought that too. I guess we must be nearly the same sort of age, though, aren't we? I don't want to be rude, but I kind of thought we might be.'

'I was born on Christmas Eve 1984,' I say honestly. 'So I'm thirty-four years old in a few days. How about you?'

'Amazingly, the exact same.'

'Yes, I know you were born on Christmas Eve, but what year?'

'That's what I said – exactly the same. Christmas Eve 1984!'

'No way!' I exclaim. 'That's crazy!'

'Don't I look thirty-four then?' Ben grins. 'Please say younger.'

'No, I mean it's crazy we were born not only on the same day, but in the same year too.'

'Yeah, I know you did. I was kidding. I don't think I've ever met anyone else born on Christmas Eve before, let alone in the exact same year. Clearly this was meant to be.'

I wonder what he means by *this*.

'I can't believe Estelle is one hundred, though.' I quickly change the subject.

'Now she *really* doesn't look it, does she? I thought she was probably in her late eighties, early nineties at a push.'

'It's odd ...' I say, as something suddenly occurs to me. 'I arrived here in Mistletoe Square on the eighteenth of December. That would have been Estelle's one hundredth birthday, wouldn't it?

Ben nods. 'It would appear so. Why is that odd?'

'Because there were no signs of it. There were no birthday cards on the mantelpiece, no gifts; you'd have thought they would have been celebrating that day, not interviewing for a job?'

Ben shrugs. 'I didn't see anything when I was in here either. All Estelle was concerned about was getting her Christmas tree in place. Perhaps they celebrated after we'd both gone.'

'Perhaps, but why then weren't there any cards the next day when I moved in?'

'Maybe she didn't want a fuss? Not everyone likes celebrations. Look at us with Christmas.'

'I suppose ...'

'Look, if it's worrying you that much, why don't we plan a joint celebration for the three of us when it's our birthday in a few days,' Ben suggests. 'I'm assuming Angela doesn't have a Christmas birthday too?'

'I don't think so. But then who knows? Everything has been so strange since I came here, I've almost stopped being surprised by things now. Does that make sense?'

'Totally. After what I've seen over the past two nights, and you've seen over the past three, I've decided just to go with the flow from now on.'

'But it is quite fun, though, don't you think?'

'Too right it is. I'm already enjoying the run-up to this Christmas much more than I thought I would.' Ben's steady gaze meets mine, and I feel my stomach do the tiniest of somersaults, which I will reprimand it for later. But it's getting harder to fight the effect Ben has on me. And I'm beginning to wonder whether it might be easier, and more fun, simply to go with the flow like he seems to be ...

'Me too,' I say quickly, glancing into the fire while I sip on my cocoa.

'I thought I was quite happy with the prospect of spending Christmas alone this year,' Ben says. 'Now, suddenly, not only am I immersed in daily tales of this house's colourful past, I've temporarily moved in with three kind, and extremely interesting women. One of whom I'm secretly enjoying spending so much time with.'

'Estelle?' I tease, my stomach flip-flopping again as I talk.

Ben shakes his head. 'Na-ah ... Angela.'

We both laugh. But when Ben looks at me again, his dark eyes hold mine and this time I don't look away – I don't want to.

'Seriously, answering that advert and moving into the house next door is proving to be one of the best snap decisions I've made in a very long time.'

'I feel exactly the same.'

'About answering your advert?' Ben asks in a low voice. 'Or perhaps about other things as well?'

'I think only time will tell,' I reply, our gazes still locked. 'As Estelle is showing us every evening, time can tell us many, many things, if we give it a chance.'

Fourteen

22 December 2018

It's strange seeing Ben at breakfast the next morning.

I'm used to either eating alone in the mornings or with Angela for company. Estelle never eats breakfast with us, preferring to take it in bed.

Last night when Ben and I both climbed the stairs and said goodnight to each other, there was a slightly awkward moment when we both walked towards our own rooms realising they weren't that far from each other.

I wondered if Angela would make Ben up a bed in one of the spare rooms on the next floor, or if she'd use the empty bedroom close to mine. It seemed she chose the latter.

'I see we're neighbours here as well,' Ben said as he paused by his door. 'Sleep well, won't you?'

'And you. Goodnight, Ben.'

'Goodnight, Elle.'

Then I went into my room and attempted to spend the next

two hours not thinking about Ben, while trying desperately to get some sleep.

It was so hard not to think about him. Aside from the fact we were both experiencing something incredibly strange yet wonderful together when we listened to Estelle's stories. There was something even stranger going on, something I couldn't yet understand. I felt like I had a connection with Ben that went far deeper and felt much stronger than simply knowing him for a few days should. And I got the feeling that Ben felt the same way.

'Ugh,' I grumbled as I turned over in bed yet again. 'Why does my new neighbour have to be quite so lovely, and quite so handsome? I'm supposed to be staying away from men.'

But as much as I tried to pretend to myself that I didn't want Ben anywhere near me, I was secretly very glad that he was now by my side during Estelle's trips into the past.

'Are you not taking breakfast with us, Angela?' Ben asks now as Angela places two plates of eggs, bacon, sausages and beans on the table in front of us.

'No, dear, I had breakfast ages ago,' Angela says, heading towards the door, 'Early riser, me, aren't I, Elle? Even on a weekend. You two enjoy.' And she leaves us to eat our breakfast alone.

'We weren't that late up, were we?' Ben lifts a coffee pot and pours us both a cup. 'Not for a Saturday.'

'No, but it did take me quite a while to fall asleep last night, so I needed a bit of a lie-in this morning.'

'Funny that – me too,' Ben says, smiling at me. 'Anything in particular on your mind?'

I can't help but smile back. That's another thing about Ben. Not only do I feel so at ease with him, but he makes me feel happy too. And only now am I starting to realise just how much I needed some real happiness in my life again. 'Just thoughts of suffragettes and Spanish flu really . . . ' I grin.

'Same!' Ben winks as he tucks into his breakfast. 'Mmm, this is great! Just how I like it – runny eggs and really crispy bacon.'

'Me too. I can't be doing with barely cooked bacon and overcooked eggs. This is spot on.'

'So, what are you up to today?' Ben asks. 'I assume there won't be any story time until tonight? Estelle seems to need the magic of the moonlight to tell her stories by.'

'Yes, that's usually what happens. Most of the time I have the day to myself and then the magic begins after dinner. I'm not sure what I'm going to do actually. Probably write up my notes on what Estelle told us last night about her mother and father.'

'Estelle clearly adored her mother,' Ben says. 'Not so keen on her father, was she?'

'No, it didn't seem like it. I wonder if something else happened she hasn't told us about yet?'

'Probably. Do you have a good relationship with your parents?' Ben asks, reaching for some more ketchup.

'It's okay,' I reply carefully. 'What about you?'

'Never knew them,' Ben says, matter-of-factly. 'I was adopted.'

'Oh.' For some reason I'm surprised to hear this and wonder how best to respond. 'I'd say I'm sorry, but sometimes people have great relationships with their adoptive parents. Better than they might have had with their real parents. Was that the case for you?'

'Yeah, my adoptive parents are great. I never knew my real mother or father.'

I'm about to ask if he's ever tried to trace his parents but, before I can, Ben changes the subject.

'You know, I don't have much on today either. I've finally got hold of a plumber this morning and he says it's likely he won't be able to come until tomorrow at the earliest – and that will be on emergency rates because it's a Sunday. So unless I want to spend the day doing tedious paperwork, I really need to think of something much more entertaining to do.' He takes a sip of his coffee. 'Perhaps we could do something together?'

'I'd like that,' I say a little shyly. 'What would you like to do?'

'Something Christmassy,' Ben says. 'I've avoided thinking about it too much this year. But now it's only days away, it feels like something's changed and I really want to get into the festive spirit. Does that seem silly?'

I shake my head. 'No, I felt exactly the same until recently. I think it must be hearing all these stories set at Christmas. It feels like I'm missing out by not joining in. But other than going Christmas shopping or visiting Santa – which I think you'll agree we're both a little old for – what else can we do?'

'Hmm ...' Ben heaps more bacon and eggs onto his fork while he considers this. 'Leave it with me. I'm sure I can think of something.'

It doesn't take Ben long to come up with a plan. His idea is for us to try and visit as many Christmas trees as we can in central London. 'It's not only the most recognisable symbol of Christmas, but it represents the beginning of all our Mistletoe Square stories too,' he says as we set off together. 'It's perfect.'

I think it's a mad idea to begin with, but as we visit Christmas trees in Covent Garden, Trafalgar Square, Leadenhall Market, all the major rail stations, and hotels such as the Ritz, Claridge's and the Savoy, my spirits are lifted and my heart is bursting with the joys of the festive season.

One visit in particular is very poignant, when we view the Christmas tree outside the Houses of Parliament in Parliament Square. But, on this occasion, it isn't the tree that catches our attention, it is the bronze statue close to it of Millicent Garrett Fawcett.

'"Courage Calls to Courage Everywhere",' I read from the banner that the tall bronze statue of a woman holds. The word 'courage' makes me think once more of the man who sat by me on Waterloo Bridge.

'I'm guessing with a banner like that she was a suffragette?' Ben asks.

'Yes, I remember reading a press release about this statue. Millicent Fawcett was an early campaigner for the women's suffrage movement. I believe she campaigned for over six decades for women to get the vote. This statue is the first of a woman, and by a woman, in Parliament Square.'

'Could have been Estelle's mother, couldn't it?' Ben looks up at the statue. 'She's wearing a similar outfit to the one Clara was wearing.'

'Yes, we owe so much to these women. I've always been in awe of what they did. But after seeing Clara last night, I really understand now how much it must have meant to them at the time.'

'Estelle definitely takes after her mother,' Ben says. 'She's just as strong and assertive as Clara was. I admire that.'

'I'm glad to hear it,' I say, continuing to look up at the statue as I speak. 'Because if you hadn't liked strong woman who speak their mind, then we may as well have said our goodbyes now.' I take a deep breath. It's time for some of Millicent's courage. 'You see, Ben, I've been oppressed too. Not like these women were – far from it. But I was in a relationship where I wasn't allowed to properly be myself. So I've made a vow that I'm never going to allow anyone to do that to me ever again.'

To my surprise, I feel Ben's hand slipping into mine, and I allow myself to turn towards him.

'Good luck to anyone trying to suppress you,' he says solemnly. 'You, Elle, are a force to be reckoned with.' He turns to look at the statue again. 'If you'd been born back when Millicent was around, I'm certain you'd have had more courage than anyone to stand up for what you thought was right.'

'That is one of the nicest things anyone has said to me in a very long time,' I tell him as he gazes into my eyes once more. 'Possibly ever.'

After our visit to Parliament Square, we decide to go to the ice-skating rink at Somerset House, mainly to see their Christmas tree, but Ben persuades me to have a little go on the ice. After about twenty minutes of us slipping and sliding and nearly toppling over a number of times, we decide, after a lot of laughter, we are much better off on dry land than frozen water. But it was rather pleasant to fall into Ben's welcoming arms when I nearly fell flat on my face a few times.

As we arrive back in Mistletoe Square and begin to climb up the steps of Christmas House, I stop and turn back to Ben. 'Thank you. I've had a wonderful time today.'

'Me too,' Ben says, pausing on the bottom step so his face is level with mine. 'You know whatever crazy stuff is going on in that house behind us, meeting you has been a wonderful antidote to all the craziness.'

'Er, thanks . . . ' I pretend to grimace. 'I think that's a compliment. It doesn't quite have the same ring as the one you gave me earlier.'

I'm joking, but Ben just stares at me. 'Oh, Christ,' he says as the penny drops. 'I don't mean you're boring, I mean you're an added bonus. No, that sounds wrong too, I mean . . . '

Surprising even myself, suddenly I lean forward and kiss him.

As I pull away from his lips, Ben looks at me with a shocked expression.

'Sorry,' I mumble. 'I'm not sure what came over me.'

Ben still stares at me. His silence, although only a few seconds, feels more like minutes. But instead of using his lips to speak, instead he wraps his arm around my back, pulls me closer to him and kisses me this time. Then, as we eventually part once more, we stare at each other.

'Are we moving too fast?' Ben asks anxiously.

'Do you think we are?'

'We've both just come out of difficult relationships. I don't want you to feel rushed. I want you to feel comfortable about us.'

'That's the strange thing, Ben, I do feel so comfortable around you. I probably shouldn't; we only met a few days ago.'

'I feel exactly the same. Like we've known each other a really long time.'

I nod.

'We thought what was going on in that house was crazy,' Ben says, glancing over my shoulder. 'But it's starting to feel like what's going on between us is a little crazy too.'

'Crazy in a good way, though?' I suggest.

Ben smiles. 'Totally in a good way.' He leans in to kiss me again, but a voice at the top of the stairs interrupts us.

'Here the two of you are!' Angela calls from the open doorway.

Tonight, Angela is gracing us with a very eighties-style

electric-blue dress. It has big shoulder pads, and sleekly cut lines, and around her neck she wears a string of big, bold, blue beads. 'I was beginning to wonder if you were coming back tonight? Dinner is ready. We need to get a move on or Estelle won't be able to tell her next story this evening.'

Ben and I both look up at Angela, and I feel like a teenager who's been caught kissing their boyfriend outside their house by their parent.

'Well, what are you both waiting for?' she says. 'It's freezing outside, come on in.'

After dinner, which as Angela predicted does feel a little rushed, we settle down as usual beside the fire with Angela handing out hot chocolates this time as our accompanying drink.

I see Ben look a little suspiciously at his mug as he's handed it, and I know he's wondering if these after-dinner beverages are how Estelle and Angela make their stories seem so real.

'I won't tonight, thanks, Angela,' I say, politely refusing to take a mug. 'I feel so full from your delicious dinner, I can't manage another thing.'

'If you're sure.' Angela looks a little put out.

'Yes, maybe I'll have one later before I go to bed if that's all right?'

Angela shrugs, but doesn't seem that fussed.

Maybe it's not the drinks after all then. I look across at Ben, who acknowledges my choice with a tiny nod of his head, while we wait for the moon to appear and shine its light onto the latest decoration whose story we are about to witness.

Tonight, as the clock strikes eight, the moon's rays pick out a decoration I remember hanging on the tree myself – it's of the three kings carrying their gifts on their way to see the baby Jesus.

'Tonight,' Estelle says in her customary fashion. 'We are returning to Christmas House in December 1936.'

Fifteen

11 December 1936

We Three Kings . . .

As the room begins to change once more, we find ourselves having to leap up as the furniture swiftly begins to disappear and is replaced by its decade's equal.

Sleek designs and smooth lines now fill the sitting room as some of Estelle's more modern furniture disappears. But not as much changes as it has in past stories. For instance, Estelle's drinks cabinet made of chrome and glass remains, simply looking a little newer and shinier. The wall between the two rooms that has always been in place, whether in 2018 or on our previous visits, slides away, and the sitting room becomes a large entertaining space with sitting and dining rooms combined.

The new armchairs that appear, look much more comfortable than their predecessors. They have large curvy armrests and white cotton covers laying over their head rests.

Antimacassars! I think excitedly on remembering their name. Covers to prevent the Brylcreem all the men used on their hair from spoiling the seats. The fireplace becomes much squarer, and is now tiled in shades of cream and brown. Over the fireplace an angular mirror shaped like a fan hangs. Of course, in 1936 we're at the end of the Art Deco period, aren't we? Where before there would have been curves, now nearly everything is angular with square edges.

The sitting room's walls are plain cream at the top, and a leafy green at the bottom, separated by a painted dado rail, and everywhere bright colours are dotted around, whether it be in the sunrise cushions that adorn the seats and sofa, or the bold patterns of some original Clarice Cliff vases I spot behind the glass doors of a wooden china cabinet.

'This is amazing!' I say, my head not able to turn fast enough to take everything in. 'It's so of its time.'

'It's so of its time if you had money,' Estelle says. 'Which we are lucky enough to have at this very moment, no thanks to my father.'

The Christmas tree has returned once more. This time it's decorated with brightly coloured balls, long pieces of silver string, and some sparse-looking tinsel. For the first time there is also the addition of some small electric lights with colourful glass shades.

The same man we met in the last story walks through the door. He's wearing evening dress – a black suit with wide, sharp lapels on the jacket, paired with a white shirt and black bow tie. Stephen looks much older than before and I do a quick bit of maths – he's eighteen years older now. But it's not just the added years and his slightly greying hair slicked back with oil that have aged him. Estelle's father looks worn down by life, as if things haven't been too easy for him over the last eighteen years.

He stands by the fire and lights a cigarette.

'Those things kill him eventually,' Estelle says matter-of-factly, without any tinge of sadness in her voice. 'Which is why I never touched them.'

'Cancer?' I ask.

Estelle nods. 'Of the lungs. He dies quite a long, protracted death – which was one blessing.'

'Estelle!' Angela scolds gently. 'That's enough now.'

'I'm sorry. But every time I see him it angers me.'

'I know, but we're here for the others this time, aren't we?' She looks over at Ben and me witnessing Estelle's anger with surprise. 'Let's carry on with the story.'

Estelle nods. 'I remember this particular evening very well – for many reasons.'

Estelle's father has now sat down in one of the armchairs and picked up his newspaper. The front-page headlines read *King to Abdicate – Duke of York to ascend throne as George VI.*

A young girl comes into the room wearing a long-sleeved red dress with white trim – it has boxy wide shoulders and is nipped in at the waist, extending into a mid-calf-length fitted skirt. Her dark hair is short, and perfectly coiffured into neat little waves held back with a diamanté clip.

'Good evening, Estelle,' Stephen says, making Ben and me jump, until we realise that Stephen is addressing a much younger Estelle who has just walked into the room.

'Good evening, Father.'

Ben and I, not quite believing what we're seeing, can't keep our eyes off this new Estelle. She really is quite beautiful. Her dark hair only helps to frame her pale but perfect complexion, and her green eyes – always so knowing – are piercingly bright, like two emeralds sparkling in a priceless tiara.

'How is your mother tonight?' Stephen asks. 'I assume you've been up to see her?'

'I have, and she's resting right now.'

Stephen doesn't seem to find anything unusual in this.

'Will she be making an appearance tonight?' he asks. 'I have some very important people coming over.'

'I really couldn't say,' Estelle says in a high-pitched, well-educated voice, like the sort you hear in old black-and-white movies. 'She looks very pale and is quite exhausted.'

'Hmm . . .' Stephen says, turning the page of his newspaper. 'We all get a little tired from time to time. But it seems to have become a permanent state for your mother.'

Young Estelle's face darkens. I glance over at our Estelle and see her face has exactly the same expression.

'Mother is ill – as you well know,' Estelle says bravely. 'She needs our help and understanding, not our blame.'

Stephen glares at her over the top of his paper. 'It is not your place, Estelle, to cast aspersions over your parents' relationship. I am fully aware of your mother's problems.' He straightens the pages of his newspaper and mumbles, 'I've lived with them for long enough.'

The young Estelle has clearly heard all this before. She ignores her father and walks over to the Christmas tree where she moves a couple of the decorations around.

'And why is that thing up so early this year?' Stephen asks, watching her. 'It's only the eleventh of December.'

'I thought it would be nice for Mother to have it up early. Rudy helped us get it from the market and Holly helped me to decorate it this afternoon.'

'Far too early,' Stephen grumbles, lifting his newspaper again.

'Will you be listening to the King's abdication speech tonight, Father?' Estelle enquires, walking back over to the centre of the room. She glances at her reflection in the mirror over the mantelpiece, but doesn't seem particularly pleased by what she sees.

'I expect so,' Stephen says, not moving from behind his pages. 'Damn ridiculous if you ask me. Three kings this country's had in the space of twelve months. Three kings in one year must be some record.'

'If the government had allowed the King to marry Mrs Simpson it wouldn't be happening,' Estelle says, perching neatly opposite her father on the edge of one of the armchairs. 'Why shouldn't you be able to marry the person you love?'

Stephen lowers his newspaper and regards Estelle. 'He's our king, for goodness' sake. He should do what's best for the country. If the government say he can't marry a divorcée then that is that. There are rules, Estelle, and sometimes you have to step up and do what's right.'

'Even if that's not what your heart desires?' Estelle asks, and I get the feeling she might not just be talking about the outgoing king.

Stephen stares at Estelle for a moment. 'In my experience, often what the heart desires is not what's best in the long run. Your brain will usually tell you much more than your heart ever will.'

'No,' Estelle says defiantly, sticking out her chin. 'Respectfully, Father, I disagree. Your heart will always tell you *everything* you need to know.'

Father and daughter glare at each other for a few seconds, neither of them giving an inch.

'In answer to your previous question, Estelle,' Stephen says eventually. 'I'm sure when the time comes this evening, I will be listening along with my fellow guests. Do you wish to listen with us?'

Estelle nods.

'Then you may enter the sitting room then and then only. Actually,' he says, as a thought occurs to him. 'Jack Tannon will be here tonight. Perhaps I should see if he would like his son to accompany him? I hear Teddy is following in his father's footsteps and is hoping to do a law degree. The two of you might find you have things in common . . .'

Estelle stares at her father – a long, cold stare that is not lost on Stephen. 'Perhaps we will,' she says eventually, in possibly the politest voice I've ever heard. 'I will look forward to making his acquaintance. Now I will leave you to your newspaper.'

Estelle stands, turns and walks slowly out of the room, while Stephen gives his newspaper a little shake, then settles down to read it.

'Come,' Angela says, gesturing for us to follow the young Estelle out of the room. 'Estelle?' She frowns. 'Estelle!'

Our Estelle jumps from where she's been standing over her father, glaring at him in much the same way as her younger self just had.

'We need to go,' Angela reminds her. 'The next part of this story?'

'Apologies,' a slightly dazed Estelle says. 'Yes, of course. To the kitchen.'

Estelle and Angela lead us along the hall towards the old kitchen and scullery.

'The beautiful floor tiles have gone!' I say as we pass through the hall and I look down at the green linoleum flooring

164

under my feet. 'What a shame. I thought the ones in your house were the originals, Estelle.'

'They are,' Estelle says, not looking down at the floor, but at the departing figure of her younger self. 'They were just covered by this dreadful linoleum – all the rage back then. The tiles are still there underneath. They reappear again ... in the nineties, I think?'

'Good,' I say as I follow the others down the hall. 'It would have been a shame to lose them.'

In addition to linoleum flooring, the hall also has a small table at the bottom of the stairs, and sitting on top of it a black Bakelite telephone. The stairs, which before were polished wood, now have a narrow, brown, patterned carpet running up the centre of them, held in place by stair-rods.

As we arrive once more down in the kitchen, I notice how much it has changed since we were last here in 1842. The 1930s have provided the kitchen with a few freestanding units painted in cream and green, that hold utensils and cooking ingredients. The big black range has gone, and has been replaced with an upright white enamel cooker that looks much more like our modern-day cookers, with gas hobs, a grill and an oven. There are various gadgets that are beginning to look more familiar on the work surfaces, such as a very basic toaster, and in the middle of all this is still a scrubbed wooden table at which a young girl, who looks a little older than the young Estelle, sits writing in a hardback book. Occasionally she gets up and checks the shelves in a large pantry at the end of the room.

'Estelle,' she says, looking up as the young Estelle walks into the room. 'How pretty you look tonight.'

'Thank you, Holly.' Estelle attempts a smile. 'Father has one of his … gatherings this evening, so I have to make an effort. What are you up to?'

'I'm attempting to plan the menus for the next week,' Holly says, gesturing at the book. She sighs. 'I'm sure my mother was so much better at this than me.'

'Perhaps,' Estelle says, perching on the edge of the table. 'You're doing a fine job, though. Ivy would have been so proud of both you and Rudy.'

'Thank you, Estelle. I do hope so.'

'You know Mother has never forgiven herself for Ivy getting sick,' Estelle continues with a solemn expression. 'She still talks about it now.'

Holly shakes her head. 'I wish she wouldn't blame herself. My aunt Mary always said that Mother would have likely caught it anyway after your mother did, so that outing didn't really make any difference to what happened.'

'Possibly,' Estelle says, not sounding entirely convinced.

'It's just such a shame that nasty bout of flu has affected your mother's poor health ever since, though.'

Estelle nods. 'Sadly, I don't think she'll ever recover now. She's going to be like this for ever, just because of a silly virus.'

Holly nods sympathetically.

'But we were very lucky to have had your aunt Mary step in and look after us, and now you and Rudy have continued the family tradition.'

'We try, but I don't think we're quite up to my mother and my aunt's standards just yet.'

'Nonsense, you're doing a marvellous job,' Estelle says firmly. 'Talking of your brother … where is Rudy this evening? Has he left you here doing all the work as usual?'

'No, he helped me to clear up after dinner. He's just popped out on some errands for your father.'

'What sort of errands?'

'I don't know – he didn't say. I'm sure he'll be back soon, though, if you're looking for him?' Holly suggests innocently.

'No, no,' Estelle says lightly. 'I just wondered where he was, that's all.'

'I'll tell Rudy you were asking after him.' Holly raises her eyebrows. 'I'm sure he'd be glad to know.'

'Only if you remember,' Estelle says breezily. 'It's not important.'

'Of course.' Holly gives her a knowing smile.

A bell rings on the kitchen wall. It's part of the same set of bells that were in the Victorian kitchen. Clearly a better way of summoning your staff has not yet been invented.

'That's your mother,' Holly says, glancing at the bell. 'I'd better go and see what she wants.'

'Don't worry, I'll go.' Estelle hops off the table. 'I was going to go up and visit her anyway. You carry on with your planning – some fish would be wonderful this week if you can get some. I do so tire of all the meat dishes Father insists on every evening.'

'I'll see what I can do,' Holly says, winking. 'Let me know if your mother requires anything more than a visit with her favourite daughter.'

'Only daughter,' Estelle reminds her. 'But thank you, I will.'

Silently, we all follow Estelle. She goes back up the flight of stairs that leads to the hall, then up the second set of stairs to the floor above the sitting and dining room. It doesn't look that dissimilar to how I know this space today. The bare floor boards are covered, like the stairs, with a narrow piece of carpet

167

that runs the length but not the width of the landing. The walls are painted a plain cream, with an occasional watercolour painting hung from a wooden picture rail, and the doors, which I know as stripped wood in 2018, are painted in a thick cream gloss paint.

The young Estelle walks towards one of the doors – the door I know as my bedroom – and knocks gently on it.

'Come,' a weak voice calls, and the young Estelle turns the handle. 'Estelle, how lovely,' the voice says. 'I was expecting it to be Holly.'

'Come.' Our Estelle beckons us all into the bedroom.

I feel a bit strange, first to be intruding into someone else's bedroom without them knowing we are here, and secondly, that this is the same room I use now, with the same view out over the square. I can't help feeling relieved when I see that the large bed, with its varnished wooden headboard that a pale and frail-looking woman is sitting propped up against, is not the same one I sleep in now.

But then something clicks – this isn't just any woman, is it? This is Clara, Estelle's mother, the strong, feisty, independent woman we met in the last story.

I'm quite shocked. Eighteen years may have passed, but Clara looks a shadow of her former self as she rests against several white feather pillows. She's frail and clearly in poor health as the dark shadows under her eyes attest to. Her dark hair, which was so carefully pinned up in 1918, is now peppered with grey and tied back in a loose ponytail at the side of her head, and she wears a short, pink frilly jacket over her nightgown.

'Yes, it's me instead.' Estelle walks over to the bed. 'Did you want Holly to bring you something in particular?'

'I was going to ask her for some fresh water,' Clara says, a little shamefaced. 'But that was only so I could have a little chat with someone. My water is absolutely fine.'

'Oh, Mother,' Estelle says, sitting down on the edge of the bed now. 'I'm sorry I haven't been in to visit you much today. I've been a little busy.'

'It doesn't matter.' Clara takes her daughter's hand. 'You're here now, and I've been quite content watching the snow fall outside my window today. The flakes are so pretty when they land on the glass. So intricate and full of detail.'

'Did you know every one is different?' Estelle says. 'No two are the same.'

'What a clever girl you are,' Clara says proudly. 'So well read for a young lady of your age. Now, entertain me some more by telling me all about your day.'

While Estelle goes through quite a dull list of events that have made up her day, from washing her hair to reading a book, I take a look around the bedroom.

It's just how I imagine a 1930s bedroom might look. Various paintings – a vase of flowers, a countryside scene, and one of a hairy little dog that looks a bit like Alvie – hang from a high picture rail that has a floral chintzy border underneath. There is a large wooden wardrobe with smooth curved edges, a matching chest of drawers and a pretty Art Deco-style dressing table with a triptych mirror. On the table are some green and pink glass bottles, and a vanity set consisting of a silver-backed mirror and matching hairbrush. Clara's bed matches the soft style of the other furniture, and, along with her many pillows that are helping her to sit up in the bed, she's covered in a sumptuous pink silk eiderdown.

Although my bed is different from Clara's, I do recognise some of the other pieces of furniture that still remain in my room today – especially the Art Deco dressing table, which I so admired when I first saw it.

'Anything else?' Clara asks when she's finished. 'You're looking very beautiful tonight, Estelle, is that for a special reason?'

'No, nothing special,' Estelle says, looking a bit shifty.

Clara observes her daughter for a moment. 'Are you stepping out with someone, Estelle?' Her eyes light up. 'Is it the young man living across the square? Please tell me it is. Your father says he's a handsome young chap and very well connected.'

'Do you mean Mr Cracker's nephew?' Estelle looks with horror at her mother. 'I don't think so. He's so in love with his reflection, he may as well just marry himself.'

Clara laughs, but that makes her cough, so Estelle pours her a glass of water.

'Thank you, my dear,' Clara says when she's sipped on the water.

'I almost forgot, Holly and I decorated the Christmas tree today,' Estelle says, clearly wanting to move the subject away from her love life. 'That took us a while. I thought you might enjoy sitting by it and looking at the pretty lights I bought from Harrods the other day.'

'You're so thoughtful, Estelle.' Clara smiles at her daughter. 'I will try and get down tomorrow if I'm feeling up to it.'

'You should try, Mother,' Estelle says quietly. 'I know you find it difficult, but you're spending more and more time up here alone in your bedroom. It's not healthy.'

'And neither am I, Estelle,' Clara says sadly. 'You know that.'

'Is that the only the reason you spend so much time up here?' Estelle asks. 'I mean … it's got nothing to do with Father, has it?'

Clara jumps at the mention of Stephen. 'No, of course not. Why would it?'

Estelle shrugs her narrow shoulders. 'I know he can be ... *difficult* at times. But that's not a reason you should have to stay up here all the time, Mother. It's your house too. If anything, it's more your house than Father's. It was your brother that inherited it from Grandpa and then passed it on to you when he died.'

'Estelle,' Clara says, patting her hand. 'You know how these things work. The man is in charge of the house, wherever it came from. He makes the decisions, not us.'

Estelle pulls her hand away. 'No, Mother, I won't hear you talk like this!' she says, leaping up. 'You fought too hard for women to become equal to men when you were young. Don't let some outdated practices overrule what you know is right now.'

'Estelle?' Clara says with concern. 'Where has this all come from?'

'It's him!' Estelle gestures down at the ground as if she might be talking about the devil rather than her father. 'I can't let him keep treating you like this.'

'Whatever do you mean?' Clara asks, but I get the feeling from her expression she has a pretty good idea of what Estelle is referring to.

'With his gambling ... and ... and ... ' Estelle stops before she finishes her sentence.

'And?' Clara asks gently. 'And what, Estelle?'

'His other women!' Estelle hisses. 'I don't want to be the one to tell you, Mother, but he goes out and visits other women.'

Clara nods calmly.

'Why aren't you shocked?' Estelle demands. 'Why aren't you upset, even?'

171

'Because I know about the other women, Estelle. I've known for a long time.'

'You have?' It's Estelle's turn to look surprised.

'Yes, but I'm interested to know how you know about them. He ... he hasn't been bringing them here, has he?' Clara looks a tad anxious for the first time. 'To the house.'

Estelle shakes her head. 'No, not that I know of.'

'Then how do you know? Is it the local gossip? Do all our friends know? Am I a complete laughing stock – first this stupid illness, and now my husband parading his whores all over town.'

Estelle looks more shocked at her mother using the word 'whores' than at anything else that's taken place so far.

'No! It's not that at all, Mother.' She sits back down on the bed again and strokes her mother's hair to soothe her.

'Then what is it?' Clara is clearly calmer, but I can see the spark of the fighting spirit the 1918 Clara possessed in her eyes once more. 'How do you know?'

'Rudy told me,' Estelle says quietly.

'Rudy ... *our* Rudy?'

Estelle nods. 'He's seen Father out and about a few times with his women, and I may have asked him to follow him a couple of times too.'

'And Rudy did that ... for you?' Clara asks, astonished. 'That goes far beyond the duties we employ him for ... Ah,' she says, an understanding look in her eyes. 'I see now.'

'What do you mean – you *see*?'

'Have you taken a shine to our Rudy, Estelle? It's completely understandable if you have – he's a handsome young man. But you mustn't become a bother to him.'

'I haven't *taken a shine* to him, Mother,' Estelle says calmly, but with a steeliness to her voice I've heard in our own Estelle before. 'I love him. And before you say anything, he loves me too. We're in love.'

Clara stares at Estelle.

'You are in love with Rudy?' she whispers.

'Yes, I am,' Estelle says proudly.

'But you can't be.' Clara's voice is still low.

'Yes. I can,' Estelle replies defiantly.

I glance over at our Estelle. She stands quietly by the window and gazes out of it, as though she can't quite bear to witness this part of her history over again.

'How long has this been going on?' Clara asks. She's calm, but I sense there's a great deal of anxiety behind her gentle voice.

'For a few months,' Estelle says. 'No one but us knows. I suspect Holly might have an idea, but she hasn't let on. If you're worried about Father, he certainly does not know.'

'That I know to be true. If your father had any idea, Rudy would have been thrown out of this house a long time ago.'

'You won't tell him, will you, Mother?' Estelle asks, looking worried.

Clara shakes her head. 'No. Of course I won't.'

'When I turn eighteen, we intend to get married,' Estelle says, her eyes lighting up at the thought. 'I know that Father will try to stop us, but I don't care. We will run away if necessary.'

Clara sighs. 'My dear child.' She lifts her delicate hand and caresses Estelle's cheek. 'What I'm about to say next I detest myself for already.'

'Then don't say it,' Estelle says, sensing what might be coming. 'I know you want me to be happy, Mother, don't you?'

'Of course I do, my love. That's all I want for you, but ...'
Clara hesitates and shakes her head again. 'No, I cannot say it.
I will not say it.'

'Say it, Mother,' Estelle demands. 'I want to know.'

'It's your father,' Clara says, after taking a deep breath. 'I'm
worried he will bankrupt us ... and soon if he carries on. He's
never been quite the same since he lost his job in publishing
and went into finance. He lost such a lot of money during the
Great Depression after investing in that American company. I
told him he shouldn't, but he was insistent that it would be a
legacy for you and his future grandchildren.'

Estelle's face darkens as Clara speaks.

'My friend Mariah came to visit me last week, and she told
me that your father is borrowing money all over town. He even
asked Bing, Mariah's husband, for money the other day. I was
mortified when Mariah told me. It's his gambling, Estelle. If
he carries on, I am afraid he will lose this house. I ... I simply
cannot have that. This house has been in my family for hundreds of years; I can't lose it. I can't. It's my home. Where would
I go, what would I do if I can't live here?'

Clara's face crumples and she begins to cry.

Estelle immediately begins to comfort her. 'Please don't
upset yourself, Mother. And please don't worry, I will make
sure that never happens.'

'But how?' Clara sobs. 'Your father's gambling is a habit I
don't think he can stop. My one hope had been that you would
marry well and your husband would provide for you and save
us from becoming homeless and destitute. But now you've
fallen for a servant, and I don't begrudge you that, Estelle,
really I don't – love is a wonderful thing – especially when it's
reciprocated, and Rudy is a lovely young man. Ivy brought her

children up well, but I do worry for both of our futures if your father carries on the way he has been of late.'

'You must not concern yourself, Mother,' Estelle says firmly. 'You always said nothing good ever came of worrying. I will make sure Father does not lose all our money or this house in any gambling game. I do not intend to marry for money or for duty, Mother. I will marry for love – just like the King.'

'My Estelle.' Clara takes her hand. 'You are such a good girl. If it were only that simple. The King is making a very hard choice in giving up his position for the woman he loves. He may live to regret it in the future, I fear.'

'But he may not,' Estelle says. 'Why can't you have both? Why can't you have love and security and family?'

'Perhaps for a lucky few, that's what they do have. But for most of us sacrifices have to be made in life to keep ourselves and our family safe and secure.'

'Like when you turn a blind eye to Father's other women, you mean?' Estelle asks quietly.

Clara nods slowly. 'I need to keep us safe, Estelle. I haven't been able to provide for us and look after you properly since you were born. I need someone to take care of me. Your father and this house is our security. Which is why your father can't be allowed to lose it. Or we will lose everything.'

Estelle stares at her mother for a moment, and then she nods. 'I understand,' she says patting her mother's hand. 'Don't you worry, Mother.' Estelle stands up and smooths out her dress. 'I will look after you. I will not allow us to lose this house, ever. Trust me, from now on, I will have *everything* under control.'

The young Estelle leaves the room and we follow her, leaving an exhausted-looking Clara to rest.

Our Estelle waits for her younger self to head back down the stairs before speaking.

'When we return to the sitting room, we have moved on a few hours,' she says matter-of-factly, but she too looks exhausted like her mother had. Living through this again is clearly quite a strain for her. 'My father and his friends are now in the middle of their poker game. They will pause shortly to listen to the King give his abdication speech on the wireless.'

'Are you all right to continue with this, Estelle?' I ask. 'It's clearly hard for you to witness it again.'

Estelle smiles. 'Thank you, Elle, for your concern, but I will be fine. It's important you, and now Ben, know all the significant moments in this house's history. Let us continue.'

She leads us back downstairs to the hall where we find the young Estelle listening intently through the gap in the door to what is currently being said in the sitting room.

Estelle slips past her younger self into the room.

The young Estelle twitches a little as her older self passes her, like a shiver has just run down her spine. But she quickly pulls herself together, and tilts her head again to listen to the conversation.

We follow Estelle into the sitting room and find the area around the fire is now vacated as Stephen and his three guests all sit around the table at the other end of the room. A velvet curtain has been pulled halfway across the gap where the wall usually is, to create a more secluded area for the men to play cards in. But we can still see most of what's going on.

Angela, unlike the rest of us, goes right up to the table and watches them closely.

Cigar smoke wafts from the card table, along with much ribbing and raucous laughter.

'So, how's business, Stephen?' one of the men asks. Like all the men he's wearing a smart evening suit, with a crisp white shirt and black bow tie.

'Can't complain, Winter. Can't complain,' Estelle's father says, studying his cards.

'You still don't regret giving up publishing, then, and going it alone?' the man called Winter continues.

'Not at all. Never enough money in it for me.' Stephen smiles slyly at the others. 'My talents are better used elsewhere.'

'Especially when authors donate their money to charity, eh?' One of the men with grey hair and a matching moustache says, lifting his bushy eyebrows.

'What are you talking about, Tannon?' a younger man with a kind face asks.

'That author fellow,' Tannon says, wafting his hand across the table. 'What's his name ... Barrie, that's it. The one that wrote *Peter Pan*. Didn't he give all his profits to the hospital or something?'

'He gave his rights to Great Ormond Street – yes. And therefore any future royalties,' Stephen explains. 'My wife was over the moon. She says it will help the hospital greatly.'

'Until people stop buying the wretched book, of course,' Tannon says. 'When they get bored of fairies then the money will dry up.'

'How is Clara, Stephen?' the younger man enquires.

'Much the same, Michael. Much the same,' Stephen says, not looking up.

'I'll have to pop in and see her sometime,' Michael says. 'As a friend, of course,' he hurriedly adds when Stephen looks worried. 'Not as a doctor – no charge.'

Stephen nods. 'Thank you, Michael. I'm sure she'd appreciate that.'

'Enough chit-chat, gentlemen!' Tannon demands. 'We sound like a lot of women gossiping away. I think the time has come to raise the stakes . . . ' He puffs forcibly on a huge cigar. 'All these notes are beginning to look quite untidy piled up in the middle of the table.'

'What do you suggest, Tannon?' Michael asks. 'My money is all on the table.'

'Property . . . ' Tannon suggests with a smirk. 'What do you say, Stephen, are you game?'

'Fine by me,' Stephen replies, his face flushed but expressionless as he attempts to bluff his way through the hand.

'Good. Good. Then I shall raise you everything on this table, plus my gold watch.' Tannon removes his gold pocket watch from his waistcoat and places it on the table in front of him.

Stephen follows by doing exactly the same. 'Michael?' he asks.

'Too rich for me,' Michael says, throwing his cards on the table. 'I've got a wife at home with a penchant for expensive dresses and a new baby on the way. I need all the money I can get. What about you, Winter?'

'Me too.' Winter throws his cards down and lifts his glass of whisky from the table instead. 'I'll just enjoy watching you two old pros battle it out.'

'What do you say, Stephen?' Tannon asks, his eyes glinting. 'What else have you to give? Or perhaps your hand isn't quite as superb as you'd have us believe . . . '

'That's what you hope, Tannon, that's what you hope. I have this house,' Stephen says slowly, and I see Estelle stiffen.

'Ooh, now, that is interesting,' Tannon says. 'When I said property, I didn't actually mean bricks and mortar. But . . . ' He considers the cards in his hand. 'Why not? I was thinking of moving soon – these houses aren't what they used to be – but owning two right next door to each other would bring a nice little earner, I'm sure.'

'Stephen,' Michael says warningly. 'I'm not sure that's a good idea. Think of Clara upstairs, and Estelle. They need this house, as do you. You can't risk it on a card game.'

'Michael, as this family's doctor I will always listen to you, in the same way I listened to your mother when she attended Clara during Estelle's birth. But in medical matters only. What I do with my money is my business, and, like Tannon says, the income from a second house would come in very handy.'

Michael lifts up his hands in surrender. 'Don't say I didn't warn you.'

'Well, my good man, are we on?' Tannon's eyes glint once more as he puffs on his cigar.

'Father!' the young Estelle calls, hurrying into the room. 'It's time for the King's Speech on the wireless.'

Stephen looks around in annoyance. 'Not now, Estelle.'

'But you said I could listen with you, and I'm sure all these gentlemen wouldn't want to miss such an important event?'

'She's right, Stephen.' Michael says. 'Our game can wait for the King.'

'Except technically he's not the King any more, is he?' Winter says as they all stand up and make their way over to the chairs around the fire. 'His brother is.'

'I like old Bertie,' Michael says, sitting down in one of the chairs. 'Family man, isn't he? Much more appropriate as the head of the Empire. I'm sure his daughter, Elizabeth, will make a fine queen one day too.'

'Hear! hear!' Angela says, pretending to pat Michael on his shoulder. 'Well said.'

Michael's hand moves to the back of his neck as if he senses something there.

Estelle gives Angela a stern look, and Angela backs away slightly.

'Women shouldn't be in charge of anything,' Tannon says, accepting a top-up of whisky from Stephen. 'It was bad enough when they got the vote.'

'Ignore him, Estelle,' Michael says, smiling at Estelle standing awkwardly by the wireless. 'Stuck in the Dark Ages is old Tannon here.'

'It's on!' Estelle announces, turning the radio up. The room falls silent as the familiar sound of King Edward VIII's abdication speech fills the room.

'A few hours ago I discharged my last duty as King and Emperor, and now that I have been succeeded by my brother, the Duke of York, my first words must be to declare my allegiance to him. This I do with all my heart . . . '

While we and the men all listen, I notice that the young Estelle has moved quietly to the back of the room, and step by step she's gradually moving closer to the card table.

The men are so engrossed in the speech that they don't notice. They all sit facing the old wireless as though it's a television set they're watching, instead of a voice over the radio.

Estelle slowly, but expertly, lifts up the two hands of cards that are still left on the table, and one by one takes a look at them, before carefully placing them back down again. She then heads over to a tall, narrow chest of drawers and opens the top drawer. I see her sorting through something in the drawer and then she takes out a playing card. Silently she moves back over to the table, removes one of her father's cards and slips the new card in between the others. Then she moves back closer to the men as if she's been there all the time.

The speech ends and the men all sit silently in their chairs.

Stephen turns off the wireless.

'Quite some speech,' he says.

The men murmur their agreement.

'Perhaps it will be the fresh start this country needs?' Michael says optimistically.

'Not if Hitler carries on the way he is over in Germany,' Tannon says, lighting another cigar. 'I can see that ending in another war for this country.'

'Baldwin won't let that happen,' Stephen says confidently. 'Not again. We've barely got over the last one.'

'Let's not think about that now,' Winter says sensibly. 'Haven't you chaps got a game to finish?'

'Yes, indeed,' Tannon says. 'Come, Stephen, old boy!' As he passes Estelle standing innocently by the drinks cabinet, he smiles. 'My dear! It's a shame my son couldn't make it tonight – he's back from Eton for Christmas, you know? I'm sure you and Teddy would get along famously together. We'll have to arrange for you to pop round sometime for drinks.'

'If you're still our neighbour after tonight then I'm certain I'd be delighted to make Teddy's acquaintance.' Estelle smiles demurely.

'Are you still here?' Stephen snaps at Estelle. 'You've heard the speech, now please leave.'

'As you wish, Father,' Estelle says, backing away as the men take their places again around the table.

Estelle pretends to leave the room, but then sneaks back

in and stands on the other side of the partially pulled curtain, listening.

'So, Stephen, ready to show your hand?' Tannon asks eagerly.

Stephen nods and I notice some beads of sweat beginning to appear on his forehead. 'I have two pairs,' he says, his voice shaking a little. 'A pair of kings and a pair of tens.' He turns the cards over on the table while keeping eye contact with Tannon.

'Oh dear,' Tannon says, smirking at Stephen. 'Oh dear, oh dear. I have two pairs also. But mine are two tens ... and two aces!'

He turns his hand of cards over triumphantly on the table.

There's a joint groan from Michael and Winter.

Stephen stares despondently down at the table, his face full of despair as he realises what he's done. What he's lost. He angrily throws his fifth card down on top of the others.

'Looks like you win, Tannon,' he says. 'Perhaps we can talk about——'

'Wait!' Michael says, staring at the table. 'Look!'

They all look at what Michael is pointing to. 'Your last card, Stephen!' he says excitedly. 'It's another king. You have three kings, that means you win!'

Sixteen

Bloomsbury, London

22 December 2018

'You changed the card!' Ben exclaims, grinning at Estelle. The Art Deco furnishings of 1936 have now disappeared, along with Stephen and his friends, and we are back in Estelle's modern-day sitting room once more. 'You changed the card to a king so your father would win the game!'

Estelle nods as she sits wearily down in her favourite chair.

'I did,' she admits. 'Luckily, I knew where Father kept his spare packs of cards. I also knew, thanks to Rudy, how to play poker. I simply made sure he had a winning hand so I could save the house for Mother.'

'Did Tannon give up his house next door?' Ben asks.

'Eventually, yes. But not because of the bet. My father and Tannon made some other arrangement in exchange for him not taking the house immediately. But when Tannon eventually moved away from Mistletoe Square, he honoured the bet, and gave the house to my father, who was poor of health by then.

Tannon worked in the city and had loads of money; he didn't need any more houses.'

'And you and Rudy?' I ask, sensing there's more as I sit down opposite Estelle.

'Rudy moved on . . . ' Estelle says sadly. 'Not long after that night, actually. He was offered a job on a farm in Norfolk. Rudy had always wanted to live in the country, and he loved animals.' She gives Alvie a stroke as he hops up onto her lap. 'The offer came out of the blue, some distant relative if I remember rightly, but it was too good an opportunity for Rudy to turn down.'

'Didn't you see each other after that?' I ask.

'He said once he got settled, I could come and visit. We talked about us getting a little place in the country one day, but sadly that day never came . . . '

Estelle looks over at the Christmas tree and the decoration of the three wise men.

'I don't know for sure, but I think my father had something to do with him leaving, because Tannon's son, Teddy, told me some years later he had family in Norfolk too. An estate with many acres, houses and farmland on it . . . '

I glance at Ben; he pulls a face.

'Was that the arrangement your father came to with Tannon, do you think?' I dare to ask.

'To arrange the removal of the man I loved to the country in the hope I'd never see him again?' Estelle asks, her eyebrows raised. 'Yes, I'm in no doubt that's what happened. Like I told you before, I detested my father – for many reasons – and that was one of the main ones.'

'Oh, Estelle,' I say, feeling for her. 'That's terrible.'

Estelle shrugs and hugs Alvie close to her. 'He was an awful man. That wasn't the only time I saved the house and my mother from homelessness. It was a blessing when he died. At least our home wasn't at risk any more. It wasn't long after that I married Teddy.'

'Tannon's son?' Ben exclaims.

'He wasn't actually that bad,' Estelle says. 'He was a quiet man, but he was kind and he looked after Mother and me. And when he died in the Second World War, I became a widow in my twenties. But at least Mother and I had the house, and Teddy left me a generous amount in his will with which we could comfortably live.'

'Did you ever marry again after that?' I ask. 'You were very young to be widowed.'

'Sadly, that happened a lot back then. There were an awful lot of us young widows. And, no, I didn't marry again. But more on that another night. This evening has quite taken it out of me. I think it's time I retired to bed.'

She leans on her cane, Alvie jumps down off her lap and Angela hurries over to help her up.

'I will see you both in the morning. Sleep well.'

'And you,' I reply. 'Goodnight, Estelle.'

Ben and I watch Angela help Estelle out of the room and then we turn to each other.

'Well . . . ' Ben says, sitting down in Estelle's vacated chair.

'Indeed,' I reply. 'Quite the story again tonight. Except this one felt much more personal, didn't it – to Estelle, I mean.'

Ben nods. 'Do you ever wonder why is she telling us all this?' he asks suddenly. 'I know we've talked about this before, but don't you get the feeling there's something more going on here than simply recalling these stories for a book?'

'I think we both know there's something more going on, but

what? What other reason could there be for Estelle to be telling us all these tales from her family's past?'

Ben thinks about this for a moment. 'I wish I could suggest something, but, really, I have no idea. If anyone else told me this was happening to them, I would think they needed help.'

'I know. I'm so glad you're here with me experiencing all this.'

'So you don't think you're going mad on your own, you mean?'

'Yes, there is that too.' I smile.

'You know I've been on some pretty odd first dates in my time,' Ben says, leaning across and taking my hand in his. 'But these trips into the past are something else.' He gets up and sits in the chair next to me now, still holding my hand. 'I'm still no closer to figuring out how they're doing it. Are you?'

I shake my head. 'I even tried not taking a drink tonight in case we were right and they were spiked with something. But that made no difference at all.'

'I saw you doing that. Good idea. But I don't think either of us really thought Estelle and Angela would drug us, did we?'

'No. That's the thing, they're both so lovely. I can't imagine them ever doing anything untoward.'

'And yet here we both are, apparently travelling back in time every night.'

'We're not really travelling back to those times, though, are we? It's just an incredibly real way Estelle has of telling us her stories.'

'A bit too real on occasions. Remember that smell in the kitchen of the Victorian house?'

'Yes, I thought you were going to throw up!'

'I wasn't that bad.'

'I think you were. The stories become so real then, don't they? Like we're actually there.'

'But we're not there, are we? We can't be. And remember,' Ben lets go of my hand while he demonstrates, 'we've both tried to touch things, but our hands just go straight through them. Like you suggested before, it's like we're in some incredibly good virtual reality game, but without the goggles.'

'You say that, and yet there's been a few occasions when I've felt the people in the stories might actually know we're there, or at least sense it.'

'Like when Estelle brushed past her old self just now?'

'Yes, and then there's been mirrors people look into and see something other than their reflections, and remember when Belle heard you say the name Ebenezer to Charles Dickens.'

'Yeah, I'm still not sure about that one, to be honest,' Ben says, remembering. He sighs. 'I'm not a huge believer in stuff like this, Elle, but it's almost like we become ghosts when we're viewing these stories. Some people are more sensitive to stuff like that, aren't they?'

'But we'd have to be ghosts from the future,' I say, thinking about his theory. 'Ghosts usually come from the past. Unless it's in *A Christmas Carol*. The ghosts come from all times then, don't they? Past, present and future.'

Ben considers this. 'If we're going down that path then we'd be more like Scrooge than the ghosts. We're the ones being shown all this by Estelle and Angela. Crikey!' he suddenly exclaims.

'What?' I ask.

'If we're Scrooge, that would mean I'm doing the same thing as my namesake being shown all these Christmases! Which makes this whole thing even weirder. What on earth have we got ourselves into here, Elle?'

'I really don't know,' I say, shaking my head. 'But I have to admit, I'm secretly quite enjoying it now I've got used to it, aren't you?'

Ben grins. 'Too right I am. But not nearly as much as I'm enjoying spending time with you.' He takes hold of my hand again.

'Flattery will get you ... everywhere!' I look up and flutter my eyelashes like a heroine in a silent movie.

'I do hope so,' he whispers, kissing the back of my hand. He then begins to kiss delicately along my arm and up the side of my neck. My eyes close with pleasure.

I'm about to turn to him so it's our lips that are touching, when a voice calls out.

'I've got Estelle settled now. So I'm just going upstairs to soak my feet, my corns are playing havoc with— Ooh la la! So sorry! Pretend I was never here!' And the door closes as Angela quickly backs out of the room.

Ben sighs.

'The thought of Angela's feet put you off, has it?' I ask, grinning.

'Bit of a passion killer.' Bens grimaces. 'What do you reckon – separate rooms tonight?' he asks, not hiding the disappointment in his voice.

'Maybe that's best for the time being. You'll have your house back soon. Maybe I can pop round and bring some festive cheer one evening? I mean, it is nearly Christmas.'

Ben smiles. 'Suddenly I'm finding myself even keener for Christmas to arrive this year.'

'That's funny,' I reply, leaning forward to kiss him. 'So am I.'

Seventeen

23 December 2018

The next morning is a Sunday, and Ben is waiting for his emergency plumber to arrive at his house. He's actually waiting in the warmth of Estelle's sitting room doing some work in front of the fire, but the plumber has agreed to call him when he arrives in Mistletoe Square.

So after I've taken Alvie for a morning walk and the plumber still hasn't called, Ben suggests I take a wander into town myself.

'As much as I enjoy your company, Elle, there's no point us both waiting in, is there?' Ben says. 'You go out and find some festive cheer for both of us. It's two days until Christmas, I'm sure there's plenty to be had. Either that or you can have a laugh at all the husbands and boyfriends doing their last-minute Christmas shopping!'

'I'd rather wait for you.' I perch next to him on the arm of the chair. The thought of going on my own out into a world

189

filled with Christmas spirit really doesn't have the same appeal as going with Ben by my side. 'It's much more fun when it's the two of us.' I put my arm around his shoulders, leaning in for a hug, but Ben swiftly pulls me down onto his lap. 'Hey!' I pretend to protest.

'I am deeply flattered you think that,' he says, looking down at me. 'Usually people hate spending time with me at Christmas.'

'Bit of a Scrooge, are you?' I ask, grinning.

Ben grimaces. 'Sadly, I was. Until I met you, that is.'

'Funny, I feel exactly the same!'.'

I reach up and pull Ben's face towards me, but it doesn't take a lot of effort as Ben is already moving in my direction.

When our lips finally part, he looks at me with an odd expression. 'What I'm going to say now might sound a bit weird. But hear me out.'

'Okay . . .'

'You know you read these stories of people finding they have long-lost siblings and they know straight away because there's a connection between them?'

'Yes?' I reply hesitantly, wondering where he's going with this.

'Because I felt this instant connection with you, and you told me you felt the same, I hoped we weren't going to find out something weird like that. Because the way I feel about you, Elle, really isn't something you want to feel for a long-lost sister, I can tell you.'

I can't help but laugh. 'Sorry, but that's really funny. I mean, you're right, we do have this incredibly powerful connection for two people that have just met. But because we have the same date of birth, if your original worry was proved to be correct, that wouldn't make us siblings, we'd have to be long-lost twins!'

'Crikey,' Ben says, pulling a face. 'I hadn't thought of that. That's even worse!'

'You needn't worry. There's no way I ever had a twin brother I was separated from at birth. My parents had so many other children they were always involved with that an extra one wouldn't have been any bother to them.'

'Really, how come?'

'It's just the way they were. You'd never know they had their own child; they were always busy doing good here there and everywhere for other people. I kind of got forgotten about a lot of the time.'

'I'm sure that's not true.'

I shrug. 'I guess you had to be there.'

'What do you mean they were always doing good?'

'Back when I was small, my parents worked, and volunteered for a lot of charities. I don't just mean occasionally, it was all the time both in this country and overseas. It was their lives. Especially my mother – I'd even go so far as to say she was obsessed by doing good by everyone.'

'That's admirable, surely?' Ben asks, looking surprised.

'Yes, of course it is. But not at the expense of your own child.'

'Perhaps you only remember it like that. I'm sure your parents loved you and cared for you the best they could. We all remember things a little differently than they actually happened when we were children.'

I stare at Ben. Then very carefully I remove myself from his lap. 'Funny, that's what everyone says,' I reply, deliberately not looking at him while I smooth down my jumper where it has twisted and risen up. 'I thought for some reason you might be different. I thought you in particular might understand, given your own situation.'

'Because I was adopted, you mean?'

I nod.

'I hardly think you sulking that your parents were not giving you all their attention twenty-four seven compares to being adopted at birth?' Ben says, his voice overly steady. 'It actually makes you sound a bit spoilt, if I'm honest.'

'Is that right?' I say in an equally cool voice. 'I was spoilt, was I?'

My voice may sound calm, but inside I'm raging. This was what everyone thought when I trusted them enough to share any part of my childhood – that I was a spoilt, only child, who wasn't happy unless she had all her parents' attention. But they weren't there. No one knew what it was like to feel abandoned by parents who were still by your side. What it felt like to have every special day in your life put on the back burner for someone else's needs. It wasn't that I didn't have all their attention, it was that I never had any of it.

'I just think in the greater scheme of things,' Ben continues, 'your personal hardships aren't really on the same level as some others.'

Ben and I stare at each other in a way we've never looked at each other before. It feels horrible, like someone has not only popped the little heart-shaped bubble we've been living in up until now, but sliced right through it with a big, sharp kitchen knife.

Slowly, I nod. 'Well, at least I know where I stand. I think I will go out on my own if it's all the same to you? I could do with some quiet. There's things I need to ... think about.'

I turn and head quickly out of the room. Then I grab my

coat, scarf and gloves from where they're hanging on a peg in the hall. I pull them on as swiftly as I can, before I throw my bag over my shoulder and head purposefully out of the door and down the steps outside.

I don't turn back to see if Ben is looking out of the window after me as I cross Mistletoe Square. I don't care. I need to be alone. I need to think ... about a lot of things.

I wander aimlessly for a while through the streets of Bloomsbury, not really knowing where I'm heading. The argument with Ben has really shaken me up.

How had I been so stupid? After everything that happened with Owen, I promised myself I wouldn't get involved with anyone else, that I would put myself first for a while. But I had barely set foot on Mistletoe Square when Ben popped up with his glossy brown hair and his kind chocolate eyes. He said all the right things, even if he didn't mean any of them, and I stupidly believed him.

But Ben was right when he said we had a connection. That wasn't just something he made up with his fancy words and his smooth voice. I felt it too. And however hard I try to deny it, as I march along in the bright winter sunshine, I simply can't.

I wish it was in my imagination. I wish I could convince myself I let Ben trick me into believing this. But I can't. Whatever this connection is, I feel it in my gut, in my heart, and in my soul. It's crazy, it's deeply annoying, but it is one hundred per cent there.

But how could it be? I've known Ben for five days. How could I have any sort of connection with him? Let alone one as deep as this feels.

That's why I was so hurt by his words back at the house.

It takes a lot for me to trust anyone enough to tell them about my childhood. Mainly because that was always the sort of reaction I got – that I must have imagined it. It was a long time ago. Perhaps my recollections aren't as clear as they should be. And, occasionally, I was spoilt.

I should have been so lucky, I think ruefully to myself. Was my childhood as awful as any of those poor individuals we witnessed in some of Estelle's stories? Of course not. I wasn't saying for one moment it was. But do I look back on my childhood remembering good times and happy memories? No, I do not. Especially at Christmastime.

Eventually, I find myself walking along a packed Oxford Street. Shoppers wearing Santa hats and tinsel around their necks hurry past me, their shopping bags full to the brim with gifts for loved ones and long rolls of wrapping paper. Restaurants I pass are full of diners enjoying a pre-Christmas meal, some wear paper crowns pulled from crackers, and a number of people look like they might have had a bit too much festive cheer, as they wobble along the pavement with happy grins on their faces, ever so slightly slurring their words as they chat excitedly to their friends and family.

For once in my life, I was able to feel just a little of what they were as Christmas approached. Now I was back to feeling like I usually did, annoyed by people bustling about, and counting down the days until I didn't have to pretend to be happy and excited any more.

Just because Ben has annoyed you, it doesn't mean you should take it out on Estelle and Angela, I tell myself as I pause outside a large department store and gaze into one of their large windows. *They've been nothing but lovely to you, and they both adore Christmas. Perhaps you should get them both something to say thank you?* But what could I buy? Like Ben, I've only known them for a few days.

Is that really all it is? I continue to stare at the window display full of suggested gifts for friends and loved ones. *Days? It feels like I've known them for a lot longer.*

Perhaps it's because we've travelled back to so many Christmases in the house's history together. In a matter of days we've covered over one hundred and eighty years. I'm beginning to feel like I know Estelle's family almost as well as I know my own.

I think about my parents again.

They are much more settled now they are older. They travel much less these days, and are more than happy living in their little cottage in Suffolk. My father has an allotment and a part-time job tending people's gardens. My mother still volunteers, but mainly for her local WI. She also helps out at the local school twice a week, and is involved in a scheme giving lifts to elderly people who need to get to hospital appointments. I'm not completely estranged from them, but it's been a long time since I've spent Christmas with them.

As a child I yearned for what I considered a normal Christmas. A simple day waking up early, rushing downstairs to find what Santa had left and then eating a huge Christmas dinner around a proper dinner table with family I only saw once a year.

But the only memories I have are of time spent in other people's homes. Or in far-away countries that barely acknowledged Christmas, let alone celebrated it. The pain and yearning I felt as a child for happy Christmas memories lessened over the years, but never fully faded away.

I allow myself to imagine for a moment what Christmas Day in Mistletoe Square could be like. In the morning there might be lots of shiny, colourfully wrapped presents waiting to be opened under the huge tree. Angela would definitely be cooking us all a delicious lunch, and Estelle would preside at the head of the table enjoying every moment. There would be crackers and board games and possibly even a singsong, and in the evening, when the other two had gone to bed, Ben and I would snuggle up in front of the open fire together . . .

No! I hurriedly stop myself. That last part definitely wasn't going to happen now. Ben and I were over.

And neither Estelle nor Angela have actually ever mentioned anything like I've just been creating in my mind. But when every one of Estelle's stories has been set at Christmas, and she clearly loves her tree so much, is it so wrong of me to secretly hope that the big day itself would be anything less than perfect in Mistletoe Square?

Maybe I should try and get Estelle and Angela a gift while I have the chance? Just in case . . .

I wander into the store and pause in front of a large sign telling me where all the various departments are situated.

Maybe Angela would like something for the kitchen? I wonder. No, I can't buy her that. It's like I'm emphasising that's how I see her. Hmm . . . what about a nice piece of jewellery? Angela is always wearing bright, colourful accessories.

Confident in my idea, I head up the escalators to the fashion floor. In the accessories department I pick out a shiny, bold necklace in the shape of a rainbow – perfect. I can just imagine Angela pairing it with one of her retro outfits.

Now for Estelle . . . Goodness, what do I buy for her? She has so many precious things around her home already. Many of the items are memories of the people who have lived there before her. What can I possibly buy that she might appreciate?

Estelle always dresses in a very traditional, classical way – matching dresses and cardigans with pearls or small delicate pieces of jewellery. Nothing I could buy for her in here would complement any of the antique pieces she favours.

I think about all the photos and paintings she has dotted about of her friends and the past residents of the house. What about a nice photo frame? Perhaps we could all take a photo by the Christmas tree and I can get it printed out for her to add at a later date to the frame. Yes, I like that idea. So I head upstairs to Home Accessories and pick Estelle out a beautiful silver frame with an Art Nouveau design that I'm sure she will like.

Happy with my choices, I purchase the gifts for Estelle and Angela. As I'm walking towards the exit of the shop I pass through the toy department. It's decorated with even more Christmas decorations than the rest of the store. There are huge displays of Lego, next to houses full of Barbie dolls. Alongside those, shelves stacked high with games, cars, jigsaws and just about any toy you can think of, all waiting hopefully to be purchased for a lucky child's Christmas stocking. But the display that really catches my eye is a huge pyramid in the centre of the department stacked high with teddy bears. Some of them wear brightly coloured bows around their necks, some full outfits, but what they all have in common are their inviting smiles and friendly faces.

I walk over to the display to take a closer look. The bears I am drawn to feel soft with realistic-looking fur, and their arms, legs and head are all fully jointed so they can move. These bears in particular all have the most beautiful dark eyes and a friendly stitched-on smile. I pick one up. This is exactly the sort of teddy bear I longed for when I was young. The sort every year I hoped to find in whatever small pile of gifts might be at the end of my bed on Christmas morning – never under the tree, there was never a tree.

There's a Santa sitting in a grotto next to the display of bears, with some children queuing up to see him, and I can't help overhearing what he's saying behind his white beard.

'And what would you like for Christmas this year, Ailsa?' he asks a young girl in a burgundy coat and black patent-leather shoes.

'A doll that eats and drinks, and then poops real poos,' she says innocently.

The Santa smiles. 'Yes, I know just the one. If you've been a good girl this year, Ailsa, then perhaps Santa will bring you one. Now what about your brother?' he says, turning to a slightly younger boy standing next to her. 'What's your name, young man?'

'Alfredo,' the boy says.

'That's his name, but we call him Alf,' his sister says matter-of-factly.

'I want to be Alfredo,' the boy insists.

'Righty ho,' the Santa says, smiling beneath his white beard. 'Alfredo it is. And what would you like for Christmas?'

'I'd like my family to all be together,' Alfredo says in a mature-sounding voice that belies his apparent age. 'My dad is in the army overseas. I just want him to come home.'

I can literally feel my heart strings being plucked one by one.

'That is a very special thing you're asking for,' the Santa says. He sounds calm, but I can tell by his eyes he's been moved just as much as I have by the boy's wish. 'I'm sure if your father can come home, he will. All families should be together at Christmas, but I'm afraid it's not always that easy.'

The Santa glances across at me watching all this with interest, so I hurriedly pick up one of the bears and pretend to be thinking about buying it.

'Why isn't it?' Alfredo asks. 'Christmas is a time to be with the ones you love. They said it on the television the other day. In the advert break.'

'I see.' Santa nods. 'And they'd be right. You should be with those you love at Christmas, and often those you love are not just family, but friends too. But sometimes it's not quite that simple, I'm afraid. It doesn't mean those people love you any less, though, just because you can't be together.'

Alfredo shrugs matter-of-factly. 'All right, if I can't have my dad home, then I'd like snow, please.'

'Don't be silly, Alf,' his sister says. 'It never snows at Christmas.'

'Doesn't mean it won't this year,' Alfredo says. 'Does it, Santa? Can you make it snow?'

I can't help smiling as I continue to listen.

'I can't promise anything, but I'll do my very best. Now you look after your sister and hopefully your dad will come home for Christmas. But if he doesn't, I want you to be a brave boy and have lots of courage, because your dad is doing a very important job in the army. He's looking after lots of people who need taking care of, and by doing that he's helping to protect us here too.'

Alfredo nods.

'Now, before I move on to the other children waiting, is there anything else I can bring you?'

I turn away from the Santa to put the bear down, but, before I do, I see a familiar face peeking through the display of bears.

'Hi,' Ben says carefully, tilting his head to the side so I can see him properly.

'Hi,' I reply, forgetting for the moment I'm still holding a teddy bear. 'Wh-what are you doing here?'

'I got bored of sitting around waiting for the plumber,' he says, moving around the display towards me. 'Angela said she'd let him in if he ever turns up. So I thought I'd do a bit of Christmas shopping before it's too late.'

'Oh, I see.'

'Actually, that's a lie. Not the plumber part, but the Christmas shopping. I wanted to check that you were all right? You left in a hurry earlier.'

'Can you blame me?' I ask, unconsciously pulling the bear in front of me for protection.

'No, not really. I want to apologise for what I said earlier. It was uncalled for and unnecessarily rude. I'm sorry. Can you forgive me?'

I look at Ben. My mind is saying *no, walk away now, Elle, as fast as you can.* But I can feel my heart pulling me closer to him. Like we're connected by an incredibly strong, but invisible thread.

I find myself nodding. 'I'm sorry too. I don't have many buttons that set me off, but you pushed the most sensitive of them earlier.'

'I know,' Ben says. 'And if it's all right, I'd like to learn more about why that happened. Like we were discussing earlier, we really haven't known each other all that long. Perhaps now would be a good time to talk? To really get to know each other better. I don't want to annoy you, Elle, or make you angry. But to prevent that happening, I think I need to know more about you and your past.'

He's right. Of course he is. I nod again. 'All right then.'

'Good.' Ben looks relieved. 'Have you eaten yet?'

I shake my head.

'Let's get some lunch, then – my treat.'

I move towards him, but Ben looks at my torso. 'Is he yours?'

I look down and I'm surprised to see the bear still pressed against my chest like a shield. 'Er . . . kind of,' I say, hurriedly lowering it. 'I . . . I was thinking of buying him.'

'Really?' Ben seems surprised.

'Yes.' I look down at the bear in my hands. 'I always wanted one just like this for Christmas when I was little, but I never got one.'

'Why not treat yourself then?'

'Oh, no, it's fine.' I hurriedly put the bear back in the display. 'It was just a thought. Perhaps Santa will bring me one this year if I'm lucky? The one they have here is really good, you know? You should have heard some of the things the kids were asking for earlier.'

'Which Santa?' Ben asks, looking around.

'The one over . . . Oh, that's odd, he was there a few minutes ago?'

'Maybe he took a break?'

Not only has the Santa gone, but the little grotto he was sitting in has completely disappeared too, so now there's only a display of children's magic sets and playing cards. Three large king cards are picked out on the advertising boards behind the display, immediately reminding me of last night's story.

'Yes, perhaps . . .'

We walk back through the store together towards the exit and a restaurant Ben suggests for lunch. But just before we leave, Ben's phone rings. 'It's Angela,' he says. 'I'd better take it – it might be about the plumber.'

I head over towards the exit while Ben speaks to Angela.

'Excuse me,' I ask one of the security guards waiting by the door. 'Do you have a Santa in the store this year?'

'Sorry?' the security guard asks, turning down his earpiece.

'Is there a Santa in the store – you know, one children can visit?'

'No, I'm afraid not. Management decided not to get one this year – too much hassle I think what with building all the grotto and everything. Shame, though – the one we had last year was great. I took my kids to see him; they loved it.'

'Ah right . . . Thank you,' I feel completely bewildered now. If there wasn't a Santa here then what did I just witness?

'All right?' Ben says, heading back over towards us.

'Er . . . yes. I think so. What did Angela want?'

'Nothing really, the plumber hasn't arrived yet. Angela just wanted to check if we'd be back for dinner tonight.'

'Right . . . ' I say as we leave the store, my mind still on the disappearing Santa Claus. 'Wait a minute, how did Angela know we'd be together? And, come to think of it, how did you know where to find me today? I could have been anywhere, and yet you knew I'd be here in this very department store?'

'Angela told me before I left the house this is where you'd be,' Ben says, also looking confused now. 'I assumed you'd been in touch with her, and told her where you were?'

I shake my head. 'Nope.'

'Well, that *is* very odd. But I guess when we've seen as many odd things as we have recently, little things like that don't seem quite so strange now.'

'I don't know,' I reply, taking one last look back into the store. 'I think there's plenty of strange stuff still going on that needs quite a lot of explanation, actually.'

Eighteen

Over a delicious lunch, Ben and I talk and talk. About our lives, our careers and the unexpected, yet quite wonderful run-up to Christmas we've both been experiencing this year.

Ben is the first to share more details of his childhood.

'So, as you already know, the people I call my parents aren't actually my real mum and dad,' Ben explains while we're between courses. 'They adopted me when I was a few days old, after my mother left me at a children's home. I know nothing of my father at all.'

'Gosh, Ben, I'm so sorry.'

'Don't be. I had a wonderful childhood. I didn't want for anything and I had kind and loving parents.'

'Have you ever wondered about your mother?' I ask gently. 'Why she left you there?'

'Sometimes. I even tried tracing her once, but she left no clues to her identity when she left me, so it was virtually impossible. I only know she requested I be called something beginning with E.'

'That's very specific, isn't it? For someone giving their new-born baby up to make requests about their name.'

'Yes, I thought so too. But my new parents just went with it apparently and that's how I ended up being called Ebenezer.' He rolls his eyes. 'Trust me to be born at Christmas.'

'Not much fun, is it?'

Ben smiles ruefully. 'No, it's not. So that's why I've never really been that keen on this time of year because it's when my mother left me. So, what's your story?'

'How do you mean?'

'Regarding Christmas. I know you feel like me about it, because we've talked about it before, but you've never fully explained why?'

I take a sip of my water, and then a deep breath.

'On Christmas Eve,' I begin. 'How did your parents differentiate between Christmas and your birthday every year?'

Ben looks surprised. 'I'm not sure. I had presents wrapped in birthday paper and not Christmas paper, and we had a cake. I sometimes had a party when I was younger, but it was never on Christmas Eve, it was always a few days before. Why do you ask?'

'Do you know how my parents kept my birthday and Christmas apart?'

Ben shakes his head.

'They didn't.'

'What do you mean? You had joint presents, that kind of thing?'

'Nope, I was lucky if they even remembered.'

Ben's brow furrows. 'Your parents forgot your birthday?'

'Not every year – it depended where we were and what we were doing that year. We travelled a lot with the various charities they were working for. Most years we barely celebrated Christmas, let alone my birthday.'

'Why on earth not? Did they have financial difficulties?'

'Not really. They were usually busy helping people that did, though.'

Sensing there's more, Ben waits for me to continue.

'Most of my memories of Christmas are of helping someone else. Nothing wrong in that, of course – it's admirable to think of others before yourself,' I add, aware of how awful all this makes me sound. 'Often we'd be dishing out meals to the homeless, or volunteering in a hospital somewhere. Some years we were abroad while they were distributing aid, then Christmas wasn't even mentioned, let alone my birthday.'

'And this happened most years?'

'Not all the time. I do have some memories of Christmas spent in this country, usually in a little flat somewhere, because we moved around a lot. But we'd always have strangers over for dinner, someone needy who didn't have a family of their own, or the means to cook themselves a warm meal. God, I sound terrible don't I? These people were probably extremely grateful to my parents for taking them in.'

'I'm sure they were. But you were a child. I can understand why you didn't see it that way. Christmas is everything when you're young. Even ol' Ebenezer here remembers that!'

I smile gratefully at him. It is such a relief to be telling all this to someone who isn't judging me for once. No one ever seemed to truly understand how I felt.

'I don't want to sound ungrateful, and I know I do, moaning like this. At least my Christmases were never dull, I suppose. And they did remember my birthday some years, even if it was a few days late. My parents are good people, I know that. But they were so busy being good to everyone else back then, I just wanted them to share some of that compassion and a little of their time with me.'

Ben puts his hand over mine on the table and gives it a squeeze. 'What a pair we make. One of us was actually abandoned at Christmas, and the other one felt like they were every year.'

'I'm just being silly,' I say, holding on to Ben's hand as tightly as he's gripping mine. 'First-world problems, as they say. I should be grateful, at least I wasn't out on the street freezing and starving like that little boy we saw in Victorian times.'

'True. Also, you didn't catch influenza and nearly die,' Ben adds, winking.

'*And* I didn't have to give up my baby on Christmas Eve to an orphanage.'

Ben looks wounded.

'No, no! I wasn't referring to *your* mother,' I say hurriedly. 'I was talking about the first story Estelle told me. The one set in Georgian times.'

'Right, yes, you did tell me a bit about that.'

'So, really, I have very little to complain about,' I say resolutely. 'This Christmas I'm going to think about all those who have passed before me that had much worse Christmases than I'm ever going to have.'

'Here's to that.' Ben lifts his glass. 'To Christmas 2018. May it give us everything we've always wanted!'

As we walk back towards Mistletoe Square, we pass by Great Ormond Street Hospital. Outside the main doors, a Father Christmas is just leaving the hospital, presumably after visiting with the children. He climbs up on a makeshift sleigh on the back of a trailer, and staff and children – some of the patients in wheelchairs and on crutches – wave him goodbye.

'I spent some time there when I was young,' I say as we pause to watch the festive scene. 'When I was a baby, actually.'

'Did you? What was wrong?'

'I had some breathing problems after I was born, I think. Luckily for me my parents were in London then, so I got the best care.'

'Yes, you did. It's a great place. Doesn't it feel strange that we've spent time with some of the people that helped to set this hospital up?' Ben says, almost wistfully. 'Clara said that Belle and her husband were heavily involved in the funding of the original hospital, didn't she?' he reminds me when I look puzzled.

'Of course, and the royalties from *Peter Pan*, which Stephen and his friends spoke about, still go to support the hospital today.'

Ben nods. 'So that links you with Estelle's family in a roundabout sort of way. Their actions helped you when you were a baby.'

'I guess they did. And now I'm helping Estelle to write the story of that family. It's a lovely little Christmas circle of life.'

Ben smiles, then he leans into kiss me at the same time as a choir outside the hospital begin to sing carols.

'Good King Wenceslas looked out
On the Feast of Stephen
When the snow lay round about
Deep and crisp and even
Brightly shone the moon that night
Though the frost was cruel
When a poor man came in sight
Gathering winter fuel.'

'"When the snow lay round about",' Ben says. 'It rarely snows these days in London. Yet it always snows on Mistletoe Square during Estelle's stories. I wish it would snow this year at Christmas.'

'Me too.' I snuggle into his embrace as he pulls me even closer. 'What harm would a little bit of snow be, and how much happiness would it bring to so many?'

When we finally return to the house later, we find Angela already cooking dinner. Tonight she's dressed more casually again in black baggy dungarees, a loose pink sweatshirt, big lace-up boots, and a pink-and-black polka-dot scarf tied in a bow on top of her head.

Neither Ben nor I feel all that hungry after our late lunch, but we don't want to upset Angela, so we sit down to dinner with her and Estelle, and try our best to look like we're enjoying the roast chicken, potatoes and vegetables that Angela has prepared.

But we clearly don't do a good enough job of pretending.

'Is anything wrong?' Angela enquires, watching us both carefully. 'You don't seem all that hungry tonight?'

I look across at Ben. He shrugs.

'Actually, we had quite a late lunch,' I admit, my cheeks flushing. 'I'm so sorry, Angela. It's nothing to do with your cooking. It's delicious.'

'As it always is,' Ben adds.

'We had a lot to talk about earlier,' I continue. 'And doing it over a meal seemed like the best idea at the time. We should have thought about you back here cooking for us.'

'Yes,' Ben says. 'We should have. It was my fault. I upset Elle, and I needed to do some serious grovelling. So I took her to one of my favourite restaurants. So sorry, Angela.'

Angela still looks a little put out, but Estelle looks pleased as punch. She casts Angela a warning look.

'I can see that the two of you have made up since,' Estelle says, looking keenly between us both. 'Which is all that matters, isn't it, Angela? *Angela.*'

Angela nods hurriedly. 'Yes, of course it is. I'm pleased you had a good time together.'

'We did.' Ben takes my hand in his. 'I think we both understand each other a little better now. Don't we, Elle?'

'Definitely.'

As I glance around the table, I see that both Estelle and Angela are now smiling just as much as we are.

'And so we move on in our Christmas stories. This time to 1962,' Estelle says a little later as she sits and waits for the moon to shine onto tonight's chosen decoration on the Christmas tree.

'The swinging sixties this time – cool!' Ben says, grinning.

'Please be quiet while we wait for the moon, thank you, Ben.' Estelle sounds like a teacher admonishing a student.

'Sorry,' Ben murmurs while I grin at him.

So while we wait for the moon to work its magic on the Christmas tree decorations, Ben and I steal flirty glances at each other, like two teenagers in a school classroom. Glances that I'm sure don't go unnoticed by Estelle and Angela.

The moon soon makes an appearance from behind the clouds. It shines through the window down onto a decoration in the shape of a snowflake, making it sparkle and shine as it hangs on the tree. And for the first time I wonder how the moon is able to shine through the same window every evening. Shouldn't it move a little further across the sky each night and therefore away from the front of the house?

But I don't have long to ponder this thought, as suddenly we're catapulted once more into the past, as Estelle's sitting room begins to transform to its former self, almost sixty years previously.

Nineteen

Mistletoe Square, London

Boxing Day 1962

Let it Snow

'Before you ask,' Estelle says, looking around her. 'Yes, I do still live here.'

'And so do I!' Angela announces to my surprise. 'You're going to meet me for the first time tonight too!'

'Calm down, Angela,' Estelle says. 'We're not at that bit yet. We need to set the scene.'

I'm not sure what I expected when Estelle said we were heading back to 1962. A retro-looking room with bold sixties flower-power prints, or some chrome and pastel-coloured plastic furniture perhaps. But what we find as some of the furniture fades away and is replaced with its sixties equivalent, is a strange mix of antique old and retro old. As though the owner of this room doesn't want to give up the past, but has had to bow slightly to the modern trends of the day.

Still remaining is some of the furniture from previous visits – the sideboard, the china cabinet and the table the men were playing cards around. I notice the cocktail cabinet has disappeared again – perhaps who lives here now doesn't drink all that much? But interspersed among this are touches of the decade we now find ourselves in – the open fireplace now has an electric fire installed into it. Above the fire, hangs a gold and wood sunburst wall clock. A large shiny green cheese plant stands in a bright-orange-and-brown pot in one corner of the room, and, in another corner, where the wireless had been on our last visit here, there now stands a boxy-looking television set with a wooden surround. The wallpaper, curtains and floor covering still lean towards the more traditional, but the cushions that are scattered on the brown leather seats and sofa are covered in the bright colours and bold prints so synonymous with the sixties.

A green velour curtain still separates the front room from the back like it had in 1936, but this time it's pulled across the opening that joins the two rooms.

And as always, since our Victorian Christmas, a large Christmas tree stands in the window of the room. It's decorated with colourful lantern lights, proper silver tinsel for the first time, and a mix of some of the traditional decorations I've noticed in previous years, along with a few more bold and gaudy baubles that befit the decade we find ourselves in.

'To give you a quick heads-up to what's going on, I live here in these two rooms,' Estelle explains quickly. 'My bedroom is behind the curtain there. The rest of the house I rent out to earn some money. I share the kitchen and two bathrooms with my tenants, many of whom are students.'

I look at Estelle to see if she's at all embarrassed by this revelation. But she seems perfectly matter-of-fact about it.

'Don't look at me like that, Elle. It was quite commonplace back then to rent out rooms in a big house like this. There was no shame in it.'

'I didn't think there was,' I say hurriedly. 'I'm just surprised, that's all.'

'I needed the money, and it was a quick solution. As I told you before, my marriage didn't last long and after I became a widow, it was just me and Mother in the house. Father had frittered away most of Mother's money before his death, and any money I'd been left by Teddy didn't last long with neither Mother nor I working. Mother had got worse and needed constant care, so I made it my mission to nurse her for as long as she lived.'

She goes over to the fire and gazes lovingly at a photo on the mantelpiece of Clara, the same one Estelle has hanging in her hall today. 'Mother died peacefully in her sleep in 1958. She was pretty bad towards the end, so really it was a blessing. I didn't see it that way to begin with, though – I was angry for both of us. While I worked my way through my grief, I became pretty much a recluse. For the first time ever I found myself totally alone in this house – it was a strange mix of freedom and loneliness.'

Estelle pauses as she remembers. She looks wistfully around the room and her gaze falls upon the Christmas tree once more and suddenly I get it. The Christmas tree is the only thing that doesn't change in this house, which is why it's so important to her. It's the one constant. The one thing that can be relied on to appear every year in a slightly different guise, but always in the exact same place.

'Then one day I had a bit of a revelation,' Estelle continues. 'Perhaps it was a mid-life crisis, who knows? But I decided I needed to get out into the world and see some of it while I still had the chance, and before I got too old. So, I rented out Holly House next door, which we still owned, to a fashion house of the time as a design studio and offices, and then as many rooms as I could in this house to tenants, and with the money I managed to travel the world for eighteen months. It was one of the happiest times of my life.'

Estelle is positively glowing at the memory.

'It wasn't as easy as it is now to travel the world – especially on your own as a woman. But I never felt I was in danger. I simply felt free for the first time in my life.'

'Why did you stop?' I ask. 'Was there a reason you came back when you did?'

'She met me,' Angela says a little ruefully. 'I was the end to her freedom.'

'Now, Angela, it wasn't exactly like that, was it?'

We hear someone putting a key in the front door.

'Here we come!' Angela says, rushing through to the hall.

'Shall we?' Estelle says, gesturing for us to follow. 'The story is about to begin.'

Estelle is just coming through the door as we arrive in the hallway. This is a slightly older Estelle than we met in the previous story – she must be what? I do a quick bit of maths in my head, but Estelle answers my question before my mind can compute the answer.

'I'm forty-four,' she says.

'You look fab, Estelle,' Angela says approvingly. 'Fab and groovy! Just like I remember you.'

This new Estelle still has long dark hair, which partly cascades down her back and is partly pulled up high on her head, but I notice an odd grey hair just beginning to mix with others. She's wearing green trousers that taper in at the ankle, a mustard-yellow polo-neck sweater and a burgundy tweed winter coat with big buttons, and burgundy leather ankle-length boots.

'You look great,' I say. 'Very on trend!'

My Estelle grimaces.

'And you have a little dog too!' I exclaim, looking at the little dog she's unhooking from its lead.

'That's Dylan, a very distant relative of Alvie,' Estelle says, smiling at the small furry dog by her younger self's ankles.

Alvie, sitting high up in Estelle's arms, looks down at the dog and growls.

Dylan looks up at Alvie and growls too.

'Can he see Alvie?' Ben asks in surprise

'Possibly,' Estelle says quickly. 'You know Dylan was named after a chap I met when I was in New York. Very good with his guitar was Bob. We had some great singsongs in his apartment with his friends.'

'Wait, you knew Bob Dylan?' I ask, forgetting all about the two dogs for a moment.

'Yes, before he was famous, though. Nice chap. I had a lot of time for him.'

I gaze in awe at Estelle. There was so much more to her than I first realised. What a very varied life she'd led.

'Shush, Dylan,' the young Estelle says. 'What are you growling at?'

A slight young man wearing a white cotton polo-neck, tight black drainpipe trousers and a black knitted cardigan comes skipping down the stairs. 'Good evening, Estelle,' he calls, as he grabs a dogtooth-check coat from a stand in the hall. 'Did you have a good Christmas?'

'Yes, thank you, Christian. It was quiet, but I like it that way. How about you?'

'Yeah, not bad. But one day with the oldies is enough for me these days. I like my independence too much. I'm glad to be back in London catching up with my mates tonight.'

'Well, enjoy yourself. You're only young once.'

'Ah, you're not that old yet, Estelle. Why don't you come with me? We're just going to a coffee shop to hang out. You'd be more than welcome.'

'That's very kind of you, but you don't want an old bird like me cramping your style. You go and have fun.'

'If you're sure?' Christian says, raising his eyebrows.

Estelle nods. 'I am.'

'Righty-ho. I'll be off then!' Christian salutes Estelle and heads towards the door.

'Christian, be careful later, won't you?' Estelle says. 'The weather forecast is predicting some heavy snow. There might not be taxicabs when you return home if it's very bad.'

'Heavy snow in London?' Christian scoffs. 'I'm from up North; any snow you might get here is just a sprinkling compared to what we get up on the hills. Don't worry, I'll be absolutely fine. It would have to snow for days here to affect me.'

'All right, but still be careful, won't you?' Estelle says with a knowing look. 'I worry about all my tenants, but especially you, Christian, as you well know ...'

'I know,' Christian says solemnly. 'I get it and I'll be careful, I promise!' He blows Estelle a kiss. 'Now, have a good evening. I know I shall!'

Estelle smiles as Christian exits through the front door. Then she sighs as she looks towards the sitting room. 'Just the two of us again, Dylan,' she says, picking up the little dog and giving him a hug. 'I hope there's something good on the television tonight. If not, I shall pick up my novel again. I'm very much enjoying this new author, P.D. James.'

Estelle and Dylan go through to the sitting room, with Dylan still clearly bothered by Alvie. Estelle closes the door behind them.

'It's Boxing Day 1962,' our Estelle explains. 'Because most of my tenants are young, they are still with their families. It's a pretty quiet house compared to what it's like usually.'

'Why do you worry so much about Christian?' I ask as Estelle is about to go through the sitting-room door.

'Don't you know?' Ben replies, raising his eyebrows at me.

'No, should I?'

Ben looks at Estelle. She nods.

'Unless I'm very much mistaken,' Ben says. 'Christian is gay.'

'So?'

'It was still illegal to be gay in this country until 1967,' Estelle says. 'Well, 1967, in England and Wales. It was as late as the 1980s before it became legal in Scotland and Northern Ireland.'

'Gosh, I hadn't realised.'

'I worried about Christian because it was quite dangerous to be gay in London in 1962. If he'd stuck to the few coffee shops and pubs back then that were secretly known to welcome the gay community, then he'd probably have been fine ...'

'What do you mean probably? What happened to him?'

'Later,' Estelle says. 'We have other things to hear about first. Now, we need to walk through this door to find things have moved on a few hours. Do not worry, you're ready to do this now. And don't be afraid; you won't feel a thing.'

We watch in amazement as Estelle walks straight through the closed door.

'Go on,' Angela says encouragingly. 'It's easy. Watch.'

And she does the same.

Ben shrugs. 'When in Rome ...' and he too follows the others through into the sitting room.

'Argh!' I exclaim, knowing I have to do the same. 'Why does this seem so strange?'

'It's all right,' Angela says, very disconcertingly popping only her head back through the closed door. 'You'll be fine – it won't hurt.'

'Really? Why haven't we done it previously then?'

'Haven't needed to, have we? The door has always been open before.'

Annoyingly, she's right. This is the first time we've encountered a closed door in all our stories.

'What about when we went outside?' I suddenly remember. 'Estelle opened the door for us that time.'

'That's because it was an exterior door – they're a lot thicker and harder to traverse. You and Ben are both ready for interior doors now – you'll be just fine. Besides, Estelle can't open this one for you, otherwise her younger self will see it open and close, and we can't be having that.'

I think about this for a moment and it sort of makes sense, I suppose. But if this is all in our imaginations, as Angela and Estelle always suggested it was, then why did that make a difference? However, I don't have time to think about it now, so I take a deep breath, close my eyes and step into the door. And just as I've been promised, I don't feel anything. I open my eyes and I'm already in the sitting room with the others.

Estelle is already by the side of her younger self, who has nodded off to sleep in front of the television with a book on her lap while Dylan sleeps soundly in his basket by the fire.

The clock above the fireplace reads just before midnight, and the television is playing the National Anthem before it closes down for the night.

Alvie wriggles in Estelle's arms and jumps to the floor, waking Dylan who growls.

'Goodness, Dylan!' Sixties Estelle says, woken by the noise. 'Whatever is wrong?'

Alvie runs underneath the branches of the Christmas tree over to the window and Dylan follows him.

'Careful, Dylan!' Estelle says, sitting up and stretching. 'You'll have the tree over if you're not careful.' She gets up and switches off the television. 'Gosh, I must have dozed off. It's nearly midnight.'

In his quest to find out exactly what Alvie is, Dylan disturbs the heavy velvet curtains that hang behind the tree in the window, so a narrow gap appears.

'How exciting,' Estelle says as she walks over to close them again and peeks through the gap. 'I think it might be snowing! Golly, it really is!' she exclaims, pulling the curtains back a little more. 'Look at those huge snowflakes. It looks like it could be settling in for quite some time.'

While Estelle stands watching the snow fall outside, Dylan continues in his quest to explain the mystery of Alvie.

'I feel like I should tell someone when it's snowing,' Estelle says, still facing the window. 'When I was a child, I'd tell Mother and we'd watch it fall together from her window. Then when Teddy was here, we'd do the same – he was a big kid at heart. But now . . .' Her voice falters. 'Now I can only tell you, my faithful friend. What are you doing, Dylan?' she says, looking round for a moment. 'Chasing your own tail again?'

219

She turns back to the window again to watch the snow fall. Our Estelle goes over and stands beside her younger self so she doesn't have to be alone.

It's such a poignant moment seeing the two of them together, I find myself getting quite emotional, and I have to blink away the tears I feel forming in the corners of my eyes.

I look over at the other two; they both look equally moved.

'It's true,' I say quietly. 'You do always feel the need to tell someone else when it's snowing. How sad if you have no one else to tell.'

Ben comes over, puts his arm around me and we all walk forwards to stand beside the two Estelles. For a few blissful moments we all stand silently watching the snow fall outside, turning Mistletoe Square into a magical winter wonderland under the glowing light of the gas lamps.

'Beautiful, isn't it?' Angela sighs. 'We could be in any decade. It's timeless.'

'Yes,' I whisper. 'The last time we saw the square in a story there were only horses and carriages outside. Now the carriages have four wheels and an engine instead of four legs and a pair of reins.'

'Brace yourselves,' Angela says now in her normal voice. 'I'm afraid I'm about to break both the magic and the silence.'

Angela continues to look out of the window, so Ben and I do, too.

'I'm dreamin' of a snowy white Christmas!' A male voice sings outside. 'Just like the ones I've never ever known!'

'Nah, it's not Christmas any more, is it?' A second voice, female this time, says loudly sounding quite drunk. 'It's Boxing Day, innit! And it won't be that for much longer. I think I just heard Big Ben strike midnight.'

'Don't be daft, you silly sausage! You can't hear Big Ben from here.'

'Yes, I can, cos it's quiet tonight.'

'Well, it was until we arrived!'

There's much raucous laughter, before we see the two fig-
ures properly for the first time. They emerge under the light
from one of the lamps, arms around each other as they make
their way very slowly across the grass in the middle of the
square, leaving two sets of wobbly footprints behind them in
the freshly laid white blanket.

'We really should be quiet, you know?' the female voice
says, slurring her words. 'It's vey, vey, vey late.'

The woman is wearing a big, red, floppy baker-boy hat so we
can't quite see her face, and the man is wearing a smart black
bowler, even though the rest of his clothes are more casual.
Neither of them have coats on, but their chosen outfits – a
tight floral dress for the woman, and a black knitted cardigan
with black trousers and a white polo-neck shirt for the man,
epitomise the fashion of the decade.

They both stop walking for a moment, look at each other,
put their fingers to their lips and say 'shush' together before
they both erupt into even more laughter.

'What about "Let it Snow!" next?' the man suggests.

'But it is snowing, innit?' the woman says, lifting her hand
to the sky. 'Look?'

As she tilts her head to look up at the night sky, we see her
face for the first time.

'Angela, is that you?' I ask, glancing over at her.

Angela nods. 'It is. I'm twenty-six there. Not aged
well, have I?'

'Nonsense,' our Estelle says now. 'You were very drunk that

221

night. You look much better now as an older, but eminently more sober woman. Even if your dress sense hasn't improved an awful lot!'

Angela begins by smiling gratefully at Estelle, and then pulls a face as Estelle finishes her sentence.

'And is that Christian?' I ask, looking out of the window again. 'It looks a bit like him – but he wasn't wearing that hat when he left the houses earlier?'

'Yep, that's him,' Angela says, looking down into the garden again.

The two partygoers have broken into a rendition of 'Let it Snow!' now and there are a few bedroom curtains beginning to twitch around the square.

'Pipe down will you?' A man calls out from a window.

'Ooh, la-di-da here, ain't ya?' Angela says, and she tries to mimic the man's cultured tones. 'Pipe down yourself!'

The man shakes his head angrily. 'You'd better quieten down soon, or I'll be calling the police.'

'We need to tone it down a tad,' Christian says. 'I do have to live here.'

'You live 'ere?' Angela exclaims. 'Well I never. I thought we was just taking a shortcut. Ain't this posh? You loaded or something?'

'No, I just rent a room, in this house here.' Christian points towards the house, and notices for the first time Estelle standing in the window. 'Uh-oh, that's my landlady. Try to look sober!'

'Crikey! She looks a bit fierce,' Angela says, attempting to stand up straight.

'No, Estelle is all right. But she won't appreciate us arriving on her doorstep three sheets to the wind.'

'You're so posh,' Angela says, grinning at him. 'Three sheets to the wind! We're pissed and there's no covering that up!'

Sixties Estelle moves away from the window and heads towards the front door.

'Bit rough around the edges back then, wasn't I?' our Angela whispers to me as we all follow into the hall.

'You do sound a little different,' I reply.

'It's all these years spent with Estelle. She poshened me up!'

'Angela, there is no such word and you know it,' our Estelle says, as her younger self unlocks the door and I feel a chill wind blow through the hall. 'I simply taught you better grammar, that is all.'

Angela pulls a face. 'Poshened me up,' she repeats, grinning.

Sixties Estelle stands with her arms folded in the doorway as Christian and Angela make their way slowly to the top of the steps giggling and still shushing each other.

'I thought I'd save you the bother of trying to fit your key in the lock,' she says sternly.

'Sorry, Estelle.' Christian bows his head. 'I didn't think you'd still be up.'

'At least take your hat off if you're going to apologise. I know you have more manners than to address a lady with your hat on. Talking of which, where did you get that hat?'

'"Where did you get that hat, where did you get that smile?"' Angela begins to sing. 'Sorry,' she says, taking her own hat off when Estelle doesn't smile.

'I think you will find it's tile, not smile,' Estelle says formally, as she eyes Angela. 'The correct lyric to the particular song you're attempting to sing.' She turns her attention back to Christian.

'I borrowed the hat,' Christian mumbles, his head still down.

Estelle studies him for a moment and, as she runs her eyes over him, I'm sure she notices, as I do, what looks like a smattering of blood on the collar of his white polo-neck jumper.

'Christian, take your hat off please.'

The young Angela glances at Christian. They both seem to have sobered up pretty quickly.

Christian slowly removes his bowler hat to reveal a large deep gash in his forehead that extends up into his hairline.

'Goodness,' Estelle exclaims. 'What happened? No, don't tell me that now, let's get you inside. I'm going to assume you haven't had that looked at professionally?'

Christian shakes his head. 'Ow!' He winces.

'Come on,' Estelle says, standing back to let him inside.

'I'd better go.' Angela turns back towards the steps.

'Oh, no, you don't!' Estelle insists. 'You are coming in with him, and once I've tended to his wound, I'm going to make us all a cup of tea, and you're going to tell me exactly how this happened.'

Estelle closes the door behind them. Then she leads Christian and Angela, with Dylan trotting along behind them, through to the kitchen. Which has now moved to where our current day kitchen resides, at the end of the hall.

'Should we go too?' I ask Estelle and Angela, surprised they haven't immediately followed.

Estelle shakes her head. 'No, not necessary. I want to move on with the story a bit.'

'But—' I begin, keen to know what happened to Christian.

'Please don't worry. All will be explained,' Estelle assures us. 'Now, back to the sitting room.'

We all walk back into the sitting room – this time I'm relieved to find through the already open door. Where we find the sixties versions of Estelle, Angela and Christian all sitting by the fire, drinking tea. Estelle is in the chair she nodded off in earlier, and Christian and Angela, wearing dressing gowns, sit opposite her on chairs they've pulled up, a bit like we all do before Estelle tells us one of her stories.

Dylan is curled up in his bed not far from the fire, and there's a wooden clothes-airer next to him with Angela's dress and hat drying on it. Now Angela isn't wearing the dress it suddenly looks a bit worn and tatty, and the hat that she wore so vibrantly looks quite grubby close up.

'Are you sure you feel all right?' sixties Estelle asks Christian. 'Not woozy or dizzy or anything like that?'

'Not now I'm sober!' Christian says jokingly. Young Angela laughs, but Estelle looks serious.

'I mean it, Christian. If you feel anything like that you must tell me. You could have a concussion. Do you know what that is?'

Christian looks blankly at Estelle and shrugs.

Estelle tuts and shakes her head.

'What?' Christian asks. 'I'm studying law, not medicine!'

'Isn't a concussion a blow to the head?' Angela asks. 'Something that can happen to your brain when you hit your head on something. Or,' she says, looking with meaning at Christian, 'your head is hit by something. My old man was a doctor,' she explains when both Estelle and Christian look at her in surprise.

'Yes.' Estelle gives Angela an approving glance. 'That is exactly right.'

'I sometimes wonder if my dad had a concussion, you know?' Angela says thoughtfully. 'His brain went a bit . . . you know, weird, and he started forgetting everything, including us. Drove my mum mad. I think that's why she left him in the end.'

'Are you talking about dementia?' I ask our Angela quietly. 'Or Alzheimer's?'

'Probably,' Angela replies. 'But like concussion we didn't know much about that back then. My dad's gambling habit didn't help either, mind. I think it was a bit of everything that finally sent my mum packing. I don't really remember much about it to be honest; I had other stuff going on at the time. I only remember her leaving.'

'Estelle, you were going to tell us how you learnt to stitch up wounds like that?' Young Angela asks now, and I realise that Christian must have some stitches in his forehead underneath the large dressing he's now wearing. 'You made a pretty decent job of it, after Chrissy here stopped whining, of course!'

'You try having a needle pushed through your skin over and over again!' Christian says. 'It bloody hurt!'

'Just as well you were still pissed, then! Sorry.' Angela glances at Estelle. 'Drunk.'

'It's all right,' Estelle says. 'I've heard worse. I spent a number of years working with soldiers. They know far worse words, I can assure you.'

'Was that in the war?' Angela asks.

Estelle nods. 'I volunteered and trained as a nurse. I worked down the road at Great Ormond Street for a while.'

'The kiddies' hospital?'

'It was a centre for casualties during the Second World War; the sick children were mostly evacuated elsewhere. The Blitz was a particularly bad time at the hospital.' Estelle's face has a pained expression as she remembers. 'Hundreds of injured people night after night. I got used to pulling glass, metal and other objects from people's heads and bodies, and then stitching them up. It was pretty routine ... Anyway,' she says, shaking her head and her memories away. 'That's where I learnt to do stitches, and I can assure you I tended to much worse injuries than you've sustained tonight, Christian.'

Christian nods sheepishly.

'So, what did happen?' Estelle asks again, clearly sensing Christian's injuries aren't simply the result of a drunken tumble.

'Got into a bit of a fight,' Christian says shrugging. 'It was nothing.'

'About?' Estelle prompts him.

'I think you know what about, Estelle.' Christian looks Estelle knowingly in the eye. 'The usual.'

Estelle nods. 'And as usual you don't want to talk about it. This isn't the first time I've had to patch your friend up,' she tells Angela. 'But this is probably the worst so far.'

'You might have been patching up a bit more than my head if Ange here hadn't come along,' Christian says, looking gratefully at Angela.

'Just doing me bit,' Angela says. 'I saw a damsel in distress and rode to his rescue!'

Christian grins.

'Is someone going to fill me in?' Estelle looks between them. 'Or do I have to guess?'

'Just tell her, Chrissy,' Angela says. 'No point hiding it now you're safe.'

Christian sighs. 'All right. I know better than to try and argue with two women! Who, may I say, are much fiercer than any foe I've ever met in a pub!'

Angela smiles at Estelle, and Estelle nods her agreement.

'Right, so I was in this pub – a pub, might I add, that I've been to many times before with no problems whatsoever. I was with a few of my mates, and things were getting a little . . . flirty, shall we say, at the bar.'

'Christian, I've told you to be careful,' Estelle says.

'I know, but this was known to be a safe pub before tonight – we'd always been all right there before. Tonight, however, they'd let some new fellas in. I don't think they knew what sort of pub it was, and . . . well, let's just say they took a dislike to what they saw at the bar.'

'How much of a dislike?'

Christian shrugs. 'Enough that it hurt.'

'You was getting the shit beat out of you, Chrissy,' Angela pipes up. 'Don't pull punches. Eek, sorry, that's a bad choice of words.'

'Like I said, things got a little heated, and there may have been a broken beer bottle or two. One of which caught me on the head.' He gently touches the dressing Estelle has applied to his wound. 'Ow.'

'But then I arrived and saved your bacon, eh?' Angela says, grinning proudly.

Christian nods. 'You did indeed.'

'What did you do?' Estelle asks.

'I was just coming out of the ladies' and I saw this scuffle. I knew immediately what was going on, on account of what was being shouted – you know the sort of words?' She looks at Estelle.

Estelle nods. 'Sadly, yes.'

'So I pretended to be your girlfriend, didn't I, Chrissy? I got all, "Please don't beat up my fiancé, we're getting married soon!"' Angela clasps her hands together in the dramatic manner of a black-and-white-movie heroine.

'She did.' Christian nods. 'It was quite convincing, after I'd got over the fact I was suddenly engaged to a complete stranger!'

'Convincing? I should be nominated for an Oscar for that

performance.' Angela haughtily sticks her chin in the air, then she grins. 'It made them stop for a moment anyway.'

'Long enough for me to wriggle free,' Christian adds, seeming to enjoy this story as much as Angela, even though he was on the receiving end of the violence.

'Then I grabbed hold of Chrissy, and started making this huge fuss of him, and said how my dad was a policeman and he'd be livid when I told him someone had been beating up his future son-in-law.'

'And that worked?' Estelle asks in surprise.

'Made them think long enough for us to leg it out of the pub and down the street! Isn't that right, Chrissy?'

Christian nods. 'So after we'd got far enough away from the pub, we decided that we'd better introduce ourselves. It seemed the polite thing to do since we were now betrothed to each other.'

Angela grins. 'So after we'd said hello properly, we thought we deserved another drink. So we went to a new pub, and then another, and, before we knew it, it was midnight and we were dancing outside there in the snow. It was a great night, though ... except for the punch-up of course.'

'Didn't you realise you had a head wound and were bleeding?' Estelle asks, looking in astonishment at Christian.

'Yeah, but I didn't realise how bad it was. I think the alcohol must have numbed the pain. I just remember Ange saying we needed to cover my head if we wanted to get into any more pubs. So I acquired the bowler hat.'

'Where from? All the shops are shut on Boxing Day.'

'I bought it from a tramp on the street,' Christian says, looking a little ashamed. 'I paid him well for it. He seemed pleased anyway.'

'What happened to your coat?'

'Left it in the pub when we ran. Don't worry, Estelle, one of my lot will have picked it up. I'll get it back. Luckily my wallet was in the pocket of my trousers.'

Estelle sighs. 'Sounds like you had a lucky escape.'

'Perhaps. Perhaps it was meant to be.' Christian grins at Angela. 'I've met a new friend tonight, that I probably wouldn't have met otherwise. A few bruises are a small price to pay for something as priceless as that!'

'Ooh, ain't you got a way with words,' Angela says. 'Ain't he got a way with words, Estelle?'

'Hmm,' Estelle says, not looking at Christian with quite the same adoring look as Angela. 'Pity he doesn't use them a bit more often to get himself out of difficult situations.'

'I'll toast to that!' Angela lifts her empty china cup and winks at Christian. 'Cheers for the cup of tea, Estelle. It's very kind of you. I guess I'd better get going soon.'

'Stay the night,' Christian says suddenly. 'It's the least I can do to say thanks. You can't be heading out now in the snow. It's freezing out there and you don't have a coat either.'

'Nah, I can't be doing that. Estelle has been kind enough already. I'm sure it's only a little covering.' Angela pulls her borrowed dressing gown around her, skips over to the window and pulls back the curtains. Then she gasps. 'Oh my Christ, would you look at that!'

'What is it?' Christian asks.

'Come and see!' Angela says holding back the curtains so everyone in the room, including us, hurries over to the window. 'I don't think I've ever seen so much snow.'

The whole square is now covered in deep, crisp, undisturbed white snow. It sits on the trees and on the benches – even the gas lamps have a layer of white on them. It looks like everywhere has been tucked up in a snug white blanket for the night. The drunken footprints that Christian and Angela left earlier on the grass have all but disappeared, and the snow is still falling heavily.

'It doesn't look like you'll be going anywhere tonight, Angela,' Estelle says, turning to her. 'You're very welcome to stay here if you wish. I'll make up a bed in one of my spare rooms upstairs for you.'

'Don't go to any bother, Estelle, she can kip in with me. She'll be perfectly safe.' Christian winks at Estelle.

Estelle merely blinks back. 'That's as may be, Christian. But Angela is my guest too, and I will treat her like I would any other guest to my house. She will get her own bed and fresh sheets, and breakfast in the morning. Is that all right with you, Angela?'

Angela looks shocked, and then pleased. 'Too right it is! I ... I mean, thank you so much, Estelle. It's very kind of you, and far more trouble than I'm worth.'

Estelle isn't the only one to puzzle at Angela's choice of words. But she simply nods. 'Excuse me, won't you, while I go and make up your room. Please, make yourself at home, while I'm gone.'

'I sure did that, didn't I, Estelle?' our Angela says now, as sixties Estelle leaves the room and Christian and Angela begin to fade away. But unusually we don't go immediately back to 2018 like we usually do. Instead the room begins to change a little as we stand there.

'What's happening?' I ask. 'Are we moving to a new story?'

'No, still this one,' Estelle says, picking up Alvie and giving him a cuddle. 'We're just moving on a few days.'

'1962 into 1963 was one of the coldest winters I can remember in London,' Angela says as the room settles down again. 'The Big Freeze it was called. There was even ice on the inside of the windows at times – do you remember, Estelle?'

Estelle nods. 'The country did suffer. The snow blocked roads and railways, there were power cuts and frozen pipes, things simply ground to halt because of the cold. We had food shortages too. Even the milkman couldn't get through in places, and they always delivered back then come rain or shine. Incredibly, even the Thames froze – people were actually skating on it.'

Angela smiles. 'Yes, I remember seeing that, and you saying to me I wasn't to go on it in case it cracked while I was out there.'

'You stayed, then?' I ask Angela. 'Longer than just the one night?'

Angela nods. 'I did.'

'Here we go,' Estelle says as both sixties Estelle and Angela re-enter the room with Dylan trotting behind them. I see his hackles raise a little when he notices Alvie again.

Angela is carrying a tea tray loaded with cups, saucers and a teapot, and Estelle is carrying a plate of neatly arranged biscuits.

Angela has clearly had to borrow a mix of Estelle's and Christian's clothes. But, as always, she carries off the slightly mismatched look extremely well.

'We'd best not have too many of them biscuits with our tea,' Angela says, putting the tray down like she's done it a few times before. 'I've heard there's already some food shortages in the shops.'

'Nonsense,' Estelle says. 'London won't go short just because of a little snow and a bit of cold.'

'It's hardly a *little* snow and a *bit* of cold.' Angela pours the tea into the cups. 'We've both seen the news.'

'Londoners are made of sterner stuff. We survived the Blitz and the war. Compared to that this is a minor inconvenience. I'm sure it won't last long.'

'We've had nearly five days of it already,' Angela says. 'It's definitely going into the New Year. Thanks for letting me stay again. My bedsit would have been absolutely freezing in this. Only one bar of my little electric fire works these days.'

'Please stop thanking me,' Estelle says, looking embarrassed. 'It's been a pleasure having you here.'

'Go on!' Angela waves her hand at Estelle. 'You're just saying that to be nice.'

'Christian enjoys you being here. He'd have gone stir-crazy here with just me for company. The weather has meant all my other tenants aren't returning until after the New Year celebrations now.'

'I hope Christian can get us some booze for tonight,' Angela says, looking towards the window. 'You can't see the New Year in without a tipple of something.'

'I have a spot of sherry somewhere, if he can't find much at the local public house.'

Angela grimaces. 'No offence, Estelle, but a tipple of sherry ain't really gonna hit the spot.' She pops a splash of milk and a sugar lump in Estelle's tea and passes it to her, reminding me of Estelle and Angela's relationship today.

'Thank you,' Estelle says, taking it from her. 'I've actually been meaning to talk to you about that.' She rhythmically stirs her tea with a silver teaspoon. 'I can't help but notice, Angela, you do drink quite a lot of alcohol.'

'Nah,' Angela says, shrugging the comment away. 'Not really.'

'I think you do,' Estelle persists. 'More than the normal amount anyway.'

'What's normal?' Angela says lightly. 'Loads of people I know like a drink or two occasionally.'

'Yes, a drink or two occasionally is fine,' Estelle continues, clearly trying to tread carefully. 'Perhaps not five or six or seven, even, and not every night, either.'

Angela puts down her cup and saucer. She wanders over to the Christmas tree and pretends to be examining the decorations, then glances out of the window as if she's willing Christian to be walking across the square with a bag and the sound of glass bottles clinking together.

'I don't drink every night,' Angela says when Estelle is silent.

'You have done since you've been here. I expect Christian has run out of different pubs to go to by now. He won't dare go to the same one in case he gets a reputation.'

Angela swivels round and glares at Estelle. 'What sort of reputation?'

'A reputation as a drunkard, or a wino, perhaps. How many names do you want me to find?'

'I'm not a wino,' Angela says quietly. 'I just like a drink occasionally, that's all. It helps me forget.'

'Forget what?' Estelle asks in an equally low voice.

'Nothing.' Angela shrugs. 'Nothing you need to know, anyway.'

'Fine,' Estelle replies, continuing to sip at her teacup. 'I don't wish to pry.'

An awkward silence falls on the room, and all we can hear is the clock's rhythmical tick above the mantelpiece.

Angela paces around the Christmas tree for a bit, pretending to look at the decorations.

'Some of these are really old, aren't they?' she asks, breaking the silence.

Estelle nods. 'Indeed they are.'

'Which is your favourite?'

Estelle thinks about this. 'They all hold special memories. Times they were bought, or times they were hung. Some of them have been passed down through my family over the years.'

'What about this one?' Angela asks, pointing to the baby in the cradle that the moon shone on for our first story.

'That is one of the oldest. I believe it was bought for one of the first trees that stood in that spot over one hundred years ago.'

'What is it about babies and Christmas?' Angela asks.

'Do I really have to answer that?' Estelle replies with a half-smile.

Angela looks puzzled, then the penny drops. 'Lordy! How stupid am I?' she exclaims, shaking her head and smiling. Then her face falls. 'Really, really stupid ...'

Estelle, to her credit, doesn't ask any questions. She just sits and waits patiently.

But Angela has a question. 'You don't have kids, do you?' she asks Estelle.

Estelle silently shakes her head.

'Why?'

'It was never the right time,' Estelle admits. 'My husband died young, and I never met anyone else. Mainly because I spent many years caring for my ill mother. I don't think I could have cared for anyone else as well. It takes a lot of time, energy and patience to care for a child, let alone a baby.'

'I wouldn't know,' Angela says, still looking at the cradle on the tree. 'I was never given the chance to care for mine.'

I turn sharply to our Angela. She looks just as sad and desolate as her younger self does right now as she watches the scene unfold.

'Why was that?' the young Estelle asks gently.

'Unmarried mother, wasn't I? They said I wasn't fit to care for my own child just because I didn't have a ring on my finger.'

'Who did?'

'My parents, the hospital I was sent away to have her in, everyone around me, basically. I should have stood up for myself. You'd think because my own father was a doctor that would have been in my favour, but, no, that just made it worse. He was an upstanding member of the community; he couldn't have his precious only child seen to be giving birth out of wedlock. Like he was so perfect – he was addicted to gambling.'

'I had one like that,' Estelle admits. 'My father was addicted to gambling too. Almost lost this house a number of times.'

'They'd have made a right pair, then!' Angela says ruefully. 'What happened to yours?'

'Died,' Estelle says without sorrow. 'During the London smog of fifty-two. He had lung cancer before that, but the smog finished him off properly.'

Angela looks with interest at Estelle. 'You don't sound like you miss him much?'

Estelle shakes her head. 'For my sins, no, I don't. He was a horrible man.'

Angela nods in agreement. 'I actually cared for mine until he let that happen to me and my baby. Then I couldn't give a shi— monkey's, I mean. It wasn't long after that he started to lose his mind a bit. I like to think of it as a punishment from Him up there.' She looks upwards. 'Is that really mean of me?'

'After what you went through, I think you can be let off a few mean thoughts. Do you know what happened to your baby?'

'No. She was adopted, that's all I know. I just hope she's happy. She'd be eight years old now. I'm sure she's better off with her current family than with me, the local drunk.'

Angela looks with meaning at Estelle.

'Would you be the local drunk if your baby hadn't been given away?' Estelle asks, not pulling any punches. 'I'm going to take a wild guess that's when you started drinking?'

Angela nods. 'Yep, I was a good girl up until then, with a promising future – that's what my parents liked to think, anyway. Then I got knocked up and I ruined everything in their eyes. I don't think they ever saw me the same after that. They didn't seem to care all that much when I moved out and came to live in the city. So here I am now bouncing from job to job, drinking myself silly to numb the pain. I'm broken, Estelle, in more ways than one, and do you know what the worst thing is?' Angela's face crumples and she begins to tremble.

Estelle, looking visibly moved, shakes her head.

'I don't know how to fix it, Estelle. I don't know how to stop.'

Angela begins to sob. Huge tears roll down her face as her legs buckle and she drops to the floor.

Estelle simply stands up and goes over to her. She lifts her up gently and holds open her arms. Angela begins to cry even harder at Estelle's simple gesture, and, as Estelle wraps her arms tightly around her to comfort her, she buries her face in Estelle's green cardigan.

'Help me, Estelle,' I hear Angela whisper. 'Please, I need someone to help me.'

'I think we can help each other, Angela,' Estelle whispers back, as a single tear rolls slowly down her own cheek.

Twenty

23 December 2018

Immediately I turn to Angela and Estelle.

They both gaze emotionally at each other across the room.

'And you did help me,' Angela says quietly. 'You helped me so much, Estelle. I can never repay you for what you did.'

'Nonsense,' Estelle says, wearily settling herself in her favourite chair. 'I only did what any good citizen would have.' She pats her lap and Alvie jumps up on to it.

'It was more than that, and you know it.'

'If anything, you helped me by moving in. I was extremely lonely then. I don't think I realised how lonely until you came along with your wacky clothes and your loud music. You brought a breath of fresh air to the house.'

Ben and I sit down next to them and quietly listen, neither of us wanting to intrude on this precious moment.

'Ha, I did a bit. We had some good years here, didn't we? Parties with the other housemates, birthdays, Christmases.

238

This was a very happy house in those days. Even if they were tough ones for me.' Angela turns to us. 'Estelle helped me kick the booze habit. I was an alcoholic – I know that now. But Estelle's kindness in letting me live here with her and Christian turned my life around. Eventually, I got a job at the hospital with Estelle.'

'I'd gone back to nursing again by then,' Estelle explains. 'Like Angela, I needed purpose in my life – a reason to get up in the morning. Angela became a ward cleaner to begin with, and then decided she wanted to become a nurse too.'

'I did,' Angela continues. 'After all, medicine was in my blood. Luckily I had the required O levels already. Before I went off the rails, I'd been quite the swot at school. So I did my training and began work a few years later at Great Ormond Street down the road. I was clean, happy, and at last I had a career and a reason to live.'

Estelle and Angela exchange a look of total understanding, that only two people who have known each other a long time can.

'This is such a wonderful story,' I tell them. 'I always wondered how you two met, and now I know. Christian is the young man in the graduation photo in your hall, isn't he?'

'Yes. After he graduated, he became a solicitor,' Estelle says. 'He actually practised next door for a while. Just like you, Ben. But eventually he moved on. He helped us a lot when we set up the foundation, didn't he, Angela?'

Angela nods. 'Yep, Christian knew what we were doing was invaluable too.'

'What foundation?' Ben asks. 'Tell us about that.'

'After we'd both been nursing for a while, Angela decided to take another step up and trained as a midwife.'

'When I'd given birth to my daughter it had been so horrific, and the nurses had been so mean to me, I didn't want anyone else to have to go through that same experience. After I did my midwifery training, I delivered a lot of babies before I decided there was still more I could do to help.'

'By this time in the late seventies,' Estelle continues, 'I didn't have that many tenants in the house. As they'd moved out I hadn't replaced them. Angela and I were both earning a fair wage and it didn't seem necessary to have strangers in the house then. We still rented out Holly House, but we both felt we could use it for something much better than a solicitor's office. No offence, Ben.'

'None taken,' Ben says amiably. 'So what did you do?'

Estelle nods for Angela to continue the story.

'We started a charity to help expectant mothers who were about to give birth, but didn't have anywhere to go after the baby was born. Perhaps they were homeless for whatever reason, or in an abusive relationship. Even though this was twenty plus years later, sadly there were still a lot of young girls who, like me, had been given an ultimatum by their parents when they got pregnant, but unlike me had refused to give up their baby.'

'Because of the complex issues of young mothers giving birth without their parents' knowledge,' Estelle explains, 'or children being born without a father there, or named on the birth certificate, we needed legal help, and that's where Christian came into his own. He gave all his services for free, and, not only that, he utilised all his wealthy contacts to help raise funds for the charity.'

'That is amazing,' I say, looking with wonder at them both. 'You are both amazing. What a wonderful thing to do.

Especially after what happened to Celeste's grandchild all those years ago. What a fabulous full circle.'

Estelle looks at me with so much pride, she looks like she might burst. 'I'm so very happy you noticed that, Elle,' she says with so much emotion in her voice I think for a moment she might cry. 'I always knew you would.'

'Remind me, who is Celeste?' Ben asks.

'Celeste was the wife of Joseph Christmas who built the square,' I explain. 'She was one of the first people to live in this house back in 1755. I told you, remember?'

'The one who was forced to give up her grandchild to a children's home?'

'A foundling hospital,' Estelle corrects. 'But, yes. That was her.'

'How long did you run your charity for?' Ben asks.

'Until we got too old to cope,' Angela answers.

'Until I got too old, you mean,' Estelle says.

'We were both getting on when we decided we couldn't do it any more,' Angela says diplomatically. 'It was around 1998, wasn't it?'

Estelle nods. 'I was seventy-nine, and you were sixty-two. By then there were a lot more laws in place to help unmarried mothers, so we were more of a women's refuge. As each woman moved on from us, we didn't take in any more, until eventually the house was empty, and it's stood empty ever since, until you moved in, Ben.'

'Then I'm truly honoured you opened it up again for me,' Ben says.

'The honour has been all ours, Ben,' Estelle says. 'Both Angela and I have enjoyed getting to know you both. Haven't we, Angela?'

'Yes,' Angela says, sounding quite emotional. 'It's more than I ever dreamed it could be.'

Ben and I glance at Angela.

'What you both did is still pretty amazing,' I say, not really knowing how to respond to her slightly odd statement. 'I'm in awe of you doing something so worthwhile.'

'Thank you, dear,' Estelle says wearily. 'You really are too kind.'

'I think it's time to get you ready for bed,' Angela says, standing up and moving across to Estelle's chair to help her up. 'It's been an emotional and exhausting trip down memory lane tonight – for all of us.'

'It has indeed,' Estelle agrees.

'Is that it, then?' I ask as Angela helps Estelle up. 'Is that all of the house's stories now that we've reached the two of you?'

'Oh, no, dear,' Estelle says, looking down at me. 'Tomorrow night is Christmas Eve, the most magical night of all. When the moon shines through the window tomorrow, I will be telling you both the most important stories of all.'

Twenty-One

Bloomsbury, London

24 December 2018

Christmas Eve

'Happy birthday!' Ben sings from the dining table, as I arrive downstairs ready to join him for breakfast the next morning.

'Happy birthday to you too!' I reply happily.

Today, for the first time in a long while, I feel totally carefree and full of joy. Not only is it both mine and Ben's birthdays, but it's also Christmas Eve! In all the years I can remember, I've never felt this happy or excited about either of those two events.

Something has definitely changed within me. Whereas before I would always feel resentment at these two celebrations because of my past, today I feel the sort of excited anticipation that I always envied others experiencing, and I know it can only be attributed to spending time here in Mistletoe Square with Estelle and Angela, and to meeting Ben.

Last night, after Angela took Estelle to get ready for bed, Ben and I sat discussing and dissecting the evening's story. We only stopped when Angela put her head around the door to say goodnight.

'That's Estelle all settled,' she said. 'She's pretty tired after everything this evening, as am I, actually. There's something very strange and a little unsettling about seeing yourself as a younger person again.'

'I can imagine,' I told her. 'Can I just ask you one more question about tonight before you go?'

'Let me guess. Did I ever try to look for my daughter?'

'Yes.'

Angela's cheery expression immediately dropped. Her bright blue eyes wandered across to the Christmas tree and the decoration of the baby in a crib.

'We did try looking for her. Both in the seventies and the very early eighties. But to no avail. There just weren't the same sort of records kept in the fifties as there are now. We even got Christian on the case, but he couldn't find anything either. And even if we had been able to trace her, how do I know she would have wanted to see me again? As far as she's aware she was abandoned by her mother.'

'But you didn't abandon her. She was taken from you.'

'They would have told her she was abandoned. That's what they usually did back then to justify their actions.'

'We could try now?' I suggested, hating seeing Angela this despondent. 'The internet makes these sorts of things much easier now.'

But Angela shook her head. 'No, it's over, Elle. We won't find her now. It's too late.' I opened my mouth again, but she cut me short. 'I really am very tired. I'm going to go to bed.

I'll see you both tomorrow bright and early. It's going to be an exciting day.'

'What's up?' Ben asks now as I pause by the sitting-room door. He walks over and wraps his arms around me. 'Your face suddenly changed when you walked into the room.'

'I just realised that I've never felt this happy on a Christmas Eve before,' I say, staring at him. 'Not even when I was a child. That's quite sad, isn't it?'

'Yes,' Ben admits. 'It is. But perhaps that's how you think you remember it?'

'How do you mean?'

'Maybe you really were excited once upon a time, but your memories of what you considered bad Christmases have over-ridden any good ones you once had?'

I think about this. 'You might be right, I suppose.'

'Of course I am!' Ben winks at me. 'Now, cheer up and give me a birthday kiss!'

'Willingly!'

'I got you a little something for your birthday,' Ben says after we've kissed for a few blissful moments. 'Actually, I got you two things. But one is for Christmas.' He looks across at the Christmas tree and underneath it I see two gifts. The first wrapped in birthday paper and the second in Christmas paper. '*And* I didn't combine them into a joint gift. That's the one good thing about us both having Christmas birthdays – I'll never do that to you.'

'Gosh,' I say, feeling incredibly touched by this small, but incredibly meaningful gesture. 'Thank you.' I'm mortified to feel tears beginning to well up in my eyes.

'Hey, don't cry.' Ben pulls me closer again. 'That's not the reaction I hoped for. You've not opened them yet. They could be awful!'

'It won't matter what's inside,' I tell him. 'They're already the best two presents ever.' And I pull him even closer to me.

'Hey, hey!' Angela says, coming into the room carrying a teapot covered in a tea cosy. 'Enough of that, it's just gone eight a.m.!'

I smile at Angela, who today is wearing full-on Christmas – a bright red jumper covered in sequins that sparkle next to the lights on the Christmas tree, black-and-silver leggings, and a glittery headband with a star and an angel on wires bobbing about on top. As always, she wears a kitchen apron on top of her outfit. But today's has a snowman on the front.

'Morning, Angela,' I say as Ben and I reluctantly pull away from each other and sit down at the table. 'How are you today?'

'Fab, thanks. How are you? You both looked pretty cheery yourselves just now when I came into the room.' She raises her eyebrows suggestively at us as she pours us both a cup of tea.

'We are feeling pretty buoyant today.' I glance at Ben. 'It's both our birthdays as well as Christmas Eve.'

'So it is,' Angela says, not looking in the least surprised. 'Many happy returns of the day to you both. What are you planning on doing today?'

'I'm not sure.' I look at Ben. 'We haven't really planned anything, have we?'

'Well, you might not have . . . ' Ben says mysteriously. 'But I might have a few ideas of how we can celebrate.'

'You really are making me look very bad today,' I say, pretending to be cross. 'First the gifts and now you have plans too?'

'Your plans do involve you being back here this evening, don't they?' Angela asks. 'Estelle is quite excited about telling you the last stories in this house's long and varied history.'

'Of course,' Ben says. 'We wouldn't miss it for the world.'

246

'Good, you know how important Christmas is to Estelle.'

'We do. Now you really must tell us if you need any help today,' I say as Angela lifts her empty tray.

'Help with what?' Angela asks with a puzzled expression.

'With Christmas? You must have lots to do today preparing everything for tomorrow.' Angela looks so mystified that I wonder for a moment if I've got it all wrong. Maybe there isn't going to be a big dinner with all the trimmings, presents in front of the fire and carols in the evening liked I hoped.

'Ah!' Angela says, grinning. 'Got ya! Yes, of course I have lots to do. But it's all under control. Don't you worry yourselves.'

'But you can't do everything,' I protest. 'At least let us help in some way.'

'Just having you both here is enough for us. Estelle loves Christmas so much that to simply have someone to share it all with this year is everything we could ever need.'

'If you're sure?'

'I am. Now, I've already got the fancy silver out ready for tomorrow. So you're getting the full works this morning for breakfast.' She lifts a white cloth on the sideboard to reveal several silver salvers with silver cloches on top, white bone-china plates, and silver salt and pepper pots and condiment dishes. 'All polished by my own fair hand,' Angela says proudly. 'I've missed seeing them.' She runs her hand lovingly over the polished silver of one of the cloches. 'And since I'm not sure when or if I'll see them again, today seemed the perfect time to bring them out in all their glory and let them shine for one last time.'

Angela turns quickly away from us, but not quickly enough so I don't spot the tears in her eyes.

'What is it, Angela?' I ask, preparing to stand up and go over to her.

'Nothing!' Angela calls in an overly shrill voice. She hurries towards the door keeping her face turned away from us. 'Enjoy your breakfast. I'm popping out for a while, so I'll see you back here this evening. Have a lovely day!' And she scuttles out of the door.

I sit back down in my chair. 'What was all that?' I ask, still looking at the door.

'I have no idea,' Ben says, sounding equally as mystified. 'But I'll tell you what I do know.'

'What?' I turn towards him.

'The smell coming from under those dishes is amazing!'

'Ben!'

'What? Angela has obviously gone to a lot of trouble to prepare all this for us. It would be a real shame not to enjoy it.'

'I suppose . . . I wonder if I should go after her, though?'

'She said she was going out.'

'I know, but she seemed so upset.' I look at the silver cloches again. 'They look old, don't they?' I stand up and go over to the sideboard. 'I don't know much about silver markings, but these look pretty ancient.' I accidentally touch one of the cloches. 'Ow! That's hot!' I jump back a little.

'Have you burnt yourself?' Ben jumps up and takes my hand.

'No, I don't think so. How could Angela have run her hand over these and not felt the heat?'

Ben gently dabs his hand at the silver. 'Blimey! They are piping hot. She must have hands like asbestos. Here.' He grabs a cloth that Angela has left for us and lifts the lid with it. 'Wow, this looks as good as it smells,' he says on discovering tasty-looking sausages and crispy bacon underneath. 'I really think we should eat this, Elle. Angela will be most offended if we don't.'

'Yes, I suppose you're right,' I say a little reluctantly, lifting a china plate from the side. But I'm still concerned about Angela. Why did she react so emotionally to the silverware, and how come she didn't burn her hand on it? But Ben is already peeking underneath at what the other cloches hide.

'So,' I ask brightly, not wanting to spoil his birthday breakfast. 'What's under the others?'

After Ben and I have tucked into a huge and totally delicious cooked breakfast, we sit at the table trying to recover from the feast we've just devoured, while we sip on refreshing glasses of orange juice.

'That is one of the best breakfasts I've ever had.' Ben lifts his glass. 'Compliments to the chef!'

'I'm so full,' I say, holding my tummy. 'I don't think I'll be able to eat again until Christmas Day.'

'Speak for yourself!' Ben grins. 'Now, would you like your birthday gift?'

'Should I?'

'Why not? It's your birthday, isn't it?'

'I wish I had something for you too,' I say, feeling pretty awful I hadn't got him anything.

'Don't worry about it,' Ben says with a wave of his hand. 'There's been a lot going on over the last few days.' He gets up and heads over to the Christmas tree, hesitating as he looks at the two gifts. 'I was in two minds which to give you for your birthday and which to give you for Christmas,' he says, picking up the larger gift, which is wrapped in birthday paper. 'But hopefully I've got it right.'

He walks back over to me and hands me the box-shaped present. 'Happy birthday,' he says. 'May it be the first of many we spend together.'

'Yes, I really hope so,' I tell him, meaning it. I may have arrived in Mistletoe Square hating Christmases, birthdays and, above all, men. But one by one, I seem to have fallen in love with all of them again.

I lower my eyes from Ben's to run my hands over the pretty paper my gift is wrapped in. 'Gorgeous paper. Very similar to the William Morris wallpaper this room was decorated with in 1918.'

Ben nods. 'I hoped you'd notice that.'

Carefully, I prise open the paper. 'It's too beautiful to rip,' I explain.

'I should have given you the paper,' Ben says, looking a little uneasy. 'I'm not sure what's inside will produce the same reaction. It seemed a good idea at the time, though.'

I look up at him, wondering what he means. But then I look down again as the paper falls away to reveal what's inside.

'It's a box,' I say, pulling a burgundy box decorated in an ornate Victorian style from the remains of the gift wrap. 'It's lovely.'

'That's only the gift box. Open it up.'

I lift the lid on the box and gasp when I see what's inside. There's a familiar face smiling up at me from the box.

'I knew it was a stupid idea,' Ben says when I don't speak. He rushes over towards the tree again. 'Look, have your Christmas present now instead. That's much better.'

'No, Ben. Wait,' I say quietly. 'It can't be.'

Ben pauses halfway across the sitting room and turns around. 'It can't be what?'

'Better than this,' I say, lifting my gift from its box. I hold it out in front of me, and then I hug it to my chest.

Ben has bought me one of the teddy bears I looked at in the

250

department store. The same bear I told him I always wanted as a child, but never got.

'You like it, then?' Ben asks, still tentative.

'Like it? I love it! Ben, you don't know what this means to me. Really you don't.'

'When you said you'd always wanted one, I knew ... no, I hoped I couldn't go wrong.'

'It's not just the bear.' I try to explain. 'It's what it signifies. It's what all of this signifies. The Christmas tree, the two presents so beautifully, but individually wrapped. It's what I always wanted, but never got.'

I stand up and walk over to him still carrying the bear. 'Thank you,' I whisper, wrapping my arms around him and kissing him with more passion than I think I've ever kissed anyone before. 'This is already turning into the best birthday ever.'

'If that's the reaction I get after a teddy bear,' Ben says, emerging from the kiss, 'then I can't wait to see what happens when I give you your Christmas present.'

After we've begun to recover a little from breakfast, we begin clearing all the breakfast things away.

We knew Angela would be mad at us clearing everything up, but we weren't going to leave everything for her to do when she got back, so we fill the dishwasher, hand-wash all the salvers and cloches, and clean the kitchen until it's immaculate.

As I finish wiping all the surfaces down, I look around the kitchen.

'There's not much in here suggesting preparations for Christmas, is there?'

'How do you mean?' Ben asks.

'I mean there's no huge turkey defrosting, or basins full

of Christmas puddings and trays of mince pies. You'd have thought Angela would have been in her element today preparing for tomorrow. She loves to cook for us.'

'Maybe that's where she's gone,' Ben says, folding his tea towel and hanging it up to dry. 'To buy everything.'

'You don't buy all the food for Christmas on Christmas Eve, especially not when there's a few of you to cook for. I remember one year we went to my granny's to stay a few days before Christmas and she was constantly baking, chopping and refrigerating everything in plenty of time for the big day.'

'Was that a good Christmas?' Ben asks, leaning against the sink.

'Hmm?' I reply, still thinking.

'The Christmas you spent with your grandmother?'

'Yes, I think it was. A bit like Estelle, she always had a massive Christmas tree in her front room. It was really exciting to have a tree for once. She cooked us a lovely dinner – you know, with turkey and all the trimmings . . . ' I smile as I remember this forgotten time I must have buried deep within me.

'What?' Ben encourages me. 'What else do you remember?'

'I remember in the evening we sang carols and my dad played his guitar . . . Gosh, I'd forgotten all about that Christmas.'

'So you did have at least one good Christmas, then?' Ben smiles.

'Maybe I did . . . ' I say, still trying to remember. 'Actually, I think we might have gone there a few times when I was really small. She lived up in Scotland, I think we took the train . . . '

'You know I could be right.' Ben walks over and puts his arms around me once more. 'You might have had more good Christmases than you think you had.'

'Perhaps I did.' I consider this for a moment. 'I know

something has shifted within me lately. Perhaps it will allow some good memories of Christmas to float back to the surface again?'

Ben nods.

'But I think this Christmas is definitely going to be one of the best.'

'How do you know?'

'Because I get to spend it with you, and Estelle and Angela. You guys are all the family I need right now.'

Ben and I spend a glorious day together among the festive frenzy that is Christmas Eve in London. We walk through the parks holding hands, drink deliciously sweet hot chocolates with cream and marshmallows floating on top, ignoring our natural instinct to have our hot drinks plain with no nonsense on top. Today we both want to immerse ourselves in everything Christmassy. Then we wander through a few Christmas markets, and generally soak up the good cheer that the capital for once is providing. Everyone is in good spirits as they pick up last-minute bits and pieces, except for a few anxious, red-faced shoppers – mostly men – who are rushing from store to store attempting to find the perfect gift for their loved ones before the shops close.

'Shall we sit for a while?' Ben asks, as we wander back into Mistletoe Square. He gestures to one of the benches in the gardens. 'I don't want this afternoon with you to end just yet.'

'Yes, I feel the same. Let's do that.'

We sit on the bench for a few minutes, mostly in silence as we enjoy the last few minutes we'll have alone for the rest of the day.

'Not too cold for you, is it, Elle?'

'Nope, not if I snuggle up to you, it isn't.'

Ben pulls me close and wraps both his arms around me.

'That better?'

'Always.'

'I was wondering . . . ' he says with a slight hesitation to his voice. 'Now, don't take this the wrong way, cos really it's none of my business.'

'That sounds ominous . . . '

'No, not at all. I was just wondering if you'd been in touch with your parents recently.'

I sit up straight, loosening myself from Ben's embrace.

'Why?'

'Because it's Christmas?' he replies, looking surprised at my frosty reaction.

I turn and rest my back against the bench, so I'm facing forwards. 'I emailed them, if you must know.'

'You emailed them? At Christmas?'

'Yes!' I'm already a little ashamed of this, and I don't need someone reminding me. 'Have you been in touch with your adoptive parents?' I ask, turning the tables.

'Yes, I rang them today as it happens.'

'Did you?' I ask, looking at him in surprise. 'When?

'This morning, while you were getting ready to go out. Just to tell them I wouldn't be coming for Christmas really, but the conversation went on for much longer than I thought it would.'

'Oh,' I reply. I'm pleased Ben has spoken to his parents, but part of me is selfishly hoping that he isn't going to announce he's spending Christmas with them after all this year. 'Why was that?'

'I'm not sure really. Probably because of everything that has been happening in the house.' Ben glances across the square to Christmas House. 'It's made me start thinking a lot about my past. Especially when Angela told us about giving up her daughter, it made me think about my own mother again, and what reasons she might have had for abandoning me.'

'You don't know she abandoned you. Angela didn't abandon her child, remember – she was taken away from her.'

'I was abandoned,' Ben says, not looking at me, but into the distance across the square. 'They confirmed it for me.'

Immediately I take Ben's hand in mine.

'I was left at a children's home on Christmas Eve, not long after I was born. No name was left, just me. Luckily I was taken in and cared for until my adoptive parents came along. And you know what else?'

'What?' I notice that Ben's eyes are beginning to mist up as he speaks.

'I wasn't even their first choice. The baby they were going to adopt got reunited with his mother again after she changed her mind. No such luck for me, though.'

Ben turns to me again, and I can see now just how distraught he is. His grief-stricken face is full of bottled-up emotion that he can't contain any longer. 'So not only was I adopted because my mother abandoned me, but I wasn't even my adoptive parents' first choice either! It seems no one wanted me.'

'I want you, Ben,' I tell him, as the tears he's fought so hard to hide for so long begin to pour down his face. 'I want you.'

Ben looks at me, a mixture of love and gratitude on his anguished face. Then before I know what's happening, he leans into my shoulder, and I find myself comforting him while he sobs.

After a few moments he sits up again, but covers his face with his hands. 'I'm sorry, Elle. I shouldn't be burdening you with all this. It's not fair.' He rubs furiously at his eyes, desperately trying to wipe away any evidence of weakness. 'What sort of a man am I? Sobbing into your shoulder like a baby.' He shakes his head, as though he's trying to shake his emotion away with it.

'Ben, I can assure you, you're more man than all my past boyfriends put together. It takes a strong man to show his feelings, to allow himself to share his emotions. We're not in the past now, you know, in one of Estelle's stories where men had to be strong and silent and not show their feelings.'

'Just as well, eh?' Ben says, trying to lighten the moment. 'I wouldn't have fitted in very well back then.'

'I'm serious. Don't you ever think you're weak because you show emotion. You're brave and strong and kind and ... and I love you,' I finish, hoping now is the right moment to tell him.

Ben gazes at me with a mix of wonder and amazement. 'If you don't know this already ... I love you too, Elle. We've known each other for six days, and yet it doesn't feel at all wrong to tell you that already.'

'I know. But how I feel about you, it scares me a lot.'

'Why?'

'Because I've been hurt in the past – badly – and I was scared of having my heart broken again. I'd made a pact with myself that I was only going to care about me from now on. But then Estelle and Angela and you came along, and I found myself caring more about all of you than I ever thought possible.'

'Elle, I would never break your heart. Because if I did, I'd be breaking mine as well.'

'Oh, Ben ...' I say, taken aback by his words. 'What have we done to deserve each other this Christmas?'

'Obviously something rather special,' Ben says as we reach for each other again. The cold of the December afternoon is the furthest thing from our minds as we embrace and then snuggle together on the bench.

'Call your parents, Elle,' Ben says suddenly, as we sit with our thoughts for a moment. 'Call them while you still can.'

'Maybe later,' I say, not wanting to think about this. 'I'm more than happy here with you right now.'

'I'd do anything to be able to speak to my real mother,' Ben continues, not letting it go. 'To find out more about why she gave me up. Don't get me wrong, my adoptive parents looked after and cared for me, I had a happy childhood and I wanted for nothing. I love them and they love me. We told each other that this morning for the first time in ... well, I don't know how long. I don't have a problem with them at all – they were there when I needed them and I'll be forever grateful. My issue is with the woman that gave up her child. If only I could find out why, maybe then I'd have closure.'

'I'll call them tonight,' I tell him. 'I promise. I'll do it for you.'

'No, Elle,' Ben says firmly. 'You'll do it for yourself and for your parents. If Estelle's stories have taught us nothing else, they've shown us family is everything, whether that's the family you're born into, or the family you choose to live with, and we need to appreciate it while we can. Especially at Christmas.'

'So,' Estelle says as we all sit around the dinner table after enjoying another of Angela's delicious meals. This time beef Wellington with green beans and fluffy white potatoes. 'How have you found living here in this house, Elle? Is it everything you expected it to be?'

I'm slightly thrown by Estelle's question.

'Er ... I'm not sure what I expected,' I reply. 'Certainly not the level of detail that I've experienced hearing all your stories.'

257

Estelle smiles. 'I do pride myself on my storytelling abilities. I am glad you have enjoyed them so much.'

'Are there many more?' Ben asks. 'I'm not sure I was ever supposed to be involved in all this, but I'm kind of glad I am.' He looks over at me, smiles and squeezes my hand.

Estelle looks at our hands clasped together on the table. 'You were always going to be involved, Ben,' she says. 'That was never in doubt.'

Ben looks as puzzled by this statement as I am. 'What do you mean?' he asks.

'Oh, nothing.' Estelle casually waves her hand.

'It's a funny thing to say, though,' Ben continues.

'I think Estelle meant that from the moment you came in and fixed the lights on the tree we could see you had a thing for our Elle,' Angela says quickly. 'Love was always going to be in the air between you two.'

'You must have known something we didn't then!' I laugh. 'The last thing I wanted when I came here was a new relationship, I can tell you.'

'Me too,' Ben says. 'But I'm glad I've got one now.' And again we exchange an affectionate look.

'That's the first part of the plan actioned,' Estelle says approvingly. 'Now for part two.'

Ben and I look at each other, this time with equally confused expressions. I'm about to ask what Estelle means, when she speaks again.

'Do you have everything you need now, Elle? To write about my family and this house?'

'I think so, yes. But is that it, then – no more stories to add? I'd hoped we'd go a bit further – we've only got to 1962. I appreciate that you and Angela must have lived here from then until now, but there must be something else that happened here at Christmas over that time.'

'Yes, there definitely is, and it's possibly one of the most important Christmases we ever had here.'

'Is that the story you're going to tell us tonight?' I ask hopefully.

Estelle nods. She glances at the clock. 'And look, it's almost time.'

I'm about to say it can't be, we only started dinner at seven, but as I glance at the mantelpiece clock with Estelle, I see it's nearly eight o'clock.

'Come,' Estelle says, standing up and heading over to her chair by the fire. I can't help noticing how easy she suddenly finds this when before she's always needed Angela's help. 'We must prepare. We have much to get through this evening.'

'Shall I help you with the dishes, Angela?' I ask, knowing that Angela always likes to clear the table before we sit down for one of Estelle's stories.

'No, no, don't you worry about it,' Angela says. 'It will all be done by the time we return.'

Now Angela was talking in an odd way. What was going on with these two tonight?

'You're both acting really weird tonight,' I say as Ben and I help Angela pull the chairs around so we can sit with Estelle next to the fire. 'And after the last few nights, that's really saying something!'

'Nonsense,' Estelle says. 'Everything is going to work out just fine. You'll see. Now,' she says, looking wistfully at the Christmas tree all lit up as usual in the window. 'Tonight, we're going back to 1984.'

'The year we were both born!' Ben says. 'Cool.'

'Indeed.' Estelle nods. 'And that's exactly what we're going to witness now. Elle's birth.'

'What?' I exclaim. 'What do you mean, my birth? How is that related to this house in any way?'

'Patience,' Estelle says, looking at me over the top of her glasses. 'All will be revealed in good time, Elle.'

Before I can speak, the clock begins to strike eight, and as always the moon shines in through the window and onto one of the Christmas tree decorations. This time, its rays light up two chubby, winged cherubs holding hands. And before I can protest further, or ask more questions, the room begins to spin as we're taken back to 1984.

Twenty-Two

Mistletoe Square, London

Christmas Eve 1984

Do They Know It's Christmas?

As the room changes, some of the furniture disappears, but not too much this time. What we lose is quickly replaced by a sofa and two armchairs in a pretty blue floral pattern. A pale cream carpet appears under our feet, and the walls, which are now painted in pink emulsion, have a floral wallpaper border running all around them.

'I remember this!' Angela says, spinning round to take everything in. 'I designed it, didn't I, Estelle?'

Estelle nods with a grimace. 'Yes, that was the last time I let you loose on your own. It was far too ... pretty for my liking.'

'That was the fashion then. Look, our old TV!' Angela rushes over to a large TV with a boxy-looking video recorder underneath on a black metal stand. 'Remember videos,

Estelle? I used to go down to the local Blockbuster video store and rent us movies to watch – you loved that!'

'I may have enjoyed the odd classic film back then. None of that modern rubbish you used to rent though. The rat pack you used to call it.'

'No, the Brat Pack,' Angela says, examining some of the videos stacked up neatly next to the TV. 'I was a little bit obsessed with Rob Lowe back then, even though I was nearly fifty!'

'The tree looks pretty,' Ben says, and we all look towards the Christmas tree, which stands in its usual place by the window. It's covered in strings of bright lights with colourful bulbs and equally colourful shades, lots of sparkly tinsel, and all the decorations that have been a feature so far in every era we've visited, along with some shiny modern red, green and gold ones.

'Doesn't it?' Angela says wistfully. 'It seems like only yesterday I was decorating it with some of these decorations.'

'Ahem!' I say as I watch them all examining the room. 'Have you forgotten something? What about me? What have I to do with Christmas 1984 in this house?'

'What did I tell you before?' Estelle says. 'Patience, Elle. All will become clear very soon.'

We hear the front door open and close, and footsteps in the hall.

'Estelle, are you home?' A familiar voice calls and another younger version of Angela puts her head around the door.

'Estelle!' She calls again out into the hall. 'Great!' she says, coming into the sitting room and heading for the TV.

This Angela looks much older than the Angela from 1962. Her red hair is a big, frizzy bubble perm, she has a few more lines around her eyes, but her clothes – a pair of workout leggings, leg warmers, and a sweatshirt that says *Pineapple Dance Studio*, are just as bright and loud as both the Angela from the sixties and the Angela we know now.

Angela pulls a video tape from her bag and pops it into the video recorder.

Then she pulls up a chair, puts her feet up on a little side table and a familiar tune fills the room, as the opening credits of the movie *Flashdance* begin to play.

'"What a feeling!"' Both Angelas sing at the same time. They're completely out of tune, but in perfect harmony with each other.

The younger Angela suddenly gets up from the chair and begins to dance flamboyantly around to the music.

Ben, Estelle and I can't help but smile as we watch her.

'Don't laugh,' our Angela says. 'I thought I looked great!'

'Angela, is that you?' Another familiar voice calls from the hall, and we hear the front door close again. 'It is you.' A new version of Estelle, who looks younger than her present self, but still much older than the one we saw last time, appears in the room. She's wearing clothes not too dissimilar from what Estelle wears today – a neat dress and button-up cardigan. But on her feet, instead of smart little shoes, she has black suede pixie boots. Her hair is now fully grey, but she wears it long, and pulled up at the sides with a butterfly bow, and she has huge gold-rimmed spectacles that seem to cover most of her face. 'What on earth are you doing?' she asks Angela, staring at her.

Angela pauses her latest dance move and slowly lowers her leg to the floor. 'Aerobics,' she says innocently. 'Just trying to keep fit – you know?'

'A brisk daily walk will do that for you,' Estelle says, looking her up and down. 'You don't need silly outfits and music to do that.' She looks behind Angela at the television. '*Flashdance*?'

'Yes – how do you know?' Angela asks, aghast.

'Angela, you should know by now I take an interest in many things, even if I don't always share it. Now, switch that television off. I need to talk to you about something.'

Angela obediently stops the video but doesn't switch off the television – she just turns it down so it's still playing quietly in the background.

'What's up?' she asks, sitting back down in the armchair.

'Is everything on track for tomorrow?' Estelle asks. 'I mean with the Christmas preparations?'

'Of course,' Angela says easily. 'If there's one thing I'm good at, Estelle, as you know, it's cooking. Christmas dinner will be everything you imagine and more this year.'

'I'm sure it will.' Estelle nods. 'Do we have enough for two more guests?'

Angela thinks about this. 'Yes, I should think so. You mean in addition to our mothers and their offspring?'

'Children, Angela, please. You know I dislike the word "offspring". Now, I know you're already catering for quite a few with everyone at Holly House, but I want to invite Tanzy and Luke along too. They've been such a great help to us over the last few weeks, and they don't have anywhere else to go. Tanzy's mother lives up in Scotland, so it's too far to travel in her current condition.'

'Sure, not a problem at all,' Angela says. 'Consider it done!'

'Wonderful,' Estelle says. She glances behind Angela at the television. 'Did they get to number one?'

'Yeah,' Angela says, following Estelle's gaze. 'Great, isn't it? So much money going to charity.'

We all look at the television and see Band Aid's 'Do They Know it's Christmas?' playing on the screen.

'Tanzy said she wants to go out to Africa and help when she's had her baby,' Estelle says, giving Angela a knowing look.

'Her heart is in the right place,' Angela says, 'but I don't think having a newborn and volunteering over there are the best fit.'

'I know, I tried to tell her, but she's adamant. She's told you about her deal, has she?'

Angela nods. 'They were trying for a baby for so long, Estelle, you can't blame them for thinking they've got to keep to their part of the bargain.'

Estelle gives Angela a reproving look. 'You don't actually believe they made a deal with Him up there, do you? *Help me to get pregnant, and in return I promise to help others for ever?*'

'Of course not. But in times of desperation, people turn to the church, don't they?'

'So now they're bound to spend the rest of their lives devoted to helping others, because she actually got pregnant.'

'It's not a bad way to spend it,' Angela says, looking at the television again. An image of a starving baby crying fills the screen, as its mother tries to comfort it.

'No,' Estelle says quietly. 'You're absolutely right.' And they both silently watch the television for a few moments together.

'Poor Tanzy,' Angela says when the song finishes. 'She really is so desperate to have a child. She told me all about it one day – how long they'd been trying, and how many they'd lost in the process. To her this is a miracle baby – especially being due so close to Christmas. What harm does dedicating her life to helping others do, if it brings her what she so longs for?'

'Angela, I don't often say it, but on this occasion you are totally right.' Estelle holds out her arms and smiles, and a very surprised Angela stands up, walks over to her and they hug. 'I've taught you well.' Estelle adds.

Angela rolls her eyes, but hugs Estelle that little bit closer.

'Now,' Estelle says, sounding much more like her usual self as she releases Angela from her embrace. 'We have a lot to do if we're to give our lovely mothers and their babies a Christmas to remember.'

'We sure do!' Angela sings.

'Now, have you got all the food?' Estelle asks. 'Do you need me to go out and get anything?'

'Don't be daft. If you're cooking for as many as I am, you don't buy all your food on Christmas Eve. There will be nothing left in the shops!'

'Good, good,' Estelle says. 'As long as it's all under control. I still have a few gifts to wrap for the mothers and their babies. So let's get to it, then!'

They both head out into the hall, leaving us behind in the sitting room.

Estelle, Angela and Ben all look over towards me, but I'm so stunned by what I've just witnessed that I can't speak.

'Elle, are your parents called Tanzy and Luke by any chance?' Ben asks quietly.

I nod.

'Did you know they knew this house?' he asks, in the same calm and controlled voice, as if he doesn't want to shock me.

'No,' I say, still trying to comprehend what I've just learnt. 'I had no idea they'd ever been here.'

'Elle, are you all right?' Estelle asks gently. 'You look a little pale. Do you need to sit down?'

I shake my head. 'Can't, can I?' I mutter, still thinking. 'The chairs aren't really here . . . just in our imaginations.'

'Elle, I know you think your parents didn't care that much for you,' Estelle says gently, as she approaches me. 'But honestly they did. You really were so wanted. So much so that your mother made that promise.'

'And it sounds like she kept her word too,' Angela adds. 'I knew she would. I remember them both so clearly. They were lovely people.'

'If Tanzy kept the promise Angela and Estelle are talking about,' Ben says, 'do you think this might be why you felt like they were always putting others before you?'

'I . . . I don't know,' I say, staring at him. 'Maybe.'

'I know it may have felt sometimes like they cared more about others than you,' Estelle says, still in the same calm, kind voice. 'Especially when they were doing their charity work. But both Angela and I know that wasn't the case. Having you meant everything to them, and they wanted to do anything they could to keep you.'

'I feel terrible,' I say, really wanting to sit down, but knowing I can't. 'Both my parents dedicated their life to helping others, and I've always begrudged them for it, when really I should have been proud of what they did. I just thought they didn't care about me or my birthdays, when really what they were doing was giving others who had nothing a Christmas to remember.'

'It's totally understandable,' Ben says, coming over and putting his arm around my shoulders. 'You don't think like that when you're a child. You only see and feel things as they are in that moment. You can't possibly see the bigger picture.'

'I'm sure they gave you a lot of love and time at Christmas

too,' Estelle says. 'Perhaps some of your nicer memories have become a little distorted over the years, because you've focussed on what hurt and upset you. It's often easier to remember something painful than it is something nice, because a painful emotion can be so much stronger.'

'Yes,' Ben agrees. 'Remember when you started talking about Christmases with your granny? You remembered that as a happy time.'

'I guess you might be right,' I say, looking round at them all. 'Perhaps I need to speak to my parents a bit more, and do some reminiscing about our past Christmases together.'

'I think that would be a very good idea indeed,' Estelle says, putting her hand on my shoulder. As she does, I feel a strange but warm and comforting feeling spread right through me.

I look questioningly at her, but she just smiles serenely.

'So, are we going back now?' Ben asks, looking around the room. 'Is that it for 1984?'

'No, we have much more to show you yet,' Estelle says. 'Both of you.'

'Both of us?' Ben looks surprised. 'How do you mean?'

'Come,' Estelle says, moving towards the door. 'We move on a few hours.'

Ben and I look at each other with puzzled expressions. But Estelle and Angela are already heading into the hall. As we begin to follow them, Ben grips my hand tightly.

'Now, what I may have wrongly assumed,' Estelle says, turning to us, 'is when we've been talking about our mothers and their babies, that you've understood it's our charity we're referring to?'

Ben and I both nod.

'Good. Your mother and father, Elle, came to us to volunteer just after she got pregnant with you. It was the first in their many endeavours to help others.'

'We were very glad of their help,' Angela says. 'Word was getting around about what we were doing by this time, and we were getting an awful lot of mothers turning up on our doorstep for help.'

Estelle nods. 'Some of the other houses and businesses were not too happy about what they considered *fallen women* with their *bastard babies* living in their fancy square.'

I flinch at Estelle's words.

'It's not a pleasant description, I agree,' Estelle says. 'But I'm afraid that's what they thought, even in the mid-eighties. They were far too quick to judge. These women weren't easy, or slutty, or any other word used to describe them. Most had fallen on hard times due to their pregnancy. The young ones had often been thrown out of their parents' houses; the older ones usually came from abusive relationships. We had all types of women, from all backgrounds. The one thing they had in common was they needed our help, and we gave it to them without question or judgement.'

'We did,' Angela says, nodding as she remembers. 'It was like one big family here, especially at Christmastime. I loved it.'

'We both did,' Estelle says. 'Neither Angela nor I ever had families of our own, so our mothers and babies were like our temporary family. Some stayed longer than others depending on their circumstances, and many kept in touch with us once they'd left.'

'That's really lovely,' I say, incredibly touched by Estelle and Angela's story. 'You talk about my mother and father helping others, but that's just what you were both doing here, keeping families together, by helping all those mothers hold on to their babies.'

Angela nods. 'Just like I couldn't.'

'Oh, Angela. I didn't mean it like that.'

'No, I know you didn't. It was all Estelle, really – she's been helping others all her life. First her mother, then everyone she nursed in the war, and then Christian, and finally me. It was no surprise she turned over her house to women in need of help.'

'I couldn't have done it without you, Angela, as you well know.' Estelle and Angela exchange a tender look. 'And, it's no more than my own mother would have done,' Estelle continues. 'Or many of my ancestors who lived here. There's a wonderful tradition in the Christmas family for helping others.'

'Yes, there is, isn't there?' I say, thinking about all the stories Estelle has told us. 'You must be very proud of your family, Estelle.'

'I am. And that is why I asked you to record their stories for me, so they will never be forgotten.'

'Of course. It will be my honour to do so.'

Estelle nods. 'Now, enough about me and Angela. We must return to you two. In a moment you will see both your mother and father, Elle. I'm warning you because this can sometimes be quite a shock for people. Everyone you've seen so far in my stories, other than Angela and myself, has been a stranger to you. This is your own flesh and blood.'

Somewhere in my mind I register the fact that Estelle has said 'this can sometimes be quite a shock for people'. *Has she done this sort of thing before?* But any questioning thoughts I might have are quickly erased by her telling me I'm about to see my parents as their younger selves.

'I'm ready,' I say bravely, and I feel Ben squeeze my hand.

'Here we go, then,' Estelle says, looking up the carpeted staircase.

The 1984 Angela comes rushing down the stairs, she grabs the receiver of the green telephone that stands on a table in the hall, and then we watch her dial 999, which seems to take for ever, as the round plastic dial on the phone whirrs fully back round each time.

'Hello, yes, ambulance, please,' she says hurriedly.

She waits for a moment to be put through, and while she does she glances anxiously up the stairs.

'Yes, I need an ambulance,' she says again. 'Christmas House, Mistletoe Square, Bloomsbury. A baby has just been born and it's not breathing very well. Ah ... uh ... Crikey, really? ... You think? ... Right, I'll do that.' And she puts the receiver down. Then she picks up a notebook next to the telephone and flicks through it. 'Where are you? Where are you?' she mutters, impatiently turning the pages. 'Right!' Then she begins the process of dialling a telephone number once more.

'It's a wonder we ever got through to anyone!' Angela says, watching her younger self. 'Bit different to today when you just press a couple of buttons on your mobile to ring someone.'

'But why are you ringing for an ambulance?' I ask looking anxiously up the stairs. 'What's going on?'

'Did you know when you were born you had some breathing difficulties?' Estelle asks.

'Er ... yes, kind of. I know I was in hospital when I was a baby. Not far up the road from here in Great Ormond Street. Wait, are you saying the baby you're talking about is me? I was born *here, in this house?*'

Estelle nods. 'Your mother wasn't due today; she was due in January. But you came very suddenly and very early.'

'Estelle and I had delivered a few babies in the house,' Angela explains. 'But we were really here for our mothers before and after they gave birth. But Tanzy's waters broke and she went into labour very quickly. She didn't want to go to hospital so we decided she would have a home birth here.'

I look up the stairs again. How can this be happening? This is all so crazy.

'Finally!' Eighties Angela snaps into the telephone. 'Yes, I need a taxi at Mistletoe Square, Bloomsbury as fast as you can – it's an emergency! No, twenty minutes isn't all right. Didn't you just hear me? I said it's an emergency! Well, get one here as fast as you can then. My name is Angela, and it's Number Five, Christmas House.' And she slams the phone down.

'Angela! How are you getting on?' Eighties Estelle calls from the top of the stairs. 'How long will the ambulance be? I've managed to get the baby breathing, but it's not easy for the poor mite.'

Angela looks desperately up the stairs, and then back down at the telephone.

'We're getting a taxi!' she calls. 'Get everyone ready. I'll be five minutes!'

Without grabbing a coat, Angela rushes to the front door.

Our Estelle and Angela encourage us to follow her, so once again we find ourselves outside on the steps of Christmas House.

Mistletoe Square doesn't look that dissimilar to how it looks today, perhaps a tad scruffier and a little more unkempt. But the gardens are still filled with the same trees, and the gas lamps that still surround the edges of the square glow in the same way they always do, whether in the nineteenth century or the twenty-first.

But I don't have time to make any more comparisons; Angela is already opening up the door to Holly House and calling in through the hall.

'Fred!' she calls. 'Fred! Are you there? Come here quickly!'

After a moment or two, a young boy of about fourteen appears at the door. He's wearing an Arsenal football shirt and blue jeans, and has bare feet.

'What's up, Ang? The women nearly had heart failure then when you called through the door. We was just watching *Cagney and Lacey* on the telly. I don't think it's a Christmas episode, but I guess it's better than *Coronation Street* they were all watching earlier.'

'Fred, concentrate. I need you to get me a black cab super-fast – it's an emergency. Tanzy has had her baby and we need to get it to hospital fast!'

Fred stares at Angela for a moment and then, as what she's saying registers, jumps into action.

'Got it!' he says, ducking out of sight for a moment then pulling on his trainers over his bare feet. 'Be as quick as I can.'

He dashes down the steps of Holly House and then sprints along the square towards the main road.

'What's going on, Ang?' a woman carrying a young baby asks, as she appears at the door. 'Where's my Fred gone?'

'Sorry, Eve, I've asked him to try and hail a cab. Tanzy's had her baby and it's not doing too well. The ambulance said they'd be a while, and when I tried calling for a taxi they said they were busy because it's Christmas Eve.'

'Crikey,' Eve says, holding her own baby that bit closer to her. 'She said she was feeling a bit off earlier. I just thought she'd been doing too much – you know what she's like. I hope it's all right. Boy or girl?'

'A little girl.' Angela smiles. 'Bonny little thing, too. But she's not breathing all that well. Estelle wants to get her to the hospital as soon as possible.'

Eve nods. 'My Fred will get you a cab. No trouble.. He's canny like that. Look, here comes one now!'

Angela turns to see a black London taxicab coming round the corner into the square, with Fred running along the pavement not far behind it.

Angela rushes to the bottom of the steps. 'Thank goodness!' she says as the cabbie rolls down his window.

'Are you Ange, by any chance?' the cabbie asks.

'Yes, yes, I am.'

'Good. That lad back there,' he says, glancing in his rearview mirror, 'nearly got himself killed – stepping out in front of me like that to make me stop!'

'We need you to go to Great Ormond Street – it's an emergency,' Angela says quickly. 'Give me a minute and I'll get your passengers.'

Angela dashes past us back up the steps, and then she re-emerges with Estelle, carrying a baby swaddled in a blanket, and a young, bohemian-looking couple.

I stare at them. It's my parents – there's no doubt about it. They look so familiar, yet so very different too. My heart races inside my chest, and yet at the same time I also feel quite numb. I think for one awful moment I might faint, but, as my father helps my mother down the steps, I find myself automatically following them.

'Are they your parents?' I hear Ben ask as I descend quickly down the steps.

But I can't speak, only watch.

My mother looks so young. Her hair that I can only ever

remember neat and short, is dyed a bright shade of auburn and cascades wildly down her back. She's wearing a long, baggy, white T-shirt, with a long black cardigan, and loose khaki trousers. Multicoloured beads and bracelets adorn her wrists. And even though it's December, on her feet are a pair of flip-flops.

She looks very young, but also drawn and quite pale.

My father is helping my mother down the steps. He also has more hair than I've ever seen him with, but it's on top of his head this time. His black hair is full and bouncy, instead of grey and thinning, and he's wearing black jeans, a thick woollen jumper, and heavy, black, lace-up boots – and is that an earring I can see in his ear lobe? Oh, my goodness, it is!

I reach out to touch him as he passes, but my hand floats right through him.

He shivers a little, before climbing into the taxi next to my mother.

'Please come with us?' my mother asks as Estelle passes her the baby – who I can't quite get my head around is actually me – now she's settled in the back seat of the cab. 'Both of you. I don't trust them at the hospital. I know if you're both there it will all be all right.'

Estelle looks at Angela and nods.

'I'll go with them now. You lock up the house and bring my bag and some things for Tanzy. She'll be there overnight.'

'Got it!' Angela says. 'I'll see you there in a few minutes.' She closes the door and the cabbie speedily pulls away. 'Right,' she says turning to Fred who's been standing on the pavement watching all this take place. 'I don't approve of how you got that cab, Fred, but the main thing is you did. Well done.'

Fred grins proudly. 'Will they be all right?' he asks, his expression changing to concern. 'That baby looked a bit blue . . . '

'I hope so,' Angela says, looking down the street after the cab, which has now disappeared from Mistletoe Square. 'You heard Estelle, though, I've got to go to the hospital with the others.' Angela glances up at the two houses. 'So I'm leaving you in charge tonight – all right?'

Fred looks surprised.

'It's Christmas Eve, Fred. Someone has to fill everyone's stocking and put the presents under the tree. I might not be back in time.'

Fred salutes. 'I can do it! Santa Fred is on the case.'

Angela looks a bit worried, but nods. 'Good. Everything is upstairs in the back bedroom. It's all labelled so you can't go wrong, okay?'

'Got it. Back bedroom. All labelled.'

'Good chap! I'll see you later tonight or possibly tomorrow morning. But I'll be back to cook the Christmas dinner whatever.'

Fred nods and Angela dashes back up the steps into the house. Fred proudly does the same next door. As both doors close, we're left outside.

'Are you all right, Elle?' Estelle asks as I climb back up the steps next to them.

I nod. 'I still can't believe that was me, though. I'm sorry I tried to touch my dad. I couldn't help myself.'

'Perfectly understandable given the circumstances,' Estelle says. 'Elle, I know it's incredibly strange seeing yourself like that, but it really was you. You were born here in this house on Christmas Eve 1984, and, as you've just witnessed, shortly after you were rushed to Great Ormond Street, where they looked after you until you could breathe properly again.'

'Yes, I understand all that, but why didn't I know this? Why didn't you say when I first came here for the job if you knew it was me? *Did* you know it was me, or is this just a big coincidence?'

'That, I can't quite reveal just yet,' Estelle maddeningly replies. 'Not until we're finished here in 1984.'

'So what's next then? Did my parents come back here to live again with me?'

'They did for a short while. But then they decided to go and stay with Tanzy's mother up in Scotland, so she could help with you. I think Luke got a job up there working for a charity, so they stayed up in Scotland for a while. It wasn't until you were old enough that they started moving around a lot with all the various charities they ended up volunteering and often working for.'

'They kept in touch with us for a while,' Angela says, 'But you know how things are, people drift apart as the years go by. They always sent a Christmas card, though, didn't they, Estelle?'

Estelle nods. 'They never forgot us.'

'Couldn't, could they really?' Angela says, smiling. 'Their only child was named after you.'

I stare at Estelle.

'I was named after you?' I ask, aghast. 'But I thought my name was Noelle?'

'It is. I was touched that Tanzy and Luke wanted to call you Estelle, but I insisted it was something else. So they went with Noelle instead for obvious reasons as your official name, and chose to call you Elle.'

'I'd have much preferred Estelle,' I tell her.

'You will always be Elle to us.' Estelle smiles at me. 'It's been wonderful getting to know you after all this time, Elle, it really has. You've grown up into a wonderful young woman.'

'Hardly young,' I quip, feeling more than a tad embarrassed by Estelle's kind words.

'Compared to Angela and myself you're but a spring chicken. Your parents must be very proud of you.'

Suddenly I feel very guilty. I'd neglected my parents of late. I'd spent too many years blaming them for things that clearly didn't happen in the way I chose to remember them. They were good people both now and in the past, and they didn't deserve my judgement on what I thought a perfect Christmas should be.

'They are,' I say quietly. 'Very proud. As I am of them. And as soon as we get back, I'm going to call them and tell them exactly how I feel about them.'

'Good,' Estelle says approvingly. 'I'm pleased to hear it.'

'I'll say hi from you if you like? In fact, why don't you both speak to them when I phone. I'm sure they would love to hear from you again. They'll be so amazed that I'm here in this house with you again.'

Estelle and Angela both look quite sad as they glance at each other.

'Perhaps,' Estelle resolutely says. 'Let's see how things go.'

What a strange answer! Especially after what they've just shown me.

'Is it time to return to 2018 now?' Ben asks, breaking into my thoughts. 'This has been an incredible story finding out Elle was born in this house and you both knew her parents. But it is Christmas Eve, and I want us to enjoy our first one together.' He grips my hand a bit too tightly and I wonder why. 'Your beautiful tree and that roaring fire. It's like the perfect Christmas scene just waiting for us to cosy up and enjoy. I think we should go back now.'

Why is Ben in such a rush?

'You two will have plenty of Christmas Eves together in the future,' Estelle says. 'Of that I'm certain. But we haven't quite finished here in 1984 just yet. You may have noticed I haven't put any gifts under our tree back in 2018? That is because I have one final gift to give you both. But first we must witness Ben's first Christmas.'

Ah, that's why? Now it's his turn, he's panicking. I squeeze his hand reassuringly just like he's been doing to mine all night.

'Don't tell me I was born in this house too?' Ben asks, grinning manically. 'Because that I really won't believe!'

He is shaking now, too, and it's not from the cold. He looks genuinely frightened.

'No, Ben,' Estelle continues calmly, 'You were not born here. But we are about to meet both you . . . and your mother.'

Twenty-Three

'What?' Ben asks suddenly, looking as pale as I was a short while ago when I saw my own parents. 'No, I want to stop this now.' He waves his arms up towards the house behind us and then out towards the square. 'This house, this square. This . . . this time-travelling. Storytelling, whatever this witchcraft is. I don't want to go on with it any more.'

'Ben,' I tell him, gently taking his hand again. 'It's fine. Really it is. I was scared when it was my parents we were going to see. But, honestly, it feels really lovely to see them as they once were. Not frightening or weird at all.'

Ben stares at me for a moment, his eyes wide with fear. 'Elle, can't you see? This is all some sort of intricate deception we've become embroiled in. Some strange illusion that we've fallen victim to. At first it was a bit of fun when all we were doing was watching some strange stories from the past. I didn't know how they were doing it, but I was impressed by the level of trickery, the realness of it all. I'd have probably walked away after that first story if it hadn't been for you. But I wanted to get to know you, and the only way I could do that was to allow myself to become open to all this . . . fantasy, illusion, I don't know what to call it, because none of it is real, is it? It can't be.'

'Actually, I think it is real,' I reply. 'I don't know how or why this is happening. But it is. Remember how you were just telling me earlier that you'd love to see your mother, to know why she gave you up so you could get some sort of closure. This is your chance, Ben. This is what you wanted.'

'Not like this, though,' Ben says, gripping both my hands now as he stares wildly into my face. 'Not like this, Elle.'

I look back at Estelle and Angela standing calmly on the steps behind us. They don't seem in the least fazed by Ben's reaction.

'Don't look at them!' Ben turns my face back towards his. 'They're the puppeteers creating this freak show!'

As Estelle is about to reply, the door opens behind her, and the young Angela appears, now wearing a coat and scarf over her earlier outfit. She carries a couple of handbag-size bags and an empty holdall. She locks the front door, and then hurries over to Holly House, presumably to get Tanzy's things for her likely stay in hospital.

The break in conversation while we watch this simple act seems to calm Ben a little; his fast, shallow breathing steadies and his hands don't grip mine quite as tightly.

'Ben,' Estelle says carefully, as though she doesn't want to startle him. 'I'm pleased you're questioning all this at last. I was waiting for one of you to. What Angela and I have asked you to witness over the last few days has been very unusual and, I'll agree, often difficult to believe. It's good you're questioning this experience – you're human, you should, it's in your nature. But please don't dismiss everything that's happened because it doesn't fit with what appears normal to you. Few things in life are ever normal. There are things going on around us all the time that can't quite be explained. So we pretend that they're not really there, or not really happening to make ourselves feel better.'

Estelle pauses to let Ben digest this thought.

Ben doesn't speak, but again I feel him relax a little more.

'It will be okay,' I whisper. 'I promise.'

Ben nods. His grip loosens and he releases one of my hands so he can stand by my side, instead of directly in front of me.

Content that she has Ben's full attention now, Estelle continues. 'Everything that's happened, from the time you both read our adverts in the newspaper, has brought us here to this very moment. All the stories we've told you have had some meaning either to us or to you. There's been a reason for everything you've both experienced, and in a very short while you will understand why. But you must let us tell you this one last story for it all to make sense.'

Ben holds Estelle's gaze for a moment, then he sighs deeply and looks down at his shoes. 'Can I really trust you, Estelle, when you say we are going to see my mother?' he asks, looking back up at her.

'You can, Ben.'

'But I've never seen her before,' Ben says, still sounding incredibly anxious. 'How will I know it's really her?'

'Trust me, Ben,' Estelle says. 'I'm not allowed to lie to you. Neither Angela nor I have ever lied to either of you – we simply can't.'

Finally, Ben nods. 'All right, I shouldn't trust you, either of you,' he says, continuing to look at them both. 'But for some unknown reason, I do.'

The young Angela suddenly comes out of Holly House. She walks down the steps carrying all her bags.

'Bloody taxis,' she says, looking round the square. 'Never one around when you actually want one. I guess I'll have to go out to the main road and try to flag one down.'

As she finishes speaking, a black cab comes trundling around the corner.

Angela drops her bags and is about to raise her hand when it stops right beside her.

'Angela?' the cabbie asks through his window.

'Yes?' Angela says, looking surprised. 'How did you know?'

'You called us earlier? Sorry it's taken a while. Christmas Eve, innit? Even Santa would struggle to get a cab tonight.'

Angela raises her eyes to the sky and whispers, 'Thank you.' Then she climbs into the cab with her bags and they drive away, around the square then out onto the main road.

'Now what?' Ben asks, but Estelle is already pointing in the opposite direction.

We follow her hand and see a young, slight woman walking slowly along the pavement. She's wearing scruffy-looking clothes that look far too big for her – baggy blue jeans held up with a leather belt, a long bottle-green cardigan, a black-and-white t-shirt with the words *Choose Life* printed on the front, and on her feet, black lace-up boots. Perched on the back of her head is a burgundy beret, and in her arms she's carrying what appears to be a bundle of clothes in a plastic washing basket.

'Come,' Estelle says, leading us down the steps to the path outside the house. 'Let us not impede her.'

As the woman gets closer to us, she keeps looking at a scrap of paper balanced on top of the washing basket, and then up at the houses as she passes them. As she gets to our house, she stops.

'Looks like this is where we part company,' she says to the

basket, and suddenly I realise that wrapped tightly in among all the clothing is a tiny baby.

'Is that Ben?' I ask quietly.

Estelle nods.

Ben just stares at the young woman.

'She's so frail ...' he whispers. 'Why is she so frail?' he demands, looking at Estelle, while the woman climbs the steps up to Christmas House. Ben is right – she does look very pale and not well at all.

'Patience, Ben,' Estelle says, still watching the woman. 'All will become clear soon. As Elle has correctly guessed, that is you in the basket, and the young woman is indeed your mother. Her name is Sarah.'

Ben stares hard at Sarah, then he follows her to the top of the steps.

'Why?' he asks her, his face pressed close to hers. 'Why are you abandoning me? Why don't you want me?'

But Sarah simply bends down to tend to her baby. She carefully makes sure he's wrapped up to keep out the cold, then she places a gentle kiss on his forehead.

'I hope one day you'll understand why I have to do this,' she whispers. 'You'll probably hate me, and I don't blame you for that. But really, this is for the best. They will look after you here. Goodbye, my love.'

'Stop!' Ben shouts as she stands up again. 'It isn't for the best. You're wrong. Right now I need you, not anyone else. I want my mother!'

Sarah is about to ring the doorbell, but she stops as though she's heard something.

'Can you hear me?' Ben asks, looking wildly at her. 'Can she hear me?' he asks us still standing at the bottom of the steps

284

watching all this unfold. 'Sarah!' he calls. 'Can you hear me? It's your son – don't leave me here!'

Sarah looks slightly puzzled as she hesitates on the steps. But something has definitely disturbed her baby, and he begins to cry.

Our Ben stares down at his younger self. 'I think you can hear me, can't you, buddy?' he says as Sarah tries to settle her child again. 'I'm doing this for you, you know?'

Baby Ben begins to cry even harder, so Sarah has no choice but to pick him up.

'Hush,' she whispers as she holds the baby close to her and rocks him to and fro. 'Hush there. Mummy is here.'

'Hi!' We turn our heads to see Fred standing on the steps of Holly House, the front door open behind him. 'Can I help you?'

Sarah immediately turns away.

Fred in his socked feet this time, pulls the door to and comes down the steps towards us.

'What are you doing?' he calls as he walks along the pavement. 'There's no one in next door right now.'

Sarah is clearly panicking outside Christmas House as Fred approaches, but there's nowhere to hide.

'Is that a baby you're holding?' Fred asks as he arrives at the bottom of the steps.

'Yes,' Sarah says, having no choice but to turn around. Baby Ben has calmed slightly now, but is still making a grumbling sound.

Fred looks up at Sarah and the baby, and then down at the basket of clothes.

'Do you need some help?' he asks. 'If you do, it's best if you come next door. Like I said, no one is home there right now.'

'Will they be long?' Sarah asks, still rocking her baby back and forth to soothe him.

'Dunno, they had to go to the hospital. Could be ages. They've left me in charge, though, so if you want to come in to ours and wait, you can?'

Sarah shakes her head. 'You're very young to be in charge of something like this, aren't you?'

Fred shrugs. 'It's only for tonight. I've got to make sure everyone gets their stocking and Christmas presents you see – all the mothers and their babies. Ange said she'd be back to cook us all Christmas dinner though – I can't wait!'

'They do that here?' Sarah looks surprised. 'Celebrate Christmas, I mean. I didn't think there would be enough money for presents and stuff.'

'Yeah, even though it's a charity they're really good. They've helped me and my mum a lot. My dad drank too much, and when he did he beat my mum. She was afraid for her unborn baby – my sister. So Estelle and Angela took us in and we've been here for a while now. It's not for ever, just until Mum can get something sorted for us all.'

'You're very lucky. It sounds really nice.'

'Like I said.' Fred looks Sarah up and down. 'They're very good here. Don't turn anyone away as far as I've seen. As long as they have room they'll look after you. And I happen to know we do have room right now.' Fred looks back at Holly House. 'Why don't you come in and wait for them? Your baby must be getting cold out here and you must be too. It's a cold one tonight.' He wraps his arms around himself and lifts his feet up and down so they are not on the cold pavement for as long. 'I think it might snow.'

Sarah shakes her head. 'No, I can't. I have to go.'

Baby Ben has settled now, and she bends to put him back in the basket again.

'Wait, you're not thinking of leaving the baby there, are you?' Fred asks, voicing his concerns for the first time, even though I think he probably guessed what was happening a while back.

'I have to,' Sarah says, standing up again with Ben still in her arms. 'I can't take care of him.'

'Then stay,' Fred says, looking worried now. 'Honestly, they're great here. They'll help you until you can get back on your feet again.'

Sarah looks back down at her baby once more. Ben is now sleeping soundly.

'That's the thing,' she whispers so as not to wake him again. 'I can't get back on my feet again.'

'Of course you can,' Fred says, slowly approaching Sarah on the steps. 'Everyone can thanks to people like Estelle and Angela.'

Fred is right. It actually is starting to snow now, as large fluffy flakes begin to fall from the sky.

They both glance up for a moment before Sarah shakes her head at Fred. 'Not me. It's too late for me.'

'Why?' Fred asks, coming level with her now. 'Why can't you?'

'Here.' Sarah thrusts Ben at Fred, so he has no choice but to take him.

Sarah pulls the sleeve of her cardigan up to reveal a thin, bony arm covered in puncture marks, scabs and bruising. The horror of seeing her arm in this state is only made worse by the delicate and perfect white snowflakes falling against her skin. 'Do you know what a junkie is?' she asks Fred.

Fred nods while arranging Ben in his arms to protect him from the snow now beginning to fall more heavily.

'Good, cos I'm one,' Sarah replies pragmatically. 'Except these days, there's a bit more danger to it than there used to be – specially when you share needles.'

Fred stares with horror at Sarah.

'Don't worry, fella, you won't catch it. Not if you're smarter than I was. Take my advice – stay well away from drink, drugs and gambling. Or they'll be the downfall of you – especially the drugs.'

'Do you have AIDS?' Fred asks, open-mouthed, while expertly cradling Ben. It's obvious he's had plenty of practice with his baby sister.

'Not yet, but I'm HIV positive. Don't worry, the little one doesn't have it,' she says looking at Ben, now sound asleep in Fred's arms. 'He was checked when he was born. I'm on borrowed time though. That's why I need to find him a good home before things go downhill, shall we say. I didn't want to involve the social, so I left the hospital as soon as I could without them knowing. My mate had heard of this place. "Go to Christmas House," she said. "They'll take care of him there." So here I am at Christmas House on Christmas Eve. Sadly, unlike Mary, there's room at the inn, it seems, but no innkeeper!' She tries to smile, but fails. 'You'll make sure he gets to them that run this place, won't you?' she asks. 'You said one of their names was Angela?'

'Yes, Angela and Estelle. But you can't just leave him here with me. I said I'd put some presents out, I didn't say I'd take care of a baby until they got back. Please stay. What's your name?'

'No names,' Sarah says, shaking her head. 'But, Angela – now that has to be a sign.'

'A sign of what?' Fred asks, looking more desperate by the minute.

'Nothing. What's your name?'

'Fred.'

'Now then, Fred, will you please take care of my baby until this Angela and Estelle get back. No, no buts!' Sarah says, as Fred opens his mouth to protest again. 'I'm leaving him here whatever you say, whether it's in that basket or in your arms. I want to be sure he's somewhere he'll be taken care of. I can at least give him that.'

'If you won't tell me your name, at least tell me his?' Fred asks, looking down at Ben.

'He doesn't have one yet. I didn't want to get too attached to him. Not that that made much difference.' Sarah pulls the blanket that Ben is wrapped in, back from his face a little so she can see him. 'I may seem like a cold, hard bitch doing this, Fred, but believe me when I say it's breaking my heart to leave him.'

They both gaze down at baby Ben for a moment.

'Why don't you name him?' Sarah says, standing back a little. 'I'd like that.'

'Nah.' Fred shakes his head. 'I ain't no good at that sort of stuff – where would I even start?'

'Look, there's this stupid tradition in my family that's been going on for years, that every child is to be named after the letters in the word Christmas – which was one of the reasons I knew bringing him here to Christmas House was the right thing to do. It was like a sign.'

'What do you mean after the letters in Christmas – like any of them?'

'No, they've always been in order apparently. First it was a C, then an H, then an R and so on. I'm the last in the line with the second S. Dunno what's supposed to happen now, really.'

'You start again?' Fred suggests. 'With C?'

Sarah shrugs. 'Maybe? The only reason I know this is because when my mother gave me away, she left this weird note that said if I ever had children I should try and carry on the family tradition.'

'You were abandoned then, just like he's going to be?' Fred asks, looking down at Ben again.

'Don't get all judgy on me, Fred,' Sarah says. 'My mother gave me up for a better life, at least that's what the letter said, and now I'm doing the same for him.'

'Have you written a letter?' Fred asks. 'That he can have when he's older?'

I get the feeling Fred is trying to delay Sarah leaving in any way he can, in the hope someone will come along and help him with his predicament. When Sarah isn't looking, he keeps glancing back to Holly House, and then along the road in case Estelle or Angela should return.

Sarah shakes her head. 'No, but you need to give him this.' She goes back over to the basket and retrieves something from the clothes.

'Along with the letter my mother wrote, she left me this.' Sarah holds up what looks like a silver locket. It's hard to see exactly what it is because Sarah has her back turned to us. 'It's just as well no one I live with saw this or they'd have sold it for drugs money. I'm ashamed to admit I nearly did a couple of times when I got desperate. But it's the only thing I have that's from my family.' She tucks the locket into Ben's blanket. 'Make sure it stays with him, won't you? At least he'll have something to remember me with when I'm in the ground.'

Sarah begins to walk down the steps.

'Wait!' Fred follows her down to the pavement. 'We haven't decided on a name yet?'

'I know what you're doing,' Sarah says, looking up and down Mistletoe Square. 'You're trying to keep me here as long as you can, until someone else comes along. I told you, call him what you like.'

'Something Christmassy?' Fred suggests.

'If you like. He was born in the early hours of this morning.'

'It's Christmas Eve so ... what about Joseph?'

Sarah shrugs.

'I know,' Fred says, as an idea strikes him. 'What if we keep your family tradition going by moving on to an E, so the names spell out Christmas Eve?'

'Yes,' Sarah says approvingly. 'I like that. You're a smart one, Fred. You'll go far. But a name beginning with E to do with Christmas? Good luck with that one.'

Sarah takes one last look at her baby and begins to walk away, her light footsteps leaving footprints in the newly fallen snow.

I feel like my heart might break as I watch her. I have no idea how Ben is coping with this.

'Ebenezer!' Fred calls out, in one last attempt to keep her there. 'That begins with an E and is to do with Christmas.'

Sarah turns back and smiles at Fred. 'I admire your spirit, Fred, but you can't call a baby Ebenezer, poor mite. No one wants a Scrooge at Christmas, do they?'

Fred sadly shakes his head.

'Why don't you call him Ebenezer, but shorten it to Ben,' Sarah suggests. 'That would work.'

Fred nods. 'Ben it is. Are you sure there's nothing that will make you stay?'

Sarah shakes her head. 'No, I'm sorry to leave all this on your young shoulders, Fred. I just know that leaving him here is the right thing to do. There's something special about that house,' she says, looking back at Christmas House. 'I don't know what it is, but I hope that one day my Ben will.'

As we watch Sarah walk away along the snowy pavement, and Fred carry Ben carefully up the steps of the house next door, somehow I know that this time when we return to Christmas House, nothing is going to be the same.

Twenty-Four

24 December 2018

'Are you all right?' I ask, turning to Ben.

Ben nods, but he looks very shaken.

'How do you feel now you've seen your mother?' I ask gently.

Ben simply shrugs. 'I'm not really sure . . .'

'It's a lot to take in,' Estelle says quietly. 'You should go back to the house again.'

'I think that's a very good idea,' I say when Ben doesn't answer. 'Angela and I can make everyone a nice hot drink and we can sit round the fire and talk about everything that's just happened.' I look around, suddenly realising I haven't seen Angela for a while.

'Where's Angela?'

Estelle looks over at the gardens, and we see Angela sitting on a bench with her head bowed.

How is she able to sit on that bench? But as I look further around the square, I realise from a few small details like the age of the parked cars, and the neatness of the gardens, that we're already back in 2018.

'Ben isn't the only one who found watching that hard,' Estelle says. 'Angela finds that particular story very difficult as well.'

Why would Angela ...? I begin to think, but Ben answers for me.

'Sarah was Angela's daughter, wasn't she?' he says calmly. 'The one she was forced to give away.'

Estelle nods.

'Which means that Angela is not only Sarah's mother, but my grandmother too.'

I stare at Estelle in shock. 'No way! That's incredible!'

Ben looks over at Angela.

Feeling him watching her, Angela stands up and walks serenely over towards the edge of the gardens, pausing on the pavement opposite the house.

'I'm sorry,' she says. 'I wanted to tell you, Ben, when you first came here, really I did. But I couldn't. We needed you to see the whole story first.'

'Did my mother ... I mean, did Sarah know when she brought me here that you were her mother?' Ben asks.

'I don't think so. Maybe if I'd been here when she dropped you off that night, things might have been different. But I was at the hospital ...'

'Because of me,' I say quietly. 'You didn't get to see your daughter, and Ben got left here, because of me.'

'No, Elle,' Ben and Angela both say at the same time. 'It wasn't your fault. You were just a baby.'

'I know but if I hadn't had to go to hospital ...'

'No one can ever know what might have happened,' Estelle

says. 'We can only deal with what did. That's the nature of life, I'm afraid.'

'All this happened because of my family,' Angela says. 'Not you, Elle. If I hadn't been forced to give up Sarah when she was a baby, she'd have had a stable home and a mother ...'

'But if that had happened then Sarah might not have had Ben?' I say, trying to take Estelle's lead. 'I guess sometimes things are supposed to happen the way they do. Even if it doesn't seem like the best thing at the time.'

'Wise words, Elle,' Estelle says approvingly. 'Very wise.'

'Perhaps,' Angela admits, still looking absolutely stricken at everything we've just witnessed. 'Addiction seems to be in my family's genes, though. I was an alcoholic, and my father was addicted to gambling. It was no wonder Sarah became addicted to drugs.'

'Doesn't look good for me, does it?' Ben tries to sound upbeat, but his face tells a different story. 'I'm clearly destined to become an addict of some kind. Best run now, Elle, while you still can.'

'I'm not going anywhere,' I say, taking his hand.

'Do either of you know if Sarah survived?' Ben asks hopefully. 'I know she said to Fred she was HIV positive, but ...'

'We don't think so,' Estelle says sadly, walking over to comfort Angela who now looks completely heartbroken. 'Back then it was rare to survive if you tested positive for HIV. Now they have drugs that can successfully treat the virus, but in the eighties, as you probably know, things were different.'

Ben nods sadly.

'I so wish I'd known all this before ...' Angela says, suddenly looking at Ben. 'Maybe I could have helped her, at least made things more comfortable for her in her last days. I can't bear the thought of her suffering in some dreadful squat. But they only tell you after . . . '

'Perhaps she got some help?' I suggest optimistically. 'She may have been admitted to a hospice. They're very good at end-of-life care, aren't they?'

'We can but hope,' Estelle says pragmatically, her arm around Angela's shoulders now.

'What did you mean when you said they only tell you after?' Ben asks Angela.

'Nothing,' Angela says, glancing at Estelle. 'I'm just a little upset that's all, seeing that again. Bless Fred, he tried his hardest. He was a good boy – he ended up working here with us for a while didn't he, Estelle?'

Estelle nods.

'Wait, is that why my middle name is Frederick?' Ben asks suddenly. 'After him?'

'Yes, it is. Fred not only provided you with your first name, but your middle name too. He's the CEO of a large children's charity now.'

'So Fred's experience here influenced what he ended up doing too,' I say. 'Like so many of the people we've met in your stories, Estelle. This house really influences the path people take in life. There so often seems to be something positive that comes from the sadness.'

'I'm so glad you understand that, Elle,' Estelle says, looking proudly at me. 'It's an important lesson for us all.' She looks fondly up at the house behind Ben and me. 'I'm extremely sorry to say that my stories are complete now, and my work here is done.' She looks at Angela, who nods her agreement. 'It's been so very special to have one last Christmas in Mistletoe Square, but now it's time for us to go back.'

'I think we've all done quite enough going back for one night,' I say lightly as I begin to climb the steps to Christmas House with Ben beside me. 'I think this Christmas Eve, it's time for nothing more than a nice mug of hot chocolate by the fire.'

'That's a very good idea,' Ben says, squeezing my hand. 'We've all got a lot to talk about and discuss. You two coming?' He turns back to Estelle and Angela still standing on the opposite pavement.

'Of course,' Estelle says as they both stand watching us. 'We're right behind the both of you ... and we always will be.'

I open up the door to Christmas House and Ben and I step inside.

'That was quite a night,' I say as the warmth and familiar surroundings of the 2018 house greet us once more. 'I'll go and put the kettle on, shall I, Angela? Then we can all get cosy again in front of the fire.' I turn around to see only Ben standing in the empty hall with the door ajar behind him. 'Where's Angela? And Estelle? Didn't they follow us up yet?'

'I thought they were right behind us,' Ben says, turning round too. 'Maybe Estelle is struggling with the steps now we're back in 2018 again?'

'You noticed that too, did you?' I walk back towards the door with him. 'Estelle always seems much more agile when she's telling her stories.'

Ben pulls the door fully open again, but there's no sign of either Estelle or Angela on the steps.

'That's odd,' he says, stepping outside. He looks all around the square. 'I can't see them anywhere.'

'What do you mean?' I ask, following him out onto the top step. 'How can they not be here?'

But Ben is right – there's no sign of either of them.

'Where could they have gone?' Ben says, looking up and down the street.

'I don't know,' I reply, my eyes scanning the square. 'They can't have simply disappeared, can they?'

I'm about to question Ben further, when suddenly it begins to snow. Huge white flakes float down from the sky, landing all around us.

'*Now* it's decided to snow?' Ben says, aghast, trying to peer through the flakes cascading down. 'Just when we're trying to find Estelle and Angela!'

A man wearing a long navy wool coat, a burgundy scarf, smart shoes and a trilby hat walks briskly around the corner of Mistletoe Square. He's carrying a briefcase and he looks a little nervous as he walks towards the house.

'Oh good!' He waves to us as he approaches. 'You are here.'

We both stare at him, and then at each other, as the man pauses at the bottom of the steps.

'Good evening,' he says, lifting his hat in greeting. 'Am I talking to Ms Elle Mackenzie and Mr Ben Harris?' I'm about to say yes, when he continues. 'Or would you prefer it if I call you Noelle and Ebenezer?'

'Who are you?' Ben asks as I wonder how he knows our real names.

'I'm sorry, I should have introduced myself first. My name is Henry Foster. I believe you may know of my uncle Christian? He was the solicitor for the late Ms Estelle Christmas, and subsequently the late Ms Angela Jones.'

Twenty-Five

Christmas House, Bloomsbury, London

24 December 2018

While Ben pours two more glasses of whisky from the cut-glass decanter, one for himself and one for Henry, I sit in front of the fire in one of the armchairs, sipping slowly on the glass of whisky that Ben has just handed to me.

As Ben sits down next to me clutching his own glass, I notice his hand is shaking a little. Henry unknowingly sits opposite us in the chair Estelle always chose.

'I love a real fire in the winter,' Henry says, warming his hands in front of the flames. 'Don't you?'

I can only nod.

'And your tree,' he says, gesturing to it. 'Is absolutely stunning, if I may say.'

'Thanks,' Ben mumbles, taking quite a large gulp from his glass.

'I'm so sorry this has all come as such a shock,' Henry says, apologising yet again as he has done so many times already since we invited him in. 'I did wonder if something like this might happen when I turned up tonight.'

'Can you start again?' I ask him. 'What you said earlier outside, it was such a shock, I can't quite take it all in.'

'Of course,' Henry says, putting his glass down on a coaster on the table next to him. 'My name, as I said before, is Henry Foster, and I work, well, I'm a partner now in Foster and Jackson solicitors – a business set up by my uncle, Christian Foster, in the early 1970s. A few months ago, before my uncle sadly passed away, he showed me this envelope.' Henry holds up an ageing brown envelope. 'Apparently we've had the original for ten years. Our strict instruction was it should not be opened until 1st December 2018.'

'Yes, I understood all that,' I say, looking at the envelope in his hand. 'But you said your uncle was known to the *late* Estelle, and the *late* Angela.'

'Yes, I believe he used to live here in this house with them both when he was a student in the sixties. I bet they had some wild times here, eh?' He grins, but quickly replaces his amused expression with a solemn one, when Ben and I don't reciprocate his amusement.

'But you said the word *late*,' I repeat. 'That would suggest . . . ' But I can't bear to say it.

'That would suggest they had passed away,' Ben finishes for me.

'Yes, that's right,' Henry says. 'Estelle passed away ten years ago, and Angela five. My father dealt with the legal affairs of both Estelle and Angela, if I may call them that? He was the one involved in drawing up what is both inside this envelope, and also inside the following three envelopes contained within this one.'

I stare wide-eyed at Ben. *This can't be happening. How can both Estelle and Angela be dead? We've just spent the last six days with them here in this house.*

'And what exactly is inside this envelope?' Ben asks for both of us.

'Now we get to the interesting part,' Henry says, not understanding why we're quite so shocked about all of this. 'As per our instructions as solicitors, this particular envelope had to remain sealed until 1st December this year. There was great excitement, I can tell you, in the office when the day finally arrived to open it ... Anyway,' Henry continues when we don't immediately share his enthusiasm. 'We broke the seal on the envelope and inside we found the first part of our instructions and a set of keys ...'

'To?' I ask, wishing Henry would just get on with it. He was obviously delighting in telling us every detail of this story.

'To this house,' Henry says, as though we should have guessed this ourselves. 'And as I was to subsequently discover, also the keys to the property next door known as Holly House. We were to come here and open up both houses again. Holly House had been shut up for as many years as our envelope, and this one we now sit in, since Angela passed away, as I said, just over five years ago. Which is when the first part of her instructions were followed by my colleagues. Christmas House was to be locked up until the first of December 2018. We were then to arrange for both houses to be cleaned and made up ready for new tenants who would arrive on ...' He pauses and retrieves a piece of paper from the envelope, which has typewritten notes. 'The fifteenth of December for the house next door, and the eighteenth of December for this one.'

I look at Ben. 'The eighteenth is the date I arrived here – what about you?'

Ben nods. 'Yes, I arrived on the fifteenth a few days before you.'

'Everything was to your satisfaction, was it?' Henry asks. 'Most of the furniture was under wraps upstairs, along with several boxes of antiques, photographs and paintings. We were given very detailed instructions of how everything was to be arranged in all the rooms in both houses. Even down to leaving out Christmas decorations in a box, but not providing a tree. If I remember correctly, we had to arrange for that to be delivered on the eighteenth at a very specific time.'

'The time I arrived . . . ' I say, again staring at Ben. 'This is so weird.'

'It is a little unorthodox, I'll agree,' Henry says. 'Oh, you're talking to each other.'

'What next?' I ask. 'What else did the letter say?'

'Only that,' Henry says. 'And then we were to leave everything alone and not bother you at all until Christmas Eve at 9.30 p.m. Which, I think you'll find is exactly the time I arrived at your doorstep.'

'Henry, I'm sorry if we seem a little shocked by all this,' I say, feeling a tad sorry for him. He doesn't know why we are finding all this quite so unbelievable. He is just doing his job, following out the instructions from a legal document, albeit a very unusual one. 'But some of the things you're telling us are quite hard for us to comprehend. You're saying that the letters inside your envelope were written, and this document was sealed, ten years ago?'

'Yes, that's right, just after Estelle passed away. The original document drawn up many years before that had simply been a will, with instructions that everything in Estelle's estate was to be left to Angela upon her death. But after the sad event of Estelle's passing, a new document was drawn up between Uncle Christian and Angela. A document that was to begin being actioned upon Angela's death, and continued to be actioned at the decreed times and dates they had agreed.'

I look at Ben. This was all getting stranger and madder by the minute.

'I'm sorry if I'm not being all that helpful,' Henry says. 'I'm only carrying out the deceased persons' wishes as they wanted them to be.'

'It's fine, Henry,' I say. 'It's not you, it's just quite a lot for us to get our heads round that's all.'

'Understandable. Should I continue, or would you like to take a moment?'

I look at Ben again. He nods.

'Continue, please,' I say. 'Is it going to get crazier, do you know?'

'I really have no idea,' Henry says, looking a little worried. 'I am not party to what it says inside the next three envelopes. Only that I've to open one and give you the next two.'

'Better get on with it, then.' Ben looks just as shocked by all this as I feel.

'Right,' Henry says. He reaches inside the brown envelope again and retrieves three white envelopes. One is typewritten, and the other two have handwritten instructions on the front. He opens up the typewritten one.

'Right,' he says, giving it a quick glance. 'I thought this is what it might say.'

Ben and I wait as patiently as we can.

'It says that although we hold the deeds for both Christmas and Holly House at our offices, from tonight you, Ben, and you, Elle, will be the rightful owners of both the houses, and you are to do with them as you see fit. There's some legal stuff that I have to get you both to sign, but that can be done at our offices

303

after the Christmas holidays.' He looks up from his paperwork, 'Congratulations, you are now both the new owners of two very sought-after Georgian townhouses in Bloomsbury, London. Quite the Christmas gift!'

I look at Ben, and then I look at Henry. 'But that's total madness! Why? How?'

'Angela left them to you in her will. Actually, I believe it was both Estelle and Angela's wish that you have them. And now, I am to give you both a letter each.' Henry passes one of the white envelopes to me and the other to Ben. 'It says for you to read them when I have left, which is absolutely fine of course.'

Henry glances at the letters and I know he's desperate to know what it says inside them.

'Don't worry, Henry, when we come and see you after Christmas, we'll let you know what they say,' I offer kindly.

'You really don't have to,' Henry says quickly. 'But I'm sure whatever it says it will help you to understand a little better. It says on my sheet here that any questions you might have will be answered in the letters. I am simply here for any legal questions that might arise. Do you have any right now?' he asks hopefully.

I look at Ben, but he's staring at the envelope in his hand.

'Thank you, Henry, but I don't think so at the moment. I'm sure when all this has sunk in, we'll have so many you'll be sick of hearing from us!'

'I doubt that,' Henry says, taking a last sip of his whisky. 'I know both Estelle and Angela were very special to my uncle – he told me so when he first showed me the sealed envelope. Any friends of theirs will always be very important clients of Foster and Jackson. Now, I must leave you and return to my own family – it is Christmas Eve, after all.'

'Of course you must,' I say, leaping up. 'I'm sorry you've had to come out on Christmas Eve.'

'Not at all. Like I said, we've all been very excited about this document in the office, so it's good to see who our mystery clients have turned out to be. It's been lovely meeting you both.'

Ben stands up. 'And you, Henry. I'm sorry if I've been a bit off. Like Elle has said, this has all come as such as shock to us both.'

'Completely understandable,' Henry says, reaching out his hand to Ben and then to me. 'I will look forward to seeing you both again in the New Year.'

Ben and I both see Henry to the door and wait while Henry pulls his coat back on, and replaces his trilby hat.

'Merry Christmas to you both,' he says, lifting his hat again to bid us farewell.

'And a very Merry Christmas to you and your family,' I say. 'Have a lovely day tomorrow, won't you?'

'We will, thank you. Christmas really is the most magical time, isn't it?'

'You can say that again, Henry,' I reply. 'This one in particular has been full of surprises.'

We watch Henry walk down the steps and along the path and then he's gone.

'Right,' I say, turning to Ben.

'Right,' Ben replies. 'Now what do we do?'

'I have no idea. I feel like I'm in some sort of strange dream.'

'Me too. I guess we'd better open our letters. Henry said that would answer any questions we might have.'

'If those letters answer every question I have right now, it will be a miracle,' I say. 'And I think we've seen quite enough of those lately, don't you?'

Twenty-Six

Ben pours us both another whisky and we sit down by the fire with our letters on our laps.

'I don't know about you, but I've what feels like a thousand questions I want answered right now,' Ben says, taking a long drink from his glass. 'And I doubt these letters are going to answer all of them.'

'Me too. But maybe we should open them first and see what they say. You never know?'

'All right, let's get this next part of the mystery out of the way, and then we can try to figure this thing out properly between us.'

'It says I should open mine first,' I say, lifting up the envelope. 'And I should read it aloud to you and you only.'

'Mine says similar,' Ben says. 'Except I should read it after your letter.'

'Right then,' I put down my glass and carefully prise open the envelope. From it I pull a thick piece of paper with a letter addressed to me, handwritten in black ink.

'It's from Estelle,' I say looking at the bottom of the second page. '"My dearest Elle,"' I begin. '"Firstly, I am sorry that I am not writing this in my own hand. Angela is noting it down for me, while I am dictating."'

'What's new?' Ben says, smiling.

'"Angela says, what's new?"' I continue to read, raising my eyebrows at Ben. 'Looks like you take after your grandmother.' I smile. '"But even though I am not writing it myself, everything I say comes from my heart. You and Ben will likely be in a state of flux right now."' I glance at Ben. 'To put it mildly.'

'"And I do not blame you at all. But what I want you both to know is Angela and I never meant to deceive or hurt you in any way. We only had your best interests and the interests of Christmas House and Holly House at heart when we came up with our plan."'

'Here we go,' Ben says.

'"As you will now know,"' I continue reading, '"when I die, I will have no direct descendants to pass my estate on to, and so I have left everything to my dearest friend, Angela. But we are both aware that there is someone who should rightly inherit Christmas House when Angela dies. This is where you come in, Elle."'

'Looks like she's leaving everything to you,' Ben says.

'I doubt that. Why would she? I'm just a stranger, whereas you are Angela's grandson.'

'That is yet to be proven. Anyway, carry on with the letter.'

'Er, where had I got to . . . ah, yes. "I knew of you of course from your lovely parents. But when I found out you were a writer, I also knew you would be the perfect person to tell both the story of my family and the story of Christmas House, since you were born here. This is something I still wish you to do, if you are happy to continue after what you learn today."'

I nod. 'I'm still going to do it,' I tell Ben. 'Everything Estelle has told me will make a fabulous book when I write it all up.'

'Good,' Ben says. 'I'm pleased to hear it.'

I continue reading from the letter. ' "Elle, you've shown so much courage. Not only in coming here to Christmas House and starting a new life, but in listening to and believing in my stories. If you think back, many of my own family and Angela's showed courage in dealing with the problems of their time. And that is how I look on you now, dear Elle, as a part of our courageous family. That is why I think you are the perfect person to inherit half of our estate. I would very much like you to have Holly House," ' I raise my eyebrows at Ben, ' "and also my collection of Christmas decorations, which, after meeting you, I am certain you will look after and cherish just like I have over the years. I know Christmas and you have not always been on the best of terms, Elle. But I hope what you have learnt in the short time we have spent together will mean you can go on to enjoy everything it represents – Peace, Love, Joy and Togetherness, not only at Christmas, but for the rest of your life too. Yours eternally, Estelle x." '

I stare at the letter for a moment, and read the last part again. Yours eternally, Estelle x. It was so final. Am I never going to see her again? It seems impossible to think she will never sit opposite me in her favourite armchair. Looking over her glasses at me, stroking Alvie on her lap.

Alvie, of course, disappeared when Estelle and Angela did. Did he ever exist at all? Just like Estelle and Angela, he seemed so real.

I look over at Ben now. 'Has that made things any clearer for you?'

Ben shakes his head. 'Not really. Only that you seem to

have inherited the house next door and some Christmas decorations.'

'They're not just any Christmas decorations, are they?' I say, looking up at the Christmas tree. 'They tell the story of this house and those who lived here.'

Just like I'm going to, I tell myself. *Over and over again, to anyone who will listen. Estelle and Angela might not be here any more, but their stories won't disappear with them. I'll make sure of it.*

'I guess they do,' Ben says. 'But what I don't understand is when Estelle wrote that letter? Henry said she died over ten years ago, and the document was drawn up and sealed shortly after that. So how can Estelle have dictated the letter to Angela if it was written just after she died?'

'I really don't know ... everything is still very confusing.'

'I thought the letters were supposed to make things clearer, but instead they're throwing up even more questions.'

'Ben, I can't explain any of this any more than you can. But all we know is, it happened. We can't both be going crazy, can we? And even if we were, we can't both have imagined exactly the same thing. I think it's time you read your letter – maybe it will help?'

'All right.' Ben sighs and begins prising open the seal on his envelope. Then he does the same as me and checks the last page to see who it's from.

'This one is from Angela,' he says. 'It's in the same handwriting as your letter.'

'"Darling Ben,"' he begins. '"It has been such a privilege getting to know you over the last few days. Even though you were not aware when you came to Mistletoe Square who I was, I was very much aware of who you were, and it broke my heart not being able to tell you."'

Ben glances up at me with a questioning look, but I gesture for him to continue.

'"For all the bad luck you consider you had when you were born, you have turned out to be a wonderful, caring, bright and clever young man, and one I would have been proud to call my grandson, if we had been given that chance together. But as you now know, sadly I will pass away before we have a proper chance of getting to know each other."' Ben looks confused once more. 'How can she have written this in the past if we ... before we ...'

'Just read the letter, Ben,' I tell him. 'I'm exhausted from trying to figure all this out.'

'Sure,' Ben says, looking at me with concern. 'It's been a long night for both of us. Right, where was I? Okay, got it. Ready?'

I nod.

'"However, I am so pleased that my last wish will be granted, just as Estelle's was to her, so we were able to plan all this together."' Ben frowns. 'Last wish? When did they get a last wish? You don't think ... ?' He looks up.

'I don't know, do I?' I say hurriedly.

Ben looks down at the letter again. '"Estelle's letter explains why she wants Elle to have Holly House and her prized collection of Christmas decorations. She knows Elle will do right by them both in the future. Just as I know you will do the right thing with the information I'm about to tell you, Ben. Why you should be the person to inherit Christmas House."' He looks up from reading again. 'Me?' he says, looking aghast. 'Why me?'

'Keep reading!' I encourage him. 'We'll never get to the bottom of this if you don't finish reading your letter.'

'"By now,"' Ben continues, '"Estelle and I will have told you and Elle all the stories of Christmas House, and you will know so much about Estelle's family. But what you do not know, Ben, is much about your own family. Although you think we were only meeting Estelle's family in her stories, what you were unaware of is we were actually meeting yours as well."' Ben looks up again. 'What on earth does she mean?'

'Please keep reading, Ben.'

'"You may have noticed that all the people in Estelle's stories had names related to Christmas, all except a few. Each of those few were your relatives."'

'No . . . ' I whisper, my eyes wide.

'"You will remember seeing your mother tell Fred that it was a tradition that each generation of her family had to be named after the letters in the word Christmas. You now know why you were named Ebenezer, why your mother was Sarah and why I was Angela. My father, your great-grandfather, was called Michael – you met him in the 1936 story."' Ben looks up at me.

'Yes,' I say excitedly. Remembering. 'Michael was the doctor, wasn't he? He said his wife was due to give birth soon. The baby must have been Angela.'

'But Angela said her father was a gambling addict,' Ben says, looking confused.

'You can be both.'

'True. Okay . . . "Tabitha, your great-great grandmother, was in Estelle's story of 1918. You will recall she was the midwife at Estelle's birth. You may remember me mentioning my grandmother was a midwife. We then go back further to her mother, Sally, and before that to Sally's mother, Iris. Iris, you might remember, was going to be taught to read in 1842 by Mrs Bow, the cook. Ronnie was her father before that, and his father was Harry. Finally, we go right back to the beginning of Estelle's stories in 1755, not long after Christmas House was built."' Ben frowns. 'But I didn't see that one. It was only you that saw that one, Elle. Oh, wait. She does mention that.' He continues to read.

'"I know you didn't hear that story, Ben. But I'm sure Elle will fill in the gaps for you when you've finished reading my letter. The baby, who Elle will tell you about, was eventually named Cromwell, after Oliver Cromwell, who history will tell you was the man who tried to ban Christmas. The name seemed most fitting for a child who was banned from his home at Christmastime."'

I gasp. 'The foundling! They must have got him back! Come on, tell me what she says next.'

'"Celeste was never going to allow a grandchild of hers to go permanently to a foundling hospital, even if that's what her new husband wanted. So she arranged with Edith, her maid, for him to be secretly looked after by Edith's sister, Merri, who already had a small family, in return for financial assistance from Celeste. It wasn't easy, but Celeste managed to keep the child's existence a secret and Jasper never found out. But what was truly incredible, and the most marvellous story, was the way Cromwell's descendants always found their way back to Christmas House over the years. Sometimes they were in the form of staff or employees, sometimes as friends or acquaintances, but they were always treated as family, and they always felt at home here – just as I did with Estelle, and I know you will do with Elle.

'"And that, Ben, is why Estelle and I wish for you to inherit Christmas House. Your seven times great grandfather, Cromwell, was the firstborn grandchild of Joseph Christmas, your nine times great grandfather. Joseph built this house and Mistletoe Square, and you, as his direct descendant, are the rightful person to both own and live in the house your ancestor was not allowed to.

'"Both Estelle and I know that you and Elle will question not only this decision, but the way in which you have both been led to it, and that's perfectly understandable. But try not to think too hard about how this happened, or worry too much about what would seem to be impossible.

'"Some things in life just can't be explained, and that's perfectly all right.

'"But this house was built by a Christmas, and if there's one time you can believe in magic, it's at Christmas time.

'"Now, I send you both all my love always and for ever, Angela xxx"'

As I wipe a tear from my cheek. Ben just stares at the letter in his hand, then slowly he shakes his head.

'What on earth just happened?' he says, looking up at me with a completely bewildered expression.

'I think you'll find you've not only just inherited this house, but a whole new family too. What Angela writes is incredible. All those descendants of that little boy, they all found their way back here to Christmas House, but didn't know their link with it.'

'That is pretty amazing. But there must be lots of descendants of this Cromwell chap dotted about. Over the decades, no, make that centuries, so many babies would have been born that would have just as much right to this house as I do.'

'Probably, but Angela and Estelle wanted you to have it. That counts for something, doesn't it? Apparently I've just inherited Holly House and the decorations on the tree – and I'm not even family!'

'Just as well really, eh?' Ben says, smiling for the first time in hours.

'What do you mean … Oh, you mean me and you? Yes, at least we're not related – even distantly! But now I realise Estelle and Angela actually were distantly – through Nora's children.'

'Angela said to ask you about that first story. Can you tell me everything that happened again?'

'Sure, I mean, I told you most of it the other day, but I can tell you it again if you think it will help?'

'Yes, please.'

I tell Ben all about the first time Estelle told me one of her stories of Christmas House. All about Celeste, Edith, Beth and Nora. How horrible Jasper had been, and how it had broken Celeste's heart to part with her grandson.

'And there was the token. Celeste presented a token to take with the baby, so he could be identified in the future. That's what they did then apparently, before records.'

'What token? You never mentioned that before?'

'Didn't I? It was a tiny little embroidery of mistletoe, holly and ivy on a red velvet heart. It also had the words "St Nicholas" stitched on it, if I remember. Celeste said it was so the baby would always know where he came from. It was really lovely.'

Ben just stares at me, and I notice all the colour has drained from his face.

'What's wrong?' I ask. 'Ben, you don't look too good.'

Ben gets up and silently goes over to the Christmas tree. He bends down and picks up the gift he said he was going to give to me for Christmas. Then he walks back over towards me and holds out the gift.

'Why are you giving me that now?' I ask. 'With everything else going on, I think Christmas presents are the last thing we need to be thinking about.'

'Open it,' he says quietly. 'Please.'

I look at him for a second and then do as he says. Carefully undoing first the ribbon, and then opening up the outer gift box to reveal nestled in white tissue paper, a small green velvet box.

I look up at Ben again.

'Go on,' he says, nodding at the box.

Carefully, I lift the hinged lid. Inside the velvet box is a large, silver, antique locket.

'It's beautiful,' I say. 'I love it. But I don't understand . . .'

'Open the locket,' Ben says, still in a hushed voice.

I do as he says, lifting the locket from the box and then opening it at the clasp.

I gasp when I see what's inside.

'It's the same one, isn't it?' Ben asks.

'Yes,' I whisper, hardly believing my eyes. Fitted carefully inside the locket is a red velvet heart embroidered with holly, ivy, mistletoe and the words *St Nicholas*. 'But how . . .'

'My mother left me the locket,' Ben says, still gazing at it in the palm of my hand. 'Remember, she gave it to Fred? My parents presented it to me when they told me I was adopted. They said it was the only thing they had that was hers. But I had no idea what the significance of the embroidery was – until now, that is.'

'The embroidery must have been added to the locket as it was passed down through your family. This is so special, Ben. You must keep it now.' I try to hand it back to him.

Ben shakes his head. 'No, I still want you to have it, Elle. You're the most precious thing in my life right now. And who knows, maybe one day we can pass it down through our own family . . . If that's what you would like of course . . . ?'

I put the locket back carefully in the box and then I stand up to face Ben. 'I can't think of anything I'd like more,' I tell him, putting my arms around his neck, 'than to live here with you, have many more Christmases together, and continue this house's tradition of a huge Christmas tree every year, with all of Estelle's decorations on it.'

We're about to kiss when I notice something odd.

'Look!' I say, staring past him up at the tree. 'The moon is shining through the window again.'

Ben turns around and we both gaze up at the Christmas tree as the moonlight falls upon two very specific decorations – the angel, which sits almost at the top of the tree, and the star, which tops the highest branch.

'How is that happening?' Ben asks, watching them both glisten in the moon's rays. 'Estelle and Angela aren't here any more.'

'Maybe not,' I say, smiling at the star and the angel as they sparkle. 'But haven't we just learnt that at Christmastime, anything is possible . . .'

Epilogue

Embankment, London

18 December 2023

Five Years Later . . .

'Sorry, can we take a detour?' I say to the taxi driver as we drive back from the school where I've been giving one of my book talks. 'Can you take me to Waterloo Bridge, please?'

'Er, all right then,' the taxi driver says, looking in his rear-view mirror at me. 'Is everything all right? You've not gone into labour, have you?'

'No,' I smile, looking down at my ever-growing baby bump. 'I'm not due yet. It's fine. I just wanted to see something, that's all.'

'Your money,' the cabbie says, taking a sharp left off the main road into a little side street.

Before Alvie had even turned up in the classroom today to remind me, I knew it was five years ago today that I sat on the bench by the River Thames contemplating my life. But I didn't know until he did that I would need to come here again.

As I sit on the same bench next to Waterloo Bridge and look out over the Thames, I remember everything that happened that strange, but magical December that changed my life for ever.

Ben and I never really figured out exactly what happened that Christmas. It was impossible – there were far too many things that happened that still can't be explained to this day.

All we knew was that suddenly we were the new owners of two Georgian townhouses filled with antiques and memories in the middle of Bloomsbury, London. We had no mortgages hanging over our heads, and hardly any bills to pay, thanks to a rather large sum of money that Estelle's estate, and subsequently Angela's, provided us with.

Everything turned out to be exactly as Henry told us. We still wondered all through Christmas that year whether it was going to turn out to be some elaborate practical joke we were both being subjected to. But no, good to his word, Henry met with us in January and we signed all the necessary legal documents that made both houses, and the remains of Angela's estate, ours. It was an unbelievable story that we couldn't really share with anyone else. The only person we could discuss it with was each other.

I stand up, about to walk back to where I asked the taxi to wait for me, when I see someone sitting on a bench on their own. They have a look of desperation about them I immediately recognise.

Without stopping to think, I head over towards them.

'Are you okay?' I ask the young, pale-faced woman. She looks frail as she huddles beneath a grubby blanket wrapped around her shoulders.

She looks at me through red-rimmed, exhausted eyes. 'What business of it is yours?'

I was used to this sort of reaction. 'It's not. But I recognise that look.'

'What look?'

'The one you had just now. I've been there.'

The woman looks me up and down. 'I doubt that very much. I recognise a designer handbag when I see one.'

'Money has nothing to do with it,' I say, realising how this must seem. I would probably have reacted in a similar way if someone looking like I do today approached me on my bench. Luckily, I wasn't in the sort of desperate state this woman was already in, but I might have been if things had turned out differently. I was very lucky that day, and I never stopped remembering that.

'Really?' The woman sneers. 'That's easy for you to say when you have it.'

'Can I help you?' I ask. 'I mean, do you have somewhere to go tonight?'

'Yeah, course I do.' She turns away from me and I see a red mark, alongside large, nasty-looking bruise on her neck.

I look down at the bulging duffle bag by the woman's feet. 'That's good to know. But if you didn't, I know somewhere you could go. Look.' I reach into my bag and pull out a card. 'They're very welcoming here. No questions asked.'

'Really?' The woman doesn't take the card. 'You'd know, would you?'

'Yes, actually I do, because my husband and I run the place. Well, we own the building it's in. We have a team of wonderful people that help us look after everything.' I put the card on the bench next to her. 'At least think about it, all right? It's safe and it's a warm bed for the night.'

The woman glances at the card now. 'That says it's

in Bloomsbury.' She laughs. 'What sort of hostel is in Bloomsbury?'

'A very special one,' I say calmly. 'And one I'm proud to be a part of. Look, I have to go now, but the offer is there. Sometimes we have to swallow our pride and let life lead us in a different direction than the one we think we're going in. Believe me, I know.'

The woman looks up at me with a disbelieving expression.

'Look on me as your fairy godmother if you like – it is nearly Christmas after all. Why not spend it somewhere where you will feel safe and warm. We have a wonderful Christmas dinner and everyone gets a present.'

'Dinner and a present, you say?' The woman picks up the card now.

'Yes.'

'"Holly House, Mistletoe Square"? What is this, a Christmas joke?'

'No, it's a magical place, all right, but it's no joke. I live next door at Christmas House. Look, I have to go now. Maybe we'll see you later?'

'Yeah . . . maybe,' she says, still looking at the card. 'I'll think about it.'

As I walk back to my taxi, I glance back to the bench to see a familiar figure walking towards the woman. He's wearing the very formal outfit of a bowler hat and a smart three-piece suit, and he's carrying a black umbrella, a newspaper and a bright red briefcase . . .

He sees me watching him and pauses for a moment. Then he lifts his bowler hat and smiles, before continuing on his way towards the bench.

'You'll be all right,' I whisper, looking towards the bench one more time, before climbing back into the taxi. 'If you have the courage to believe . . . '

I get the taxi driver to drop me off on the edge of Mistletoe Square and then I walk back across the garden towards the house.

I pause, as I always do when I pass one of the benches.

The bench took a while to arrange and get permission for, but as I read the inscription that's written on the brass plaque pinned to the back of the bench, I'm so glad we persevered.

Sarah
Here only briefly, but never forgotten.
In our hearts always and for ever.

After I've stood in silence and thought about Ben's mother for a few moments, I turn my attention to two small fir trees, which stand either side of the bench.

We planted the trees at the beginning of 2019 when Henry presented us with both Estelle's and Angela's ashes, and the request that they be scattered in the Mistletoe Square gardens.

After the initial shock, we sorted permission to both scatter their ashes and then plant two Christmas trees in their memory – which seemed appropriate and something that they both would have liked.

'Happy birthday, Estelle,' I say to one of the trees, and I lay some flowers at the bottom of its trunk. 'Don't worry, I hadn't forgotten. You didn't need to send a reminder in the form of Alvie. I'll never forget this day and the two of you. And I'm so glad you approve of everything I've done with the knowledge you shared with me.'

Again, I stand for a moment in silence, remembering everything that happened that Christmas of 2018, and the two people who were so very much involved, and were still so very much missed by both Ben and me, and as I do it begins to snow.

I smile up at the sky as the flakes fall lightly down onto my face. 'Of course it's snowing. It always snows in Mistletoe Square, doesn't it?'

Eventually, I leave the bench and the trees and begin to walk back through the square to Christmas House, pausing again to look up at the house I'm lucky enough to call my home.

'She's back!' I hear an excited voice call, and I see my daughter Stella's face disappear from the sitting-room window as she rushes to the front door to greet me.

'Hello, you two,' I say, greeting both Ben and Stella in the open doorway as I climb to the top of the steps. 'I'm sorry I'm a bit late. Have you been waiting long?'

'Yes!' Stella says impatiently. 'Daddy won't let me finish the tree until you get back, and now it's snowing too!'

'Patience, Stella,' Ben says. 'I promised you could go out in the snow once we've finished the tree. And you know Mummy always puts on the angel and the star.' Ben leans over Stella to kiss me. 'And she's here now, so you don't have to wait any longer.'

'I think maybe the time has come for Stella to do it this year,' I suggest, hanging my coat up on the stand in the hall. 'I'm not sure I should be climbing ladders in my condition.'

'You're probably right,' Ben says, putting his hand on my stomach. 'How's little one today?'

'Kicking away as usual.' I head into the sitting room where Ben has already made up a roaring fire. 'He or she is going to be a feisty one, I think!'

'A bit like their sister, then.' Ben smiles at Stella as she grabs the angel and the star from the chair ready to put on the tree.

'Your parents phoned earlier; they're definitely coming for Christmas this year.'

'Wonderful, I'm so pleased. It wouldn't be the same without them now. I stopped by your mum's bench when I walked across the square. Have you been polishing the brass plate again? It looked very shiny.'

'I have, actually. And I've ordered the flowers for us to put there on Christmas Eve like always.'

'Good. I thought you might have. I left some for Estelle's birthday today too. Also, in case I forget, there might be a new resident next door tonight.'

'Oh, really?' Ben raises his eyebrows. 'Have we been doing our guardian angel bit again?'

'No, I think one angel in the family is plenty, don't you? I may have passed someone our card, that's all. She looked like she might need help.'

'Legal help or just a roof over her head?'

'Possibly legal as well as the roof. I'm not sure yet. Your services may well be required. We'll find out if she turns up. Right, missy,' I say to Stella. 'Let's get this tree finished, shall we?'

Ben helps Stella climb the ladder so she can just reach the top of the tree.

'Can we put the angel at the top this year, Mummy, please?' she asks, looking at her. 'I love this decoration – she's the prettiest.'

'I'm afraid not, my darling,' I say, watching her from below. 'You know the star and the angel always go together at the top of our tree – it's our family's tradition. They're both equally as important as each other, and,' I whisper, 'both equally as missed.'

'You know your name means "star",' Ben tells Stella as he helps her place the star on top of the tree.

'Yes, I know you told me last year.' Stella rolls her eyes dramatically, making both Ben and me laugh. 'I should have had a name beginning with V, but you wanted to name me after your friend Estelle – her name meant star too, and you call me Stella because it's a bit different.'

'That's absolutely right,' I tell her. 'There will only ever be one Estelle, won't there, Ben?'

Ben nods as he helps Stella place the angel right next to the star.

'And there will only ever be one Angela too,' he says, glancing down at me. 'Perhaps a V next time?' he suggests, looking at my bump.

I nod as I watch them climb carefully back down the ladder together. 'Yes,' I agree, gently stroking my blossoming tummy. 'I think that's another tradition this family should definitely continue.'

'*Now* we switch the lights on?' Stella asks impatiently.

'I'll do that,' Ben says, giving me a knowing look. 'Just in case.'

While I pull Stella up onto my lap in front of the fire, Ben kneels down on the floor ready to flick the switch.

'Are you ready?' he calls. 'Three, two, one!'

This year's Christmas tree is immediately flooded with light, and, as we all silently admire its beauty, I can't help but notice that, as always, the star and the angel shine just that little bit brighter than all the rest of the decorations.

Just like they always will do . . .

Merry Christmas!

324

Christmas Names

Angela tells Ben in her letter that many of the people in Estelle's stories had Christmas-related names. How many Christmas names did you spot in the story? (I've given a meaning if not immediately obvious.)

Main Characters:

Noelle (Elle)

Ebenezer (Ben)

Estelle – Star

Angela – Angel

Alvie – 'Friend of the Elves'

1755

Joseph Christmas

Celeste – Heavenly

Jasper – Bringer of Treasure

Nora – Light

Edith – Blessed

Beth – Bethlehem

1842

Robin Snow

Carola – German, meaning Carol

Timothy – 'Tiny Tim' from *A Christmas Carol*

Belle – Scrooge's first love from *A Christmas Carol*

Nanny Avery – Avery means 'Ruler of the Elves'

Mrs Bow

1918

Clara – from *The Nutcracker* ballet
Stephen – St Stephen's Day (Boxing Day)

Ivy
Dr Fraser – Fraser is a type of fir tree

1936

Holly
Rudy – Rudolph
Mary
Bing (Crosby!)
Mariah (Carey!)

Winter
Tannon – A name evolved from the German for 'fir tree'
Teddy – short for Theodore, which means 'Gift of God'

1962

Christian

1984

Fred – Scrooge's nephew from *A Christmas Carol*
Eve – Christmas Eve!
Tanzy – Tanzanite, the birthstone for December

Luke – the story of the Nativity is contained in the Gospel of Luke

Others

The children visiting Santa:
Ailsa – 'Elf Victory' – and Alfredo – 'Elf Counsel'

Merri – Edith's sister

Acknowledgements

If you're reading this before 25 December, may I wish you a very Merry Christmas! Or if you're reading in the middle of the festive season, then Happy New Year! And if you've chosen to read this Christmas story in the middle of summer ... then I hope you're enjoying some beautiful weather!

Whatever time of year you're reading this book, I really hope you've enjoyed it. It's the first time I've written a Christmas story, and although there's a little bit of magic in all my novels, this time I've really enjoyed allowing the very special magic of Christmas to flow through the pages.

Writing a novel is usually a very solitary experience – only you as the author truly know what's going to happen to your characters. But when it comes to the editorial process and the production of the book, there are many more people without whom the stories you love to read would not find themselves to their rightful homes – snuggled up on your book shelves! So I'd like to send my thanks and much gratitude to:

All the wonderful elves that help to produce my books at Santa's workshop – otherwise known as my fab publishers, Sphere and Little, Brown. With special mention going to chief elves Darcy Nicholson, Ruth Jones, Brionee Fenlon and Zoe Carroll.

My magical Fairy Godmother – otherwise known as my always amazing agent, Hannah Ferguson.

Those that continue year after year to share the magic of Christmas with me and make it a little more special every year – my husband, Jim, and my children, Rosie and Tom.

And the unique gifts that keep on giving throughout every year – my gorgeous dogs, Oscar, Sherlock and Ted.

And to you, if this is the first of my books you've read, or even if it's the fourteenth! (Yes, at time of writing in 2023 I have fourteen published novels out in the world!) Thank you, my lovely readers, for allowing yourselves to believe in magic, not only at Christmastime, but the whole year through.

Much love to you all,
Ali x

Extract quoted from the abdication speech of Edward VIII, broadcast after his abdication, 11 December 1936, official website of the British monarchy, archived from the original https://web.archive.org/web/20120512065623/http://www.royal.gov.uk/pdf/edwardviii.pdf

'A perfect, sparkling, summer read' Cathy Bramley

Ali McNamara

Cornish Clouds and Silver Lining Skies

This uplifting summer novel from Ali McNamara

will make you laugh, cry and feel like you

have your toes in the Cornish sand . . .

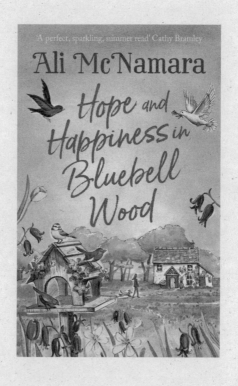

A gorgeous novel from Ali McNamara, packed with her trademark blend of humour, romance and just a little magic. Welcome to Bluebell Wood!